The Shakespeare Secret

Also available by David Nix

Jake Paynter Series
To the Gates of Hell
Devil's Ride West
Dead Man's Hand

The Shakespeare Secret

A Novel

David Nix

alcove
press

Books should be disposed of and recycled according to local requirements. All paper materials used are FSC compliant.

This is a work of fiction. All of the names, characters, organizations, places and events portrayed in this novel are either products of the author's imagination or are used fictitiously. Any resemblance to real or actual events, locales, or persons, living or dead, is entirely coincidental.

Copyright © 2025 by David Nix

All rights reserved.

Published in the United States by Alcove Press, an imprint of The Quick Brown Fox & Company LLC.

Alcove Press and its logo are trademarks of The Quick Brown Fox & Company LLC.

Library of Congress Catalog-in-Publication data available upon request.

ISBN (hardcover): 979-8-89242-152-2
ISBN (paperback): 979-8-89242-252-9
ISBN (ebook): 979-8-89242-153-9

Cover design by Lynn Andreozzi

Printed in the United States.

www.alcovepress.com

Alcove Press
34 West 27th St., 10th Floor
New York, NY 10001

First Edition: July 2025

The authorized representative in the EU for product safety and compliance is eucomply OÜ Pärnu mnt 139b-14, 11317 Tallinn, Estonia, hello@eucompliancepartner.com, +33757690241

10 9 8 7 6 5 4 3 2 1

For all my sisters whose talents go disregarded.
May we open our eyes to you and kick down the doors.

1

London, November 16, 1591

The serpent offered Eve the key to all knowledge, but the price was death. Mary Herbert, Countess of Pembroke, reflects on this tragic absurdity as she falls headlong into a snake pit.

With the lift of two fingers, Lord Pembroke draws Mary's attention as they proceed toward the Presence Chamber of Whitehall Palace—and Her Majesty. Such is Pembroke's way, a man of small gestures and guarded words that belie the power, calculation, and restrained menace beneath the surface. He regards her with sharp gray eyes against an otherwise blank expression.

"Remember. Your three-year absence from Court is cause for suspicion." His voice is a growled whisper. "Chin low and do not meet her eyes. My family remains too near the succession to give reason for Her Majesty's disfavor."

"Thank you, Lord Husband." She fails to restrain her growing pique and squeezes his elbow until he winces. "However, might I remind you that I am no longer that naive maiden you married fifteen years ago. And I have been known to Elizabeth since my childhood—a fact you cannot claim."

His right cheek tics, a reaction that under more casual circumstances might reveal a soft smile. "This I know, my lady countess. I press, though, because our reputation at Court demands it."

"Of course."

Mary understands Pembroke's relentless strategy. Elizabeth runs her court with a hand of velvet iron, good-humored and gracious until she is not. While other nobles often fall out of favor with the queen for overstepping boundaries, her husband avoids censure through discretion and abject humility in the queen's presence—though he sometimes rages about her in private. The intrigue and innuendo so studiously practiced by other courtiers remains a barred and bolted door to Mary, which she much prefers.

"The Lord Pembroke and Lady Pembroke."

The liveried herald nasally intones their titles as Mary and her husband enter the queen's presence with steady, stately steps. Through subtle cuts of her eyes, Mary assesses the battlefield. Lining the chamber walls are the fixtures of the court—ladies-in-waiting, advisers, peers who have come to pay homage—all seeking the queen's favor while navigating personal ambitions that sometimes lay at odds with the Crown. This, and the army of servants, soldiers, and court musicians, overstuff the room to an elbow-jostling state. A hundred competing perfumes mask the creeping odor of overheated bodies, aided by an array of scented candles and the strewing herbs that crunch beneath Mary's shoes. Elizabeth does not abide the scent of stale sweat, but the counter effect leaves Mary slightly nauseous.

The crowd thins before the throne, revealing a clearing occupied by the queen and those who have her ear. This elite group includes the Lord Chamberlain and the enigmatic Robert Cecil standing in for his ailing father. Cecil's rise to prominence since Mary's previous visit to Court proves a source of intrigue. His diminutive, hunchbacked frame and lack of a title until his recent knighthood should have relegated him to the margins. Yet he has always left an impression on Mary as a man in constant motion—his asymmetric gait propelling him along a path that keenly cleaves the affairs of state. That trait has fashioned him into a man to be reckoned with—a man ruthlessly loyal to the queen and devoted to destroying those who mean her harm.

Mary pauses with her husband, a dozen steps short of the throne, to await the queen's invitation. To show humility, she avoids the queen's gaze by studying the court musicians packed into one corner, with instruments at the ready. All are men but for a startling exception—the beautiful and infamous Emilia Bassano who is mistress to the Lord Chamberlain. This is quite a coup as the Lord Chamberlain is first cousin to the queen, the son of a Boleyn sister. She has grown in beauty since Mary last saw her, with wavy midnight-black hair; sparkling brown eyes; and plump lips, softly parted. Her bright yellow skirt and deep red bodice illuminate the young woman like a war beacon within a court of fainter flames. A true Helen of Troy with a thousand ships at her command. The musician briefly studies Mary before deferentially lowering her gaze.

Envy nibbles at Mary's edges—and not for the girl's beauty. What Mary wouldn't sacrifice to frolic in fields of art without the iron constraints of nobility! As a child, she constantly shadowed her eldest brother, Philip, and they had composed impromptu poetry for each other's amusement. Philip's later circulation of epic verse and sonnets written for his mistress had cemented his reputation as England's finest poet. His most ambitious work, though, had been a translation of the Psalms into soaring verse—an undertaking known only to Mary and a few others. His untimely death five years prior had hurled Mary into a pit of darkness. It had been her decision to continue his translation of the Psalms that had lifted her out. Since then, her sharpest recurring fantasy features the abandoning of her role as a lady of estates to wander England as a poet and a bard.

She shakes her head gently over the impossibility. Station and sex render that dream a barred and bolted door as well. Instead, she limits her artistic talents to acceptable pursuits—translations and the bestowing of her patronage on a gaggle of male poets whom her brother had claimed were her inferiors. How she misses Philip! He had understood her plight. He alone had known the true depths of the suffocating well she inhabits.

The tug of her husband's elbow forces Mary to swallow mounting frustration. She drops a perilously deep curtsy, holds it until her forward knee quivers, and returns upright. She fixes her attention on the queen's feet, studying the woman's emerald shoes festooned with gold bangles. As always, Elizabeth's fashion declares her femininity while reflecting her princely grandeur.

"Lord and Lady Pembroke."

The queen taps one of the shoes twice, clearly inviting a response. Pembroke slides a half step forward, leaving Mary off his hip.

"Your Imperial Majesty, Prince of the Realm, and Avenger of England." He speaks in that same sonorous voice, but now it fills the hall. "We, your faithful servants, come to swear fealty and offer adulation for the anniversaries of your accession and your magnificent defeat of the Spaniards three years past."

Mary briefly marvels at her husband. Such a grandiose statement from most nobles would ring hollow with flamboyance designed only to satisfy court protocol. From her husband's mouth, though, it resonates with sincerity alien to the abilities of his peers.

No wonder he has avoided the famous displeasure of Elizabeth for three decades.

"A delight as always, Lord Pembroke." The queen's response, though, carries a sharp edge that pricks Mary's ears. She fights to keep her hands steady under Elizabeth's iron regard. "As for you, my dear Lady Pembroke . . ."

Mary curtsies again. "Your Worship."

"Let me see you."

Mary stands straight-backed, watching the queen's lips as they purse in consideration. Elizabeth circles her thumb with her forefinger three times before closing the hand into a loose fist.

"You have changed little these past three years, to your credit. However, I would have you explain your extended absence from Court. Most noblewomen trip across the threshold in their eagerness to grasp at my attention. Why have you not?"

Mary and her husband have rehearsed her defense dozens of times since her recent arrival from Wilton House. "My abject apologies, Your Majesty. Circumstance rather than intention sent me from London three years past. The loss of my parents, brother, and uncle, as well as a month at death's door left me hollow, and the crush of Court began unspooling my health again. Only recently have I reclaimed the vigor to undertake the challenge once more. I humbly beg your pardon for my reprehensible lack of homage to the Crown, circumstances aside."

The thin set of Elizabeth's lips softens, and she raises one nearly unseen eyebrow. "I knew as much, and your frankness is a welcome respite from the acid flowers that drip from most tongues. And you must know, I too mourned for your family, may the Almighty rest their souls. I loved your uncle and counted your mother among my dearest friends for her candor. That trait clearly persists in you."

"Thank you, my Queen. Your concern for my family touches me deeply."

Elizabeth flicks her hand but again closes it to a fist. "I would question you on *another* matter, though."

Uncertainty flutters in Mary's breast. Another matter? Have they not anticipated everything? Mary lifts her gaze to blink into the piercing eyes of the queen. Elizabeth tilts her head to one side.

"Regarding your procession into London not one week ago with nearly one hundred in your train. Though I did not witness it, many recounted to me the spectacle of it. The regal nature of it. As if fit for the entrance of royalty."

A chill wind slices through Mary, and Pembroke tenses by her side. The queen's implication is clear—that perhaps Mary considers herself equal to Elizabeth and wishes others to believe the same. Mary's resemblance to the queen—red hair, proud nose, regal beauty—does her no favors in completing the illusion. In desperation, she pins her attention to the queen's gold-bangled shoes, harkens back to those idyllic days of wandering the meadows with Philip, and unleashes the public poet within her that must otherwise remain caged.

"Your Excellence, my sovereign Queen. History elevates the great princes of the world, the towering kings, the invincible warriors who stand against the whelming tide of the adversary and snatch triumph from defeat with sword and iron will. Against such luminaries, chroniclers will not record my arrival on this globe nor my inevitable departure from it. My existence will fade like a plucked flower, crushed underfoot and forgotten."

She draws a breath.

"Conversely, those exalted regents and soldiers of old pale beside your glory this day. You are the prince who scattered her enemies on the waves, who laid to waste the indestructible

Spanish Armada, who delivered her people from calamity and destruction with unbowed resolve and a mother's love. No trivial procession, no vacuous finery, no faint imitation of glory can ever compare to your indomitable feats. Time will forget me anon, Your Grace. Your magnificence, though, will illuminate the pages of history for as long as the words of men endure."

Mary remains frozen as the court holds its collective breath. After a few yammering heartbeats, the shoes shift. "Come forward, Lady Pembroke."

Mary moves woodenly to the queen. Astonishingly, Elizabeth leans forward to kiss her cheek. The musky fragrance of damask rose powder, Her Majesty's favored scent, washes away the nausea and settles Mary's stomach. The queen begins to pull back before pressing her cheek to Mary's in a startling maneuver.

"Let me tell you what I know, Lady Pembroke." The queen's whisper is faint, an intimate thrum in Mary's ear. "Men endure only through the persistence of the female sex, and that is *our* secret. We must exert our will within the shadows of men or possess no will at all—and we must exceed them at their own game."

Mary cuts her eyes toward Robert Cecil, who alone perhaps overhears the remark. One corner of his mouth quirks upward, but his eyes remain blank. The queen leans back against her chair and lifts her voice. "You freely wandered my court as a child as your mother withheld the leash, but you have long since disappeared into your husband's estates. I would see more of you in times to come, Countess."

"Yes, Your Majesty."

"More specifically, I would see you remain this evening to dine with a gathering of notables so that you might lend credence to your fealty. Do you understand?"

"Yes, my Queen."

"Very good." Queen Elizabeth flicks a wrist. "Oh, and my players will stage a pleasant diversion for us. I remember well your love of a good play, a conceit we share."

"You recall correctly. I offer my sincerest thanks."

Mary curtsies again and returns to her husband's arm. Before her head clears, they have left the Presence Chamber. She ventures a glance at Pembroke to find him shaking his head. Rather than offering reprimand, he pecks the same cheek the queen had kissed and produces a rare half smile.

"Well spoken, Mary Herbert. Well spoken, indeed."

Though Mary appreciates the approval, she is only happy to have survived another encounter with the one person who could crush her with a word. As they return to the great hall to wait, however, familiar heaviness begins settling on Mary's shoulders and invading her soul, just as it had three years earlier.

"Lord God," she whispers. "Not again. Not now."

2

Having been on the run since the age of nine, Jane Daggett holds loosely to new places, novel occupations, and fresh acquaintances. She does not expect the city of London or her new job as mistress of the wardrobe for a company of players, the Queen's Men, to change that trend. In fact, the prospect of visiting the *by God* Queen of England's court on just her second day of work has Jane considering possible paths of flight. However, she cannot draw her eyes away from the looming presence of Whitehall Palace as the barge approaches the shore. The collection of grand halls and noble apartments stands clear of plainer surrounding structures, buffered on each side by large gardens and various outbuildings.

No sooner does the barge thump the Whitehall landing than the troupe leader, John Dutton, leaps onto the stones and squares to face his company mates. Though nearly fifty, he retains a handsome face and a violent vigor. He expels a misted breath in the bitter cold and levels a finger at them.

"No fighting, no cursing, and no fondling the kitchen maids. One cross word from Her Majesty, and I will run you through."

Though the players grin, the flatness of their eyes tells Jane all she needs to know. Dutton is deadly serious and, so she's heard, expert with a sword. As the players begin shuffling off the barge,

Dutton seizes two of the younger men by their respective shoulders and turns them toward Jane.

"Simon. Will. Help . . ." He snaps his fingers. "What's your name?"

"Jane Daggett."

"Right. Help Miss Daggett cart the props and wardrobe to the tyring room. And do not dally."

The conscripted men shuffle back to the barge, toss a pair of sacks atop a heavy chest, and seize the handles, one on each end. The man called Will peers sidelong at Jane. His gray eyes are wide set and brimming with warm intelligence, offsetting a proud, straight nose and a small mouth with upturned corners. An earring adorns his left ear, marking him as a gentle scoffer of tradition. This small act of rebellion appeals to Jane. His lack of gray hair but deep laugh lines place his age anywhere between twenty and thirty—an enigma. "Mistress, can you manage the remaining sack, or shall I call for a team of oxen?"

"Gods, no. I will carry it myself."

"As I suspected. Off we go, then."

She must demonstrate to them that she is strong. Her best defense against ill-intentioned men, she has learned, is to show them that any unwanted advance might cost them an eye, a finger, or some other precious member. So far, the strategy has worked. Mostly. Jane hefts the largest sack and flings it across her back. She is no stranger to hard work, but the pendulous shifting of the bag as she climbs threatens to send her tumbling back down the Whitehall Stairs and into the muddy Thames.

She follows the company through an arched gate into a narrow outdoor passage, where they dodge liveried servants hurrying between the great hall and the kitchens. The entire company funnels into a large pantry on the right side of the passageway. Dutton shoos out a bug-eyed kitchen maid and faces his group.

"As most of you know from our previous visits, the great hall lies across the passage, with an antechamber suitable for entrances and exits behind the screens. I shall serve as bookholder when not on stage. The tyring house will establish here as usual. That's you, Miss Daggett. Understood?"

"Yes."

"What?"

"Yes, sir!" Her shout echoes into the passageway and flings Dutton's eyes wide.

"Shout again and I will . . . I will . . ."

"Run her through?" says Will drolly.

"Yes. That. And we shall dispense with the song and jig after the performance as the nobles find it less amusing than do the common hordes."

A few of the players groan until Dutton shoots them a baleful eye to silence the disappointment. Just then, a man with a hatchet face and an enormous ruff emerges behind Dutton.

"You are late," he barks.

Dutton wheels on him. "We are here now, steward. When do we go on?"

The steward curls one side of his upper lip. "This moment, but only if it pleases you. I am certain Her Majesty will not mind waiting while the rabble assembles."

Dutton shrinks from the little steward and grunts. "We shan't keep her waiting."

"I will alert the queen of your magnanimity."

Before Jane knows what is happening, the players raid her garment sacks and the chest, which sits precariously atop a barrelhead. They file out the door in a rush, dragging the chaos with them. The last to leave, Will, slows and lifts his chin to her.

"It is customary for the mistress of the wardrobe to lay out the garments for easy retrieval and to turn a blind eye when a player drops his hose. I am sure you already know this, but do as you like."

Then he is gone. Jane swallows hard and spreads the garments across various foodstuffs and sundries while wriggling her nose. They reek of the sachet powder that keeps moths at bay. She freezes when Dutton begins introducing the play beyond the wall with a booming presentation. An abrupt jolt of pure joy tremors through her, and memories of watching a dozen traveling troupe performances rush through her recollection. Despite the chill air and fading light, she scrambles into the passageway. The mammoth gray stones of the wall block her view into the great hall, hiding the queen and her nobles. However, the voices of the players drift through open windows some twenty feet above her head. She soon falls into the story's embrace while avoiding players who rush in and out of the pantry for costume changes.

The Queen's Men present a play new to Jane. The story features a pair of soldier brothers who wager that each can win the hand of the beautiful daughter of a wealthy landowner. After a series of comic misadventures and outlandish deeds performed to impress the fair maiden, the brothers learn that she has secretly wed their youngest brother, who had the good sense to remain at home to woo her. Although the remarkable skill of the players pleases Jane, she grimaces over the simplistic plot and the flat portrayal of the young woman. The fair maiden is in turn emotional, easily duped, and capricious. The boy playing her speaks with a shrill twittering voice for comic effect. Despite periodic applause and laughter from the audience, Jane fails to shake her disappointment over the characterization of the fair maiden. The finest steel is forged by the hottest fire, and the punishing rules of society plunge women into the heart of the coals. The portrayal of the female sex as weak and wilting completely misses the obvious point—that every woman is constructed of steel because she would otherwise not survive.

Jane knows better than to suggest any improvements to the players. Unsolicited suggestions have gotten her expelled from more than one village, the last running her out with accusations of witchcraft. Only the kindness of her employer, Mr. Burnham, had saved her. The old man had spirited her away beneath the nose of a mob and had given her enough money to survive in London for a time. Unfair, she knows, but dangling by the neck from a tree is not a future she relishes. Jane's tendency to say the wrong thing at the wrong time, or the right thing in the wrong way, will spell her doom if she can't learn to bridle her tongue. Still, she clings to the perfect stories that live in the wilderness of her head. There they must remain, though, if she wishes to survive. This hard truth threatens to end her as surely as any mob could.

During the stretching final act, in hopes of catching a glimpse of the queen in all her terrible glory, Jane creeps to the antechamber door and slips up behind the offstage players. She has never laid eyes on the sovereign before but has heard breathless stories. Does her face really shine like the moon? Does she truly breathe fire? However, Jane can see nothing past the pack of players—save a remarkable female musician tucked into one corner. She pads back into the pantry as the players take their bows to warm applause. A voice rising above the rest knifes through her.

"Well conceived and masterfully executed, men."

A tremble wracks Jane. *Can it be?*

"No players in all of England grace the stage with more proficiency and good humor than do the men of my company," the voice continues. "Now, make haste to the kitchen for well-earned repast. And let not the master cook denigrate you, as is his wont."

A chorus of "Your Majesty" and "Your Grace" confirms the speaker's identity. Jane presses her back to the wall to escape the glory that is Elizabeth, Queen of the Realm. The company rushes to the pantry within moments, giddy and flush with triumph. Jane remains one with the wall as the men disrobe from their costumes amid a rising stream of banter.

Dutton returns last and shoves a crimson garment into Jane's hands.

"John Garland tore this, the fool. Ensure its repair by Thursday next."

He departs the pantry without another word, leaving Jane to study the garment with dawning delight. Only titled nobles may wear crimson, but players have been granted an exception by the Master of Revels for costume use. Servants of nobles do a brisk business selling the glorious castoffs to player companies. Jane has never mended such a startling garment before. She briefly considers her empty stomach, but the lure of the spectacular cloak overpowers her immediate need for food. After packing scattered costumes into the various sacks, she retrieves her sewing kit and examines the torn cloak with a squint.

"I need better light," she says aloud.

Perhaps the antechamber might prove sufficient. Upon reaching the door, she jerks her head up to find a tall man barring her way. He wears blue livery, a copper breastplate, and a sheathed sword. He cocks one eyebrow and frowns.

"Absconding with a nobleman's frock, are you?"

Jane's spine goes bolt straight. "Gods, no. I am the mistress of the wardrobe for the Queen's Men, seeking better light that I might mend this costume."

She shoves the cloak nearly into the man's face, forcing him back a step. His lips soften. A deep pit marring his left cheek speaks of past violence that stands at odds with the gentle lay of his features. "Of course. I humbly beg your pardon, mistress. The warming house atop the stairs is kept ablaze with light and is presently unoccupied. Might I suggest that venue?"

Jane looks over her shoulder to find the chamber of which he speaks, marked by a single torch burning in a sconce outside. "That will do, good sir."

He strides around Jane and leads the way to the warming house, where he pauses to push the door open. As the man has claimed, the cozy chamber is bright from a hearth fire and a trio of candles. And it oozes glorious warmth. Jane slips inside and shoves a chair toward the fireplace.

"I will stand watch outside," says the man.

Jane frowns. "Why?"

He smiles again through the diminishing crack of the closing door. "There are many about who would think nothing of ravishing a lovely maiden left alone."

The door thuds shut, leaving Jane with the twin glow of the fire and a rare compliment. She shakes her head to rid herself of the sentiment. Years of fleeing the displeasure of her neighbors has taught her to dismiss kind overtures, for they eventually turn sour in the face of her oddness. She should expect no different from the handsome guardsman.

3

Most people arrive at Court to be seen and to curry favor with the queen. Emilia Bassano comes to wage war. Her rules are simple: Cede no ground, take no prisoners, and trust no one. Every appearance is just another battle that marks her arduous campaign from obscurity into the borderlands of acceptance. Instead of a sword, though, she wields a lute and a razor-sharp wit. Neither is proving helpful at Whitehall Palace this night. On any other evening, she might enjoy the attentions of her lover, the Lord Chamberlain—Baron Hunsdon. However, in honor of the queen's Accession Day, Lord Hunsdon has arrived with a highly vigilant Lady Hunsdon clutching his arm like a bear handler in charge of the leash. From her perch at the corner of the great hall, Emilia tries to ignore how Lady Hunsdon is lavishing the affection on her husband that she typically withholds when Emilia is not present.

"If it helps, Lord Hunsdon appears terribly uncomfortable."

The whispered comment in Emilia's ear comes from Alfonso Lanier, a recorder player and her cousin by marriage. She nods.

"Let us hope."

"'Twill not always be thus, Emmy. Your time will come."

His encouragement breaks through her doldrums. She looks sidelong at him. He cuts a fine figure in a green doublet, brown breeches, and his customary boots. "Again, let us hope."

She cannot help but smile, though. While most of her extended family is content to fashion musical instruments and play at Court, Alfonso harbors grander ambitions. He wants a knighthood and actively works toward that goal. In that sense, he and Emilia are birds of a kind. She wishes to become a lady—welcomed at Court as an equal rather than a barely tolerated appendage of the luminary who shares her bed.

As a lady, she could write poetry for entertaining guests in her home and bestow patronage on artists of her choosing. She even dreams of publishing poetry despite the deep social mores discouraging it. The notion of resisting such damnable obstacles stirs her blood, but she cannot feed her impulses without first achieving the status of a lady. Despite three generations of Bassano family service to the court since their arrival from Venice, though, Emilia remains simply an intriguing interloper of foreign ancestry. Earning the favor of the queen as a precocious fourteen-year-old had seemed simple then, but as she faces the ripe old age of three and twenty, the climb has become much steeper.

Now, the aging of Lord Hunsdon emboldens other noblemen, forcing Emilia to fend off unwanted advances with increasing frequency. To them, she is simply a high-step courtesan, free for the taking, trapped halfway between their disregard and their lust. "Halfway"—the most discouraging word in the English language. Purgatory, Dante called it.

"Your Most Eminent Majesty! My noble lords and ladies!"

The announcement draws her attention to the leader of the Queen's Men introducing the play. Determined to forget her struggles for a time, she concentrates on the player.

"With abject humility and deep gratitude," says the man, "we present a comedy of misguided aspirations, adventurous competition, and capricious impulse. Thus begins our tale, set in a grand country house inhabited by a wealthy landowner and his comely daughter."

As usual, Emilia is soon caught up in the story—one new to her. She watches and listens attentively, noting the skill of the players, the flow of the story, the cadence and depth of spoken lines. By the time the third act commences, however, she has already relegated the play to an ever-growing mound of mediocre offerings—pleasant enough for a diversion but falling short of the spectacular work for which she yearns. After the performance has closed to restrained applause and a dismissal from the queen, Alfonso taps Emilia's wrist.

"Your verdict? A hanging offense or merely worthy of a stiff fine?"

"Does my expression betray me so blatantly?"

"Only to those who have heard your past diatribes on such matters. Shall I fetch a rope, then?"

"Most likely." She rubs her forehead with an index finger. "The playwright clearly believes that childish characters and an elementary plot may be plastered over with an excess of swordplay, bumbling, and shouting. I could have written better."

"Though I do appreciate swordplay, bumbling, and shouting," he says, "perhaps *I* could have written better."

She jabs her elbow into his ribs. "Remain in your depth, sir."

"I will endeavor to do so."

She swings her focus toward the Lord Chamberlain to find Lady Hunsdon still clinging to her husband's arm and peering down her noble nose at Emilia. She stands up abruptly.

"I must have air."

Emilia stalks toward the passageway beyond the great hall in order to find the stars, the cold be damned. Upon entering the antechamber, she collides with a man lingering just around the corner. As if waiting for her. She beats back a grimace.

"Lord Cumberland. My apologies."

The smolder of his eyes betrays his intentions. "When will you discard that relic, Hunsdon? I can show you *sterner* stuff worthy of your talents."

Cumberland is devilishly handsome, selectively charming, and an unrepentant carouser. He has been attempting to pluck Emilia's maidenhood since she was thirteen years old and under the protection of his wife. Lady Cumberland had sent Emilia to Court as an act of mercy. Emilia bites back revulsion and reminds herself to play her game of war. She flashes a smile that has tamed greater men. "Sheath your sword, my lord, lest your sternness dislodge your codpiece and shock the finer ladies present."

He seizes her elbow and pulls her into his body and wine-soaked breath. "'Twould be no shock to many, and I would have you join that pleasant association."

"I would have you unhand me. Thus freed, your hand might remedy your present condition."

Cumberland releases the elbow and shows her the back of his hand. "Perhaps this would do."

Emilia leans toward the raised hand. "If you intend to strike me, sir, then do not fail to draw blood. How else will you demonstrate your talent for assaulting ladies?"

"You are no lady," he growls, and pushes past her into the great hall.

Rage flashes within Emilia. How long must she suffer men who consider her as they would a prized horse—a creature suitable for riding and little else? She sails through the open door into the darkened passageway and massages her temples while muttering curses beneath her breath.

"Trouble, my lady?"

She finds an armed man watching her. His blue livery marks him as belonging to Lord Pembroke's guard.

"None intent on pursuing me just now."

The man studies her briefly and taps the hilt of his sword. "The warming house is unoccupied save a seamstress. While I stand here, no man shall enter."

Emilia considers his invitation to find refuge, even if for just a minute. She rubs her upper arms to fend off the invading chill. A fire would be nice. A respite from lascivious lords and judgmental ladies. She walks toward the guardsman, and he opens the door.

"Thank you, sir."

"At your service, my lady."

She steps into the glow of the small chamber, clinging to the warmth of the guard's respectful address. Her gaze locks with that of a slender young woman possessed of blonde tresses, a pleasant face, and impossibly large blue eyes. Her gray dress of coarse linen marks her as of lesser status than even the court servants. The girl leaps from her chair, spilling a crimson cloak and a sewing kit. She curtsies with head dipped.

"Beg your pardon, my lady. I shall depart immediately."

Without thinking, Emilia strides toward the girl and holds up a palm. "Please, do not go. It would please me to share the warmth with another. Also, you should know that I am no lady."

The girl tilts her head with eyes narrowing. "You are the lady musician. No?"

"Yes, but I possess no title."

The girl's eyes fly wide, and she claps her hands together. "But you are a musician! How grand! I am absolutely green with envy."

Emilia lips soften. "What is your name?"

"Jane Daggett, newly appointed mistress of the wardrobe for the Queen's Men, here to mend a cloak."

"How old are you?"

"One and twenty, but only just. With your youth, I must seem an old maid to you."

Emilia grows a smile. "I am nearly two years your elder, but thank you for the beneficent lie."

"'Twas no lie, miss. Your beauty gives me the notion to cover my face."

"Nonsense. You are lovely, and your frank manner nourishes my soul."

Jane rolls her eyes. "My frank manner has produced no end of trouble for me. Now, it is you who lies."

Emilia laughs, to her surprise. She likes the blunt young seamstress. She motions to the vacant chair. "Sit, please. Do not shirk your work on my account."

Jane plops down. "Thank you, Miss . . ."

"Bassano. But you may call me Emilia."

Jane's cheeks flush as she ducks her head to resume the mending while Emilia settles into a chair near the fire. In the ensuing silence, broken only by the soft crackle of flames, she considers the absurdity of the situation. With the forces of Court arrayed against her, she has found a moment of peace with the unlikeliest of people. She must relish it, for when she leaves the warming house, the brutal war begins anew.

4

The play's disjointed story and the press of nobles leave Mary uneasy. As the players exit the stage, the guests return to scattered huddles of whispers and innuendo, stirring court intrigue beneath Elizabeth's very nose. The queen appears to ignore the phenomenon, but for what purpose? She is entirely too astute not to recognize what they are doing. More likely, she is providing them with enough rope to hang themselves.

Harsh whispers pull her attention to the great hall antechamber, where she finds Lord Cumberland gripping the Bassano girl's elbow. He raises a hand to her before stalking back inside, leaving the young woman to slip away in anger. Mary sees Cumberland join Robert Cecil and the new court favorite, young Lord Southampton, in hushed conversation while Southampton's hovering mother tries to eavesdrop. Mary blinks with mounting disorientation as she studies one conspiratorial huddle after the next. Joining a group would not only counter her husband's strategy of disengagement, it would sap her soul. Not joining, however, might arouse the queen's suspicions further—that Mary's aloofness marks her as one with visions of equality to Elizabeth. Waves of conflicting speculation crash together in Mary's chest, drawing it tight. Her breathing becomes labored and shallow. She needs to escape. She needs to breathe.

"I must step outside."

Her words to Lord Pembroke emerge as a broken whisper while she clutches his sleeve. His brow creases with irritation, and words of denial begin forming on his lips—but die there. He peers intently into Mary's eyes before the irritation recedes.

"I will make an excuse," he whispers. "I posted Captain Dansby to watch the Whitehall Stairs."

Relieved and grateful for empathy, Mary also understands her husband's implication. She will find refuge in the long passageway outside the hall, guarded by a man who loyally serves House Pembroke. She tenderly kisses his hand. "Thank you, Lord Husband."

Mary flees the great hall through the antechamber and into the passageway. She inhales deeply the chill night air and expels it as a frosty stream. The sound of a throat clearing draws her attention to Dansby, Pembroke's captain of the guard, standing beside a closed door. He bows and approaches.

"May I be of service, my lady?"

Mary motions toward the door. "Why do you stand watch there?"

Dansby grows a sheepish smile. In better light, she might see his cheeks flush. "'Tis a warming house for guardsmen and travelers."

"Then why do you not use it?"

He shifts his stance. "It is presently occupied by two young women. The tyring woman for the Queen's Men and the Bassano lute player."

"Did they ask for your protection?"

"No. I merely thought it prudent."

Mary dips her head to him. "You are a good man, Captain Dansby."

"Thank you, my lady."

"I would not mind the warmth of a fire just now."

"As you wish."

Dansby marches ahead of Mary and opens the warming house door. When Mary enters, Miss Bassano leaps to her feet to drop and hold a deep curtsy. Her black curls bounce, and her dark eyes sparkle in the firelight, just as they had at their last encounter several years prior.

"My lady!"

A young woman with long, fair locks and a crimson garment spread across her lap stares at Mary with alarm. "You are a lady? Truly?"

"She is the Countess of Pembroke, Jane," whispers the musician loudly. Then Jane erupts from the chair, nearly propelling the garment into the fire, and falls to her knees.

"Begging your pardon, m'lady." Her voice trembles. "But you are too kindly of countenance to be a noble."

The girl's forwardness stuns Mary initially. Then she lets loose an indecorous laugh for the first time in months. "Rise up, you two."

The girl scrambles to her feet, and Miss Bassano releases her curtsy. Mary regards the latter first. "I hear you now play the lute and the Lord Chamberlain with equal dexterity."

Her cheeks flush. "My lady, I—"

Mary lifts a palm. "I meant to offer a compliment. You have my admiration for both skills, Miss Bassano."

"Thank you, Countess."

"I am Jane Daggett," blurts the younger woman, "newly appointed mistress of the wardrobe for the Queen's Men, hired only yesterday by John Dutton because his former mistress of the wardrobe eloped unexpectedly and left him in dire straits, and I have never before met a noblewoman." Her large eyes grow rounder still, and she slaps a hand to her mouth. "Oh, greatest apologies, my lady! I should not speak unless first addressed!"

Mary suppresses another laugh. She has not felt so amused in—well, a very long time. She glances at the discarded garment that lies inches from catching fire. "I recognize that splendid cloak, I think. Worn by the King of the Franks on stage, if I recall."

The girl startles as if just remembering the garment. She stoops to snatch it away from the flames. "It was torn by John Garland, you see, and as I am the new mistress of the wardrobe, I must mend it or be discharged."

Mary extends a hand toward Jane's vacant chair. "Then you must avoid getting discharged by all means. Carry on."

Jane bobs her head, retrieves her scattered sewing implements, and settles back into the chair. Miss Bassano lifts a pair of sweeping eyebrows at Mary. "My lady. Take my chair while I obtain another."

Before Mary can decline, the young musician is pushing a third chair toward the hearth. With a sigh, Mary settles into the offered seat. After Miss Bassano sits, she stares into the flames while Jane continues drawing thread and watching Mary sidelong. Such are the consequences of Mary's title. One day, she was the fifteen-year-old daughter of a knight; and the next, a countess married to the wealthiest man in England. Initially, she had chafed against the newly raised barrier between her and nearly everyone she knew. However, time and experience had revealed to her a coping strategy—by prying open a door in the wall when needed.

"I witnessed Lord Cumberland pressing you earlier," she says to Miss Bassano. "He seemed overly familiar with you. A sentiment you did not appear to share."

The musician turns her narrowing eyes toward Mary. Calculating what she can safely say, no doubt. "My father died when I was just seven, but not before he'd arranged for my education in the household of the Countess of Kent. Later, I went to live with the Countess of Cumberland for two years . . . before coming to Court."

Mary senses a story in the young woman's pause. "What is your opinion, then, of Lord Cumberland?"

Miss Bassano's eyes narrow further. "I . . . well . . ."

"I believe him to be a faithless dog unworthy of his exemplary wife," says Mary. "That is *my* opinion."

Relief ripples across the young woman's face, and her lips curve into a conspiratorial smile. "I agree. He has been trying to bed me since just after I first bled. In that he has failed but persists in his attempts."

Mary looks at Jane to find her eyes still wide as she stitches the cloak by touch alone. The girl blinks rapidly and ducks her head to her work. Mary checks a smile and again regards the musician. "It seems, Miss Bassano, that we have landed here from a shared need of escape."

The musician frowns with incredulity. "From a man, my lady?"

"Not *a* man," she says. "From the eyes of men, writ large."

"They pester you as well?"

"No. Worse."

"Worse?"

Mary watches the dancing flames and sighs softly. "They disregard me as little more than a fixture of my husband's holdings, ignorant of my work with pen and parchment. They see me as a sturdy piece of furniture that serves its intended purpose but is capable of nothing further. And then there is Her Majesty. I believe she views me with suspicion for reasons I do not know. Her full favor seems always just out of reach."

The musician hums understanding. "The difficulty of earning the queen's favor I know well. However, I believe men misjudge you at their peril."

"Why would you say so?"

"I heard your speech to the queen earlier today. Your words were brilliant, poetic, powerful. No man could have spoken better, perhaps not even your departed brother, whose poetry I greatly admire."

Mary's chest warms with Miss Bassano's fervent explanation. The compliment is a rain shower on the parched plains of Mary's soul. "You have my deepest gratitude. Given your understanding, I suspect you share my plight. Do you compose music, then?"

"Some, but I prefer to dabble in poetry. Alas, it matters little. Neither of us may publish much of what we write without risk of public censure and social disaster. I must instead find contentment in deploying my verbal talents to rid myself of unwanted advances, such as those from Lord Cumberland."

"If I might pry, what exactly did you tell the man to send him scuttling away in such a huff?"

With her cheeks flushing anew, the musician recounts her conversation with the lord. Mary shakes her head with admiration. If only she could muster such defiance! A giggle from the seamstress draws her attention.

"*Lest your sternness dislodge your codpiece and shock the finer ladies present,*" the girl quotes. "How terribly glorious!"

⁂

Aware that she has drawn stares from the ladies, Jane again slaps a hand over her mouth. Heat rises up her neck to invade her cheeks. "My humblest apologies! Again, I have spoken out of turn."

The lifted eyebrows of the countess settle. "Do not apologize, Jane. I, too, found her verbal jousting amusing. Though Miss Bassano is a poet, she possesses a playwright's sharp wit. Perhaps she might have mended the miserable play we saw this evening."

"You found it wanting also?" says Emilia.

"In ways too numerous to count."

Jane knows acutely that silence is not only her social obligation but also her best defense against another banishment. However, she plunges headlong into the gap between knowing and doing with enough enthusiasm to guarantee disaster.

"I can count the ways," she blurts. "The maiden's head was as empty as a week-old milk jug; the brothers were clearly sired by ogres; and the story seemed as if the pages had been scattered to the wind and then reassembled with no care for order."

She shrinks into her chair, certain of a set-down for so carelessly spewing her opinion. Instead, the countess arches her eyebrows again.

"When put that way, I quite agree. The writer meant the maiden as nothing more than a prize to be won, but I found her in turn the object of pity and annoyance. The boy playing the role appeared determined to make her a buffoon. No woman of my acquaintance is so vapid or feeble of emotion, regardless of station."

"True," says Emilia. "The playwright gave her the words of a fool and the feelings of a child, as if he cannot abide a woman whose talents lie beyond the bedchamber or kitchen. The men were little better, strutting and crowing and belittling in a manner unbecoming of the so-called gentlemen they were. This might have been tolerable if their actions had made any sense whatsoever."

Lady Pembroke sighs. "A pity. The premise of the tale enticed me, but the result left me wanting. A different hand might have produced something of true quality."

"Yes. The play should have been much better."

Jane's soul sings with agreement. As she listened to the play from the stairwell, her imagination had crashed through the brambles and briars of the script with thoughts and notions about what the playwright should have written instead. As she draws stitches and listens to the ladies lamenting the play's shortcomings, the collected notions bubble in her mind and spill over onto her lips.

"What if . . ." Jane clears her throat. "What if the daughter of the wealthy landowner was *not* a prize? What if she was not . . . what word did you use, my lady?"

"Vapid?"

"Yes. What if she was *not* a prize because she was intelligent and strong-willed? Because she spoke her mind too freely?"

A crease forms above the bridge of the countess's nose. "Tell me more."

Jane glances at Emilia with apology. "What I mean to say . . . what if suitors *avoided* the daughter because of her sharp wit? And they called her a shrew? What if the wealthy father was forced to allow a scoundrel to marry her? To tame her?"

"Yes, of course!" Emilia's dark eyes flare with interest. "And then, what if the daughter waged a war of words with the would-be husband, as his equal, and said everything aloud that a woman should not? That a woman cannot? Such frankness has saved me much distress from the unwanted affections of men. They cannot cope with a woman who speaks unvarnished truth and raises a bright candle to illuminate their indiscretion. They have not been equipped for such a formidable adversary."

Jane's thoughts become a maelstrom, spinning her notions into paths of new invention. She thoroughly forgets her place. "Yes! The husband tries to tame his misbehaving wife, certain of success. But what if she instead tames him? Tames the scoundrel!"

The countess blinks at Jane and Emilia with an inscrutable expression. Wonder? Interest? Disappointment? The last takes hold. "A wondrous tale, but never to see the light of day. If only women could write plays for the public and not just for entertaining guests."

Jane dares look into the countess's eyes, unblinking, though she knows it to be disastrously improper. "Begging your pardon, my lady, but you are noble. Why could *you* not write such a play?"

The countess offers a sympathetic smile. "Fair question. But you see, our men would not allow it. Society would not allow it. No company or playhouse would dare stage a play from a woman's hand. If they did, the public would not attend. More importantly, only Her Majesty is allowed to write rhetoric. We must content ourselves with translations and private musings, and even those must not stray from religious subjects. Any attempt of a woman to write a play, especially a woman of high station, might be perceived by the queen as a claim of equality." She stares at the flames and taps a finger on the arm of her chair. "I have known Her Majesty since I was a child, and one truth is certain. She does not abide claims of equality from her subjects. Such claims, even if unintended, have resulted in banishment from Court or imprisonment in the Tower for even the highest ranks of nobility."

Jane dips her head to draw the final stitches. Though deflated by Lady Pembroke's argument, the notion of *her* story of the strong-willed shrew on stage fails to fade. How grand would that be? She remains powerless to change the situation, given that she barely knows her letters and can neither read nor write more than her name.

If only!

Lady Pembroke's solid reasoning against a woman writing a play has nearly convinced Emilia that it shouldn't be done.

Nearly.

But not quite.

The fire that ignited within her as Jane delivered a plot continues to spread. The very idea of capturing such counter behaviors on paper, to be staged before an audience, leaves her breathless with excitement. In the silence following the countess's argument, a notion surges into her mind, only to encounter the brick wall of her third rule of war: trust no one. She rises from her chair, walks to the opposite wall, and leans her forehead against the cool stone surface. Opposing desires tear at her, rending her soul into jagged pieces. She caresses the wall with her fingertips, finding it unyielding, unreproachable. Its steady presence lends her the calm to make a choice.

"My lady." Her forehead remains pinned against the stone. "If I may ask, why have you remained so long away from Court?"

Only the gentle gutter of licking flames interrupts the cascading silence. Finally, a chair creaks behind her.

"I remained away because I cannot abide the court. The whispers. The machinations. The delight many take in harming their peers for nothing more than an affirming word from Her Majesty. The queen I would visit every month if it were her alone. However, the fortress of intrigue surrounding her would destroy me if I tarried too long within its poisonous walls. I must remain absent or else unravel."

Emilia expels a slow held breath. She believes the countess. But why? Emilia grasps for the reason but fails to touch it. Nevertheless, something of Lady Pembroke's manner whispers gently to Emilia's desire to step away from the battle for just a moment, to find an ally to lean against for a brief rest. She turns from the wall to face the countess and the seamstress, aware that her chin is trembling.

"Do you mean what you say?" The question emerges as a ragged whisper.

Lady Pembroke nods firmly. "I do."

"Do you swear?"

"By my troth as the Almighty is my witness."

Emilia walks back toward the fireplace and grips the back of her chair. She can contain the notion no longer.

"What if . . . *we* . . . wrote in secret. The three of us."

Jane's eyes fly wide. Lady Pembroke tilts her head. "A play?"

"Yes. And what if we found a playwright or theater owner to take credit for the work so we might remain anonymous?"

Jane slaps both hands to her mouth to stifle an outburst. The countess inhales sharply and leans forward in her chair, as if ready to rise. She perches there, unmoving, as she struggles toward a response. "A playwright would never agree to it. I know many, and none would set aside his hubris to accept such an arrangement. As for theater owners? Men of grand indiscretion and greed who cannot be trusted to keep a secret, let alone their sacred word."

Jane stands from her chair, clutching the cloak. "But what about . . ."

When she clamps her mouth shut, Lady Pembroke holds out a hand. "We are alone here. Speak your mind."

Jane clenches her free hand into a bloodless fist. "What about a player? A man who knows the stage? A man of good humor and uncommon kindness?"

Emilia straightens and blinks with epiphany. "Of course. A player would know the workings of staging a play. Entrances, exits. Oratory and stage presence. Costumes and foul papers and rehearsals. And Jane, you already know many of them. Do you have one in mind?"

"Perhaps. Maybe."

The countess frowns softly. "The risk is so terribly great. And to what end?"

Emilia understands the reservation. Lady Pembroke risks her status and reputation, perhaps her freedom. However, Emilia risks her very life but still cannot dismiss the impossible. "To what end, my lady? The greatest poets of the land speak of your poems, but your voice remains silent outside the confines of your estates. Just imagine it, then. The day when you attend the playhouse to watch the unfolding of a tale written by *your* hand. To hear the players speak the words *you've* penned, to express the feelings *you've* given them. To witness men and women of all stations watching, rapt with attention. And the applause—oh, the applause! To hear a thousand hands thundering appreciation for the gift of the play—the gift *you* gave them. Just imagine it. What better end might there be for one such as you? For the one so disregarded as little more than a jewel on her husband's hand."

A vivid flash of possibility appears to rip through the countess, for her face brightens. "And if we are discovered?"

"How could we be? Who would suspect three women of joining forces to write a play? Who could conceive of it?"

Jane shivers with agreement, her eyes sparkling. If anyone knows what it means to be disregarded and dismissed, it is certainly her. Lady Pembroke bows her head and pinches the bridge of her nose. Then she rises slowly to join Emilia and Jane in standing.

"This is what we will do, then." Her countenance burns with erupting authority. "I will arrange a clandestine gathering within days. I will bring the implements to capture a story. We tell no one—*no one*—not even those we love most. We will pursue this path until we succeed or decide to abandon the venture. Do you agree?"

Emilia's smile stretches the confines of her cheeks. "I do."

Jane's large eyes run wider still, but she bobs her head.

"Very well. Then let this shadow sisterhood commence, and may God preserve us."

As if in confirmation of the decision, a log snaps in the fire to throw a shower of sparks onto the hearth. Emilia wonders if it is an omen. Has she made a terrible mistake by trusting two strangers of far different stations? She hopes not but cannot shake the nagging suspicion.

The grizzled man watches with interest from the shadows as the Countess of Pembroke leaves the warming house with her companions in tow. They do not notice him, he is certain—not even the alert guardsman. Decades of stealth on behalf of his patrons have fashioned him into darkness, silent and unfelt.

The guardsman leads the gentlewomen into the great hall while the commoner disappears into the kitchen pantry. The watcher emerges from his shadowy nook, melts through a different doorway, and slips over to the empty council chamber. He pulls up a chair at the table to consider what he has witnessed while drumming his fingers on the oaken slab. His vigil from the fringes had paid dividends when the countess left the festivities with a determined stride and entered the warming house. When she emerged perhaps an hour later with two companions, the women had been chattering as if old friends. As if equals. He knows this to be deeply untrue. Through a source within the Queen's Men, he has identified the commoner as their mistress of the wardrobe, a girl recently arrived from Oxfordshire. The other is the infamous Emilia Bassano, paramour of the Lord Chamberlain.

In the relative seclusion of the shrouded chamber, he wrestles with the nature of the improbable companions. Why a seamstress and a courtesan? The girl has come of late from Henley-on-Thames, a well-known hotbed of Catholic recusancy. Whispers circulate that the Bassano's are Protestant in name only. Given their Venice roots, they likely harbor papal sympathies. Are they corrupting Lady Pembroke? Or has she sought *them* out? He can't decide but smells a rat. Popish plots always begin that way—innocuously until there is blood.

With a firm nod, he rises to return to the great hall for continued observation. He will focus his scrutiny on Lady Pembroke in the coming days and then report the strange meeting to his patron. The man will demand details, not guesswork. The spy is only happy to oblige. His long-burning desire for justice and retribution far outweighs the silver he earns for the work.

5

A chorus of "my lady" greets Mary when she enters the nave of Temple Church with Dansby shortly after sunrise on a chill November morning three days after the remarkable meeting at Whitehall. She cranes her neck at the domed ceiling supported by sharp arches and delicate columns. She marvels again at the leering grotesques of stone ringing the circle—faces with lolling tongues and evil grins, and one with a ratlike creature consuming his ear. As always, the place evokes magic, a realm of dreams and terrors engaged in an intricate dance of possibility. Mary cannot help but smile.

She drops her brief study to find Jane and Miss Bassano waiting patiently alongside a vaguely familiar young man. Mary lifts an eyebrow at him.

"Alfonso Lanier," says Miss Bassano. "A court musician, my cousin's stepson, and a friend. He escorted me here from the palace."

The man's presence concerns Mary. What has he been told about the purpose of the meeting? As if sensing her unease, Lanier dips his head. "My lady, I thank you for inviting my cousin to pray at your side. You do her great honor, and God knows, she needs the practice."

Miss Bassano elbows him and smirks. "Ignore this man. He knows nothing. About anything."

The coded message relieves Mary. Though she has said little to Dansby, the captain clearly suspects that the meeting is not about praying. However, she doubts there is a more discreet man in all of England. Mary turns to Jane. "Who escorted you, then?"

Jane's cheeks flush and she curtsies again. "I walked, my lady."

"Walked? In this chill? From whence?"

"Southwark. I crossed over London Bridge and purchased sewing needles along the way for Mr. Dutton."

"Southwark? Does not London refer to that place as Rogue's Retreat?"

"I have not heard it called such. Though the severed heads mounted on pikes at the South Gate threaten to turn my stomach."

"Regardless, is it not terribly dangerous for a woman to walk alone along that route?"

Jane's big eyes widen. "Is it? I make a similar walk to Shoreditch nearly every day. Perhaps that explains the drunkards who follow me closely until I clock them with my walking stick." She hefts her short staff to underscore the point.

Mary blinks with disbelief. "None of the Queen's Men help you?"

"They are busy, and Southwark is quite out of their way."

"We shall remedy that." The clandestine meeting saddles Mary with enough guilt without the prospect of adding an injury to Jane to it.

Jane lowers her chin. "You should not bother with the likes of me."

"I am a countess. I do not bother with anything that does not please me."

"Thank you, my lady."

Rapid footfalls draw Mary's attention to a priest emerging from the chancel. The man, whom she has not met, lifts his brows and creaks to one knee.

"My lady countess." He clearly recognizes her, though she wonders how.

"Rise up, Father . . ."

"Nicholas, my lady." When the man rises, a warm grin paints his face, accentuating his expansive forehead and wide-set eyes. "My predecessor named you as our most esteemed supplicant, and I witnessed your arrival at Court. Have you come to pray, then?"

"You already know me well." She motions to her party, which has drifted to a halt. "Miss Bassano and Miss Daggett join me on this early morn. Captain Dansby and Mr. Lanier provide for our protection."

The priest bows curtly. "A warm welcome to you all. I am the Master of the Temple, at your service."

Jane curtsies, which appears to amuse the priest. He grins again and cuts his eyes toward Mary. "The Chapel of St. Anne, as is your custom?"

"Indeed, if it is otherwise unoccupied."

"If it is occupied, I shall throw the brigands out. Now, follow me, please."

Father Nicholas mounts a set of stairs on the south side of the nave with a single glance over one shoulder. Upon reaching the top, he dips a hand into his robes and produces an enormous ring of keys. After trying two keys in a heavy door without success, the priest finds the correct one. He presses the door open and bows to the countess.

"My lady. Merely call out if you require my services."

Mary halts before the door and cocks an eyebrow at Dansby. He sets down the small box and two leather tubes he has been carrying beneath one arm. "Mr. Lanier and I shall remain in the nave until you call, my lady."

"Thank you, Captain."

"Yes," says Emilia as she flips a hand toward Lanier. "Run along and play."

The man chuckles. "As your highness commands."

Mary smiles at the youthful banter and watches the men descend the stairs. She stoops to retrieve the implements, hands the tubes to Miss Bassano, and enters the chapel with her companions trailing. Mary sweeps an arm to encompass the chamber.

"The Chapel of St. Anne. Though humble, it has become my sacred refuge in London. There is no place its equal for the weary heart. Barren women over the past four centuries have come here to pray for a miracle that might undo their grief. Though the Lord has blessed me with children, my prayers are not so different. We all pray for tranquility, regardless of what happens."

She watches her companions study the narrow room, whose blocky simplicity contrasts with the delicate detail of the nave. According to Father Nicholas's predecessor, the chamber had been bolted onto the Temple Church as an afterthought, several centuries earlier, to house nuns. As usual, Mary experiences deeply the chapel's femininity. Set to the side of grandeur, unassuming, an afterthought, and yet working minor miracles day by day. If this does not represent the lot of a woman, then what possibly can? She places the box on the lone table and begins unloading its contents—a capstan inkwell, four goose-feather quills, a penknife, and a pounce pot. Meanwhile, Emilia pulls a roll of paper from one leather tube as Jane pushes three chairs against the table—one next to Mary and the other two on the opposite side.

"Be seated, please," Mary says.

Miss Bassano sits first while Jane flips her attention between the chair and Mary. She clenches her fingers into twin fists and jumps into the chair as if it is a torture device. The girl is clearly unnerved, likely for many reasons. Mary turns to the musician.

"Miss Bassano, I have a question."

"It would please me, my lady," she says, "if you would call me Emilia."

Mary nods. "Very well. When we are alone, you and Jane may call me Mary. When in the company of others, we should avoid the semblance of familiarity if we are to mask our secret association."

Jane giggles before slapping a hand over her mouth and mumbling another "m'lady" through her fingers. Miss Bassano—Emilia—grins at the seamstress before reengaging Mary. "You have a question, you said?"

"Yes." She drums her fingernails on the oak tabletop. "Can your Mr. Lanier be trusted?"

Emilia shrugs. "Can anyone be trusted? Can *you* be trusted? Nevertheless, I trust Alfonso with my deepest secrets. We understand each other well. We guard each other's backs."

Mary finds that she believes Emilia's claim. The young woman is too shrewd to give her trust lightly. She looks at Jane, who ducks her chin. "Do *you* trust me, young Jane?"

The girl rocks her head back and forth while studiously avoiding eye contact with Mary. "I want to trust you, m'lady. I don't much know how."

"Why not?"

Jane places her palms face down on the tabletop and spreads her fingers, as if to keep herself from flying through the ceiling. "It's just that my parents died of fever when I was a child, and I have been alone for most of my life. Since then, I've tried to be quiet everywhere I go. But then I get to know people a little, and I begin to offer my opinions and eventually say something I should not, and they send me away—or chase me away or consider hanging me from a tree."

The girl's admission stuns Mary. How could anyone hold malice against such a bright and frank spirit? She shakes her head. She knows very well why. The unsolicited opinions of any woman not named Elizabeth Tudor can only invite trouble from those who consider the female sex simply well-dressed livestock.

"So, Jane, have you no friend in all the world?"

Jane peers up at Mary from beneath her brow. "Just one. Mr. Burnham, my employer at Henley-on-Thames. When a local family decided I was a witch, which I am certainly not, the kindly man spirited me away with words of solace and enough coins to make my way for a time in London."

"Is he a potential suitor?" Emilia asks.

A giggle erupts from Jane. "No. He is near sixty and more like my grandfather. Otherwise, I have no friends."

Overcome by Jane's story, Mary reaches across the table to touch the girl's hand in a move that surprises them both. "Perhaps we might change that."

The wells of Jane's eyes overflow instantly. "Yes, my lady."

Mary briefly squeezes her eyes shut to keep her own tears in check, and retrieves a quill. "Enough unpleasantness. We have come to write a play in secret, so let us conspire."

The startling notion of having friends, let alone those who are her betters, rattles Jane to her core. In an act of self-defense, she long ago rid herself of the need for female friendship. That ground has lain fallow for so long that it cannot possibly bear fruit. Can it? Left alone, she might stew all day on the puzzle, if not for Emilia.

The lady musician taps the cleft of her dainty chin. "Jane has already provided the grand sweep of a plot. Perhaps we might begin with the setting and give flesh to our two lovers and the scheming father."

"Excellent," Lady Pembroke says. "Have either of you a suggestion for the story's location?"

Emilia clicks a fingernail on the table while staring at the ceiling. "What about Venice?"

Lady Pembroke purses her lips. "Yes, yes. Have you been to Venice?"

"I have not. My only venture to the continent was in the service of my ward, the Countess of Kent, on the occasion of visiting her brother, General Bertie. He was serving as the English ambassador to Denmark at the time. We resided the summer at the Danish court in Elsinore, where I remained thoroughly entertained by a pair of overly amorous courtiers, Rosenkrantz and Guildenstern. It took a directive from the general to warn them against soiling my virtue, an intervention for which I am now grateful. I was only twelve at the time and brutally unaware of the ways of men."

"Do you suggest Denmark, then?"

She shakes her head and laughs. "No. I am rambling as I stroll the fields of memory. Venice is a superior choice with respect to my knowledge. You might know that my clan hails from there, invited by Henry the Eighth some fifty years ago to serve as court musicians."

"I have heard this."

"Well, then you might not be surprised to learn that hardly a day of my life has passed without some tale or remembrance of Venice, Padua, Treviso, or Bassano del Grappa. So vivid are the descriptions that I know those places as if connected by an unseen thread."

"Venice it is. We might save Denmark for another tale."

"Yes. Venice." Then Emilia holds up a hand, her features pensive. "Perhaps Padua. It is smaller than Venice and nearer the farms. A much more likely habitation for a wealthy landowner or a minor lord."

"As you suggest." The countess scratches the paper with the quill. "Might you offer suitable Italian names?"

Jane was acquainted with an Italian man called Petruchio for a time. He tried to bed her one day and then helped his neighbors run her out of town the next. She thinks to offer the name but swallows the suggestion. Besides, Emilia is smiling with amusement.

"'Twixt my family in England and Italy," she says, "I am awash in Italian names. I might offer Katherina as the shrewish young woman. My Uncle Augustine often claims that my tongue is as sharp as that of his great-aunt Katherina from the old country. She was said to have been a beauty who burned suitors to ashes with her acid tongue. Oh, that I could have met her!"

Lady Pembroke writes again, probably the name: *Katherina*. Jane admires its stately elegance. However, the acid tongue and burning of suitors concerns her. Such a personality doesn't feel quite right.

"You disagree, Jane?"

The question from the countess tugs Jane from deep consideration. "Apologies, my lady. Why do you ask?"

"I am not accustomed to the present wrinkle of your brow. You seem distressed."

She stares at the floor. "I do not wish to counter Miss Bassano's ideas."

The musician lifts Jane's chin with two fingers until they lock gazes. The knotting of the young woman's brow matches the grim set of her lips. "Jane, dear. I know well the sting of disregard, and perhaps disregard is the extent of your experience. However, I pledge on my dead father's honor that I will never treat you thus. It was you who set this sisterhood to sail. We must hear your voice, or we become less than those we condemn."

"Emilia speaks the truth," says Lady Pembroke. "Come. Share your concern."

Jane inhales a stuttered breath to contain an erupting sob. She swallows the emotion and nods. "Well, it seems to me that women who speak out of turn are despised, as I well know. Stories are told of them that cannot be true. Some are made to be witches. I do not wish this fate to befall our Katherina. I do not wish her to be hated."

The chapel falls silent as Jane stews in her companions' sad-eyed regard. She turns her face away in shame. She does not want anyone's pity.

"Yes, of course." Emilia's response is warm and measured. "Strong indeed. But not reviled from the opening act."

Lady Pembroke rolls the quill between her thumb and forefinger. "That is settled. Now, what about our scoundrel? He must be a little cruel to engender sympathy for Katherina, but not a monster. Not despicable."

"He must be a worthy opponent," says Emilia. "Otherwise, Katherina will be seen as a browbeater. Her verbal victories must be well earned. And his name must work in the story's favor. It must alert the audience to his shady nature at the first mention of his name."

Raw with emotion, Jane can contain herself no longer. "What about Petruchio?"

Lady Pembroke expels a short laugh. "Petruchio. Oh, indeed! His very name suggests putrescence and all things putrid."

"A perfect name," adds Emilia. "Thank you, Jane."

The seemingly genuine praise from finer women heats Jane's cheeks. It is like the sun, though—warm and life giving, but too much will surely burn her. She has very little time to inhabit the sensation because Emilia is intent on moving forward while Lady Pembroke scribbles notes. The musician stands from her chair to pace.

"The father must be at his wit's end to accept such a suitor. This will allow his daughter's strength to appear more practical. And there should be a second plot intermingling with the first, so we must leave space for other characters and scenes."

Jane can see it in her mind's eye. The overwrought father, the swaggering Petruchio, the resistant Katherina. But where is the incentive for any of them to allow such a disaster to occur? An idea strikes her.

"What if the father has a sweet and beautiful younger daughter whom he will not allow to marry until Katherina is wed? And what if Petruchio has a friend who wishes to marry the younger daughter, and he convinces Petruchio to court the older sister?"

Lady Pembroke blinks and produces a half smile. "Brilliant, Jane. You thought of that just now?"

"Yes, my lady."

"Remarkable."

Mary writes for a few minutes more before stopping to flex her fingers and pull a clean sheet of paper. "We have a basis, I believe. Now, for the plot." She meets Jane's eyes squarely, and Jane fights not to look away. "Tell us what is in your head, as you did in the warming house. You clearly see the grand sweep in your mind's eye."

Jane wavers and stares at the tabletop. "Yes, my lady. I will do my best."

"I know you will."

Over the course of the next two hours, Jane unspools the plot that wanders in her brain and discusses it with her companions. A half hour into the process, Lady Pembroke begins writing in earnest. Emilia cuts a new quill and takes over for the last of it while the countess massages her cramped hand. More than once, Jane falls briefly silent, questioning everything. *What is happening here? Is this real? Are two highborn women whom I barely know truly listening to my ideas and nodding and smiling and recording them in ink?* It seems a dream.

After they have captured the bones of the script and a rough version of the scene where Katherina and Petruchio first spar, Lady Pembroke rises from her chair to stretch her lower back. "We have done well, but perhaps should leave it here for now. We have much to think about."

Emilia sets the quill into the inkstand. "It is just as well. Alfonso is likely growing hungry, which makes him grumpy, and I prefer him as he is."

Lady Pembroke eyes Jane with one eyebrow arched. "Speaking of men, have you given more thought to the player who might help us?"

She bobs her head. "I have."

"Do you trust him?"

"I think so." She spreads her hands. "He is humorous without making fun and kind without expecting reward. So, yes."

"When will you see him next?"

"Monday in Shoreditch when the troupe meets to rehearse."

Lady Pembroke rolls the marked papers and slides them into the second leather tube. She extends the tube to Jane. "Show these to him. Measure his reaction. However, do not breathe a word of our identities. For all he will know, these papers are the product of a male hand."

Jane rises from her chair, accepts the tube, and curtsies. "Yes, my lady."

Emilia collects her discarded cloak. "When will we meet next?"

"How about Wednesday?" says Lady Pembroke. "Jane might give us some sense of the mysterious player's reaction to the scene."

"Wednesday it shall be."

The countess sweeps a hand toward Jane. "From now on, I will send Captain Dansby to retrieve you in Southwark for our meetings here and then return you home or take you to Shoreditch, beginning today."

Jane's cheeks again grow warm at the thought of riding behind the handsome guardsman. "You need not, my lady."

Lady Pembroke lifts her spine to peer down her regal nose at Jane. "I will do as I please, and sending Dansby to fetch you pleases me." A slight smile breaks the hard set of her lips. "After all, we cannot proceed without you."

Jane drops another curtsy, perhaps her tenth of the day. Her thighs will ache tomorrow, for sure. "Thank you, my lady."

Minutes later, she is sitting behind Dansby on his horse, blushing from her toes upward and wondering how long it will take the captain to realize how truly odd she is. It always happens that way eventually.

∽

"How went the *praying*?"

Alfonso's curled lip tells Emilia that he knows very well she hasn't prayed a word. She stopped praying the day her dying father announced he was pawning her off to be raised by strangers. She learned then that God cannot possibly care enough to listen to a girl such as her, one too full of desires and ambitions to be loved by the father of all fathers. She stabs Alfonso's shoulder with three fingers.

"You know very well how it went. Now, help me onto my horse."

Alfonso grips her by the waist and hoists her onto the saddle of her dapple-gray mare. He swings onto his cream-colored stallion and nudges it into motion as Emilia draws her mount alongside his. She peers ahead along the Strand, past the bend of the Thames that will lead them to Whitehall Palace, wracked by a storm of chaotic feeling. The meeting has spiraled her spirits ever upward until they soar. However, the prospect of trusting strangers to keep a dangerous secret stands at odds with her rules of war.

"You appear troubled."

Alfonso's observation does not surprise Emilia. In the service of music, she has spent more time with him over the previous few years than with any other person—Lord Hunsdon included. She hates that she is so transparent to him and therefore at his mercy. Alfonso, though, has never used his knowledge of her secrets to his advantage. Still, Emilia is not stupid. With proper incentive even the best of allies will sell a friendship to the highest bidder.

"I am not troubled," she says. "Simply thinking. 'Tis a thing done by women from time to time, though universally eschewed by men. Perhaps I might teach you how it works."

He rolls his eyes, and the curled lip returns. "You are correct, but not accurate in your assumption. Some men practice the art of thinking. Sometimes, anyway. For example, I was just thinking to myself, 'Alfonso, what do suppose those women were doing if not praying?' I think it still. I wonder if you might illuminate my ignorance on the matter."

Emilia flashes a grin, though his probing unsettles her. "You know that illuminating your ignorance is one of my favorite pastimes. That said, we were simply attending to Lady Pembroke at her request."

"In a chapel, but not praying."

"As I said."

"Then to what end?"

Emilia eyes Alfonso sidelong. "It matters not. Countesses do not answer to the likes of us. They do as they please."

He lifts his chin to her. "And what pleases your current countess?"

"Nothing I would repeat to a man."

Alfonso grunts and stares ahead until the road begins bending toward Whitehall. Then he expels a sigh. "I accept that you wish to keep a secret and understand why. But I do worry."

"About what?"

The lines above the bridge of his nose deepen as he studies her. "Do you fully trust the countess? Or the seamstress, for that matter?"

Emilia considers his question as her horse passes a man cursing a broken-down cart. "I think so."

"Think so? You hesitated long."

"You know my rules, Alfonso."

"Cede no ground, take no prisoners, and trust no one. Do you not violate at least one of those in this case?"

She nods, thankful for his concern. "I do, hence my hesitation."

"You should be careful then."

She pokes out her lower lip in a mock pout. "What is wrong? Do you think my high-strung friends will brand me a Catholic because of my Italian roots, or a Jew because of my Jewish ones?"

He glances around with alarm and shakes his head, clearly unamused by her jest. "Whatever they choose to brand you, Emilia, I worry that the courtiers whose favor you crave will become the very instruments of your destruction. They have done worse to others. They will do it to you if it conveniences them."

Emilia looks ahead again, unable to meet his eyes. She cannot disagree with his reasoning, unfortunately. She wakes every morning with the same anxiety, the same fear, in the forefront of her thoughts. "Do not worry overmuch. I can control the courtiers."

"Can you?"

"I think so."

Alfonso sighs again and falls mute. As she makes her way toward Whitehall, Emilia ruminates over his valid concern. She can manipulate those she knows well, but what about those she doesn't? Her project with Lady Pembroke and Jane is exactly the sort of association that could bring her down when she least expects it. Prudence tells her to quit playwriting immediately and wash her hands of such far-fetched notions. Her soul, however, whispers a different message.

You must try.

You must fly.

You must not quit the dream—not yet.

6

While haunting John Dutton's door in Shoreditch, Jane grips the leather tube ferociously until her fingers grow numb. The two-mile walk from Southwark, across London Bridge, has given her ample time to contemplate the potentially dire consequences of her actions, which is a rarity for her. Typically, she veers into trouble without the luxury of planning it. Today is different. The scent of disaster had grown stronger with each step nearer the gathering of the Queen's Men, and now she is at the door. Once the plan lurches into motion, she risks banishment from another town at the hands of those offended by her notions and opinions. To that end, she had packed all her belongings into a bag earlier and has lugged it along with her.

"Jane! Why do you stand there like a hitching post?"

The caustic question in her ear startles Jane into dropping the tube. She falls to her knees to recapture it and clambers up to find Dutton filling the doorframe.

"I . . . uh . . . my apologies, sir. I only just arrived."

He flings a thumb over his shoulder. "Come inside, then, girl. You are late, and the crimson cloak requires mending."

She yanks the cloak from the top of her bag and whips it open. "'Tis already done, sir."

Dutton raises an eyebrow and studies the garment with a frown. "I see. Well, then come along. We've a new frock to assemble for the part of a spurned goddess. My wife will provide direction."

Jane trails the troupe leader inside. She blinks upon finding the great room filled with the entirety of the Queen's Men, gathered into knots of two and three as they pore over foul papers and props. John Garland's eyes light when he spies the cloak still clutched in Jane's hands.

"Ah! My royal raiment rendered repaired. How resplendent."

John Singer smirks at his side. "'Twill not straighten your kingly staff, Garland, which remains beyond repair."

"Your wife did not protest over its shape when last I paid her a night visit."

"My wife is fond of relics and stray dogs. As you are both, her lack of protest surprises me little."

Jane hurries past the bantering Johns in search of Mrs. Dutton. She met the woman only once; the day Jane joined the troupe just before the performance at Whitehall. The sound of singing leads her to the kitchen, where she finds the older woman mincing turnips. Mrs. Dutton stills her knife and smiles.

"The new tyring woman has returned! Those old vultures did not frighten you away?"

Jane sets her bag on the floor. "No, ma'am. I have endured much worse."

"As have we all, muffin. Now, I suppose you'll be wanting to use the table as a sewing bench."

"If you don't mind."

"Not at all."

Mrs. Dutton brushes her hands against her apron and disappears from the room. She returns with two bundles of cloth—one creamy cotton and the other pale green silk. She spreads them across the table. "I will describe what my husband conceives, but I trust you to bring it to life. Is that agreeable?"

Jane nods happily. She loves sewing nearly as much as inventing stories. The fashioning of a garment from a mound of cloth makes her feel like a minor deity, the creator of life from dust. She wonders if God felt that way after creating the world. If so, then why did he bother to rest? For Jane, the act of creation does not empty her, but instead fills a well of need that she cannot describe with anything as mundane as words.

After Mrs. Dutton explains the framework of the costume, Jane sets to work. As the hours pass, though, she finds herself glancing more often at the leather tube resting forlornly on the floor beside her feet. By early afternoon, the tube has begun openly reprimanding her.

Remember your assignment, Jane.
Your new friends are counting on you, Jane.
Time to blunder into trouble, Jane.

When she can disregard the tube no longer, she sets aside her thimble and needle, massages her fingers, and breathes deeply in and out.

"Right, then. Here we go."

Jane retrieves the leather tube and stands from her chair. Mrs. Dutton has abandoned the kitchen for other chores while the murmur of conversation and rehearsed lines continues to drift inside from the adjacent hall. Jane returns to the great room, where she spies Will in the far corner, pitching lines back and forth with Simon Jewell. She waves her hand in an attempt to gain his attention, but he fails to see her.

"Will," she calls. Still, he does not notice. Jane lifts the tube over her head and calls out, "Will Shakespeare!"

The room slams into silence as all eyes turn her way, including Will's. He lifts his chin. "Miss Daggett?"

"I must speak to you about this . . . tube."

Robert Wilson, who is standing near Will, drags him to his feet. "Run along, Will. The young and pretty mistress of the wardrobe wishes to consult you over a tube."

"She grips it tightly, Will," says Singer. "A hopeful sign, I'd say."

John Towne shoves Will toward Jane. "Shall I fetch some wine for you? Perhaps a troubadour?"

Jane lowers the tube to her breast and cringes over the lewd suggestions. She has done it again. Given the opportunity for discretion, she has invited ridicule. Though Will's face is newly flushed, he strides to Jane with a wry grin and offers her an elbow.

"Perhaps we should step outside, Miss Daggett. I fear our youthful vigor might incite apoplexy in our elderly colleagues."

She grabs his elbow in self-defense and follows him outside through a gale of guffaws and protests. Once on the street, Will leads her down the narrow cobblestone lane to a small fountain, withdraws his elbow, and invites her to sit. She settles on the cold stone lip and eyes the thin layer of ice coating the water behind her. Will plops beside her with a respectful arm's reach separating them.

"I apologize on my friends' behalf," he says. "They are jackasses, but mostly harmless."

A smile steals over Jane's face. "They have not wounded me. And none of them are a match for me in a fair fight."

Will throws back his head and laughs. "Indeed. Indeed. The brashest of men are often overmatched by the demurest of women, and so they devote themselves to constructing the illusion that it is the other way round. Most women see through the pathetic ruse, though. Especially my wife."

"You are married?"

He rolls his eyes and clutches a hand to his chest. "Blissfully so." He drops the hand to his lap. "Which reminds me. Do I detect a provincial accent? Wiltshire or Hampshire, perhaps?"

Jane studies the stones beneath her shoes, wishing her past would stay where she'd left it. His finger taps the stone in the gap between them to draw her attention.

"I meant no offense, Miss Daggett. I am a Warwickshire man myself and hold only fondness for your manner of speech. It reminds me of home."

She shakes her head. "I took no offense. It is only that my past is better left behind me."

He expels a sigh. "That I understand. Leaving things behind."

"You left home to become a player?"

"Unfortunately. My entire family views players as somewhere between charlatans and cutthroats."

"Even your wife does not approve of your profession?"

Will stares down the street as if watching for someone. "She approves of the funds I send home each month but would rather I join the family whittawer business in Stratford, where she might better descry my whereabouts."

Jane has rarely considered the prospect of marriage, but the distance of several counties between spouses seems less than ideal. Her curiosity gets the better of her. "Your wife wishes you to live in Stratford, yet you remain here instead. Why?"

Will faces her, all trace of his characteristic grin vanished. "Country life is not for me, Miss Daggett. Nor for you, I assume, as you are here in the heart of London rather than in . . ."

"Tisbury."

"Ah. So, Wiltshire it is. Do you miss it?"

Jane lifts her gaze to the leaden sky. "Not yet."

Will's grin returns. "Good girl. We will make a proper heathen of you soon—we and your certainly endless supply of suitors."

Suitors? Jane cuts short a laugh. "You overestimate me, sir. I have no suitors. I am far too odd."

"Aren't we all? But surely, you must dream of someone."

To Jane's surprise and alarm, the image of Captain Dansby astride his stallion flares in her mind. Her cheeks must be reddening, for Will laughs.

"Aha! There is someone." He winks at her. "I wish you well in that endeavor."

"No," she says. "The man is far above me and worthy of much better than a strange country girl."

"Do not belittle yourself, Miss Daggett. Every woman is a jewel, and every man a would-be thief. Love opens even the dimmest of eyes."

Jane wants to believe Will's claim, but is he not his own worst detractor? "Is love not enough for you and your wife?"

"She is my joy, my moon, my stars, but I am here *because* I love her. We are best at a distance. When we come together, she and I are like newly caught fish—good at first but then beginning to raise a stink over time. So, I am a London player while she plays the country wife."

His last comment reminds Jane why she has come. The leather tube becomes a lead brick in her hand. She grips it tighter and clears her throat. "Do you ever aspire to also *write* the plays?"

Will chuckles softly. "No. A thankless job on a ridiculous schedule for little pay. The most successful playwrights in the land live in abject poverty on the meanest of streets. As I must support a family, playwriting is not for me. However, I do aspire to become the bookholder for a player company and to even purchase a share of a troupe. Or perhaps even a share of a playhouse. That would be grand. And I do dabble in poetry from time to time. Nothing serious."

Will's disinterest in playwriting but desire to rise up in the theater provides Jane with the perfect opening to enact the plan. *Be bold,* she tells herself. *Be direct.* She sets the tube in her lap and gathers her wilting courage.

"I have a proposal. I have here a play written by an anonymous writer who wishes you to represent it as your own. You keep the pay for its sale plus ten pounds from the playwright. And you claim right of bookholder for its staging."

Jane has vomited the proposal in a single, rushed outpouring. When Will frowns with apparent disbelief, she wonders if she has been *too* direct. It would not be the first time. When he laughs, she jumps up to flee, but he catches her wrist.

"Do not run, seamstress. Again, I meant no offense. I thought you were jesting but see now that you are sincere in your offer."

Jane settles again onto the stone lip. Her hands are shaking. "I am."

"Right, then. Why me?"

"You are kind."

Will smiles. "My great curse. Will you break my legs or hex me if I refuse?"

It is Jane's turn to laugh. "Of course not. I am not a witch."

"'Tis a shame. I know too few witches. Now, tell me about the play."

"I can show you." Jane retrieves the papers from the tube and sets them on the stone lip. "This is the scene where the lovers first meet. It begins the story of a father who allows a scoundrel to court and marry his headstrong daughter in an effort to tame her, but she turns the tables on her would-be suitor."

Will's eyebrows arch. "Good story notion. May I read what you have?"

Read the papers now? In her presence? The urge to snatch up the parchment and run away overcomes Jane. She shoves the anxiety aside, dips again into her dwindling well of fortitude, and reluctantly withdraws her hand from the papers. "If it pleases you."

Will picks up the papers and reads through them with astonishing speed. As he does, his brow unknots, and the thin set of his lips curves into a smile. When finished, he flashes her a grin. "Brilliant dialogue. Katherina is a gem. She speaks her mind in a manner very much reminiscent of my wife's."

Jane blinks with astonishment. "You like it?"

"Immensely. However, the scene has some technical problems. Entrances and exits mostly, but I can repair those. Otherwise, the foul papers hold little of the typical chicken scratch or cramped revisions. The writer clearly maintains an excellent grasp of the plot in his head to unwind it so cleanly."

Jane's cheeks heat with his praise of the storyteller. His praise of *her*, though he remains ignorant of that fact. She turns her face away to hide what she assumes is the mother of all blushes. Will grunts beside her.

"Apologies, Jane. Did I give you offense?"

She squelches a giggle before it can erupt from her throat, and faces him again with a smile. "No, sir. Just the cold, I think. You will represent the play as yours, then?"

He exhales a column of frosted air and purses his lips. "Will you reveal to me the identity of the writer?"

"I cannot."

"A nobleman, perhaps?"

"I am allowed to say nothing."

He nods slowly. "Very well, then. I will do it. I admire anyone willing to release their words into the world. If only I were as brave about my poetry."

In a fit of elation, Jane falls headlong into the familiar trap of offering unsolicited opinions. "You should write poetry for others to see."

"I doubt it is any good."

"Even so, you would regret the failure for only a day. If you do not try, you might regret it for a lifetime."

Will squints at her. "How old are you?"

"One and twenty."

"When did you become so wise?"

Jane averts her eyes. "Now, I question *your* judgment."

Will stands, rolls the papers, and presses them into the leather tube. "May I keep this? I must copy it into my own hand to avoid suspicion, and I can add stage directions in the process."

Jane rises to face him, still surprised that he is accepting the proposal. "Yes, but I must have it back by midweek."

"Excellent. I shall copy it this evening. In the meantime, we should return to Dutton's place before we invite scandal."

"That seems prudent."

As they walk back toward Dutton's house, Jane considers the ramifications of what has just happened. The sisterhood, so secret at first, has already spilled into the inclusion of three men—Dansby, Lanier, and now Will—and she barely knows any of them. Has she made the fatal mistake that will again send her on the run? She hopes not but will keep her bag packed just in case.

7

Bereft of sleep but driven by winds of opportunity, Will sails up to the Mermaid Tavern in Cheapside and bursts inside. A cloud of smoke huddles near the ceiling like a colony of spectral bats, reflecting the light of dozens of candles. The funk of tobacco joins the scent of roasted crane and bustard to permeate the place with fond memories of late-night gatherings past. He rubs his eyes and scans the far corner favored by the Queen's Men.

John Garland and John Singer lounge at a table with a pair of older women who frequent the theater and pay full price for balcony seats. Beyond them, at another table, Dutton sprawls in a chair while regaling a seemingly uninterested Lionel Cooke. As much as Will dislikes Dutton, he is fond of Cooke. The two men helped found the troupe eight years earlier at Queen Elizabeth's directive, but where Dutton is hard and driven, Cooke remains devoted to enjoying his work. Head down, Will marches across the tavern toward the men. Dutton sees him coming.

"Shakespeare. You missed rehearsal, young oaf."

Will spins a chair around and straddles it to sit. "I was up half the night and overshot the morning."

"What was her name?"

Under other circumstances, Will might respond with a name that is sure to stir Dutton's mounting ire. However, the roll of paper in his fist thrums like a mandolin. Through his fingers, he senses the banter between Katherina and Petruchio, as if they are trying to climb from the page. Despite his misgivings about claiming the play as his own, he remains committed to the plan for reasons both selfish and loyal.

"Her name was Muse," he says.

Cooke cocks an eyebrow, but Dutton's scowl remains. He swallows a gulp of wine. "You bed Greek goddesses now?"

"No. Just English ones. I leave the immortals to you of higher standing."

Dutton smirks, clearly soothed by Will's flattery. "As you should. Now, about missing rehearsal."

"It was for a good cause."

"Oh? What cause?"

"Your pocketbook."

Dutton downs another swallow. "What have you to do with my pocketbook besides earning a revenue share despite your disregard of rehearsals?"

Will bites back a sharp reply and finds a more tempered response. "I can obtain a new play on the cheap."

"How cheap?"

"Two pounds."

The troupe leader sets down his glass and his eyes light with interest. "Two pounds? Less than half the standard payment? Where will you find such a play?"

Will spreads the papers on the table, careful to avoid the wineglasses. Dutton eyes them with a frown. "*The Taming of the Shrew*. What is this?"

Will stabs the papers with an index finger. "A two-pound play, gentlemen. An early scene, anyway, with the rest to come."

"From whom?"

Will leans back in his chair and weighs his options. He can snatch up the papers and call it a jest or he can plunge ahead with a lie that deposits a thin layer of grime on his soul. The whispers of Katherina and Petruchio from the pages cement his decision.

"From my hand."

Cooke tips his head in surprise, but Dutton narrows his eyes. "A play written by you? I find that unlikely given your country origins and general lack of education."

Heat rises swiftly in Will's belly. Though Dutton's suspicions are on the mark, is not Will a poet? Had he not wooed his wife, the most beautiful girl in the county, with the written word? He tamps down his pique and smiles. "Nevertheless, here it is."

Cooke retrieves the pages and holds them up in the candlelight for a better view. Dutton simply shakes his head. "Playwrights attend Oxford and Cambridge and pay their dues for years before selling a play. You are barely literate."

Will fights to relax the grit of his jaw. "I attended public school in Stratford-upon-Avon until the age of fifteen, and my headmaster was an Oxford man who earned a larger wage than did the esteemed instructors at Oxford itself. I learned rhetoric and literature and drama. I lack nothing that others claim."

Dutton leans back in his chair, with arms folded, and rocks his head back and forth. Before he can summon a rebuttal, Cooke blurts a laugh.

"This is quite good, I'd say. *Asses are made to bear, and so are you.*' Delightful!"

Dutton ogles Cooke as if his troupe mate had misplaced his mind. "You find it literate?"

"Perfectly so." Cooke grins at Will and taps the page he has been reading. "I knew you dabbled in poetry, young buck, but this is rather unexpected. You must toil by night, as evidenced by your general dishevelment and missing of rehearsal today."

Will beats down the urge to snatch the papers and run while simultaneously basking in the warm regard from a veteran player. He finds the latter intoxicating. "I am grateful for your words of praise, Lionel. 'Tis not easy toiling by candlelight night after night."

"Right, right." Cooke ducks his head again toward the papers.

Dutton's frown deepens. "Lionel . . ."

"Hush," says Cooke with an upraised palm. Will and Dutton sit in awkward silence as Cooke reads through the remaining pages with an assortment of grunts and chuckles. On reaching the end of the final page, the old player plants the pages on the table and stabs them with an index finger.

"We must have this play, John. Else another troupe will nab it from us."

Dutton uncrosses and recrosses his arms. "I don't know . . ."

"Do not spear me through the heart, friend. We are short of material, and this is . . . this is . . ."

"Rubbish?"

"No, John. It is fresh. The woman speaks like a certain someone of our acquaintance who expects a new play from us for Christmas."

Will jerks his head back. *"A certain someone of our acquaintance."* Could he be speaking of *her*? Dutton clearly has the same response for he slaps a palm on the tabletop.

"Do you mean to say that we might present this play to Her Majesty? Is that the color of your madness?"

Cooke peers intently at Dutton. "These pages are good. She would find the banter enjoyable. I am certain."

Dutton glares at Cooke briefly before the clench of his jaw softens. He lifts an eyebrow and the slimmest of smiles takes hold of his lips. He slowly cuts his eyes toward Will. "Very well. We will set aside Marlowe's commendable play and will instead stage *your* play for the queen the day after Christmas. As such, we require finished foul papers by the thirteenth of December to present to the Master of Revels for approval. Can you meet that timeline, I wonder?"

Will's breath hitches and he nearly coughs. *The thirteenth of December is only three weeks away.* Few playwrights can maintain such a pace, and he has no notion of who the writer is. "Your timeline leaves little room for grace."

Dutton's smile hardens. "If you are not up to the task, Shakespeare, then you may take back your papers and abandon the mad notion of writing plays. I will not hold it against you. In fact, I did not expect it of you in the first place."

Will's ire expands to drive out the alarm that had seized his chest. The urge to prove Dutton wrong, even by way of a ruse, overwhelms his good sense. He pops up from his chair. "I will meet your timeline, but with a caveat."

Dutton chuckles. "Oh? You would demand a caveat of me?"

"I wish to act as bookholder for the play. After all, I will know it best by the time it is written."

Dutton shakes his head adamantly. "A thousand times no. I will continue in that role, particularly given that I might need to revise it extensively to make it remotely worthy of the queen's audience."

"But . . ."

"Take my offer or take the papers. Your choice, lubberwort."

Will knots his hands into fists and wrangles his umbrage into submission. "Very well. Foul papers in three weeks and you the bookholder. However, you will not need to revise, I assure you."

"Excellent!" Cooke claps his hands together. "May I show these pages to John Garland and John Singer?"

Will swallows hard. "I suppose so."

Cooke cackles as he snatches up the papers and joins the other players at their nearby table. Will watches with concern when Cooke passes the pages to Garland. The cart is in motion now and rolling downhill at speed.

"Shakespeare."

Will returns his attention to Dutton. The man's hard smile has faded into something more feral. The troupe master leans his elbows onto the tabletop to close the gap between them.

"From whom did you steal these papers?"

Will beats back a sudden tremor. He needs an accurate lie. "I did not steal them. The words on the pages were penned by my own hand."

"Perhaps. However, if you are lying to me, I will unearth the truth. In fact, I know just the man to dig. He wields a nasty spade."

Will sways to his feet before gripping the chair, spinning it around, and shoving it beneath the table. "Do what you must. I will do as I must."

Without another word, he makes a beeline toward the tavern door to avoid revealing his alarm. Dutton is a close supporter of Lord Essex, a man grasping for control of state security and all the spies attendant to it. As a result, Will believes Dutton's threat. Only after leaving the tavern does Will begin to consider that he has already failed. If the mysterious playwright proves unable to produce an entire play in three weeks' time, he is doomed regardless of Dutton's digging.

8

Mary has always cherished the divide between not knowing a thing at all and knowing it for certain. In those precious moments just before ignorance gives way to understanding, hope for the best of outcomes reaches its zenith, whispering of better worlds and stranger days. Reality rarely matches the anticipation, though.

As Mary looks across the table in the Chapel of St. Anne into Jane's open face, she suspects the high watermark has already passed. The girl's eyes look as those of a hog before the knife. Emilia, sitting beside Mary, must realize the same.

"You may as well give us the dread news," says Emilia.

For an instant, Mary considers ordering Jane's silence. All brilliant outcomes fade in her mind before the inevitable truth. The player has found their effort wanting, and the dream is over before it has begun. She chides herself for allowing her hopes to have soared so high. It was foolish.

"He did not care for the scene," says Mary. "That is your news. Right?"

Jane shifts her fraught gaze from Mary and Emilia before shaking her head. "Ah, no. It pleased him greatly."

Mary straightens in her chair, only now realizing she has slumped. "I see. Then it was the Queen's Men who cast it aside."

Jane shakes her head rapidly, more anxious still. "No."

Emilia leans onto the tabletop to snatch one of Jane's fluttering hands. "No? They did not toss it out?"

"No." Jane closes her eyes. "I mean to say, yes, they did not toss it out. They want to . . ."

When Jane freezes, Mary gently grasps Jane's other hand despite her heart trying to erupt from her chest. "They want to do what, sweet Jane?"

"They . . . they want to purchase the script. They want to stage it."

Emilia lets loose a tempered squeal. "In truth? Do you mean what you say?"

Jane nods, but the terror crowning her features fails to abate. Mary tamps down her rising exuberance. Clearly, Jane has more to say. She squeezes the seamstress's hand. "Tell us the rest. You need not fear."

Jane expels a half-held breath. "They want to stage it by Christmas."

"By Christmas?"

"At the palace. For the queen. And they require the completed foul papers three weeks hence."

Silence descends on the room as impossibility sinks its claws into each of them. Visions of days and nights scratching parchment race through Mary's mind. She speaks without meaning to do so.

"That is too soon. We cannot possibly achieve such a goal."

Jane ducks her eyes and nods agreement. When Mary turns her attention to Emilia, however, she does not find dejection. The musician's mouth has drawn tight, and her eyes flash like twin torches. She flares her nostrils, lurches from her chair, and paces to the same wall as she had during the previous meeting. Rather than planting her forehead there, Emilia wheels on Mary and Jane and wags an index finger.

"I have been told all my life what I cannot do by those who claimed to know better. My parents. My wards. My aunts and uncles and cousins. Patronizing ladies, loathsome lords. They have all instructed me in great detail about the vast length and breadth of what I am not allowed to do." She pauses to breathe. "As God is my *witness* . . ." Her voice rises to a crescendo on that last word. "I will not tell *myself* what I cannot do. I will not join that unholy parade. I refuse to clap myself in stocks of my own volition and discard the key."

Though Emilia's outburst surprises Mary, it sings to her soul. She rises to her feet, leaving her fingertips in contact with the table's oaken surface. "You truly believe we can do this?"

"I know we can."

A smile tugs at Mary's lips, against all reason. "I . . . I agree."

Emilia appears unready for that response. "Do you really?"

"I do. As you said, we must not engage in our own degradation. There are scoundrels enough to do that without our willing participation." She eyes Jane, who has stood as well. The girl's eyes remain as wide as saucers. "What say you, Jane?"

The seamstress nods. "I say we are lunatic, but I have a sudden notion to bay at the moon."

Mary laughs. "We continue, then. How often can we meet?"

"As long as Court remains at Whitehall Palace," says Emilia, "I can slip away every two or three days without arousing suspicion."

"And you, Jane?"

The whites of Jane's eyes fade slightly. "I will come every day if my lady wishes, but only after completing my duties for the Queen's Men at Shoreditch."

The unhesitating agreement of her accomplices buoys Mary's spirits in a manner that startles her. When has she last felt this degree of passion? This brand of resolve? Five years, at least. Not since Philip died.

"Very well. I will ask Father Nicholas for a key to the chapel so we need not bother him with our comings and goings. Now, let us reclaim our seats and sally forth."

Emilia returns to the table to sit as Jane lowers herself onto her chair. Emilia taps a finger on the tabletop. "We jumped over the first scene. How do you see it, Jane?"

Jane stares at the ceiling and begins unspooling the beginning of the story while Mary prepares her quill and ponders the obstacles before them.

Three weeks. An entire play. We are novices.

She clenches her jaw with determination and pushes apprehension to the margins. However, over the course of the next hours, her sense of dread fails to leave the field.

9

Three weeks later

As a creature of crowded rooms, Emilia typically does not relish isolation. She is surprised, then, that a few minutes of solitude in the chapel before her fellow playwrights arrive soothes her. She sits at the oaken table, caressing the pages beneath her hand, touching the wonder of what she has created. The acute sense of fulfillment aches in its intensity. For the space of a glorious writing session, she had become Katherina, and the woman's residue still lingers in Emilia's essence. Has she given life to Katherina, or is it the other way around?

Only the creaking of the door yanks her from the mystery. "Hello?"

Emilia finds Mary entering the chamber, with Jane slouching in her train. "Lady Pembroke. Jane."

The two women settle at the table, Jane with more comfort than she had initially. The hectic sessions have clearly lifted her confidence, and well they should have. Her ability to spin flights of imagination continues to astonish Emilia. Mary and Jane appear tired, but joyfully so. Mary runs a finger over Emilia's latest pages.

"Do we have here Katherina's final speech?"

Emilia puts her hands together and pulls them to her breast. "We do."

"Wonderful. Jane, has your player finished scribing all other pages into his hand? This Will Shakespeare?"

"Yes, my lady. He lacks only what Emilia brings just now."

"And his alterations?"

Jane frowns and averts her eyes. "I cannot read, my lady, so I must trust him. He avows to have added only stage directions so that players without lines do not stand around like heaping mounds of dung. His words. My apologies."

Mary chuckles softly. "Then it is just as we had hoped. Do you still trust him to guard our secret?"

Jane hesitates, but only briefly. "Yes, my lady. I believe him to be a man of his word."

She turns her attention to Emilia. "And what of Mr. Lanier?"

Mary has asked that question at nearly every gathering, so Emilia is prepared. "He continues to pry, but not overtly. I chide him for his curiosity and tell him nothing."

"Good, good." Mary looks again at the pages. "Can we see what you've written for our dear Kate? What is her response when Petruchio compels her to say what duty women owe their husbands?"

Reluctance overcomes Emilia, though she knows it should not. Handing over her words to others is as if baring her breast in preparation to take a knife. But Mary gathers the pages gently. She is also a writer. She understands. Mary stands and begins reading—aloud.

"Fie, fie! Unknit that threatening unkind brow, and dart not scornful glances from those eyes. To wound thy lord, thy king, thy governor: it blots thy beauty as frosts do bite the meads."

Mary speaks the words with deep sarcasm, as they had decided. When pressed for her opinion, Katherina spouts back what society demands of her, but with a tone that mocks the very foundation of the message. As Mary continues reading the speech, she rolls her eyes as Katherina would. She stalks the floor dramatically as Katherina would. She flings the lines like daggers, as Katherina would. At one point, Jane cackles with glee. Emilia shares her amusement and luxuriates in the sound of the diatribe. As the speech unwinds, a smile fully invades her cheeks until they can retreat no further. She envisions a crowd of listeners understanding Kate's double meaning and mocking appraisal of the absurdity of men's expectations. She imagines them cheering on her railing defiance. The final words sting like hornets as Mary's sarcastic rush becomes a flood.

"Then vail your stomachs; for it is no boot; and place your hand below your husband's foot. In token of which duty, if he please, my hand is ready: may it do him ease."

Emilia jumps up from her chair and clutches her breast. *"Why, there's a wench! Come on and kiss me, Kate!"*

Mary and Emilia fall into laughter over Petruchio's response to Kate's speech. Jane leaps up and applauds. "If I had rotten fruit or a dead cat, I would surely heave it—at Petruchio."

Emilia wipes a tear from her eye and gathers her composure. Her heart is near bursting. "You approve, then?"

"It is perfection," says Mary. "All women and most men will understand the jest. The densest of men, as with Petruchio, will simply hear a recital of what they already believe. Katherina will have the final word, and in telling her husband what he wants to hear, with no intention of submitting in truth, she will have taken hold of what she wants. She will control Petruchio, with him the puppet and her the puppeteer. Perfection."

Relief washes over Emilia. Her life has been a long run of imperfection, interrupted only by holy moments when the lute comes alive in her hands. Everything else is marred in some manner, even if minor. When others call Emilia beautiful, she shields from them the hidden blemishes of her body and soul, in hopes of not proving them liars. She knows the truth—that so-called perfection is a rung that, when reached, reveals yet another rung on an endless ladder to oblivion. Emilia knows that Kate's speech could be improved. She could spend the rest of her days tinkering over a word here and there, never content, always reaching for the next rung. However, she agrees with Mary's praise. The speech is a form of perfection sufficient for her to loosen her grip on what is done and to begin a search for new poetry and prose. It is enough, and enough is in most ways perfect.

"Thank you," she says. "And thank you, Jane, for not pelting me with dead cats."

Jane giggles. "My toss is weak, so you are safe from me."

Mary rolls the papers and holds them to Jane. "Take these to Mr. Shakespeare on the morrow, so he may copy them and finish scribing out the promptbooks for rehearsal."

As Jane accepts the papers with a curtsy, Emilia clenches and unclenches her fists. "Then to the Master of Revels?"

"Then to the Master of Revels," says Mary.

"And if he does not approve the play?"

Jane's jaw goes slack as comprehension crowns her features. One man, Edmund Tylney, holds absolute power over which plays might be staged, and if so, what lines must be struck. The man is famously overdressed but generally protects the player troupes from critics. More importantly, he had personally formed the Queen's Men at the queen's behest a decade earlier. Mary simply nods and smiles.

"If Tylney does not approve, we still will have accomplished what we endeavored to do. We will have written a play suitable for a playhouse. We should take pleasure in that."

Emilia disagrees. "A play is not a play until it comes to life on stage. If Tylney does not approve, then we will have failed. I mean no offense to you, my lady."

Mary's smile fades, but only just. "Passion never offends me. And perhaps you are right. I have been schooled to accept small victories while denied the chance for greater triumphs. Your refusal to settle for such crumbs may yet inspire me."

"And me," says Jane. "I tire of what falls from the table."

"Then let us pray," Emilia says, "That Edmund Tylney's judgment of plays exceeds his taste in clothing, and that his goodwill toward the Queen's Men still holds."

Although her accomplices offer agreement, and Emilia holds out hope, she cannot dismiss the potential reality of having failed to become enough—again.

Mary revels in the afterglow of her secret rebellion until her coach rolls to a stop at the entrance of the Pembroke family's London residence. The looming shadow of Baynard's Castle reminds her of the giants she faces. Built up from a manor house ninety years earlier by the queen's grandfather, the hulking structure presses against the north bank of the Thames, casting an imposing shadow over all who dare pass beneath its palisades. Mary despises the place. More a fortress than a safe haven, its dank corridors drain her spirit day by day. She much prefers her beloved Wilton House and Ramsbury Manor, deep in the countryside and far from the poison court. At least they don't stink of sewage day and night. However, when the queen granted her husband the right to use the castle some years ago, he'd had no choice but to accept. Baynard's is the premier residence in all of London outside

Elizabeth's court, and to reject the queen's gift is to challenge the Crown's judgment. Such challenges never end well.

Mary sighs as the coach door opens. The usually present Dansby is ferrying Jane to Shakespeare's house with the final pages and then will return her across London Bridge to Southwark—just as Mary had promised the girl. The young footman facing her, though, appears eager to fill the role. Mary notices his attempt to hide a smile as he offers a hand and a scraping "m'lady."

"Thank you, Harold," she says. The young man flinches at her use of his name, but dutifully completes his task.

With her feet firmly on the pavement, Mary strides through the castle's great arch and into the courtyard. A tall figure standing in the sunlight brings her to a skidding halt. She offers a brief dip of her hips.

"My Lord Husband."

Pembroke's hooded eyes betray no sign of emotion, a skill he deploys to his advantage against friends and rivals alike. Mary tries not to resent his use of the tactic against her and instead turns it on him by meeting his gaze without speaking. He breaks first.

"You have just arrived from Temple Church? Again?"

"Yes."

"Without escort?"

"Captain Dansby accompanied me," she says, "but I sent him on an errand before we returned."

Pembroke purses his lips. "You pray with inordinate frequency these days."

Though his expression has barely changed, Mary recognizes the subtle shift. Suspicion. She wrestles her rising angst into submission. "Prayer dispels the darkness, as you know."

Pembroke's hard stare softens, and he takes two steps toward her. "Are your feelings as they were before, three years past?"

They are, though it is not prayer but playwriting that has kept the darkness at bay. He must never learn the truth. "I am holding fast, husband. Thank you for inquiring."

Pembroke tips his head to one side. "Do you pray alone?"

"Other women join me."

"Who, might I ask?"

"No one you would know." Mary stops her fingers from clenching into fists. "Women who visit the chapel in search of a miracle."

"I see." Pembroke's gaze hardens again. "Do you seek a miracle, Mary?"

"Always, but you know that about me."

"I do." He shakes his head slowly. "I also wonder. On most days your mind is a strongbox to me, locked, chained, and beyond my ken."

It is a challenge. He does not believe her story of piety, and rightly so. He possesses an uncanny knack for spotting lies, and Mary is a poor liar. Unbidden, the lines of Kate's final speech come to Mary, and the fictional woman whispers to her.

"Tell him what he wants to hear."

Mary knots her fingers together at her waist and feigns weariness. "I attend to prayers publicly for the sake of appearances, Lord Husband. I show my face often at Temple Church to demonstrate that I am a good Protestant, a good wife, and a humble subject of the Crown. I do so to please the queen, as she is watching me."

Her husband's brow smooths, and he shrinks the space between them. "I commend your wisdom, then. However, perhaps you should pray less often. Elizabeth might consider too much piety an equal threat."

"Of course."

Apparently satisfied, Pembroke touches her brow with his lips. "I go now to the lion's den to spar with our rivals. Good day, good wife."

When he steps past Mary toward the road, she tucks her chin and massages her forehead. Disarming her husband's suspicions will prove challenging. By the time Mary leans into motion again, she has already decided to shift her strategy. She will have Dansby carry word to Emilia and Jane to avoid further meetings at the chapel until Christmas Eve, at which point a visit to the church will not only be appropriate but expected. But dread dogs her heels. Pembroke is not a man easily fooled. However, quitting when she has come so far would open the floodgates of darkness. Forward remains her only option, no matter the cost.

The spy lurks in the shadows of Whitehall, invisible to most and disregarded by all. The muffled voices of the queen's advisors leak from the council chamber, always adamant and sometimes strident. Without the queen in attendance, the great men of the court are ablaze with opinion and confidence. He chuckles softly. It would take a single iron glare from Her Majesty to render them stammering boys. Regardless, he only cares about the opinion of one man—his employer.

His patience pays dividends after more than two hours, when the doors burst open and the advisors file out, led by the Lord Chamberlain, Baron Hunsdon. The spy ducks into an alcove as the muttering men stalk past, oblivious to his presence. Questions about his visit to Whitehall would only complicate his employer's maneuverings. He does not wish that for one of the few courtiers he deems worthy of his respect.

As the voices trail into silence, the spy slips into the council chamber to find Robert Cecil madly scribbling on a piece of parchment. He waits until the queen's de facto secretary sets aside his pen and finally notices him. A brief flinch of surprise immediately gives way to a narrowed but curious gaze.

"Mr. Harwood."

The spy bows low. "Sir Robert."

"No one noticed you?"

"Not a single eye."

"Good, good." Cecil massages his writing hand. "I assume you've something to report."

"I do."

Cecil waves toward the line of chairs adjacent to his. "Come, then. Tell me."

Harwood removes his cap and settles into a chair midway down the table, near enough for discreet conversation, but not so close as to insinuate equality with Cecil. Although his employer concerns himself little over rank, Harwood has not survived so long in a hostile world without abundant caution and timely deference. Cecil appears to notice, as evidenced by the uptick of one side of his mouth.

"You may proceed."

Harwood clenches his cap in both fists on the tabletop. "I wish to report the puzzling activities of a certain noble subject near to Her Majesty: the Countess of Pembroke."

Cecil's eyebrows lift. "Mary Herbert?"

"Yes, sir."

"That is unexpected. She shuns court intrigue like the plague."

Harwood knows this but has formed a strong suspicion. "Perhaps she avoids notice for a reason."

"Go on."

Harwood sets aside his cap and leans toward Cecil on his elbows. With precision and an economy of words, he tells of the initial meeting at the Whitehall warming house, not two hundred steps away, and then describes the several gatherings at Temple Church. Cecil listens with the unblinking stare of a bird of prey. When Harwood finishes, the little man leans back in his chair and absently tugs his left earlobe.

"A countess, a courtesan, and a seamstress for a player's troupe. Accompanied by a soldier loyal to the countess and a court musician. Very odd. And all three women attended each meeting, but no others did?"

"Yes."

Cecil pushes up from his chair and begins pacing back and forth along the far side of the table. Harwood finds this unnerving, particularly given the man's irregular gait. Cecil circles a hand in the air while still walking.

"The Master of the Temple, Father Nicholas. Has he not claimed that Catholics might be spared from Hell by the Almighty?"

Hope flares within Harwood. Cecil is treading the same line of logic he has been following for weeks. "Yes, Sir Robert. He says so even though the queen surely disagrees."

Cecil spares him a chilly glance. "I do not make a habit of assuming what Her Majesty believes, nor do I question her closely on religious matters. I value my neck too highly to invite her debate. However, despite her uncontested courage, she is often troubled by the Catholic plots against her."

Harwood squeezes his fists with relief. Cecil understands. "Rightly so. I suspect a popish plot is brewing that involves these women. What say you?"

Cecil stops pacing to face him. "Lord and Lady Pembroke are good Protestants in all ways discernable—that much is true. Yet

Lady Pembroke spends most of her days away from Court and far from those who might assess her more closely. As of the Bassano woman? Her family descends from Venetian Catholics not three generations past." He runs a fingertip slowly across the tabletop, as if checking for dust. "What do you suppose they do when meeting at the church?"

Harwood has hoped for this question, as it sharpens the point of his conjectures. "They carry parchment and ink in and out. The soldier and the seamstress take the papers elsewhere afterward. I tried to follow, but the man—Captain Dansby is his name—he is too vigilant. They always travel toward Shoreditch, though."

"An unseemly place, to be sure." Cecil returns to his chair and sits. "They are clearly delivering missives. Letters to unknown parties."

"My suspicion exactly. Letters for priests. Instructions to papists for concealing priests. Perhaps Catholic dogma meant for schooling the followers of the pope."

Cecil's brow knots. "You believe they are writing religious tracts?"

"Why not? Lady Pembroke is sister to a poet. She might possess rudimentary writing skills suitable for the task."

Cecil grunts. "I believe her skills to be far above rudimentary. Do not underestimate her."

"I do not, which is why I report to you now. She appears more than capable of mounting a plot, or worse, a rebellion. Lord Pembroke is the wealthiest man in England, with a distant claim to the throne. Who knows how widely this plot has infected the kingdom?"

Cecil hums softly. "You make a good point, Mr. Harwood. As with the spider, the gravest threats are often posed by the most silent of creatures. Despite their prestige, Lord and Lady Pembroke studiously avoid attention and intrigue. I wonder why."

Harwood nearly rises from his chair in triumph. "I agree wholeheartedly, Sir Robert."

Cecil must have noticed Harwood's depth of his approval, for he lifts an eyebrow. "I hired you by reputation, John. However, I am little acquainted with you. I'd like to know why you are so keen to destroy papists."

Heat crawls up Harwood's neck. He has managed to avoid that question so far but has known he cannot guard his past from one as astute as Robert Cecil. He averts his eyes to study his hands.

"My father was Stephen Harwood. Have you heard of him?"

"The name sounds familiar."

"He was a brewer in Stratford, not far from here. Bloody Queen Mary sat the throne and sent her bulldog, Bishop Edmund Bonner, to silence loud Protestants. I was seven years old when they kicked down our door and hauled away my father."

Cecil grunts softly. "That was before my time, but I've heard tales of those dark days. What became of your father?"

"They burned him." Harwood swallows the lump in his throat. "My mother made me watch while she wailed vengeance into my ear. The smell of my father's smoking flesh never leaves me. I vowed to kill the queen and the bishop when I came of age, but Mary died too soon, and Bonner perished in prison."

"You were robbed of your retribution, then?"

He nods and looks up at Cecil. "I was. So, instead, I hunt those who carry on that cursed faith—the faith that murdered my father."

"You don't do so out of loyalty to Her Majesty?"

"She is not Catholic. I care about nothing else."

Cecil nods and lays his palm on the table. "I understand but advise you to keep your fervency in check. Too much too quickly will drive the plot underground."

Harwood's ears perk. "So, you believe there is a plot?"

"There are always plots. And I will destroy anyone who threatens Her Majesty—Catholic, Protestant, or heathen. Doubt not my words."

Harwood trembles with agreement. "What would you have me do, then, in service of your vow?"

Cecil casts an assessing eye on Harwood until the urge strikes the latter to shrink from the room. He instead squares his shoulders and lifts his chin. A smile crawls across Cecil's face.

"I must swear you to a secret, John. Are you prepared for the consequences?"

Weakness invades Harwood's knees, but he steadies them. "Yes, sir."

"When Walsingham was alive, he formed a secret brotherhood called the Bond of Association." Cecil has lowered his voice to nearly a whisper. "The sole purpose of the brotherhood is to hunt down and kill anyone attempting to harm the queen. Upon his death, I inherited the role as master of the association. Do you understand?"

Harwood swallows the lump in his throat. "I do."

"Good, good." Cecil waves a diffident hand back and forth, as if miming a religious ceremony. "I hereby induct you into the association. What the rest of us know, you will know. What you learn, you will tell us. Do you agree?"

Pride swells in Harwood's chest. "Yes, sir. It is my honor to serve."

"You must never breathe a word of the association or its activities to anyone. Am I clear?"

"Perfectly clear."

Cecil bobs his head. He plunges a hand into his purse, pulls out a handful of silver coins, and pushes them across the table. "Continue watching to determine what these women are—Catholic or Protestant, patriot or plotter."

Harwood collects the silver, rises to his feet, and bows low to his employer. "Thank you, Sir Robert. I will not disappoint you."

"Good hunting, John."

Relief surges through Harwood as he spirits himself away from Whitehall. Cecil shares his suspicions and not only trusts him to uncover the truth but invites him into his inner circle. Armed with burgeoning confidence, he vows to expose whatever plot the women are hatching, no matter the time and cost involved. Cecil will be pleased. Better yet, his dear father will smile down on him from Paradise.

⁂

The late hour and Dutton's fondness for ale sends Will again to the Mermaid with the final pages of *The Shrew* firmly in hand. Jane, in the company of the blue-liveried soldier, had shown up at his door as night was falling on the day of Dutton's deadline. After scrawling the final lines in his own hand, Will had gone to Dutton's house, only to find him absent, and then rushed straight to the tavern. He is breathing hard as he arrives. As usual, the troupe master haunts the table at the farthest corner from the door. On this night, however, his two tablemates are not of the Queen's Men, though Will recognizes one on sight.

Robert Greene.

A groan slips from his throat as he makes his way to the table. Perhaps the most prolific writer in London, Greene is best known for his acid-tongued pamphlet attacks on his rivals and his cozy association with the criminal underworld. Like Will, he comes from humble origins but has risen in society through a sharp wit, focused intellect, and malicious cunning.

The three men look his way as he approaches. Dutton and Greene frown while the third man, a hulking brute, glares solemnly at Will through piggish eyes. The big man's features look as if they've been removed and then hastily reassembled at some point, no doubt the product of repeated blows. His expansive scarred knuckles indicate that he serves up more violence than he consumes. Will avoids the man's scrutiny to find that Dutton's frown has grown deeper.

"Shakespeare. What do you want?"

Will extends the roll of paper in his left hand. "I am delivering the final pages of the play."

"Could your business not wait until morning?" Dutton tilts his head toward Greene. "I am drinking with friends."

Will nearly turns away but instead steps up to the edge of the table. "This is the date you imposed for the play's completion. I seek only to uphold my agreement so you might deliver the manuscript to the Master of Revels in a timely manner."

Dutton eyes the pages before scowling and snatching them from Will's hand. It occurs to Will that Dutton might have come to the tavern to avoid taking the final pages so he can scuttle the play without their fellow players objecting. A surge of pride courses through Will—for his fortitude and for the determination of the mysterious playwright. Or playwrights. Will has become convinced that the foul papers are the product of two hands, not one. But whose? Will's expression must betray his pleasure, for Dutton grows a mischievous grin.

"Where are my manners?" He motions to his left. "You, of course, recognize the distinguished Mr. Greene."

"I know him by sight and reputation, but we've never enjoyed the pleasure of an introduction."

Greene is a man possessed of seedy handsomeness, like a fine racehorse that has run too far without rest. His dark eyes spear Will as he stares down a razor-thin nose. "Yet I knew not one iota about you until Dutton began speaking your name to me a few weeks past."

With a flash of insight, Will deduces that Greene is the friend that Dutton mentioned—the man who intends to unearth Will's secrets. Any affinity Will might feel for Greene as a fellow country bumpkin evaporates. Greene is a viper by reputation, and Will knows it to be true as he faces the man. He dips his chin to Greene and tries to appear innocuous.

"I greatly enjoyed your *Pandosto*, Mr. Greene."

The writer's nostrils flare as he looks Will up and down. "So, you are Dutton's upstart. I was expecting someone rather more imposing given that you claim equality to university-educated wits."

The direct jab stirs Will's ire. He should hold his tongue, but he has never claimed to be wise. "Perhaps you recognize a kindred spirit given your arrival here on a manure cart."

Greene simply nods to the brute, who rises to his feet and stabs out a meaty paw to grip Will's throat. "Apologize, toad."

Will pries at the fingers without success while his closed airway fights for relief. When spots begin to gather before his eyes, he shoots a panicked plea at Dutton. The troupe master waves a hand.

"The poor player that he is, his understudy is worse. Please release the man's throat so I need not replace him."

Greene flicks a wrist, and the brute unhands Will. Will crumples to a chair grasping his throat and inhaling ragged breaths. The giant sits as well but leans toward Will.

"Apologize. Toad."

Will croaks a response. "My apologies for impugning your pedigree, Mr. Greene."

Greene lifts an eyebrow and smiles drolly. "I forgive you. However, you must apologize to my large and violent friend. As the brother of my mistress, Em, he devotes himself to my health and honor."

Will rubs his throat and dips his head toward the man, who seems dispassionately unoffended. "I beg your pardon for my thoughtless remark, Mr. . . ."

"Cutting Ball," says the brute.

Will blinks. "Cutting Ball? That is your name?"

When the man begins to rise again from his chair, Will holds out a palm. "A fine name, sir. One destined for literature. Perhaps I will assign it to a noble character in a future play."

Ball sits but his iron gaze fails to leave Will. Under the withering glare, Will solves the puzzle. Em Ball had been the mistress of the great comedian, John Tarlton, before he died. She is a woman whose dubious reputation is exceeded only by her brother's, for he is a notorious cutpurse and cutthroat. And now, they are both devoted to Greene, one in the bedchamber and the other on the streets. Will swallows, finding the action difficult with his mangled throat.

Meanwhile, Greene appears amused by the theatrical scene, as evidenced by a lopsided smile. He chuckles and extends a hand to Dutton. "Let me see what *brilliance* Shakespeare has produced."

Dutton hands the pages to him. "Not original. Amateurish. I find the heroine unbelievable and absurd."

Greene hushes Dutton with a finger and reads the pages in silence. His face remains an unyielding mask. Upon finishing, he meets Will's eyes. "This is good, Shakespeare. Too good for a country yokel with no education."

Will bristles again but recalls how much he enjoys breathing. "With apologies to your large friend, are you not of country origins as well, Mr. Greene?"

"I am but possess university degrees and talent." Greene spouts the reply as if he keeps it near at hand for quick retrieval when asked the question by his betters. "I am a writer, not a puppet on a string. You, sir, are clearly a fraud, having copied this from another."

Will manages to keep from grinding his teeth over the accuracy of Greene's guess. "I am a writer as well. I have composed sonnets for some years now, though kept for private amusement."

Greene laughs. "You write sonnets, you say? I scarcely believe it."

"I speak the truth."

"Then compose some lines for me." Greene leans toward Will. "This table is, after all, private, and I seek to be amused."

Fire courses through Will's veins. Since his arrival in London three years earlier, men like Greene and Dutton have dismissed him as an oafish player and no more. A man of no station, no talent, and no possibility. He recalls his discussion with Jane at the water fountain, when she had encouraged him to capture his poetry for others to enjoy. She believes in him. Cannot he do the same? Against his better instincts, Will gains his feet and grips his shirt as he glares at Greene.

Preeneth thy feathers, magnificent crow,
Lord over London with pinion outspread.
Cast thine aspersions on the wretched below,
Surfeit thyself on cadaveric dead.

He remains standing, half in wonder that such words have come to him so easily. Dutton and Greene both frown and blink. The latter lifts his chin.

"Am I the crow, then?"

"I do not assign roles," Will says, "but merely invent the lines."

Greene slouches in his chair and regards Will while letting the frown marinate. "We shall see what you are, to be certain. I will find you out. I possess the means, associates, and determination to expose you naked before the world."

Dutton nods agreement. "It is as I said, Will. You reach too high. Your words or not, when the queen disparages the play, I will have her know that you claim it."

"As you wish." Will inclines his head. "Mr. Dutton. Mr. Greene. Mr. Ball."

He turns away and strides toward the tavern door, trying not to appear hurried, though he spins in a maelstrom. The men correctly called him an imposter but without proof. Nevertheless, he wants the play to succeed if for no other reason than to humble those who would view him as a footstool. More than that, the play is very good. Though Dutton mentions the dire consequences of the queen not liking the play, Will fears the opposite. What if she approves? What if she requires more? How can he continue the ruse without knowing whether the mystery playwrights are willing and able to continue? And if they are, how long can he conceal the truth from a man so well connected to the city's criminal element? If he knows anything for certain, it is this: Robert Greene does not make idle threats, and he aims his dagger squarely at Will Shakespeare's heart.

10

Christmas Eve, 1591

Jane steals into the nave of Temple Church and slams headfirst into a wall. The barrier is not of stone or wood, but of bodies in motion and chaotic sound. She freezes three steps inside the great doors, her eyes rounded to their boundaries. The nave, normally empty save Father Nicholas or a stray candle lighter, crawls with strangers of all ages and stations, talking, praying, singing, laughing. The assembly cloaks the church in a tapestry of human emotion. A gentle hand against the small of her back reminds Jane that Dansby is still behind her.

"'Tis Christmas Eve, Jane." His calming breath tickles her left ear as his lips nearly touch them in a whisper. "They come to honor the Christ child, as is customary. The chapel, though, remains your refuge."

She inhales a shuddered breath and leans into motion. The other visitors pay her no heed as she mounts the stairs and enters the now familiar Chapel of St. Anne for the first time in nearly a fortnight. Mary and Emilia interrupt their whispered conversation to acknowledge her arrival with nods.

"Jane, you've come." Emilia's smile reminds Jane of the warmth she has missed since their last meeting and confounds her anew that a woman of such station is pleased to see her. Jane curtsies.

She is becoming very proficient at the maneuver, which she counts as a benefit. Perhaps it is a skill that will save her from disapproval in the future. Nothing demonstrates deferential apology like a well-executed deep drop.

"Miss Bassano. Lady Pembroke."

Only then does she notice the tight lines that cradle Mary's eyes. Her clear anxiety threatens to inflame Jane's doubt, but it is too late to run. Dansby has already closed the door behind her. In the hanging silence, the news she has been keeping for a day and a half erupts from her lips.

"The Master of Revels signed the final pages of *The Shrew*. It is an allowed book."

Allowed book.

Two words that transport a play from the land of *maybe* into the world of *is*. An official title that elevates a work from obscurity to the hallowed planks of the London stage. Relief ripples across Mary's features without fully erasing the lines along her eyes. She nods once, settles into a chair, and motions to the empty seats. Jane joins Emilia, across from the countess, to wait in silence. Mary's pause is brief.

"You are certain of this?"

"Will . . . Mr. Shakespeare told me yesterday. John Dutton is furious, and I am buried beneath a stack of garments, and the entire troupe is in a frenzy."

Mary's lips tighten. "Why a frenzy?"

"Because Dutton made the players recite lines for a different play, sure that the Master of Revels wouldn't approve *The Shrew*. Now, we all scramble to catch up."

Emilia leans her face into her hands to massage her temples, and groans. "This is disastrous. Their lack of preparation will reflect poorly on the play."

"I think the same," Mary says. She cuts her attention between Emilia and Jane. "Which underscores the reason I called for this final meeting. *The Shrew* is to be staged at Court two days hence for Her Majesty. Once we leave here, the bones will have been cast, and the cart set in motion down a treacherous road."

Emilia lifts her head to peer at Mary. "What are you suggesting?"

"That if we so choose, we can stop now while knowing we have written a play worthy of the London stage. That we might find all the satisfaction we desire in having birthed a noble creation. Tylney owes Pembroke money. I can stop this play from seeing daylight with a single word to him and no explanation. He will do as I ask."

Emilia shifts in her chair. "I must confess that second thoughts pester me. They have for days. What if the play is not liked? What if the queen reviles it?"

"Yes," says Mary. "What if the truth becomes obvious—that a woman wrote the words? That the lines and plot are fundamentally lacking in quality? The fiasco with the Queen's Men only increases the odds of such an outcome."

Jane has been literally sitting on her hands to prevent them from tremoring. As the commiserating silence stretches between Mary and Emilia, her body fails to cooperate. A cascade of memories rushes through her—of ridicule and exile; of fleeing from an unpleasant past toward a frightening future; of days on the road, wracked with hunger, until a new place offers refuge that she knows is only temporary. She should leave such a momentous decision to her betters, but the sum of Jane's experience disallows it. Her blunt and dogged nature won't stand for it. She yanks her hands free and slaps them on the tabletop.

"No."

Mary and Emilia stare at her, startled. Mary cocks her head. "Jane?"

Jane digs her nails into the oaken table. "With apologies to my ladies, I have been running away for most of my life. Running from one place that doesn't want me to the next, never looking back, never wondering if I could have stayed. If I could have fought for my place there. If I could have found a satisfying life." A sob erupts from her throat. "I tire of running. For the first time, I want to stay. I want to fight for the present. I have found"—another sob—"friendship."

Emilia drops a gentle hand onto Jane's wrist. "Sweet Jane. You have no concerns, then?"

Jane shakes her head. "I fear disaster, just as you do. And if we quit today, I will be no less than I am now. But I will regret my cowardice for as long as I live. I don't want to quit. I don't want to run anymore. I want to become more than what I am."

Mary's eyes brim with tears that escape, trailing unhindered down her cheek. She carefully wipes them away with the back of a hand.

"Then let us vote as the Lords do when at Parliament." She nods to Emilia and then smiles at Jane. "If you wish to allow the play to continue, raise your right hand."

Three hands reach toward the ceiling without hesitation. A warm wind blows through Jane's soul, a westerly breeze that drives her toward the hope of something better. However, pure terror pushes back.

Two days!

What if my companions' fears are justified?

What if the Queen's Men fail?

The haunt of Mary's and Emilia's eyes mirrors Jane's. The day of reckoning is at hand, and the axe hangs ready to fall. However, even that scenario lends Jane some solace. They will rise together or fall together.

Together.

For Jane, such a thing is wondrously new.

⁂

The two days fly like a sparrow driven before the autumn gale.

After arriving at Dutton's house, Jane makes camp at the kitchen table, with needle and thread, to construct a half-dozen costumes on Dutton's orders. Evidence of frantic frustration leaks from the common room in the form of heated exchanges and mounting disagreements. Sometime after midnight, the troupe departs the house for a more secretive location. To work on Christmas Day is all but illegal, and the neighbors cannot possibly miss the strident activity. Where they go, Jane has no idea.

Toward midmorning, she lays her head on the table in an attempt to sleep. Every time slumber comes upon her, so do the nightmares—shadowy, grasping creatures that drag her before the queen, to be sentenced and hung from an impossibly tall tree. As the rope tightens, she jerks awake. Eventually, she gives up and resumes working.

The holy day passes as a numbing train of stitches and angst. Mrs. Dutton occasionally forces her to eat and drink, but otherwise leaves Jane to her labors. While she is sewing the final costume, a dreamless slumber overcomes her, and her cheek hits the tabletop.

"Jane! What is this?"

Jane bolts from the depths of sleep to panicked disorientation in the space of a stuttering heartbeat. Her bleary eyes focus on a looming Dutton. He shakes the unfinished costume in one hand.

"Well?"

"My apologies, sir! I am nearly finished."

He tosses the garment at her face. "You will need to do so on the barge. Now gather the wardrobe. We must fly!"

Jane throws the new costumes into a pair of bags and hauls them toward the common room. She stops short at the threshold. The Queen's Men are all gathered there, slumped into chairs or against various walls, their faces gray with exhaustion. Jane swallows dismay.

God help us.

"Up!" shouts Dutton. "Her Majesty will not wait for laggards."

The players climb to their feet and file out the door, carting props and the heavy chest. With no other recourse, Jane hoists the two bags across her shoulder and trails them. The day is cold, but a breeze overnight has scattered the normal pall of wood smoke and has washed the sky blue. The chill increases as they travel the Thames by barge toward Whitehall. Jane settles on the bags and continues stitching the final garment while trying to ignore the general lack of banter among the men. When she glances at Will, he looks away. Only when the barge touches the landing at Whitehall Stairs, do the players' spirits begin to stir.

"Let's go, lads," says Lionel Cooke. "We've faced worse a hundred times and slayed the crowd nonetheless."

"Here, here," adds John Singer. "Draw your swords."

Dutton is still peeved, though. "Move your indolent feet. Make haste!"

The troupe mounts the stairs and invades their traditional tyring room—the pantry. As before, the players snatch garments faster than Jane can lay them out. As they leave, Jane finally catches Will's eye. He frowns and shakes his head before disappearing through the door. In their absence, Jane's thoughts spin into disastrous flights of fancy, and she paces the small pantry until her skin tries to crawl off her bones. She bolts outside and inhales deeply of the chill air to calm her anxiety.

Without conscious thought, Jane approaches the antechamber and wiggles through the waiting players until she can view the musicians in the far back corner of the hall. Emilia is there, staring blankly and stroking her neck slowly as she does when wracked with concern. Then the queen is speaking, unseen, her great and terrible voice uttering momentous and maybe ominous things. Jane stumbles back through the collected bodies and falls to the ground in the passageway. She stares at the cobblestones beneath her trembling hands.

What have we done? she thinks.

Jane has devoted her life to avoiding notice, to melting into crowds, to hiding her peculiarity beneath a cloak of anonymity. But only moments from now, her invented story will be revealed to the queen—raw, naked, and unmasked for royal judgment. Jane fights back nausea, and only the empty state of her stomach prevents her from retching.

A pair of hands grip Jane's arms and lift her gently to her feet. She raises her head and finds Dansby towering over her, so perilously close.

"Come," he says.

Dansby guides her along the passageway to the pantry and encourages her to sit on a crate. He studies her face until she turns it away in shame. He must already know that she is strange. Now, he sees her cowardice as well.

"You've never asked about my scar."

Jane looks back at Dansby to find him lifting his pitted cheek in her direction. She blinks in confusion. "Pardon me?"

"Most new acquaintances wait no longer than a few days to ask what happened to me. You have not."

"I decided long ago that scars are personal. Only the bearer should decide when and if to tell the story."

Dansby chuckles. "A worthy creed, Miss Daggett. In that vein, may I tell you what occurred?"

Jane has wondered about the injury and cannot resist his offer. "I would be honored."

"Very well." He picks up a costume that has fallen to the floor. "When we defeated the Spanish Armada at Gravelines, I was aboard the *Mother Mercy*."

"You fought against the Armada?"

"I did. I would do so again. For England. For the queen." He taps the hilt of his sword. "My men and I stood on deck, ready to board enemy galleons. We came up on one, broadside, but the Spanish monster rode so high in the water that boarding became an impossibility. However, while its cannons fired over our decks without harm to us, ours began ripping its hull to shreds. I sheathed my sword and went below decks to help load shot. The beast had just begun to list when one of our cannons backfired and threw a slug of iron through my cheek. I remained barely within my senses as our quarry slipped beneath the waves."

Jane peers closely at the healed wound, imagining how it might have looked in the immediate aftermath. The shattered flesh. The shock. The pain. "I am sorry for what happened to you. Your courage is admirable, sir."

Dansby shakes his head. "Not at all. I was afraid, Miss Daggett."

"You were?"

"Terrified, in fact. We all were. However, we knew the stakes of failure and what must be done to avoid it. We attended to our tasks. We did the work." He extends the costume to her. "As you will now. I have faith in you."

Warmth spreads through Jane's chest and heats her neck. She accepts the costume and holds it to her breast. "Thank you, Captain."

"Call me Dansby."

He bows to her and leaves the pantry. In his absence, Jane realizes her hands have stopped trembling. She perks her ears as the first lines emanate from the high, overhead windows across the passageway—and she hopes for the best.

༺ ༻

Mary maintains an iron grip on her husband's knee and stares at the wall behind Elizabeth's head while the queen speaks. She will later recall not a single word of what Her Majesty was saying. Then, without fanfare, John Dutton is atop the platform, to introduce the play. Mary's heart tells her to leave before disaster strikes, but she cannot look away. With her avenues of escape sealed shut, she casts a silent prayer into the void and gives herself to the maelstrom.

To Mary's astonished relief, the Queen's Men rise to the challenge. Their lines are crisp and well timed. The banter is lively. The movement across the stage is dynamic. The noble audience leans forward in their seats with rapt attention, mewing on cue and laughing when they should—especially when Katherina and Petruchio wage their war of words. She notices a stumble here and there, but only the playwright and players could identify the mishaps.

When Mary dares peek at Elizabeth, she finds the queen relaxed in her chair, with the hint of a smile on her face. But despite all the positive signs, Mary remains uneasy. The teenager playing Katherina speaks his lines shrilly, undermining the character's strength, even though entertaining the listeners. By the end of the second act, Mary realizes what is going wrong. The performance is all but devoid of the satire and sarcasm it needs, as if Dutton has sucked it from the script like marrow from a bone. Petruchio's acts of manipulation and physical deprivation are staged as worthy pursuits rather than as the dastardly acts they are.

Mary sinks lower into her chair with each passing scene as smoldering chagrin sinks its claws into her. Kate's final speech, designed to accuse society of debasing women, instead plays as an act of obeisance that not only excuses Petruchio's tactics but lauds them. After the final lines of the play are spoken, however, the nobles stand from their seats with applause, a practically unheard-of response from those who consider the showing of approval in public a mortal sin. The queen taps her fingers to her palm, wearing that slight smile, no different from the one she wore during Mary's previous visit.

However, Mary notices a subtle difference that drags her deeper into confusion. She considers what she sees and can make no sense of it. The dichotomy of disappointment and accolade, anger and pride threaten to rip Mary in two. Without a word, she leaves Pembroke behind and exits the hall through the antechamber. Captain Dansby is waiting in the passageway, as she had instructed him. He tips his head toward the river.

"The warming house, my lady."

He leads her to the familiar chamber and opens the door. Jane and Emilia are standing together, clearly waiting for Mary. They curtsy in unison, and then Jane takes a step forward. Her eyes are red and puffy, her shoulders rounded.

"They butchered it, my lady."

Emilia cannot agree more adamantly. She stalks to the wall opposite the fireplace and back again, pushing scenes of the presentation through her memory like brackish water through a sluice. For a moment during the first act, Emilia's dwindled hopes of triumph had risen from the ashes of crushed expectations. A phoenix resurrected by the skilled and determined efforts of the Queen's Men to set the stage on fire. But only for a moment. One by one, Katherina's lines of rebellion had become shrewishness, and her acts of resistance had been twisted into shows of naivete and compliance by nothing more than the way the words had been spoken. Emilia squares on Mary.

"Kate was all wrong. Her manner of speaking was all wrong. Her tone was all wrong. It was all so very wrong."

Jane bobs her head at Emilia's side and sniffles. Mary's lips are thin and tight, her eyes burning. "Go on."

Mary's nudge shoves Emilia into motion again, marching her between the twin walls of stone while she waves her hands and pours forth indignation. "Nearly every day, I witness helplessly the men of Court stuffing their wives into the narrow confines of social strongboxes, locking them tight, and losing the key. Kate's final speech? It simply congratulated them for such prudent actions. Dared them to expand their dominion, to hold their women in tighter check."

She slaps the wall with a palm and spins to face Mary and Jane. "Why did we even try? We knew they would find a way to foul Katherina. To break her spine. To steal the spirit from her body."

In the echoing silence that follows, Mary appears to explore the depths of her own disappointment. "It is as you both claim. I witnessed the same."

Jane plops onto a chair and expels a defeated sigh. Emilia sets a hand on the young woman's shoulder. "It should not be thus. Our Kate deserved better."

Mary hums and the grim set of her features loosens. "However, . . ."

The single word trails away. Emilia cocks her head. "My lady?"

Mary looks into the fire, her brow knotted with thought. "However, and for reasons I know not, Her Majesty loved the play."

Jane lifts her head and Emilia stares. She raises open palms to the countess. "How do you know?"

"Dansby," Mary says. "After I arrived at Whitehall today, the captain relayed something one of the queen's guardsmen shared with him. A man Dansby fought alongside some years ago."

Jane rises to her feet. "What did he say?"

Mary touches her neckline below her ruff. "He said that when the queen is enjoying a play, she tends to unlatch the first toggle or two of her dress."

Emilia blinks rapidly. "Did she unlatch a toggle, then?"

"No," says Mary. "Three toggles."

Emilia's consternation trends toward bewilderment. The queen liked their play? Three toggles' worth? How could she, given what happened to Katherina?

"Jane Daggett? Where the devil are you?"

Dutton's irate call rushes down the passageway outside and burrows beneath the door, invading the small chamber. When the man roars again, Mary closes the gap and pulls Emilia and Jane into a huddle.

"Let us meet a final time at Temple Church, three days hence, to discuss the meaning of these events, away from prying eyes and ears. We will decide if anything is to be done or if the matter ends."

Jane curtsies on wobbly knees. "Yes, my lady."

Emilia deflates as the implications become clear. Her flirtation with playwriting might soon come to a halt. As for Katherina? She may be silenced forever. She dips her head.

"As you wish, Mary." Emilia touches Jane's sleeve. "You should go. We will wait a moment before leaving in your wake."

Jane drops a second curtsy and pushes her way through the warming house door. In her absence, Emilia has nothing to say to Mary, and the countess seems just as tongue-tied. *Does she feel as I do?* Emilia wonders. *As if my soul is cleaving in two?* Regardless, she fears for the survival of either half.

After waiting perhaps a minute, Emilia returns toward the great hall, anxious and wringing her hands. However, a man waits for her in the now-empty antechamber: Lord Hunsdon, the cousin of the queen. Her benefactor, whose bed she warms. How has he managed to escape the clutches of his wife? The anxiety abates enough to allow her to smile.

"Henry."

"Emilia." He steps forward to grasp her hands. His hair is fully gray, and his face deeply lined, but he retains the handsome features of his youth and an uncommon vigor for his age. "You appear flummoxed."

She looks at him sidelong. "Where is Lady Hunsdon?"

"Bundled off toward home. We are quite safe from her jealous eyes." He scans the passageway behind Emilia. "Where did you go in such a rush after the play?"

Emilia shrugs. "Just to the warming house for privacy in which to relish the presentation."

Hunsdon narrows his nearly colorless blue eyes at her. "Not meeting with a younger man, then?"

She stretches her neck to kiss his lips. "I would not, Henry. You well know my fondness for you."

"Fondness for the income I provide you."

Emilia shakes her head. For a man of such importance, his lack of confidence regarding her fidelity never ceases to astonish her. He remains the only man with whom she has been intimate, yet he questions her repeatedly. She tamps down mild pique. "When others invent stories of my sexual exploits, I ignore their slander. When you question me as if you believe those stories, I am wounded."

Hunsdon gathers Emilia in his arms and kisses her forehead. "My apologies, dear. I am well past my youth and more aware of my frailty with each passing day. Everyone at Court whispers of it."

Emilia chuckles softly. "They do. Lord Cumberland called you a relic to my face."

Hunsdon grunts. "Though he is a jackass, he is not wrong. Why else would a young beauty give her affections to an old married man?"

This time, she cannot help but smile at his doubt. "You do keep me well, I freely admit. However, while most men trumpet their privilege with great fanfare and repetition, you question your worth, in the quiet of an empty chamber, to a girl far beneath your station. Such a quality is rarer than gold."

"You could say the same of a father. Is that how you love me? As a father?"

Emilia turns away to begin leading him by one hand in the general direction of his chambers. "Oh, you of little faith. Allow me to remind you of how unfatherly you are, before I send you back to the queen."

⁂

From his customary crevice deep along the Whitehall passage, Harwood lurks like a denizen of the stones as he watches his quarry enter the warming house. Minutes later, they leave again—the seamstress first, then the courtesan, then the countess. He shakes his head in disbelief.

Right beneath the queen's nose! The audacity!

The women have made a habit of convening at every opportunity, so why not here? Why not now? And what manner of plot are they brewing? After waiting for the Pembroke guardsman to vacate the passageway, Harwood slips into the still-crowded hall. He ducks his head but cannot help but overhear why they buzz. *The play! Oh, the play!* With his focus firmly on Lady Pembroke and the Bassano woman, he had not paid much attention to the players. Were not plays foul practices anyway? Fit only for heathens and Catholics? So his mother had told him, and she had been a saint.

Harwood finds the corner recently vacated by the musicians and lounges there until Cecil spies him. A subtle tilt of Sir Robert's head sends Harwood into an adjacent chamber. He waits quietly for some time before Cecil slides into the room and shuts the door behind him. The secretary folds his arms and cocks an eyebrow.

"They met again just now," Harwood tells him. "Same place as before."

Cecil's arms loosen, and he rubs his forearms while staring blankly at the stone floor. "Is that so? Not two hundred steps from Her Majesty?"

"Yes, sir."

Cecil grunts. "What does your gut tell you?"

Harwood is surprised to find that he does have an instinct—one that has only nibbled the corners of his mind until now. "The seamstress is the key."

"The least important of the lot?"

"Yes, sir. I have learned from my spy inside the players troupe that she was run out of Henley-on-Thames with accusations of witchcraft. She only escaped with the aid of her employer, a Mr. Burnham. A well-regarded tanner of the town, it seems."

"Have you laid eyes on this man?"

"Not yet."

Cecil lifts an index finger. "Tell me. Why would a man risk his reputation and his livelihood to help a girl with all the status of a stray dog?"

"I wonder the same." Harwood risks a smile. "What would you have me do next, Sir Robert?"

Cecil returns to the door and puts his hand on the latch before looking once more at Harwood. "I would have you devote a share of your observation to the girl, then. And see what you can learn about her employer. We will speak again later."

Cecil is gone before Harwood can thank the man for his continued confidence in him. Buoyed, he leaves by a different door, more determined than ever to please Cecil and his dead father.

༄

The Queen's Men storm the Mermaid with jubilation over having pulled *The Shrew* from the fire at the last minute and staging it to a warm response from the queen. Will isn't having any of it, though. Unable to escape the accolades of his troupe mates, he has been swept along from Whitehall, across the Thames, and into the tavern, while offering only minor resistance. Glum recollection circles his brain. They had gutted the play's satire, ripping the brilliant beating heart from the script. He had seen it coming for two days but had been powerless to stop Dutton's campaign of neutering. Cleary, the troupe master had intended to erode the play as a swipe at Will, to knock him down a notch by watering down Katherina's character. Will remains surprised that Dutton's plan had both succeeded and failed. The revised Kate had muted the play's brilliance but had resonated with a noble audience quite accustomed to the degradation of women.

"Smile, lad!" Lionel Cooke blasts Will on a shoulder raw from congratulations. "This night is your triumph."

Fortunately, Will doesn't need to respond because of a crescendo of raised voices. He looks up to find a half dozen of Lord Strange's Men occupying the corner table beloved by the Queen's Men.

"Move your carcasses!" bellows Dutton. "Get thee to your proper place."

Richard Burbage slowly rises to face Dutton. Though not well acquainted with the man, Will finds him impressive. Younger than Will by several years, Burbage has already stamped himself as the most popular dramatic player in London, and with reason. His wide shoulders and stocky frame exude power that erupts as he moves like an athlete on stage. His voice carries through the largest of venues like a trumpet cutting the air. His renditions of powerful characters move crowds to tears, a phenomenon Will has witnessed firsthand. Burbage's recent defection from the Lord Admiral's Men has generated no end of gossip among the troupes of London.

"Mr. Dutton," says Burbage, "Our proper place will be at Whitehall on the morrow to see to Her Majesty's satisfaction, which should be sorely lacking in the aftermath of enduring the Queen's Men."

Will drifts closer to the conversation as Dutton's face reddens.

"Fear not, little man," Dutton says. "We left her satisfied. Three toggles' worth."

Burbage's brow knots. "So, the rumor is true." He lifts his chin toward a different table, which Will finds to his chagrin is occupied by Robert Greene and his mountainous bodyguard, Cutting Ball. "Mr. Greene. You owe me five pounds."

Greene makes an obscene gesture at Burbage. "We never shook on it. I owe you nothing."

Burbage laughs before reengaging Dutton with a steely gaze. "Nevertheless, we remain here. Go sit with your disreputable friend, if you please."

Dutton growls and stalks toward Greene's table. "We shall have to burn that table later to rid it of lice."

Will moves with the rest of the Queen's Men to occupy the tables surrounding Greene. Though Will avoids eye contact with the man, he has Greene's attention.

"Shakespeare!"

Will finally meets Greene's glare. "What?"

"Take your bows, boy, while you can," he says with a barely disguised snarl. "Who's the crow now?"

"Yes," says Singer. "Take a bow. You are, this night, a playwright."

His fellows push Will to his feet, and he bows curtly before plopping down again. It is bad enough that the play is not his work, but the gutting of Katherina has rendered it unrecognizable. Bows are superfluous. Dutton seizes a cup of ale and drains it in a single shot before grabbing a second cup and raising it high.

"Hear, hear!" His voice is raw with restrained outrage. "Who knew a country oaf of no education and even less standing could amuse the queen with the strokes of his pen? Let us all toast to the day ignorance triumphed over class, when buffoonery bested common sense. Let us all lift our cups to William Shakespittle—may he be struck by lightning."

His fellow players cut their eyes from Dutton to Will. Some raise their cups half-heartedly, clearly taken aback by Dutton's animosity toward Will's triumph. Will is beyond that. His shame and ire rise in tandem, equal oxen paired to a punishing cart. He glares at Dutton, further bewildering his troupe mates. Dutton's nostrils flare. He downs his second cup, wipes his mouth with a sleeve, and shakes the empty vessel at Will.

"Do not look at me so, boy. I know you pilfered the play. Fortunately for you, I was able to repair its flaws. Nevertheless, you are a thief, and I will find you out."

Awash in a sea of disgrace, fury, and noise, Will breaks. He jumps to his feet, sending his chair tumbling. He grips the table's edge with such force that his nails crack. "As God is my witness, John Dutton, I have stolen nothing!"

"Sit down and shut your mouth."

Will pushes away from the table. "I will not. Never again. From this moment forward, I remove my services from the Queen's Men."

Dutton grows a smile as he silences groans from some of the players. "Let him go, lads. Who would hire such an oaf?"

It is a good question. Quitting the Queen's Men in a huff will not do Will's career any favors. What has he done?

"I will hire him."

Will turns to find Burbage standing again at the table in the corner, watching him. Will cocks his head. "Pardon?"

"Do you have another play in the works?"

The correct answer is "No." Or perhaps "Allow me to consider it" while he tracks down Jane to learn if the mystery playwrights have additional plans. However, neither answer comes anywhere near his lips.

"Of course."

Burbage nods with approval. "Excellent. Lord Strange's Men move into the Rose Theatre less than two months hence. We require material. Can you have something for us by the first of February?"

Again, all correct responses flee Will's brain. "Yes. Yes, I can."

"Good, good. And another by, say, first of March?"

"Indeed." Will stops to allow his runaway mouth to fall silent. His brain finally resumes its normal function. "May I act as bookholder?"

Burbage waves a hand. "Of course. For every play you write."

"And can I own a share of the troupe?"

Burbage chuckles. "One hill at a time, Mr. Shakespeare."

Only then does Will take note of the cacophony that has erupted at his back. He turns to find various of the Queen's Men threatening Dutton with bodily injury for having chased Will away. For the first time in days, a smile creeps over his face. His time under the punishing thumb of Dutton is behind him. Fields of opportunity lie before him. His smile fades when a hand grasps his sleeve—a hand belonging to Robert Greene.

"Dutton is sometimes a fool, but he is right about you. I have people delving into your activities even as we speak." Greene leans nearer, his ale-soaked breath washing across Will's face. "These are not the kind of people whose attention one would desire. Mind your back. Knives have been known to slip in just . . . there."

He stabs three fingers to the left of Will's spine, just behind his heart. Will yanks his arm away from Greene's grasp and strides to the corner table. He doffs his cap.

"May I join you gents?"

"Yes, of course," says Burbage. "You are with us now, it seems."

"And very grateful, thank you."

"My pleasure."

Only then does Will consider the promises he has made. He must speak to Jane, but how can he? She is with the Queen's Men, and he doesn't know where she lives. He leans toward Burbage.

"I don't suppose you could use a mistress of the wardrobe, could you?"

"The Rose employs a tyring man for that job." Will's jaw goes slack before Burbage raises an index finger. "However, we do require someone who can sew costumes and watch the admission collectors to make sure Henslowe treats us fairly. Do you know of such a person?"

Will's dread dissipates somewhat. "I do."

"Very well, then. Now, let's raise a glass to our newest playwright."

As Lord Strange's men hoist their cups to Will, he prays silently for the health of the true playwrights—whoever they might be.

11

Usually, a lifetime requires a lifetime. Emilia has lived one in three days. From the whiplash of the play at Whitehall to the cusp of the final meeting three days later, Emilia's mood has swung wildly by the moment, a ball-and-chain flail wielded by a demon to impact everyone who steps inside its range. Riding beside her in the coach as it nears Temple Church, Alfonso still wears a persistent wince from having taken more than a few blows. He points through the window to a familiar blue coach.

"Lady Pembroke has already arrived."

"I am not late," Emilia says curtly.

"I did not accuse you of such, but merely observed that her ladyship is early."

"Your observation spilled over to your lips and thus became accusation."

Alfonso heaves a sigh. "Apologies." He cuts his eyes at her. "Will you not tell me why the play has affected you so? Raging one moment, giddy the next?"

Another retort leaps to her tongue before she swallows it. Shame heats her cheeks. Alfonso has been patient and mostly understanding. What if she were to tell him the truth? That she is the playwright? That she conspires with a countess and a seamstress to tread sacred spaces where women aren't allowed? That her soul is torn between victory and vexation? And what might he think of her if he learns the truth? She looks away. She cares too much about what Alfonso thinks, which annoys her more than it should. When the coach rolls to a stop, she finally makes eye contact with him.

"Worry not for me, Alfonso. I am simply too much in my head these past few days, nothing more."

He must sense her remorse, because he ventures a smile. "A dangerous and wondrous land, the inside of your head."

She cannot hide her smile. "Which is why you should not enter. You are ill-equipped for the perils there."

"I do not disagree."

Alfonso exits the coach and helps Emilia down. However, he has the good sense to walk behind her as they enter the church. She passes a stone-faced Captain Dansby and mounts the stairs as Alfonso greets the soldier. After pushing through the chapel door, Emilia finds Mary and Jane waiting. A fading echo tells her that Mary has been speaking. Emilia joins them with a less than dainty thud into her chair.

"What have I missed?"

Mary's lips are a thin line, but the smile of her eyes welcomes Emilia. "I was sharing my qualms with Jane."

Jane's head bobs, her eyes wide and her brow uncharacteristically wrinkled in consternation. Emilia's lips draw into a frown. "Might you share those with me?"

"Of course." The countess folds her hands on the tabletop. "We appear to have survived our playwriting experiment without harm. Our secret remains intact. The play was much loved despite the disappointment of Kate's spirit and the misdirection in the final scene." She expels a sigh and looks at Jane. "Perhaps we have accomplished our mission. Perhaps this is the end."

When Mary returns her attention to Emilia, she has one eyebrow lifted in question. *Oh, and what a question!* Emilia quickly revisits all the arguments that have raged in her mind for quitting, for continuing, for ripping her clothes and screaming. Perhaps Mary is right. Is this, then, the end of the dream? Emilia blinks as she becomes aware of Jane's expression. She hadn't thought the young women's remarkable eyes capable of conveying such sorrow. It dismays her.

"Jane," she says. "What . . . what are you thinking."

Jane catches Mary's eye, and the countess nods. The seamstress turns her face to stare at a blank, stone wall.

"I come from nothing and have accomplished nothing." Her words tumble forth so softly that Emilia cranes her neck to better hear. "For as long as I can remember, I had assumed I would continue to be nothing for as long as I drew breath and would eventually die nothing." Jane swipes a tear with the back of her hand, still staring at the wall. "These past three days, though, I can think of nothing else but what happened that night. I know Dutton made mince of it, but *The Shrew* was my story. On a stage. Before the queen. And she liked it very much. Since then, I have walked around these same streets as before, but clouds carry me. I lift my chin like a noble lady and meet the eyes of those I pass. Hardly a minute goes by that I do not remember that I have accomplished something I never thought possible for one such as me. And I smile. I smile until those around me think me mad. But I don't care."

Jane peers into Emilia's eyes. "But now? I apologize for my melancholy, but I am deeply saddened. I . . . I don't relish returning to what I was. A nothing."

Empathy floods Emilia, overtaking her bleak feelings in a cleansing rush. She stabs a hand across the table to clutch one of Jane's. "Hear me, Jane Daggett. You are not nothing, no matter what comes next. You are a bright light, a sparkling imagination, a beautiful spirit. And I, too, cannot keep the play from my thoughts for more than a heartbeat. I . . . I cannot open my hand to let it go."

She looks at the countess. The hard lines of Mary's expression have melted to release a soft smile.

"I had suggested an ending," she says, "because it is prudent. Rational. Safe. However, I secretly hoped you would disagree, and you have. I thank you for the courage to scoff at safety and carry on. My father, God rest him, was a humble knight who forever refused to leave the field, though bloodied and beaten, much to my mother's chagrin. I am his daughter, formed in his likeness and keen to remain on the field of battle. I needed only to learn if I still had allies."

Euphoria elbows aside the darker emotions that have buffeted Emilia for three days. She clenches her fists to keep her hands steady. "I am with you, my lady."

"You know my thoughts on the matter," says Jane.

Mary's smile broadens. "It is done, then. We will try again. Though we cannot continue meeting as we have. We must solve that problem."

Emilia agrees, but a more immediate issue holds her attention. A sliver of doubt pricks Emilia's joy as a vision of Kate's final speech at Whitehall revisits her. She tries not to frown. "You saw how Dutton eviscerated Katherina. How he robbed her of rebellion and denied her victory. Yes?"

Mary and Jane nod.

"Can we accept such a price?" Emilia asks. "That the bookholder might twist our intent to suit his fancy?"

Jane draws a hitching breath, as if to speak, but halts to wring her hands and mouth silent words. Mary's head tilts. "You have something for us, Jane?"

The seamstress nods. "Will Shakespeare has quit the Queen's Men."

Alarm seizes Emilia, opening a back door for disappointment to reenter. Mary's clouding features surely mirror hers. Emilia rubs her neck. "This is a setback. We need a company if we wish to stage a play."

Jane waves her hand as if shooing away a fly. "He has joined another troupe—Lord Strange's Men. And he has dragged me along to work for them."

Mary's eyes light. "Lord Strange's Men, you say? An elite company, better now that young Burbage has joined them. Who serves as bookholder?"

The smile Jane has clearly been suppressing breaks across her face like the rising sun. "Will does, for any play he brings them."

Emilia gasps. "Any play?"

"Any."

"And they will stage what he brings?"

Jane's smile fades. "Yes."

"This is wonderful news!"

"Oh. One more thing."

"Yes?"

"Burbage asked for a play by the first of February."

"February!" Mary blurts.

Jane fades into her chair like a rabbit shrinking into her warren. "And another by the first of March. Will has agreed."

Reflecting Emilia's roiling reaction, Mary cups her hands over her nose and mouth and closes her eyes. She massages the side of her nose while drawing long, steady breaths. Emilia waits while wrangling her warring emotions into a semblance of calm. After a few moments, Mary lowers her hands to the tabletop. They are balled into fists.

"Then Mr. Shakespeare has decided for us. We will produce a play in four weeks and then another four weeks after that."

With Mary's pronouncement, Emilia's conflict dies a shocking death. What rises in its place is the familiar determination that has driven her deep into Elizabeth's court. *A new play! Two!* "More comedies?"

"No." Mary says. "My mood for comedy has dissipated. The players failed to understand our subtleties. The audience proved none the wiser. Not even Her Majesty. No. Not that. We require something of more depth. Of a type more in demand."

More in demand? More depth? "You speak of a historical?"

"I do. Everyone from the lowliest peasant to the most pompous lord drips with patriotism since our defeat of the Spanish Armada. A historical about English glory should ply that love of country to our advantage. We have no end of subjects at our fingertips."

Jane, who has watched the exchange with her characteristically wide eyes, breaks her silence. "Oh yes, my lady. When I arrived early today, Father Nicholas showed me the rose garden just outside, which looks like nothing more than the leftover bones of the devil's supper, but he assured me the roses bloom white and red, and that some say the Civil Wars began just there when some who did not really wish to get involved were forced by the Duke of York to pluck a rose to show which house they followed, and there were many angry words exchanged."

Jane stops to draw a breath, her cheeks having flushed during the blurted explanation. Emilia can't help but smile.

"The Civil Wars," she says. "What a rich subject."

Mary snaps her fingers. "That is *our* subject, then. We will write of the conflict between the houses of Lancaster and York and how it brought Her Majesty's family to the throne. Our library at

Baynard's Castle holds a copy of Edward Hall's history of the families Lancaster and York that I might study."

The notion of writing about such historic and dramatic events immediately seizes Emilia's imagination. Doesn't Hunsdon keep a copy of Holinshed's *Chronicles* in his chambers?

"I have a source as well," she says, "which I might peruse at my leisure when the Lord Chamberlain is away or too exhausted to ask questions."

Mary quirks an eyebrow at Emilia. "Very good. Perhaps we should . . ."

Jane shifts so abruptly in her chair that it nearly tips over. She catches herself and beams a smile at Mary and Emilia. "May we start now? Right now?"

Emilia smiles back, amused and enthused, but Mary laughs. "I brought paper, quill, and ink for just such an eventuality."

―――

Mary writes furiously as she and Emilia create the bones of a story from what they recall of the famous conflict. She will study the history tome later to shore up details. Mostly, however, they identify the characters—heroes, villains, and those who straddle the fence.

Unsurprisingly, Jane knows little of the history, but she interjects questions as fast as Mary can write. Why did the Duke of York claim the throne? Why was the Duke of Gloucester so important? What can you tell me about his wife? Who is Jack Cade? And a hundred more. Mary attempts to temper her smiles. Jane is voracious in her pursuit of understanding, like a wineglass barely used but begging to overrun.

As the session wears into a second hour, the expansive plot solves an immediate problem. They have enough for two plays.

Mary and Emilia decide that the first play will feature the political intrigue and infighting that led to war, and the second will cover the conflict itself. With the decision still fresh, the first part grows so unwieldy that they must cleave it again. Three plays now. Emilia grows pensive.

"How will we manage three plays at once? Given that our regular gatherings here in such a public venue already draw suspicion. Alfonso quizzes me on the subject daily."

Mary agrees, given her husband's wary gaze of late. Their time at the Chapel of St. Anne is over. A stab of regret pricks Mary's heart. She will miss this humble place that gave birth to an audacious dream. She rises from her chair to pace, one hand supporting her elbow and the other massaging her chin. Three plays. Three minds. Three locations. Two writers. One conduit for funneling the results to Mr. Shakespeare. Suspicious men on all sides. What to do? She returns to the table and leans on it.

"Here is what I propose. Emilia writes the first part, for it contains the French wars and courtly intrigue, including Jane's story of choosing the roses from Temple Garden. I write the second part, beginning with King Henry's marriage to Margaret and ending with York staking his claim and igniting the first battle. We collaborate on the third."

Emilia's eyes grow sharp, and she nods twice. "And what of the means of accomplishing this without meeting together?"

Mary has already given much thought to the how of it. "We use Captain Dansby as a courier. He will carry papers discreetly between Baynard's Castle and Court in his capacity of attending Lord Pembroke, and will deliver foul papers to Jane, wherever she might be."

She cuts her eyes toward Jane, hoping to find agreement, but encounters instead the young woman's eyes large with injury and threatening tears. A flash of insight reveals to Mary the cause. Her plan neatly excises Jane from her role as storyteller. Which will not do. The seamstress's grasp of possibility and her spiraling imagination were chiefly responsible for *The Shrew*'s success. They cannot afford to cast her aside, nor would Mary choose to do so. She extends a curled forefinger to lift Jane's drooping chin.

"Can you sew a fancy dress? One worthy of Court?"

Jane cocks her head and pinches her brow. "I made the costumes for *The Shrew*. Like those?"

"Yes, just like those." She pauses to consider the absurdity of what she will suggest, but plows forward anyway. "Every midweek day, Lord Pembroke leaves for Court before the sun rises and returns at dusk. I will send Captain Dansby early by barge on those days to meet you in Southwark. He will bring you by water to the landing at Baynard's, where you will begin assembling a new gown for me. You will, of course, require my guidance as you work in my private chambers."

Jane's brow unfolds and her eyes brighten. "And we will talk of the plays?"

"And we will talk of the plays. We need you, Jane. Emilia and I write the words and speeches, but you see the grand sweep and the smaller tales in your mind and fold them together in a manner that neither of us can match."

Jane's tears do come but frame a smile. "Thank you, my lady. I will not disappoint you."

"Of course you won't."

Emilia loudly expels a breath. "The complexity concerns me, though. Can we do this? Can we continue without exposing ourselves to ridicule or worse?"

Mary knows the answer like she knows her husband's face. "We must, and not just for us. For all the women who are denied this opportunity because they lack the idle time, lack the wealth, lack the education."

"Women like me," Jane whispers. "Those who cannot read."

Of course, Mary thinks. *Why did I not think of this before?* She rifles through her satin reticule, withdraws four silver coins, and extends them to Jane. "A first payment for your upcoming labors."

Jane shakes her head and blushes. "I cannot . . ."

"You must, but with a stipulation."

Jane eyes the coins. "Stipulation?"

"You must use half of it to engage a tutor who will teach you to read. Perhaps your Mr. Shakespeare will serve, or another of the literate players."

Her blush deepens and she gingerly accepts the coins. Her smile spreads to stretch the confines of her cheeks. "Thank you, my lady."

Jane's joy shames Mary that she had only just now seen to the young woman's education. Perhaps the natural intelligence behind those wide blue eyes has helped Mary forget that Jane cannot read. However, the girl's reaction also brings Mary rising delight. She can be so much more than an illiterate seamstress. But what will she become? The world carves out few niches in which women might flourish, and none for learned peasant girls. No matter. Knowledge nourishes the soul, even if it does not produce wages. Understanding is its own reward—and often the only reward.

When Emilia and Jane agree to Mary's plan, they stand aside from the table to leave. Mary considers embracing them, but a lifetime of noble reserve holds her at bay. She curses herself for it as the young women break free of the awkward parting to disappear down the stairs. Mary remains for a moment to drink in once more the austere wonder of the chapel. Beneath the surface of her calm, a storm roils, opposing currents of exhilaration, determination, and dread.

Oh God. I must write a five-act play in four weeks, without aid.

The coursing realization should ignite her panic, but it does not. Quite the opposite. Remarkably, the darkness that has dogged her footsteps since her arrival in London is absent at last.

One final miracle from St. Anne.

12

On the first day of February, the sun finally cleaves through leaden skies after three weeks of conspicuous absence. Though most people welcome its arrival, Jane offers a silent prayer in favor of more clouds. The three hundred bodies crammed shoulder to shoulder in the courtyard of Cross Keys Inn emanate heat as they stamp frenetically and roar with delight over Richard Burbage's last outdoor performance with Lord Strange's Men before they take up residence at the Rose Theatre. Jane, of course witnesses none of it. She is confined to the cramped tyring house with a dozen players who await their entrances. After months of winter chill, Jane finds the air close and stifling.

As she helps John Hemings shrug into an armor plate, she is painfully aware of the trails of sweat that plaster her bodice to her breast. Hemings stares respectfully skyward to spare Jane any discomfort. She yanks the lower strap of the armor tight.

"Done, sir."

"And done well, Jane."

Hemings shoots her a grin before slipping through the curtain to join the ongoing scene. Despite the close quarters, Jane can't help but smile. The players of Lord Strange's Men have offered Jane nothing but kindness during her month of service to them, a departure from the more jaded Queen's Men. Hemings's wife, Rebecca, had befriended Jane immediately when Jane and Will came aboard. She is Jane's age, confident, comely, and with two babes in arms—a world apart from Jane. However, she makes it clear that Jane hasn't simply joined a new company; she has been adopted by a family. Will notices the difference as well and frequently tells Jane as much. Even now, he booms his lines from somewhere beyond the curtain, drawing a laugh from the pressing crowd. Her chest swells with pride for her fellow conspirator.

During the respite, she considers how her life has been upended again. The previous month remains a blur of rehearsals, sewing, mending, several tutoring sessions from Will, and four crossings of the Thames to meet with Mary at Baynard's Castle.

The last looms largest in her mind. Hours on end virtually alone with Mary as Jane labors on the most spectacular garment she has ever created. The to-and-fro barge rides over the water, with Dansby lingering by her side, his calming presence invading her senses. She still cannot determine who terrifies her more—the countess or the ever-attendant captain. She is leaning heavily toward the latter and chides herself once more for having adopted the rather curious new conceit of perfuming her dress before he arrives.

She blinks away her distraction as Burbage finishes the final speech. The audience responds with a ramping roar of approval. She has heard that when the troupe begins staging at the Rose in a week, they can expect a crowd three times larger. And the first play they will stage is one of her stories. This also terrifies her.

As the milling bodies stream toward the exit, Jane peeks through the curtain. The stage occupies one side of a cobblestone courtyard that is surrounded on three sides by the three-story inn, each floor ringed by a balcony where watchers still linger. She likes the place, but the Rose is a stone's throw from her lodgings in Southwark. No more perilous treks across London Bridge and the whole of the city. On the other hand, no more chest-to-back horseback rides with Dansby. What was Emilia's Italian phrase? *La rosa senza spine non può stare:* "There can be no rose without thorns." As if her thoughts have summoned him, the blue-liveried captain appears in the courtyard at the edge of the stage. He lifts an eyebrow and motions toward the innyard exit.

Her heart races as Jane scrambles from the tyring house and down to the cobblestones. She follows Dansby through a narrow archway that leads to the rear of the inn. It occurs to her again that this is her lot with Dansby—always following after a man who is far her superior, while in the service of other business. He is not for her, nor she for him. Still, she takes comfort in the fact that he has not belittled her oddness—yet. When he halts in the lot behind the inn, she sidles up to him. He extends a pair of leather tubes to her.

"Foul papers for two plays—the countess's and Miss Bassano's."

Only after Jane accepts them does she take note of what he said. *He knows?* When did this occur? Who else knows? Dansby touches her wrist and smiles.

"Do not be alarmed, Jane. I guessed from the beginning what you were about in the seclusion of the chapel. I have served her ladyship too long not to know when she falls headlong into writing. Yesterday, she confirmed my suspicion."

Jane blinks with disbelief and glances around for eavesdroppers. She leans toward him and lowers her voice. "She simply told you that we are writing plays?"

"Not exactly. I asked her directly so that I might better serve the cause."

Jane shifts back and forth and wrings the tubes in her hands. *He knows.* "Can I ask . . . that is to say, what do you . . . ?"

She drops the dangled question into the mud at their feet. He leans nearer still. "I am awestruck by the notion. I found your play brilliant, though I felt a mind to mash Petruchio's nose for his ill treatment of Katherina."

Warmth rushes through her body, driving out a giggle. "As do I."

"As you should. Will I see you next midweek day at dockside?"

"I will be there."

"Good. Until then"—he sets a finger to his lips—"we keep the secrets and serve the cause."

When Dansby bows curtly, Jane's knees nearly buckle. He spins away, his cape billowing, and strides toward the stables. She stares after him, grinning but awash with confusion. What is his game? What does he want from her?

"Who was that man?"

Jane pivots and lashes out at the voice in her ear. The tube in her right hand connects with Will Shakespeare's temple. She gasps with dismay, but he simply rubs the side of his head and smiles.

"I've never before felt the weight of words quite so literally."

"My apologies, Will. I did not . . ."

He waves a dismissive hand. "Think nothing of it. Again, though, who was that man in blue? He seems terribly familiar."

A murder of crows erupts in Jane's gut. "No one of concern, I assure you."

"And yet you appear concerned."

She shoves the tubes into his face to extinguish the maddening line of questioning. "These are new acts for both plays. This completes the first."

Will narrows his eyes and gingerly retrieves the tubes from Jane's tremoring hands. "Of course. And not a moment too soon.

Burbage has been hounding me for the final lines. I will scribe them into my hand and use the originals as kindling, per usual. Then on the morrow, off to the Master of Revels for approval."

She clasps her hands together at her waist to stop them from trembling. However, her voice betrays her. "You should hide those before we are seen."

"Indeed." He smirks and turns to leave before glancing at her over a shoulder. He motions to where Dansby has just disappeared inside the stable door. "Allow your heart to want what it wants, and brook no disagreement."

Heat rises in Jane's cheeks. "That man is of no interest to me."

"I know the glow of ardor when I see it, Miss Daggett. And you are a terrible liar, by the way."

He slips back into the innyard, leaving Jane alone. She pins her attention to the stable door and finds her feet in motion. But why? To what end? She halts, though, when an older man steps into her path. Jane's breath catches before she lunges toward him and throws herself into an embrace.

"Mr. Burnham!" She belatedly realizes the public immodesty of her action and leaps back from her former employer. "Oh, Mr. Burnham! My deepest apologies for the impropriety. My feet have outrun my thoughts again, and as you well know, I am wont to stumble when caught by surprise. Oh, I am monstrously pleased to see you all the way from Henley-on-Thames! Why are you here?"

Burnham grows a wide smile that creases the deep scar running along his jawline, the remnant of a horse's kick that nearly killed him in his youth. His hair has grown whiter still, a thick blanket of snow covering his head. "The pleasure is all mine, Jane, and I would take offense if you withheld such warm greetings."

"You are too kind." She cocks her head. "Did you come in search of me?"

"Yes and no." He pats his belt, where he typically keeps his coins. "I arrived in London a few days ago to attend to various matters, but had a notion to inquire of your welfare. I had given up finding you and attended today's play on a lark. Imagine my surprise to find you employed by the player company and peeking from the curtains after the play. Now, look at you! Hale and hearty and . . . filled with a glow I have not seen before."

Tears spill from Jane's eyes, and she begins to sob. Burnham gently collects her in his arms and caresses her back with a tanner's broad hand. "There, there, sweet child. What troubles you?"

She shakes her head, likely leaving a trail of phlegm on his shirt. "You are one of the few who has shown me true kindness despite my strange ways. I failed to express my gratitude when I ran from Henley-on-Thames."

He hums low, his voice vibrating from his chest into her ear. "You just did, so think nothing more of it."

Jane pulls away and pushes dirt with her toe. "I will never forget what you did for me, though. You saved my life."

He simply nods. "Well, you must tell me how you came by such an auspicious position. The London theater! What that must be like."

Jane finds herself eager to answer his question. She spills the story of her search for work, her time with the Queen's Men, and her recent defection to Lord Strange's Men. She breathes not a word of her association with a countess and a musician in the secret writing of plays. If Jane could confide in anyone, it would be Mr. Burnham. However, having just learned that Dansby knows her secret has left her defensive. Perhaps in time she might tell the old man. Just not today. Burnham listens to Jane's tale with amazement and delight.

"My heart soars for your success and good fortune," he says when her narrative finishes.

"'Twould not have been possible without your aid." She swipes moisture from her nose. "I would have been a rotting corpse dangling from a high branch if not for you. You are a saint."

He laughs from his belly. "You've a low threshold for sainthood, then. I simply help people find their way, and from time to time, I make a difference. Nothing more."

Jane wants to disagree but abruptly remembers the money he had pressed into her hand the day she fled. She plunges the same hand into her pocket and withdraws a fistful of coins saved from her work. She pushes it toward him.

"The money I owe you, sir."

He deflects her hand. "That will not be necessary. It was a gift."

Jane thrusts the coins at his face. "Consider this a gift, then. You would not deny me the pleasure of returning a favor, would you?"

"Ah." He purses his lips and nods. "I would not."

Burnham accepts the coins and stows them in his belt.

"Jane Daggett! Where are you?"

Burbage's call from the innyard causes Jane to jump. She curtsies to Burnham. "I must help pack the garments. Will I see you again?"

"Perhaps." He steps near to lightly kiss her cheek. "Remember, Jane, you are second to no one. You are a treasure."

He saunters away with a final wave, and Jane returns toward the innyard, relishing the fortuitous encounter. If Burnham makes a habit of helping others find their way, he is very good at it. She wonders how he grew such a large heart in the sometimes-callous backwater of Henley-on-Thames.

~~~

Harwood is torn over which man to follow from Cross Keys Inn. The player? The old man? His gut sends him after the soldier instead. He knows the Pembroke guardsman will be returning to Whitehall along the roads, which allows him to follow at a distance without fear of notice or losing his prey. As he rides, Harwood considers what he'd witnessed after the play. The seamstress had met the soldier in seclusion behind the innyard, where he had given her a pair of courier's tubes. She had transferred those to the player—the Shakespeare fellow. Then, the old man had appeared as if on arrangement. The seamstress had seemed to know him well, though Harwood could not overhear their conversation from his vantage point. She had clearly given him money, but why? Was it related to the documents? Did they contain plots or heresy? Harwood chews his lip in thought. The old man's distinctive scar brings to mind one described by Mountford Scott the previous year, when he was tortured. The Crown had executed the Catholic priest a week later, before a name could be produced. Could this be the same old man? Another Catholic plotter? Given his familiarity with the girl, it seems likely.

The soldier arrives at Whitehall after nightfall. The gathering gloom has allowed Harwood to close the distance and tie his horse to a post near the stables. This proves fortunate, for it allows him to witness the guardsman handing a letter to a court page, with a stern shake of his finger. Harwood bolts through an adjacent passageway in time to intercept the page. The young man skids to a halt, his eyes wide at the stranger who has materialized in his path.

Harwood pulls a dagger from his boot and picks at his thumbnail with the tip as he glares at the page.

"I will see that letter."

The alarmed page's eyes dart left and right. "But sir, I have strict orders to deliver this to Miss Emilia Bassano and no one else."

As Harwood steps toward the man, he spins the dagger around a finger and catches it by the hilt. The page stares in horror at the blade aimed at his neck from inches away. Harwood leans closer.

"I will deliver the letter to Miss Bassano. There need not be bloodshed." The page blanches and places the letter in Harwood's waiting hand. The letter is comfortably thick and heavy. He taps the flat of the blade against the bottom of the man's chin. "Off with you now. Not a word of my presence, or I will visit while you sleep."

The page turns tail and runs, disappearing in an instant. Harwood hurries to a candle sconce and holds the letter to the light. There are no visible words, but he recognizes the seal. Lord Pembroke's. And because Lord Pembroke has been at Whitehall for weeks, the letter's author is clear. The Countess of Pembroke. Mary Herbert. Elation swells his chest as he trots through the maze of Whitehall to Cecil's chambers. There he paces for perhaps an hour before approaching voices draw his feral attention. Robert Cecil and one of his aides slow when they spy Harwood.

"Mr. Harwood?" Cecil's greeting is cool and questioning.

Harwood's excitement gets the better of his discretion, given the presence of the aide. "I have something, Sir Robert."

Cecil's eyes light, and he closes the gap to accept the letter from Harwood. The little man eyes the seal with clear recognition. He lifts a finger without turning toward his aide.

"Ellis."

"Sir?"

"Fetch Gregory and Phelippes with haste, and have them bring their instruments. You will find them at the barracks."

"Of course."

Cecil brushes past Harwood to open his chamber door with a key. He motions, again without glancing back. "Come along, John. Tell me about this."

Harwood enters, a bit cowed by entering his employer's chambers. It reminds him of the time he fell into the River Stour as a youth and only survived by the goodwill of a stranger. Out of his depth; at another's mercy.

He shakes away his discomfort to describe to Cecil the meeting behind Cross Keys Inn. Cecil listens with hawk-eyed interest while caressing the sealed letter. He is still asking clarifying questions when a knock sounds. Cecil lifts his chin to the door.

"Let them in. They are associates."

Harwood opens the door, and two men enter. He has seen them around Whitehall but doesn't know their function. Cecil does the introductions.

"Thomas Phelippes, seal breaker. Arthur Gregory, cryptographer. John Harwood, spy."

They all nod to one another. Cecil extends the letter to Phelippes. "Open Lady Pembroke's letter, if you will."

Harwood watches with interest as Phelippes uses a candle and a pair of thin, fine-bladed knives to heat and lift the seal unbroken without changing its appearance. Cecil removes the letter and begins scanning it with a speed that impresses Harwood, quickly flipping through the nine or ten pages. His forehead wrinkles in concern, and his frown deepens. He sets the pages on a writing desk.

"Gregory, what do you make of this?"

The cryptographer carefully considers the first several pages. "The writer mentions the Civil Wars, houses of Lancaster and York. Then she continues in the form of a conversation between two people. No, there are three." The man's eyes dart up from the pages and he nods. "This is clearly a cipher. A code."

Cecil grunts approval. "As I suspected. A replacement code?"

"I'd wager so." Gregory taps the first page. "The Duke of Gloucester rebuking his wife over her desire to become queen, only to be undermined by a treacherous priest. The writer discusses a plot but replaces names with figures from history. A common cipher technique."

"Of course." Cecil puts his hands behind his back and begins the ungainly pacing that so unnerves Harwood. "Mary Herbert has been known to send letters to friends in cipher as a lark. An amusement. Substituting musical measures for letters of the alphabet. She uses a different cipher here, but with more dire consequences."

Gregory flips through a few pages a second time. "The Duke of Gloucester could be Lord Pembroke. If I recall correctly, he is of similar power and stature to the Gloucester of days gone by."

"Which would make the duchess none other than Lady Pembroke." Cecil stops pacing. "Lady Pembroke is under the influence of a rogue priest. Catholic, no doubt."

Gregory hums and nods agreement. "My thoughts exactly, Sir Robert. Lady Pembroke seems to be describing to her associates how she tries to influence her husband to seize the throne, guided in her persuasion by an agent of the pope."

Harwood's finds his jaw slack and closes it. This is exactly the type of disaster he has feared and has committed his life to averting. Phelippes, meanwhile, leans over the letter, his eyebrows knit in concentration.

"It reads like a script. What if this is simply a play about the Civil Wars and nothing more?"

Gregory bursts into laughter. "Don't be a simpleton, Thomas. Women don't write plays. They do engage in subterfuge regularly and sometimes dabble in treason."

"I agree," says Cecil. "What better way to mask a plot than to dress it up as an amusement? Very clever."

Harwood can hold his tongue no longer. "What shall we do, then? Lady Pembroke plots beneath the queen's nose inside the walls of her residence. Surely, we must act."

Cecil holds up a hand. "Patience, my bloodhound. The queen will require proof. More than a ciphered letter. Phelippes will replace the seal and deliver the letter to Miss Bassano's chambers to avoid arousing suspicion. Meanwhile, you will leave on the morrow for Henley-on-Thames. Infiltrate the populace. Win their trust. Learn what you can about those who employed or helped the seamstress when she resided there. Determine why they chased her out."

Elation builds again in Harwood. His master has released him for a hunt and put him on a scent. This he knows how to do. "What of the old man at the inn?"

"If he is involved," Cecil says, "he will turn up."

Harwood ventures a smile. "If not, I will root him out like a fox from its den."

The thought of how he might do this adds a spring to Harwood's step as he takes his leave from his fellow provocateurs.

❧

Loud, infernal banging drags Will from a dead sleep into a semblance of waking. He lurches from his cot and falls to the floor. He widens his eyes in an attempt to focus. Surely, someone has driven a spike through his skull as he slept. Where is he, anyway? Oh yes. In his rented room after a night of drinking and carousing with Hemings and Burbage in celebration of their performance at Cross Keys Inn. But why is he on the floor? There was something . . .

"Mr. Shakespeare!" his landlord calls out as he pounds the door again. "Are you in?"

Will climbs to his feet, sways, and holds the sides of his aching head. Has he not paid the rent? "A moment, please."

He rubs the dirt on his shirt before sniffing his fingers and wincing. No, not dirt. He tucks half his shirt in, lurches to the door, and yanks it wide. "What in God's name, Gipson?"

The squat-faced man had made clear to Will, when renting him the room, that boarding a player was all but beneath his dignity. As he faces Will, though, he practically scrapes. "You've a visitor outside."

The manner in which he emphasizes the word *visitor* ignites visions of dire scenarios in Will's muddled head. His wife come down from Stratford? Dutton to threaten him? Greene's bruiser who nearly choked him to death? "What sort of visitor?"

Gipson leans in and whispers, "A great lady."

Will blinks without comprehension. A lady? To see him? His thoughts begin to clear, and he remembers his shirt. "Give me a moment to clean up."

After throwing on a less stale shirt and jacket and splashing his head with water, Will carefully descends two flights of stairs behind the jittery landlord. Standing in his way at the bottom is a towering footman wearing orange livery.

"William Shakespeare?"

Will steadies himself. "In the flesh."

"Her ladyship, the Dowager Countess of Southampton, wishes a word."

Still baffled, he smooths his sleeves and follows the man outside to a waiting coach. The driver curls a lip at Will while the footman opens the coach door. When Will hesitates, the man shoves him toward the opening. Will mounts the step and comes face to face with the countess, still comely, though older and long widowed. She motions to the bench opposite her. He sits gingerly, already sensing the axe on his neck. This can't be good. Though his sensibilities are still dulled, Will makes eye contact with the woman as she regards him coolly. The many rumors he has heard of the woman circle his brain. That she works the court efficiently to maintain control of her income. That she does not abide betrayal. That she carries on affairs with younger men. Mostly, however, he recalls that her handsome young son, Henry Wriothesley, is one of the queen's new favorites as he cuts a swath through Court with the help of his oldest ally, Robert Cecil. Everyone who is someone in London wishes to wed, bed, or otherwise befriend the young Lord Southampton. No, this can't be good.

"My son loves the theater." Lady Southampton's abrupt statement causes Will to flinch. "Though you likely know as much."

Will does recall that the young Earl of Southampton has attended every Queen's Men appearance at Court and has shown much enthusiasm over the performances. "Yes, my lady."

She eyes him further. "He especially enjoyed your play about the shrew. For days afterward, he spoke of nothing else, spouting dialogue from memory until I shut my ears."

Will blinks again, but not with surprise. *The Shrew* is a precious gem worthy of adoration. No, he is simply taken aback by having the play ascribed to *him* by a noblewoman. He shoves aside the unseemly truth and ventures a smile.

"Thank you, my lady. I am deeply honored by Lord Southampton's interest in the humble blather of my pen."

"Not blather, Mr. Shakespeare." She lifts her chin to regard him anew. "My son's infatuation with your words notwithstanding, I found the play fresh, the lines lyrical, and the character of Katherina fascinating, even though the player mishandled her lines something awful."

He blinks in astonishment and bows in his seat. "Thank you, my lady."

She waves a hand. "However, I have not come to critique your play, but to make a proposal."

Will swallows hard. Proposals from nobles cannot be easily refused and often come at a stiff price. Or so he's heard. He fights to maintain the smile but fears he resembles a cat preparing to cast up a hairball. "A proposal. I count it my good fortune."

"You seem a man knowledgeable in the ways of love and poetry."

Though he is not the playwright she believes him to be, he cannot disagree. His torrid affair with his wife, Anne, was primarily a product of his fluidity with words. Lately, heeding Jane's urging, he has begun to plot an epic poem featuring the love affair between Venus and Adonis, but with gender roles reversed. "I have my merits on both accounts, my lady."

"Let me drive directly to the point, then. Although every woman in England pines for his bed, my son remains disinterested in marriage. No marriage, no legitimate heir. I am too old to stand idly by and wait for grandchildren."

Will nods. "I see. Even noble sons disappoint their mothers."

"Do you disappoint your mother?"

"I am a player with no interest in my father's glove-making business. She wakes up every day disappointed."

This elicits a smile from the countess. "Ah, the truth. I find that refreshing."

"Well, I am a poet, and all poetry is truth." He disregards his guilt over the audacious lie of his playwriting. That's different.

Her smile fades as she is again all business. "In that capacity—as a poet—I propose that you write a series of poems encouraging my son to marry and produce an heir. Sonnets, perhaps. Given his interest in your play, such lines from you might tip the balance in my favor."

Will tries not to panic. A countess wishes him to write highly personal poetry for her earl son, believing Will to have authored something he did not. How can he? The memory returns to him of Jane's encouragement while they sat at the fountain near Dutton's house. She believes in him. His wife does as well. Does he believe in himself? He clenches his right hand into a fist.

"Not to be crass, my lady, but might I inquire of the pay?"

She lifts her chin. "Produce for me two sonnets for my review, and I will pay you two pounds for each. Should I approve, I will commission more."

Four pounds for a few dashed lines? As much as a playwright might receive for an entire play. "I will begin immediately, my lady. How shall I send them to you?"

"I will send Perkins to retrieve them in one week."

"Perkins?"

She motions toward the coach window. "The giant who fetched you from your lodgings."

"Ah." Will ventures another grin. "Will he break my arms if I am not finished?"

She emits a laugh akin to a bird's twitter, before frowning. "Oh no, Mr. Shakespeare. He will break your legs. You need your arms to write my sonnets."

Will waits for her to betray the joke, but her steady gaze never wavers. He swallows hard. "One week, then. Two sonnets."

"We have an accord?"

"It seems so."

"Excellent." She taps the door, and it opens. As Will rises to leave, she halts him with a vice grip on his forearm.

"My lady?"

She tilts her head and narrows her eyes. "One question. Robert Greene is painting you as a fool, as a stealer of words. Please assure me that he is not correct."

Will's nostrils flare, and he grits his teeth. "He is not correct. I have stolen nothing."

"I am counting on it, Mr. Shakespeare."

He bobs his head and stumbles from the coach. Perkins seizes the back of Will's collar to keep him upright. He thanks the footman and stands aside as the coach clatters away along the cobblestones. His soul is in danger of rending in two over his duplicity. However, a new thought barges into his head to dislodge the guilt. He has claimed to be a writer. If he pens sonnets approved by a countess, then he will render his claim true.

Abruptly sober and basking in the glory of that epiphany, he marches upstairs and retrieves his quill. First, he must copy the lines of his mysterious benefactors' foul papers to be shipped to the Master or Revels. And then? His inner muse is awakening, and he desperately wishes to commune with her.

13

Six days after pressing into Dansby's hands the final lines of her play, *The First Part of the Contention Betwixt the Two Famous Houses of York and Lancaster*, Mary understands now that playwrights and mothers suffer under the same curse. The pride of sending a child or a play into the world is eroded by the creeping suspicion that the effort has failed miserably. She squirms in her box seat at the Rose Theatre, waiting for confirmation of her worst fears.

"Do you experience discomfort, my lady?"

The innocent question from her lady-in-waiting, who sits to her left, freezes Mary. She smiles politely. "I am grateful for your concern, Lady Dalia. However, I am quite well."

The flatness of the girl's eyes tells Mary that her lie is not convincing. Captain Dansby clears his throat from behind her. "Does my mistress desire the use of a second cushion?"

"No, but thank you."

To dismiss the questioning, she turns her attention to the floor below. The groundlings continue to swell into the pit—men, women, and children alike. They talk and laugh and shout and jostle one another as they pack shoulder to shoulder in the standing area. She wonders how they continue to fit when all the free space appears to have vanished. The thatched roof high overhead does little to absorb the cacophony. Two men begin brawling in the midst of the crush, sending bystanders tumbling into their neighbors. The crowd administers swift justice by beating the men over their heads with walking sticks, bags, and fists until the men come to a sensible understanding. Mary exhales as the tension subsides. She is glad of Dansby's presence. Though her father was of modest means, Mary remains a foreigner in the world of the working class. Their rough and tumble manners repel and entice her all at once. What it must be like to be free of the bonds that constrain her every look, word, and gesture.

She studies again the odd structure of the Rose. It is roughly circular, but unlike the Temple Church nave, it is not truly round. The building's many flat sides hold three levels of box seats for those who can pay more than a penny. Mary has paid six pennies for her cushion and second-tier box, which faces the stage dead center. She glimpses through the stage doors a frenzy of activity as the players prepare. And as Jane works. She is there, somewhere, no doubt as anguished as Mary and Emilia are. Mary scans the box seats for the lady musician who has become, against all odds, a confidante.

She finds a few court acquaintances instead, who wait with lifted chins and pending judgment. Mary exchanges a nod with Lady Southampton, who sits with her handsome young son, the earl. He is leaning forward with elbows on knees, clearly enraptured. The smile on his face is far out of place for one of such high station. Lord Pembroke would condemn him for it. Mary finds his reaction gloriously appealing.

Only then does she spy Emilia. The beautiful musician enters a first-tier box, off to one side of the stage, in the company of Alfonso Lanier and two other men who can only be blood cousins. Their black, curly hair and Italian jawlines show how closely all Bassano apples fall from the same remarkable tree. She waits until Emilia makes eye contact and smiles. Mary dips her chin briefly—a faux pas for a woman of her station to one without a title. However, the young woman deserves it. Even from here, Mary recognizes the elated exhaustion that mirrors her own.

The six-week period since the staging of *The Shrew* has reminded her of the labor of childbirth in its relentless inevitability. Writing at night to avoid her husband's suspicions. Clandestine meetings with Jane to wring out the plots. Two dozen missives and manuscripts sent and received, carried by the loyal Dansby. The managing of her multiple estates and Baynard's Castle, each with its own clamoring list of needs. Her weekly appearances at social events in order to satisfy the queen's pleasure. The neglect of her young children. Oh, her poor children! Do they still recall that she is their mother? During other times, the crush of responsibility and guilt would have thrown Mary headlong into a dark abyss.

But not today.

The elation of giving birth to fiction buoys her spirits like nothing she has ever done. As crowd anticipation rises to a fever pitch, Mary continues to drink in the buzz despite a queasy stomach.

And then, Will Shakespeare enters the stage. He welcomes the crowd and speaks words of introduction that Mary can barely follow through her nervous shifting. Then a pair of trumpets sound from somewhere, a fanfare. Most of Lord Strange's Men enter the stage in a rush, half from each of the opposing doors. The lines she has written and rewritten, dreamed about and obsessed over, begin to emerge.

As by your high imperial Majesty
I had in charge at my depart for France,

As procurator to your Excellence,
To marry Princess Margaret for your Grace,
So, in the famous ancient city Tours,
In presence of the Kings of France and Sicil,
The Dukes of Orleance, Calaber, Britaigne, and Alanson,
Seven earls, twelve barons, and twenty reverend bishops,
I have performed my task and was espoused.

The player kneels before continuing his lines, and the play is rolling in furious motion. Mary falls into a trance, her eyes unblinking. She follows the flow of the players, the entrances and exits, the movement of props. Only when she becomes aware of Lady Dalia's stare does she realize she is whispering the lines. Mary presses her lips together, but the words echo in the deep well of her enraptured soul. Her spirit threatens to fly through the thatched roof and beyond.

Will Shakespeare has done it.

He has staged what she, Emilia, and Jane have intended. She squeezes Lady Dalia's hand in a death grip when Queen Margaret faces Henry to save him from surrender during the final scene.

What are you made of? You'll not fight nor fly.
Now is it manhood, wisdom, and defense
To give the enemy way, and to secure us
By what we can, which can no more but fly."

She—for Mary sees the young man playing the part of Margaret as all woman—she does not browbeat. She does not whine. She does not cajole. No. She commands. She is strength. She is power. She is the spine that props up her husband to keep him from folding. A tear leaks from Mary's eye, and she rubs it away too aggressively.

And then the crowd is applauding. They cheer. They stamp their feet. Even the nobles rise to offer approval. Lord Southampton is shouting with joy, his commendations lost on the sea of happy outpouring that engulfs the Rose. Mary is also on her feet, though she does not remember standing. She locks gazes with Emilia, whose cheeks are wet with tears. The young woman's luminous smile could bring down a king, slay a kingdom, subdue a nation.

"This is it," her smile says. "This is why. This is what we'd hoped for. What we've dreamed."

How long the adulation continues, Mary can't say. The players return to the stage to bow, not once but twice. There is no jig, but the crowd appears not to care. A jig would only detract from what they have witnessed this day. In time, the groundlings begin to file out, elated over the performance, deflated that it has ended and the real world calls them back to drudgery.

"Shall we, my lady?"

Mary notices Dansby's offered elbow and takes it. As they weave their way along the narrow passageway and down the stairs, reality begins to invade Mary once more. She owes Will another play in three weeks—the continuation of today's story. Emilia has set aside her play to help Mary in the endeavor, thank God. She might not survive otherwise. Can she continue the impossible juggling act of home, family, queen, and dreams? Will her candle melt to nothing before she can deliver on her commitment?

"It must not."

"My lady?"

"Nothing, Captain. Carry on."

She has no choice but to succeed. A promise is a promise. And every woman in England—dead, living, and yet born—relies on her success, starting with Emilia and Jane.

⁂

Emilia's tears begin during the fourth act and do not abate until the crowd is half dispersed. Though it is Mary's play, she has helped mold the plot and has contributed no less than three score lines. She basks in the uncomfortable afterglow, questioning her entire existence. After nine years of scrambling for status at Court, the prize she has anticipated pales against the bliss that imbues every fiber of her being. What has she been doing all this time? Has she truly believed that acceptance by her betters could compare to this? To the joy of creation? To the adulation of a thousand strangers from every walk of life? No judgment. No poison glances. No whispered rumors of whose bed she's warmed, true or not. The epiphany rattles her. She cries with pure jubilation and a profound sense of regret. Jubilation over the play. Regret that she still desires the approval of those at Court and cannot shake free of it.

Alfonso says nothing as the Rose empties. At some point, though, she feels the comforting presence of his palm against the small of her back. Cousins Andrea and Jeronimo converse by her side as if nothing is amiss. As Bassano men, they know better than to ask why a woman cries after a performance of any kind. They understand the elation of art and don't question her reaction.

"The play was nothing short of magnificent." Alfonso's comment startles Emilia in the near-empty and strangely quiet space. She looks at him to find the warm smile that inhabits so well his strong French features. He pushes his fair hair away from one eye. "I particularly enjoyed one line. What was it? *'Small things make base men proud. True nobility is exempt from fear. The first thing we do, let's kill all the lawyers.'* It sounds like something you'd say."

Emilia flinches. It was something she *had* said. To Mary, in a letter suggesting the line's inclusion. She doesn't know whether to embrace Alfonso or stamp her heel onto his toes. "Yes. A good line, that one."

"I would commend the playwright for it . . ." He eyes Andrea and Jeronimo, who are still waging a debate about Civil War history. He leans toward her ear. "However, I suspect the playwright already knows my opinion on the matter."

Emilia cuts her eyes at him. *What did he just say?* His smile has turned wry. He dips his chin and ducks his eyes, as if to a superior. She draws a sharp breath. *Does he know? How could he?* She twists her rising panic to her advantage, harnessing it as a spear of anger. She grips his jacket and pulls him toward her until her lips are nearly in his ear.

"If what you suggest is true"—her whisper is harsh and primal—"then I would be at dire risk. Exposure would ruin me in all ways. It would end me."

Alfonso pushes her gently away. His smile is gone, and his features have softened. "Nothing could possibly end you, Emmy. And rest assured, I would cut out my tongue before placing you in peril."

His assurance rings true. It is Alfonso, after all. He has been her confidante since she was a child. The panic that is struggling to reassert dominance muddles her response, though. "Can I truly trust you to keep your word?"

Pain ripples across his face, and his eyelids flicker as if struck. He leans farther away and straightens his spine. "I am not the court. I am not the high and mighty Lord Hunsdon, who remains wholly unworthy of you."

Alfonso stands up and leaves. Emilia scrambles after him, with Andrea and Jeronimo asking befuddled questions in her wake. She ignores them and tries to keep up with the stalking Alfonso. Regret floods her gut over questioning his loyalty. Over doubting his integrity. But what choice does she have? She is well out of her depth in perilous waters. If she falters for even a moment, she will drown. She must take every precaution to guard her secret, even if it hurts Alfonso.

Alfonso. Her only true friend at Court.

Regret breaks free of its cocoon to emerge as self-loathing. It is a creature with which Emilia is all too familiar.

⁂

One time, while on the road between a village that had expelled her and a destination she had not yet found, Jane had become lost in a mist so thick that it had invaded her lungs. Wracked with coughing and not knowing where to go, she had fallen into a repetition of wandering aimlessly and huddling against the moist earth. The chaos following the play feels much the same. She hears the crowd's approval as if from a distance. She watches the players slapping shoulders and shaking hands. She helps the tyring man round up the scattered costumes and then scrubs the gore of pig's blood from the stage with hands that seem not her own. All the while, a clarion call rings through the fog.

You did this, Jane Daggett. Nobody knows, but you did this. God help you.

She and the tyring man have just pushed a trunk into the gap beneath the stage when a hand touches her shoulder. She spins to find Will standing over her. She notes with surprise that the theater has emptied. Even Emilia has gone. Will curls a finger to beckon and walks toward the outside door. Still numb, she follows him. She steps out of the building into the half-light of a sun just set. He waits for her to approach before leaning close.

"I wish you to offer congratulations to the playwrights on my behalf."

Jane blinks with confusion. "Playwrights?"

His eyes go half lidded. "Playwright, I meant to say. Singular, of course."

She doesn't believe him. He had meant her to know. Before she can comprehend the ramifications, Richard Burbage appears and whacks Will across his back.

"A triumph, Will. Absolute and devastating success." Burbage doesn't bother to disguise his elation. "I cannot wait to stage the second part. Do you remain on track to deliver the final lines in three weeks?"

Will flashes his eyes at Jane but smiles for Burbage. "Of course. I work tirelessly to meet expectations."

"Good." Burbage belts him again. "Very good."

"Do not believe him."

Jane yanks her head around to find the source of the new voice. Two men step into the huddle as if they own it. The smaller man is faintly familiar to Jane, but not the scowling brute. Burbage eyes them as if he'd just scraped them off his boot.

"To what do we owe the pleasure, Mr. Greene?"

The gritting of Burbage's teeth indicates his extreme lack of pleasure. The man, somebody named Greene, offers a smile that brings to Jane's mind an open latrine.

"A success indeed." He jerks a thumb at Will. "But this man is a fraud, as I have told you. I will prove my case. Mark me."

Alarm nearly buckles Jane's knees. Dansby knows, and now this man? But how? And just who is he? Will stabs out a hand to grip Jane's wrist. Perhaps he means to steady her, but the clench of his fingernails speaks warning.

"Always a delight," he says to Greene.

Greene lifts an index finger and levels it at Will's nose, not inches away. "You are an upstart, Shakespittle. A word stealer. I will unmask you."

Jane watches as Will's slumping spine goes bolt straight. "Here I stand. Come when you have proof of this claim, or cease speaking to me."

When the brute steps toward Will, Greene restrains him with a gesture. Greene's eyes narrow at Will and then at Jane. She begins to wither beneath the reptilian stare before a smile crawls across Greene's face. He cocks an eyebrow at Will. "As you wish. Speaking to you always erodes my intellect anyway." He jerks his head toward his companion. "Come, friend. Let's not bother this poor man until we have proof. Then you may kill him, if you like."

The brute pushes a meaty fist into his palm and nods to Will. "Until later, worm."

Burbage boldly stalks after Greene, loudly advising him to mind his manners lest the players of London turn against him. As the heated conversation drifts out of earshot, Jane flings Will's grip from her wrist. She squares on him and points at the departing men.

"How?"

"How what, Jane?"

"How does that man know? Who is he?"

Discomfort flits across Will's face before his annoyingly charming smile returns. "Do not worry, fair seamstress. Robert Greene is a blowhard, and Dutton is a pompous ass."

Jane wrinkles her brow. "Dutton? What has he to do with this?"

Will winces, probably because he's offered too much information. After a stretching pause, his taut shoulders deflate as he releases a breath. "Very well, Jane. Dutton and Greene are determined to expose me as a fraud."

Jane wobbles again, but Will steadies her. She stares at him with rising alarm. "Do they know about us . . . the playwrights? The playwright, I mean?"

Will's brow draws down. "No. But they have the means to dig for the truth. Dutton is loyal to Lord Essex. Lord Essex has the queen's favor most of the time. He battles with Robert Cecil for control of the spies and pays men like Dutton to hunt down rumors and innuendos. In short, they do not lack the funds or motivation to root out the identity of our mysterious benefactor."

The admission blows through Jane like a gale. "What will we do, then?"

"Just take care. In the worst scenario, your playwright can simply take credit while I am made to look the fool."

"No." Jane shakes her head hard enough to rattle her brain. "That cannot happen."

"Why?"

"It just can't. You must believe me."

Will regards her for some time before rubbing his eyes. "I see. The stakes have been raised beyond your ability to wager."

Jane nods, wishing he were wrong. Will places a finger to his lips, gives her a wink, and returns to the theater without a word. Jane remains outside, wracked with questions. Should she tell Mary? Or Emilia perhaps? Should she grab her packed bag and run? Her shoulders slump. No. She can't. Not yet, anyway.

Jane trudges back into the Rose, hoping she has made the right decision but strongly suspecting that she is again wandering into an impenetrable fog.

As Will returns to the Rose, he considers the newfound complexity of his life. His ongoing fraud covers him with a mantle of guilt that he must hide from his new troupe mates. And Robert Greene's persistence is worrisome. The fact that he is so near the truth is concerning, as is the violent demeanor of his bodyguard. Now, he must also keep Jane calm, lest she panic and the playwrights withdraw. Without original plays, he cannot act as bookholder. If he is not the bookholder, then he is just a player. He wants more. Much more. Will walks through the door, distracted, when a vice closes over his shoulder. He jerks his head around, expecting to see Cutting Ball with a knife or a clenched fist. Instead, he finds a giant footman wearing orange livery and a deadpan expression. What was his name? Oh yes. Perkins.

"Her ladyship, the Dowager Countess of Southampton, wishes a word."

Will exhales with relief. "Now?"

The footman tips his head slightly to one side. "What do you suppose?"

"Right." Will follows the footman back outside, passing a frowning and mumbling Jane along the way. The man leads him to an adjacent street and a familiar coach, opens the door, and motions Will to enter. He climbs inside to again find himself face to face with Lady Southampton. He dips his head. "My dowager lady Southampton."

She lifts one eyebrow and appears to study the makeup still clinging to his face. "An excellent play, Mr. Shakespeare. Another of yours?"

He swallows hard. "Indeed."

"I *would* suggest including the Southampton family in the story, but my husband's ancestors were humble London drapers at the time of the Civil Wars. Perhaps in a future play?"

"Er, perhaps." He tries to smile calmly but is certain he comes across as nauseated instead. He knows what is coming. The countess does not make him wait.

"Have you produced what I commissioned?"

The agreed-on delivery time isn't until the morrow. Fortunately, he has anticipated the possibility of another all-night drinking binge with his new friends. He digs into his vest to produce a piece of parchment, trifolded, and places it in her waiting palm. Lady Southampton holds the paper at arm's length and leans back in her seat. Her eyes narrow to a squint, and she begins reading. Out loud.

"*From fairest creatures we desire increase, that thereby beauty's rose might never die.*"

Will squirms as she continues reading the first sonnet. It is one matter to read the words himself. When hearing them from another's lips, he considers how poorly he has written. How he should have done better. How much the countess will despise his effort.

"Bravo, Mr. Shakespeare." She smiles while reading the page again in silence. "Brilliant. Just as I had hoped. And the other sonnet?"

"Simply turn the paper over, my lady."

"Ah." She reads aloud again, subjecting Will to the torturer's rack a second time. He turns his head half aside, as if in anticipation of a slap to the cheek. However, Lady Southampton's smile does not fade when she finishes. "Well done, Mr. Shakespeare. You play to his worst fear."

"I do?"

"Yes. How did you know that the prospect of growing old and losing his beauty keeps him awake at night?"

Will blinks, not believing his luck. "Do not we all fear the same?"

Lady Southampton's smile fades, and she leans toward him. "Let me tell you a secret. Perhaps men fear old age. Not women. It is only then that men take up younger mistresses and stop clamoring for our company in bed. Only then do we become truly free. Free to orchestrate our own plans."

"Such as, say, encouraging your beautiful but carefree son to produce grandchildren?"

Lady Southampton laughs. "So, we understand each other."

"I think we do, my lady." Will feels as if he has not only escaped the execution, but he has gone to town on a bacchanalia with the executioner. He nearly floats from his seat. Meanwhile, Lady Southampton taps the door. When it opens, Perkins fills the doorway. "Pay Mr. Shakespeare four pounds."

"Of course, my lady."

As Perkins retrieves the coins, the countess raps Will's knee with a closed fan. "I expect two more. And as you are quite busy writing your next play, I shall allow you three weeks to complete them."

Will does his best to bow while sitting, which is an awkward gesture at best. "As you wish, my lady."

He rises and steps down from the coach. Perkins presses the coins into his hand and eyes Will coolly. "Until next time."

"Of course, Mr. Perkins."

Will wanders back toward the Rose, his knees loose and his heart full. Guilt has gone on holiday, replaced by sublime contentment. He tosses the coins in his hand, and their jingle is the sound of acceptance. He had been paid for his work. He is a compensated writer. No one can take that title from him now. Yes, his life is complicated and might eventually land him in jail or the morgue. Oh, but it is a wonderful chaos. And surely, his life cannot get any more complicated.

14

June 11, 1592, four months later

Whereas summer infuses the countryside with the scent of field, flower, and tree, it is an altogether different animal in London. The rising heat bakes the fecund waste that gathers in the Thames until the resulting stew permeates the city with a noxious stench that drives most people away from the water's edge. Emilia is not most people. She holds a kerchief over her nose, undaunted, as her coach clips along the south bank of the Thames toward the Rose.

She and her companions have covered most of the six miles from Greenwich Palace with unimpeded progress. Soon, she will see her play again. *Her play!* Emilia's world is bliss. A month after staging the first part of the York and Lancaster saga, Lord Strange's Men staged Emilia's play, which she had titled simply *Henry the Sixth*.

It had been a stunning triumph.

She cannot help but smile while recalling the raucous crowd response and Henslowe's bubbling enthusiasm as he'd counted and recounted the box. During the three months since, *Henry the Sixth* has played a dozen more times, a financial monster. She has attended three of those stagings. Her only regret is that it had kicked aside the two York and Lancaster plays. In fact, the players had opted to open the second of those plays, *The True Tragedy of Richard Duke of York and the Good King Henry the Sixth*, at Cross Keys Inn between performances at the Rose. A lesser woman than Mary Herbert might have taken offense over it. However, the countess remained effusive in her letters to Emilia as the collaboration continued.

The four plays are a product of their combined minds and hands—hers, Mary's, and Jane's. Who writes the prose, crafts the poetry, and spins the plots matters little. Still, Emilia cherishes *Henry the Sixth*. How many candlelit nights had she spent pouring out lines in the solitude of her apartment? How many days did she while away as words and actions danced in her head? Too many to count.

"We near London Bridge."

The comment from Alfonso stirs Emilia from her musings. "Pardon."

Alfonso is leaning toward the window. "I spy the bridge. It crawls with people."

"Doesn't it always?" Jeronimo chuckles at his own joke. Her cousin has joined Emilia and Alfonso for a startling reason. He likes the play too. He has become a devotee of William Shakespeare's work. Jeronimo swipes dark curls away from his eyes. "Perhaps they come to watch the play as we do."

"Perhaps." Alfonso's response holds a note of concern.

Jeronimo pulls Alfonso away from the window to wave a finger in his face. "And why not? That Shakespeare fellow produces remarkable plays."

"Oh yes." Alfonso peers at Emilia. "That Shakespeare fellow. He is the one."

"Of course, he is the one. Such language has not been heard on the London stage before, I'd wager. I've seen nothing like it."

Alfonso nods while continuing to watch Emilia. He wears an impish smile. "One must wonder about the source of his muse."

Emilia cuts her eyes at Jeronimo, who fails to notice Alfonso's tongue-in-cheek commentary. She shoots Alfonso a glower and a subtle headshake. This merely encourages him.

"It must be a woman," he says.

Emilia nearly chokes. What is Alfonso doing?

"Undoubtedly," Jeronimo says. "How else could he portray his female characters so finely, so richly? He plays them like a mandolin such that they fill the stage with wit and depth. He must know a woman of similar mettle, I'd say."

"Of that, I have no doubt." Alfonso's smile nearly overflows. "What do you think, Emmy? Is it a woman?"

She wishes to slap his cheek, but that would invite uncomfortable questions from Jeronimo. She knots her fingers together instead. "Of course, it is a woman, dullard. Behind every man of note and inside every worthy endeavor, you will find a woman who toils in silence to make all things possible. But then, you already know this."

Alfonso laughs. "I do. God help me, I do."

Jeronimo waves a hand. "Regardless of his muse, four rousing plays in four months is quite the feat. A comedy. Three histories. Will Shakespeare is the talk of London, and he a humble player from the country. Who could have guessed?"

"You are right," says Alfonso. "Who could have guessed?"

Emilia is overcome by discomfort and the need to box Alfonso's ears. She leans her cheek against the window to hide her reaction from Jeronimo. How she wishes that everyone knew *her* name instead. Knew that the lines belonged to three women who labored in secret. Knew that they are, even now, working on two new plays. But this cannot happen. The fact that *she* knows must be enough.

Emilia continues to stare outside before turning her attention to the visible sliver of road ahead. She blinks twice before understanding what she sees. Only then does she realize that the rising din belongs to a crowd. No. Not a crowd. A mob.

"Alfonso." She points ahead.

He already has his door ajar and is leaning out for a better view. "My God."

Jeronimo slides over to look. "What goes on?"

Emilia cracks her door for a better view of what lies ahead. She immediately wishes she hadn't. The mass of men spilling from London Bridge onto Bank Side two hundred strides distant seethes like a disturbed ant hill. Many carry sticks, torches, or stones. She spies the flash of several swords. The men's cheeks are flushed with rage, matching their shouts of vengeance. Alfonso pounds the side of the coach and shouts to the driver.

"Turn it about, man! Turn it about!"

The coach immediately swings rightward to the edge of the cobblestone road before lurching into a left-hand turn. The four horses crowd a building, pressing haunches to the walls as they strain to pivot the vehicle. With the coach now perpendicular to the road and nearly stopped, Emilia watches the crowd surge away toward the location of the Rose. Even as she tries to understand what the mob is doing, a knot of men breaks free and runs down Bank Side toward the struggling coach. They wave sticks and shout incoherently. Alfonso reaches across Emilia and pulls her door shut.

"Remain inside no matter what happens!"

Then, he is out the opposite door and onto the street with his sword drawn. Jeronimo leaps to his side with his sword at the ready.

Emilia grips the seat as the oncoming men slow their advance. However, they do not stop. She counts seven, all armed with bludgeons of one kind or another. The coach lurches forward, blocking her view of the coming conflict. She presses against the window in time to watch Alfonso belt a man across his temple with the flat of his sword. Jeronimo plunges his blade into another man's leg. The rest of the attackers halt and begin to circle her companions. When one man tries to dodge past toward the coach, Alfonso brains him with the butt of his sword. The coach jerks again, and her view of the battle is lost. Frantic, she slides to the other window as the vehicle begins to gain speed away from the mob.

"Alfonso! Jeronimo!" She doesn't intend to shout but cannot restrain her cry. A few hammering heartbeats later, she decides to leap from the coach to . . . to what? Help? The door flies open, nearly pulling her out. Alfonso pours through the opening and takes her with him. Jeronimo flies up behind, kicks a man in the face, and slams the door. The coach lurches again as the horses respond to the driver's frantic lash. Jeronimo thrusts his head through the window curtain.

"They fall away."

He slumps onto the opposite bench, gasping for breath. Only then does Emilia become aware that Alfonso has pressed her to her back on the narrow floor, shielding her from whatever might come through the door. His back is heaving; his exhaled breaths flow past the nape of her neck. He holds her in a clench as if she might fade away at any moment. She slips her arms around his waist and presses her cheek against his temple.

"Alfonso?"

Her whispered question brings him up to his knees. He searches her face, her form. "Are you injured?"

Is *she* injured? "I should ask that of you."

Alfonso helps her to the bench and sits beside her. He runs his hands over his midsection, his face, his head before wincing. His fingers come away with a pink stain. "A knock to the head. Nothing more."

"I, too, am well," says Jeronimo. "Just in case either of you wondered."

Emilia's cheeks heat. "I am pleased for your safety, Cousin, though your Bassano bravado has clearly spared you from harm."

"Clearly."

The reality of what has just happened crashes back into Emilia's senses. They were attacked. Alfonso could have been killed. She grabs him by the collar of his jacket. "What is happening back there?"

He shakes his head. "A riot. Angry shouts, most of them about strangers in the city. They clearly hold a strong dislike for foreigners. Why they go toward the Rose, I know not."

Emilia's heart falls with a thud. Jane! She is at the theater. What will become of her? She reaches for the coach door. "We must go back for Jane!"

Alfonso stops her hand and frowns. "Given your Italian origins and foreign appearance, we cannot."

"What can we do, then?"

"Not much." He releases a sigh. "We return to Greenwich and pray that the whole of Southwark does not go up in flames. We pray for Jane and her troupe."

At his pronouncement, Emilia deflates and slumps against the corner of the bench. Everything has been going so well. Until now. Is this God's punishment for her deception? For her pride? For treading where she is prohibited? For chasing after respect from those who will never give it to the likes of her?

No, she decides. God is not punishing her. He just doesn't care. It is clear that the Almighty has already given up on Emilia Bassano.

༄

Jane is haggling with the walnut seller on Bank Side Road on behalf of Burbage when it all falls apart.

"Have you any more than these?"

The old woman stares at Jane as if she's just grown a second head. "More than six bags?"

"Yes."

"That's all I keep."

Jane starts counting coins in her hand. "If you kept more on play days, you would sell at least twice that. The crowds love walnuts for eating and for throwing at the players."

The woman frowns. "I've only ever kept six bags."

Jane's next comment dies on her lips. The steadily rising din she hadn't been minding abruptly ticks up. She looks left toward the bridgehead to find a mob of shouting men flowing onto Bank Side and turning her way. She blinks with confusion. What are they doing? The old woman snatches the bags off the table, retreats to her shop, and slams the door. Only then do the fine hairs of Jane's neck stand on end. The red-faced men shout with anger and wave sticks at Jane.

Visions of her last day at Henley-on-Thames wash over Jane, freezing her to the pavement. That crowd had looked much the same, hurling the word "witch" and proclaiming a desire to hang Jane from a tree. She had run, then, and had avoided the mob long enough for Mr. Burnham to spirit her away. But he is not here now.

"Run, girl!"

Jane finds that the walnut seller has poked her head through an upstairs window. "What?"

"'Tis a riot, idiot child. They will lay hands on you with ill intent should they catch you."

Jane runs. She veers away from the oncoming mob and arrives at the Rose with her lungs heaving. She yanks the door handle with all her might, but the door is barred. She pummels it with both fists. "Let me in! Let me in!"

Her pleas are of no use. The roar of the mob drowns them in a sea of wrath. She casts a glance over one shoulder to find the leading edge of the mob not a hundred strides distant on Bank Side, a malicious wave of humanity bearing down on her. They hurl stones through shop windows, shattering glass and terrorizing those cowering inside. Jane belts the door a final time and dashes across the thoroughfare to a mound of discarded barrels, crates, and scrap lumber. She hunkers behind the mound, ankle deep in mud as the mob draws nearer along the road. Their incoherent voices sharpen into a chant about the need to expel strangers by force. Jane gulps. Isn't she a stranger? She is strange, at least.

She prays that the men will pass by, knowing that angry young men have a penchant for assaulting women to appease their wrath. Her prayer goes unheard beneath the commotion. The mob stalls practically before her on Bank Side when a half-dozen mounted marshals meet them. Down along the road, she sees more mounted men coming, many in uniform and all bearing arms. The rioters begin hurling stones and epithets at the lawmen, daring them to come nearer. When the mounted ranks grow to twenty, the marshal's men take up the crowd's offer. As one, they kick their horses into motion and barrel into the mob with swords and pikes flashing. The mob breaks apart in the center only to congeal around the mounted men. A pitched battle ensues. Screams and powder shots reach Jane's ears even as she presses her palms over them. Her lips move in constant prayer.

She startles when a man flops before her in the mud, and she presses her back against the broken staves of a barrel. The man blinks up at Jane, clearly surprised to find her there. Blood leaks from his skull to drench one eye. He can't be more than sixteen, given his wispy mustache and lack of a beard. Whatever anger he might have arrived with has melted into pain and terror. Jane's heart turns over in her chest. She has been in his place before. She knows terror and pain. Before she can stop herself, Jane removes her scarf and crawls to the boy.

"Here. Let me tend to your head."

The young man stares with wide-eyed surprise as Jane swabs away the blood and draws the scarf tight around his crown. In no time, she has staunched the flow. She finds the boy staring at her as if she is an apparition.

"Did my mother send you?"

Jane furrows her brow. "No. I am certain that I don't know you or your mother." She lifts a hand toward the street. "Are these men searching for me?"

The young man frowns. "Uh, no. Who are you?"

"Jane Daggett, seamstress for Lord Strange's Men." And secret playwright, but she does not share that.

His mouth drops open. "Oh, I so enjoyed *Henry the Sixth*. And *The Shrew*. I liked that as well."

Jane beams with pride before remembering that a horrific battle still rages just a few yards away. "Why do you riot?"

The boy reclaims a measure of his indignation, and he squares his shoulders. "We are apprentices and protest the foreigners taking our jobs. Two days past, the marshal's men arrested a felt maker's apprentice who dared to speak up. Took him in front of his wife and children. We had no choice but to come."

"But why are you *here*? On *this* road?"

Jane feels her question is silly, but the young man nods as if she is a sage. "We assembled with the pretense of attending the play today so we could come to Southwark. Most of the strangers live here."

Jane's frown grows deep. "And you wish to do what? Kill all those from foreign lands?"

The boy stares with startlement, perhaps only just realizing the stakes of what he has undertaken. "Oh no. We wish only to frighten them away."

She peers through gaps in the woodpile to find that the mob is slowly dissipating under oppression of the marshal's brigade. A group of men wearing fine coats ride at the periphery while the rioters scatter.

"The Lord Mayor!" No sooner does the young man cry out the name than he runs away, following his brothers-in-arms back toward the bridgehead. Jane emerges from her hiding place and clambers back onto the road as the marshal's men wade around her.

"Miss!" Jane turns to find one of the finely dressed men watching her. "Are you party to this chaos?"

She glances down at her dress and shoes, now caked with mud and stained with blood. She must look the part. "No, my lord."

He waves her away. "Get thee home before these scoundrels do you harm."

Jane agrees, but it is not her rented room she has in mind. She hurries across the road and returns to the Rose. The door remains barred, bursting her pique. She kicks the door until her foot stings.

"Let me inside!"

⸺ ⸻

"Brace yourselves, lads! They're coming in!"

Kemp shoulders his low-centered bulk against the door, where Hemings joins him. When the shout comes again, Will wedges himself in front of his troupe mates.

"It's Jane Daggett, fools! Move aside."

When they draw back, Will unbars the door. Jane pours herself through the crack before he drops the bar back in place. Jane leans over with hands on knees, panting. When Will touches her back with concern, she springs erect and plants a finger against his chest.

"Why did you not let me inside?"

"I did, just now as you can plainly see."

"I meant before."

"Before?"

"When the mob came down the street."

Will's neck heats with shame. "We thought you had taken shelter, so we barred the door and prepared for an invasion." He motions toward various deadly stage props—pikes, swords, and axes—and the many buckets of water meant to douse fires. "We did not know, Jane. You have our deepest apologies."

The other players mumble similar regrets and dip their heads to the flushed seamstress. Jane sniffs and ducks her eyes, clearly embarrassed by her outburst.

"'Tis quite all right. The mob has gone back over the bridge, and the marshal's men guard the road."

Will heaves a sigh and rubs the back of his neck. The theater will not burn tonight, anyway. He pulls Jane away from the door. "How did you escape the madness?"

Jane breathlessly describes how she hid from the mob and aided an injured man after the skull crackers arrived. Will is surprised by her bravery, but then again, not really. The seamstress is a well of contradictions, secrets, and hidden mettle. He wonders what she hides from him—besides the identities of the playwrights.

"And a man, the sheriff himself I believe, ordered me to go home. So, I came here."

Will apologizes again for not hearing her attempts to escape the chaos. Then he smiles. "But look at you. Hale, hearty, and intact after a riot. It is a story you might tell until your old age."

Her expression goes slack, and she peers upward and to the side as if hearing a distant sound. "Yes. Yes. A story."

Burbage steps into their huddle before Will can quiz Jane about her wistful reaction. He slaps Will on the shoulder. "Jane's adventure notwithstanding, we have emerged unscathed." He pauses to purse his lips. "For now. I worry for the morrow, though."

His new friend's dread tone intrigues Will immediately. "The morrow? You fear another riot?"

"No." He paces back and forth with his hands behind his back, as if preparing to deliver an ominous line to an audience. "Jane said the apprentices had assembled on the pretense of watching a play. Regardless of their intent, I cannot help that we will be blamed for this."

Will's heart sinks. Of course. Though the queen and various nobles sponsor the players troupes, other powers at Court never cease seeking a reason to call them into question. It does not help that Kit Marlowe and others lace their plays with political innuendo intended to poke the nobility. In fact, have not his mysterious playwrights already done the same?

"What then, Richard? Which course do we take?"

Burbage shakes his head slowly. "We can only wait. If there are ramifications, we will be the first to know. In the meantime, we stage *Henry the Sixth* on the morrow as we had intended today. We do not stop until we are made to stop."

While Jane and the other players nod and smile at the bravado, Will stands mute. Burbage's words sound less to him like a plan and more like a dark prophecy.

～

Harwood arrives from his long investigation at Henley-on-Thames, by way of Whitehall, as a mass of men retreats over London Bridge toward the city proper. Bloodied heads and those carrying the injured tell him that a battle has occurred. But why? He presses his horse through the flowing current of beleaguered men, ignoring their curses. They are mostly young and not dressed in rags. Workers, then. Apprentices, perhaps.

On reaching the south end of the bridge, Harwood encounters a wall of mounted marshals who glare at him with steely eyes. The sheriff, swathed in clothing that surely violates the Sumptuary Laws, lifts a finger to impale Harwood from a distance.

"Turn about, man. This way is closed."

Harwood grits his teeth. Sure, he wears traveling clothes that have seen better days. However, he chafes at the insinuation that he is as common as the men scurrying over the bridge at his back. He stiffens in his saddle. "I am no laborer, sir. I demand passage."

"I demand you turn about." The sheriff's lip curls with annoyance.

Harwood had hoped to gain entry to the south side of the river on the strength of his merit. He grunts over his failure. Now, he must resort to the game men like the sheriff play—bandying about names to puff up his importance. He pushes his mount closer to the human wall, causing a few of the defenders to redouble their grips on bloodied swords. He ignores them.

"I am in the employ of Sir Robert Cecil, secretary to Her Majesty."

"I know who Robert Cecil is. I suspect you tell me lies."

"I do not lie, but perhaps we might go together to Greenwich and quiz Sir Robert directly."

Harwood smiles when the sheriff falters. Weak men are always quick to bluster and quicker to buckle. Harwood pushes his horse forward until he draws alongside the sheriff. He casts a disdainful eye over the befuddled man's finery before sniffing. "Tell me what happened here that I might report it to my employer."

The sheriff frowns while his men cock their eyebrows at the upstart challenging local authority. Then he lifts his chin. "Apprentices of the city came to Southwark to attend a play at the Rose. *Henry the Sixth*, or so I hear. They chose to riot instead and battered the shops of Bank Side. We exacted a price for their malice and sent them home."

Interesting. "Why did they riot?"

"Does it matter?"

"The 'why' always matters as much as the 'what.'" Harwood glances down Bank Side to find glass and stones littering the road. "What has the play to do with this?"

The sheriff lifts his lip again, as if encountering a foul odor. "The theater is rife with subterfuge and heresy. Playwrights spread innuendo that emboldens the rebellious."

Harwood nods. Subterfuge he understands. "Very well, sir. I will make a report."

"You need not bother. The Lord Mayor has gone to write a letter to Lord Burghley as we speak. Cecil will know soon enough."

"Nevertheless."

Harwood tips his cap to the man and spurs his horse along the road. His annoyance over arriving at Whitehall only to learn that the court had moved to Greenwich has faded. If he'd traveled directly to Court, he would have missed the opportunity to be the first to report the unrest. He leans forward and drives his tired mount with new urgency over the six miles from Southwark to the palace. Night falls before he arrives.

Within the hour, he has tracked down Cecil and been summoned to a secluded room used for storing kitchen ware. He bows before entering the cluttered space.

"Close the door, John, and make a report."

"Yes, sir."

Harwood first reports what he witnessed in London earlier. Cecil has not heard the news, but doesn't appear terribly surprised.

"The rabble of London chafe beneath the Lord Mayor's authority. I blame him for it, the odious man." He waves his hand. "My father will attend to the matter, I am certain. Now, what of our popish plot to the west? What have you learned?"

Harwood lifts his spine with pride. He has uncovered information that he is certain will please his employer. "I established myself as a merchant there, buying and selling beer."

"Yes," Cecil says. "Your father was a brewer, God rest his soul. Continue."

Harwood dips his head, acknowledging Cecil's mention of his martyred father. "As you know, no one earns trust faster than a trader of spirits, and drunken tongues soon become loose. I employed those tendencies to slowly gather information from servants and friends of the old Catholic families. After a time, I uncovered a pattern."

"A pattern, you say?" Cecil leans nearer.

"Yes, Sir Robert. The families regularly attend the parish church as any dutiful Anglican would. However, they do an outsized business with a local tannery."

Cecil's eyebrows shoot up. "Burnham? The seamstress's former employer?"

Harwood cannot help but grin. "The very one. They overpay for the goods he offers and purchase more than they can possibly use. But that is not all."

"Oh?"

"I learned that the seamstress was to be hanged as a witch, but Burnham helped her escape. Not only that, the townsfolk did not hold the act against him. Now, what kind of man could so immediately change the minds of a mob?"

Cecil chuckles. "A sheriff with an army at his back. Or a priest."

Harwood resists the urge to embrace the man. He is so terribly quick to understand and sees what Harwood does. "My conclusion exactly. Burnham is a priest, no doubt. The seamstress likely aided him in his secret and profane duties. And now, she connects herself to Lady Pembroke."

"Yes. My little birds report that she crosses the river to attend to the countess every midweek day. As a courier for the Catholics, perhaps?" When Cecil begins to pace, Harwood knows his next assignment will soon follow. Without stopping, his employer waves a finger in the air. "Lord Pembroke is here at Court while his wife hides away at Baynard's Castle, plotting. Perhaps it is time for me to plant a seed."

"A seed, sir?"

"Yes. If Mary Herbert hides something, she will make a mistake eventually. Plotters always do. A properly planted seed will incite a level of doubt and panic that will hurry along the process." He stops to face Harwood. "In the meantime, rest here for a day or two under the care of my staff. Then return to Henley-on-Thames and catch this rogue priest in the act. Do you understand?"

Harwood stretches taller still. "I do, Sir Robert. I will not disappoint you."

Cecil smiles. "You never have. Good hunting, John."

As he leaves his employer, Harwood considers his good fortune. He has earned the trust of a powerful man who shares his quest to punish Catholics and honor the memory of his dead father. He is determined to succeed for all of them.

                                               ⁂

She is a woman, therefore may be wooed. She is a woman, therefore may be won. She is Lavinia, therefore must be loved.

Mary lifts her quill from the page and reads what she has just written for Demetrius in her new play about the Roman emperor Titus Andronicus. A smile crosses her face. The lines are perhaps overly grandiose in their sentimentality, but is not that the flaw of so many plays? Sentiment worn childishly on the sleeve? Left to their own wits, most people find a means to express deeper sentiment when love is on the line. Should not the plays they attend do at least as much? Mary has read many of the lines from Emilia's new play, where gender is turned on its head, and she chuckles over them. The story is about two gentlemen of Verona, but they have yet to think of a suitable title for it. Regardless, Mary and Emilia have Jane's endless imagination to thank for the twists and turns of both tales.

A rapping on the door of Mary's bedchamber snaps her attention to the pages before her. She snatches them up and indelicately shoves them into the hollow below the false bottom of her writing desk. She rises to her feet and gathers a calming breath.

"Who knocks?"

"Captain Dansby, my lady."

Mary's breath hitches with unspecific dread. She strides to the door and pulls it open to find the captain of the guard standing rigidly. She steps into the hallway and closes the gap between them to inches.

"Have you learned anything?" Her voice is a whisper, barely enough for Dansby to hear. He gives a subtle nod and turns away. As he walks down the narrow hallway, he glances back over a shoulder with a lifted eyebrow. Mary follows at a discreet distance. When he ducks into another room, she scans the hallway for spying eyes. It remains empty. She steps into the room and closes the door. The chamber is narrow and long, used by Lord Pembroke when he conducts meetings of business and state. It would remind her of the blessed Chapel of St. Anne but for the three narrow windows that overlook the gate yard below. In the event of a siege, the thick glass panes would be broken to make way for arrows and musket shot. However, Baynard's has never been besieged, so the windows serve only to light the room and provide a bird's-eye view of anyone entering or leaving the castle. Mary joins Dansby near one of the windows.

"Tell me what happened yesterday, Captain."

He stares down into the gate yard, where his horse remains hitched to a post. "I spoke to many in Southwark who told a similar tale. A mob of apprentices crossed from the city during the early afternoon with the pretense of attending *Henry the Sixth* at the Rose. They rioted instead and caused much damage to property thereabouts."

A lead weight forms in Mary's chest. *Henry the Sixth*? The Rose? Why? "What was their purpose in rioting?"

Dansby breathes a sigh. "The same sordid tale, my lady. Fear of outsiders taking their jobs. Fear of their strange ways and religions. Fear of coming change."

Mary considers his answer while gathering the courage to ask the question she has dreaded. "And what of our girl, Jane? Was she caught up in the violence?"

When Dansby nods, Mary's knees nearly buckle. Dansby holds out his forearm for her to grasp. A slight smile graces his face, though. "She is well and unharmed despite the fright. When I visited her at the Rose, she remained a bit flustered but continues to work."

Mary sighs relief and pats her chest. Jane is unhurt. "Then the Rose still stands?"

"Yes, my lady. Though the mob's pretense was to attend a play, they never reached the playhouse. The marshal's men scattered them and beat the rioters back across the bridge."

"We can give thanks for that at least."

"Indeed."

A flash of movement below the window catches Mary's eye. Upon spying her husband striding through the gate yard, she ducks away from the window. "Lord Pembroke has returned early. I must go to him."

"Of course."

Mary leaves the meeting chamber and walks briskly toward the stairs. Halfway down, she meets her husband as he climbs. He wears an expression of war—the one she never welcomes. When she stops, he continues past Mary, but not before clutching her arm and pulling her in his wake. Pembroke returns to Mary's bedchamber with her still in his grip. He drags her inside and bangs the door shut. She invites steel into her backbone and lifts her chin.

"What troubles you, Lord Husband?"

Pembroke cocks his head from side to side as he scrutinizes Mary. She fights the urge to slouch under his glare, knowing how he despises weakness.

"What have you been doing, Wife?"

Moisture prickles her forehead and upper back as a wave of unease sweeps over her. Surely, he notices. She remains as straight as a ship's mast. "Of what do you speak? If you accuse me, I ask that you claim it directly."

Pembroke emits a grunt that lies halfway between annoyance and approval. "Very well. Only this morning, I was party to a troubling conversation with Robert Cecil at Greenwich. A conversation about you, dear Mary."

A bead of moisture rolls slowly down Mary's spine. "He speaks of me? What possible care could he have about me?"

Her husband's brow draws down. He opens his mouth to speak, but halts. He releases her arm and waves his hand. "He was not specific, which is why I ask you."

"What exactly did he say?"

Pembroke peers down his nose at Mary. "He suggested that I keep my wife on a tighter tether. To take stock of her acquaintances and activities. What do you suppose he means by that?"

The panic Mary has held beneath the surface nearly breaks free. Nearly. She contains it with a force of will that would cow her husband if knew the mettle behind it. There is too much at stake for weakness. She cannot fold. She must not.

"Who knows Cecil's mind but Cecil?" She forces a smile through the rigid confines of her tensing cheeks. "Perhaps he speaks of the poets I gather here in London and at our country estates. Though the queen loves poetry, I fear that Cecil disapproves. He is too driven for such frivolity."

Pembroke lifts one side of his lip. "Poets. Those wastrels who dangle from your purse strings while penning veiled mockery of the very nobles who pay their wages? If that is his meaning, his point is valid." He rubs his chin. "But I wonder. Is that the sum of his concern? His warning appeared more dire than the folly of poets."

Umbrage rises in Mary. Her dear departed brother had been a poet. She is a poet. "Do you consider me a fool, then? A mocker? A wastrel?"

The stone of Pembroke's expression softens. "Not you, Mary. You are above such frippery."

The urge to tell him about her clandestine playwriting surges within her. To tell him that she is exactly what he despises. To dare him to set her down for it. She quells the feeling, though. She cannot throw away everything she, Emilia, and Jane have built simply to poke her husband's eye. Instead, she dips her chin. "I thank you for your regard."

Pembroke purses his lips in clear consideration and gives a curt nod. "Watch your step, Mary. The court is on a knife's edge after the unrest yesterday across the river. You have heard?"

"I know some."

"Then you know that the queen and her counselors will be more vigilant than ever for threats. You have done well these past months avoiding Her Majesty's censure. However, Cecil clearly has his eye on you, and he holds the ear of the queen between his thumb and forefinger. Do not allow a slip, no matter how frivolous, to send us both tumbling."

The mention of the queen reminds Mary of what she stands to lose if discovered. Would Elizabeth consider her activities a declaration of equality with the throne? And does Cecil suspect the truth? But how could he? Has Jane told Will Shakespeare the truth? Or worse, has Emilia let slip their secret to Lord Hunsdon? The queen's cousin? Mary loathes herself for such questions—for doubting the discretion of her sisters. She gathers herself and smiles at Pembroke.

"I will do as you say. I will take care to remain in Her Majesty's good graces."

"Good, good." He lifts a finger. "Necessary but not sufficient. We must leave nothing to chance. You must remove yourself to the country within a fortnight to calm Cecil's suspicion."

Mary swallows hard. "The country?"

"The Ramsbury estate, perhaps. That property requires your attention anyway."

The thought of abandoning Emilia and Jane during the flower of their combined creativity sags Mary's spirit. How can they continue while separated by such a distance? Where will Mary find her joy? However, the hard planes of her husband's expression brook no disagreement. She knows him well enough to recognize that he has set his defenses and will not be moved. She buries her resentment and drops a curtsy.

"I will do as you command, Lord Husband."

When he reaches a comforting hand toward her, she disregards it and leaves him behind in her chambers. She has much to do before her impending exile.

15

"Trouble always rides three abreast"

When Emilia's father grumbled that claim long ago, her seven-year-old mind had envisioned three horsemen and wondered what was so dismaying about men on horseback. Then her father had died, the family had barred her estranged mother from taking Emilia, and she had been shipped off to live with strangers. *Three abreast.* Since then, whenever trouble arrives, Emilia remains alert for the second and third riders.

The first horseman came in the form of the riot that put her life in peril. The second is the letter in her lap from Lady Pembroke, stating that she is leaving London in two days, apparently under duress. She makes a veiled warning to Emilia to remain clear of Robert Cecil, and makes no mention of how their playwriting venture might continue. As for the third rider—she glimpsed him on the horizon some weeks ago, but now she is certain of his arrival.

Emilia sets the letter aside and places both palms over the flat of her stomach. How long before it begins to grow round? How long can she wait before telling Lord Hunsdon that she is pregnant with his child? This wasn't supposed to happen with a man of his age. She shakes her head and stands from the chair, unable to remain still. She snatches the letter, crumples it in her fist, and feeds it to a candle until it is ash. She paces her apartment from one wall to the other twice, three times. The lavishly appointed chamber is suddenly a prison. She pushes through the door and strides down the long hallway of Greenwich Palace in search of relief. Where is Alfonso?

She finds him where she often does on warm summer days. He sits on the green grass of the expansive lawn near the river, paper and pencil in hand as he composes new music for the queen's pleasure. He must be deep in thought, for he startles when her shadow falls over him. He places a hand to his brow to shield his eyes from the sun shining behind her.

"Emmy. You surprised me."

She indelicately plops into the grass at his side and pulls her knees up to rest against them. After a moment, Alfonso's hand falls on her arm.

"What has gone wrong?"

She swings her head to engage him and finds his face is lined with concern. "Why do you assume anything is amiss?"

Alfonso rolls his eyes. "Really, Emmy? I have known you all your life. I have watched you go to war against the entire court of England in a quest for respect. I have never seen you as defeated as you are now. So, out with it or I will call in the torturer."

Emilia looks away again toward the river. A barge drifts by, serene, detached, unaffected—everything she is not. The explanation lodges in the back of her throat. She swallows and tries again.

"I am with child."

Silence stretches between them. She dares not meet Alfonso's eyes for fear of his disapproval. He clears his throat. "You are certain?"

"Since I was fourteen, I have bled with the regularity of a water clock. The last time was two months ago. This morning, I vomited my breakfast. I never vomit, Alfonso. Never."

Alfonso sets aside his papers and slides in front of her. He wears a grim smile. "Perhaps it is simply a plague and not a child."

She glares at him. "This is not a good time for jesting."

He drops his gaze and nods. "You are right. But I must ask. Is it . . . is it . . ."

"The Lord Chamberlain's child?" Her cheeks heat as her ire rises. "Of course. I know most others believe me to be a whore, but I have come to expect better from you."

He stares at her with horror. "No, Emmy. I did not mean that. Forgive me. I simply thought he was no longer able to father children."

"As did I and everyone else at Court." She expels a sigh. "Clearly, I was mistaken."

Silence grows between them again before Alfonso steps into the gap. "I must ask another question."

She suspects what he wants to know and lifts two fingers. "Ask then."

"Do you wish for this child?"

Emilia blinks at him, momentarily frozen. She thought she knew until he asked the question. Abruptly, though, her will has changed. "Yes. I do wish for it." Tears well in her eyes, and she squeezes them away. "What will I do?"

Alfonso nods resolutely, his jaw set. "You must tell Hunsdon as soon as possible."

The horror of his suggestion descends on Emilia. "What if he disowns the child? What if he disowns me?"

"That is a possibility. I cannot lie."

Emilia pushes the heels of her hands against her eyes. "What if I traveled to Venice to stay with relatives and returned after the child's birth. He need never know."

"And what of the child? Would you give it away to avoid Hunsdon knowing?"

His question strikes Emilia's heart like a dart—sharp, deep, and painful. She imagines handing a child—her baby—to a family member for safekeeping. The thought threatens to reignite her nausea. "No, I could not."

"I did not think you could." Alfonso inhales deeply and expels a long breath. "There is another option."

She lowers her hands to better see him. His expression is guarded, but she needs a miracle. "What would that option be?"

"You could marry me, Emmy. We could raise the child together. I would support us."

The suddenness of his suggestion snatches away Emilia's breath. She is very fond of Alfonso. In a world where she is the consummate outsider, the inscrutable girl of dubious foreign ancestry, Alfonso understands her implicitly. The notion of converting their long friendship into a formal union entices her. However, she would lose her place at Court. She would be forced to abandon every hard-won tread on the staircase toward nobility. And what if Hunsdon accepted the child? Does he not love Emilia? If so, how can he not love their child? She closes her eyes briefly before peering intently at Alfonso. She squeezes his hand.

"Your offer honors me. However, I will do as you first suggested. I will tell Lord Hunsdon the truth. I believe he will accept the child and perhaps find delight in the matter."

Alfonso's features sag, and he shakes his head. "I applaud your honesty. However, I do not believe Hunsdon will respond as you hope. He is not worthy of you, Emmy. No man can ever be worthy of you."

The strength of his compliment warms her, driving her to place a palm against his cheek. "It is *my* life, Alfonso. My decision. I will do what I must to protect both my position at Court and the child."

Alfonso studies the grass that separates them. "When will you tell him?"

"Not yet. I will wait until the quickening to be certain that the pregnancy holds. Before my condition becomes obvious."

His head sags lower. "You will do as you must, then."

The haunted sadness in his eyes speaks to a wound that surprises her. She pulls her hand away from his cheek and rises to her feet. "I am sorry, Alfonso. Sorry I burdened you. Sorry if I have wounded you or disappointed you. I don't want to lose you."

He collects his papers and climbs to his feet. "You cannot lose me. Do not add that possibility to your list of burdens." He holds an elbow to her. "As you are expecting, too much sun might not be ideal for you. Shall we take you back indoors?"

Relief floods her soul. She loops her hand through his elbow and leans against him. "Thank you."

As they stroll toward the palace, Emilia is at war with herself. She knows what she must do to secure a position for herself and her child in higher society. Yet her place at Alfonso's side brings the comfort she craves. A world that is content to send trouble in threesomes also takes delight in denying her the joy of having everything she desires. She is no different from the characters in her plays, then, cast about by the winds of fortune and blind to whatever disaster looms just over the horizon.

The Mermaid Tavern has become packed so tightly that Jane feels trapped. Another mob. Another dark day. The mingling smoke of lantern and tobacco threatens to choke her. Her heart races like a chariot. As she slips through the bodies of the assembled players and those who work the playhouses in search of the door, a hand gripping her elbow draws her attention. She finds Will Shakespeare staring at her with a furrowed brow. His breath reeks of ale, indicating that he is deep in his cups.

"Are you well, Jane?"

"I cannot seem to breathe."

He nods with a knowing smile. "My wife sometimes suffers the same malady in crowds. Come."

He shoves his way through the crush of bodies until reaching the open stairs that lead to the next floor. "Sit here, then, above the fray."

Jane climbs to the fourth step and settles there. "Thank you, Will."

"Cannot have the troupe's seamstress absent for our day of reckoning."

His tone indicates mirth, but the tight lines around his eyes speak of deep concern. He turns to face the bar as Philip Henslowe crawls on top of it. From her perch, Jane can see him clearly across the tops of three score heads. The owner of the Rose appears uncharacteristically grim. The crowd falls silent, a concerto of held breaths. Henslowe waves a paper over his head.

"A friend of the playhouses has secreted me this copy of the Privy Council edict regarding the riot a fortnight past.

He holds the paper at arm's length, narrows his eyes to a squint, and begins to read. *"A letter to the Master of the Roles, Sir Owen Hopton, Knight John Barns, and Richard Young, Esquire. Whereas Her Majesty is informed that certain apprentices and other idle people and their adherents that were authors and partakers of the late mutinous and foul disorder in Southwark of a most outrageous and tumultuous sort . . ."*

Jane listens with growing trepidation as the edict describes a curfew and heavy restrictions on the apprentices, and therefore everyone else by association. Lawmen are given expanded powers to maintain a night watch and prevent any nighttime trouble by force, if necessary. When Henslowe pauses for a breath, Will Kemp belts a relieved laugh.

"That is not so bad! We stage plays during the afternoon, well before nightfall."

Others seem to agree, as evidenced by scattered whispers. Henslowe glares at the player until the crowd falls silent again. "Hold your tongue, Kemp. I have not yet recited the worst of it."

"Out with it, then," says Burbage.

Henslowe continues. *"Moreover, for avoidance of these unlawful assemblies in those quarters, it is thought you shall take order that there be no plays used in any place near thereabouts as the Theater, Curtain, or other usual places there where the same are commonly used, nor no other sort of unlawful or forbidden pastimes that draw together the baser sort of people from henceforth until the feast of Saint Michael."*

An anxious murmur ripples through the crowd. Will climbs the steps to stand beside Jane, and pounds the railing. "What's this, Henslowe? No plays until the end of September? Three months?" He hurls an empty mug against the landing, causing Jane to wince. "We are all buggered now. Our children will go hungry."

His declaration unleashes a firestorm. The assembly divides into knots of furious conversation, a cacophony of outrage and worry. Players of Lord Strange's Men and the Lord Admiral's

Men begin to assemble beside the stairs. The latter troupe has shared the Rose with the former, so Jane has come to know many of them well. Anxiety carves a swath across the features of each man. She shares their dismay but for different reasons. Captain Dansby informed her just a day ago that Lady Pembroke is leaving London on the morrow. This likely spells the end of her dream time as a secret London playwright and the loss of what could only be called friendship with Mary and Emilia. She also realizes that she will not see Dansby again, and her heart sinks. She has come to cherish his kindness as he delivers her across the river and back again. In her feverish imagination, she has often wondered what it would be like to have the regard of such a wondrous man. Now she will never know. The cart of her life is rolling untethered downhill at an increasing pace, and the wobbling wheels are coming off.

"That is not the worst of it, lads." John Hemings's warning draws the attention of the other players—and of Jane. "There are reports of the plague abroad in the land. 'Twill be only a matter of time before it reaches the city."

Burbage strokes his chin and shakes his head grimly. "Our troupe does not possess the funds to survive until September, let alone longer should the plague descend."

"Nor do we." This from Edward Alleyn, principal player of the Lord Admiral's Men. "Our coffers have nearly emptied since the riot. Only the mounting of a tour would allow us to remain solvent."

Hemings rubs his forehead. "Lord Strange has already made it clear that he will not fund a tour this season. His tight purse strings doom us."

"The Lord Admiral has declared the same," says Alleyn. His features have fallen further. "We cannot perform without the patronage of a nobleman, per the law. If neither of our patrons will support us, then this edict has ended us."

As one, the assembled players regard the floor, hollow-eyed. After a pause, Will Shakespeare slaps the railing a second time to draw their collective attention.

"I will find another patron," he says. He slurs his words slightly and winks at Jane. Will Kemp blurts a laugh.

"Oh, is that so? The great Will Shakespeare will simply dig up a noble patron on a moment's notice to spare us the indignity of starving? Who might that patron be, then? King Arthur, perhaps?"

"Or Old King Cole," says another.

"Or maybe one of the dead dukes from your latest play?"

As the players laugh and offer ridiculous suggestions, Jane watches Will seethe. He slaps the railing a third time and then rubs his hand to ward off the sting.

"No, you wastrels. Lord Pembroke."

The players freeze for a heartbeat before bursting into laughter.

"Pembroke?" says Hemings. "He thinks all playwrights are scoundrels."

"And is he not correct?" Will waves a hand. "More importantly, is he not married to Mary Herbert?"

Every face instantly grows pensive. Burbage nods. "Of course. Lady Pembroke. She is a patron of poets and has attended our plays at least a dozen times these past months. Do you know her?"

"I do not." He raises both hands to quell any complaint. "But I know someone very near to the countess."

Kemp folds his burly arms. "Who, then?"

Jane stares at Will with dawning alarm. He cuts his eyes at her. "Leave everything to me and wait for my report."

Jane's jaw falls agape. Has Will guessed the truth at last? Or some portion of it, anyway? She has no time to fret, because as Will stumbles down the steps, he grips her arm.

"Come, Miss Daggett. I require your assistance."

The players part to allow Will and Jane to pass, their features crowned with bewilderment. When Jane breaks free of the Mermaid, in Will's wake, he stops to face her.

"Do I guess correctly, Jane?" His words continue to slur.

Jane inhales a stuttered breath. "Correctly? About what?"

"That you know Mary Herbert, the esteemed Countess of Pembroke."

"How would I possibly know her? I am but a lowly seamstress in the service of a player's troupe."

Will grins and shakes a finger at her. "You are a terrible liar, Jane Daggett, and I like that about you. Don't ever change. Regardless, we are doomed if I am wrong."

Jane blinks at the mud at her feet and rubs her temples. She does not like that everyone's future depends on her. However, the thought of not losing her unexpected friendships appeals to her. And then there are the plays. And Captain Dansby, astride his horse in a blue uniform, looking like William the Conqueror in his magnificence. She shakes away that last vision and, deflated, lets her hands fall to her sides.

"Yes."

"Yes what?"

"Yes, I have met the countess. I sewed a new dress for her."

Will whoops and nearly falls into the mud before catching his balance. "I knew it! We must go to her immediately."

Jane folds her arms across her chest. "What makes you believe she will grant me an audience unannounced? I am just a seamstress."

Will's grin grows wry. He grips his vest with his right hand and stands straight, though wobbling a bit. *"Defer no time; delays have dangerous ends.'"*

It is a quote from one of their plays. A line suggested by Jane, having remembered its use by Mr. Burnham. She taps her foot several times before letting her arms drop again. "*Henry the Sixth*, act two, scene three. Very well. Let us go to Baynard's Castle before the day escapes us."

Will lifts his brows dramatically. "Baynard's Castle! Oh my!"

She grabs hold of his vest and drags him stumbling along after her. "First, though, we must sober you up. I will not have you casting up your accounts on Lady Pembroke's shoes."

Will laughs, but Jane is far from amused. She fears that her uninvited invasion of Baynard's will spell the end of her friendship with Mary sooner than later.

Every household move is a small military campaign, complete with objectives, logistics, and a chain of command. Mary runs the preparations like Hannibal crossing the Alps. She drives her army through an impossible set of obstacles and drags them onward when they grow weary. She alone is exempt from rest. Without her dogged persistence, the endeavor flirts with delay. This reality and her desire for competence drag Mary from bed before sunrise on the last uninterrupted morning before they leave Baynard's for Ramsbury. As a result, she has been at work for hours when Captain Dansby announces visitors. Mary's brow furrows in perplexity. Who would come calling on the day before her departure?

"Can they be sent away?"

Dansby dips his chin and leans nearer than is his custom. "It is Miss Daggett and—"

"Oh, Jane."

Mary pushes past Dansby on her way to the gatehouse. Since Pembroke commanded her to leave London, Mary has fretted over the seamstress. She sent a letter with every intention of finding Jane for private conversation, but the list of tasks has kept her buried. Her plan has been to remain in contact with Jane and Emilia and perhaps find a way to keep their partnership alive. As she steps into the gate yard, though, Mary realizes how naive she has been. The poor girl is only just learning to read and write. How would she correspond? And where would Mary find her now that the Privy Council has closed the theaters? Her chin droops as she understands the truth. Jane has come to bid her farewell. As she crosses the garden, Mary looks to the gatehouse to find Jane standing in its shadow. But she is not alone. Mary frowns and closes the gap.

"Miss Daggett." She regards the man standing beside Jane. "Mr. Shakespeare, I presume. We've not had the pleasure of an introduction."

When Mary holds out a hand, Shakespeare gently takes her fingers and dips his head until it nearly touches her knuckles. "My lady."

Of course, she knows his face. He has filled multiple roles in each of their plays, and quite well. He possesses an affability that endears him to the audience and fellow players alike. However, little of that is on display as he fidgets before Mary. She feels much the same and struggles to maintain a veneer of calm. Why has he come with Jane? Has the seamstress confessed to him the source of the manuscripts? Is this why Cecil warned her husband? Because he knows as well? Mary holds her suspicions at bay and faces Jane.

"What brings you here today?" She fears the answer, whether it is a farewell or an unmasking.

Jane drops a formal curtsy and leaves her chin dipped in deference. "If you recall, my lady, it was I who stitched your new gown over the spring."

A measure of relief seeps into Mary. Jane pretends to barely know her. She is telling Mary to treat her as nothing more than hired help, a virtual stranger. Which is what she wants Shakespeare to believe. Which means he doesn't comprehend Mary's role in producing the manuscripts. Mary keeps her expression blank and nods.

"Of course. It has become the finest garment I own." Mary means what she says. The slate-black damask dress, bodice embroidered with a tangle of roses, and soaring lacy ruff put to shame the efforts of the other ladies at Court. She offers Jane the warmest smile she dares given the ongoing subterfuge. "You should know that the queen herself complemented the dress."

Janes blushes crimson and curtsies again, nearly to her knees. She is playing the role she occupied during that first meeting in the warming house—an overwhelmed girl in the presence of one of her betters. Jane ducks her eyes and motions to her troupe mate. "You may know that Mr. Shakespeare has been writing plays these past six months."

"Yes," says Mary to Shakespeare. "I have greatly enjoyed your work. You have my congratulations."

The man cocks one eyebrow at Mary, exposing a hint of his affability. "If only your congratulations were deserved, my lady. I feel more akin to an imposter, stealing glory from those who toil in darkness. However, I am truly grateful for whatever fortune sends my way."

His response should alarm her, but she cannot help but smile. "Are we not all imposters, in some way? For all we know, you are a nobleman, I am a French princess, and Jane is a secret playwright."

Jane's jaw falls open briefly before she closes it. Shakespeare lifts his other eyebrow and grins. "Yes. For all we know. Though I assure you, I am no nobleman."

"Nor am I French."

"I am certainly not a playwright," Jane blurts. "Only now, Mr. Shakespeare is teaching me to read and write."

"I commend you both on that account," Mary says. "However, I suppose you haven't come here to discuss your education."

She pauses as Jane and Shakespeare exchange glances. Mary's curiosity threatens to bleed into her expression. This meeting has not veered toward either of her worst-case scenarios of farewell or exposure. Shakespeare nods at Jane and engages Mary.

"Of course, Lady Pembroke. If you have not yet heard, the Privy Council has shuttered the theaters and all plays in London for at least three months."

"Yes. Lord Pembroke informed me that an edict was likely."

Shakespeare shifts from foot to foot, a country boy for an instant, before reclaiming his player's bearing. "I come on behalf of my fellows to request your patronage that we might tour the country during the closure. We fear for our children's health if we do not work."

The request is nothing she has expected. Patronage for a player's troupe? Her husband had sponsored a troupe two decades past but had quickly tired of it. Though she sponsors a number of poets from her own purse, Mary has never considered resurrecting a player's troupe in the name of House Pembroke. But why not? The notion flowers quickly inside her, blossoming into an epiphany.

Of course! This is how she can keep her playwriting torch lit—by creating a reason to remain involved with a player's troupe through the closure. The urge to provoke her husband adds to the appeal. He denigrates her poets? Well, let him attack her players, and she will have words with him.

"I must convince my husband, for the law prohibits me from sponsoring a company in my own name." When Shakespeare and Jane expel held breaths, Mary holds up a palm. "That said, perhaps I should refuse such a bold request. What if I do refuse?"

Mary half expects Shakespeare to turn on her. To reveal what he knows to coerce Mary's support. To dangle the prospect of blackmail. However, he instead dips his head.

"I am grateful for the heady experience of these past months. If your patronage is an unreachable star, then I shall return home until the edict is rescinded, to care for my wife and children as best I can. I will find a way, my lady. Please accept my apologies for such a brazen request, and do not hold Miss Daggett at fault. The idea was mine, and her aid was only at my insistence."

Mary blinks rapidly. She is overcome by his gentle goodness, his deference, his consideration of sweet Jane. She watches him until he dares to look at her.

"I will convince Lord Pembroke. Until then, I will have my captain of the guard provide you with sufficient funds to begin mounting a tour."

Jane's blue eyes go wide and glimmer with tears. She drops an impossibly deep curtsy. "Thank you, Lady Pembroke."

Shakespeare bows with a flourish. "Yes. Our deepest thanks, my lady."

"No," she says. "My thanks to you. I do love the theater and find it my pleasure to bring back to life Lord Pembroke's Men. You may expect regular correspondence from me on the matter."

Jane and Shakespeare offer effusive gratitude as they back away from Mary toward the road. Jane lifts a hand. "I wish you the best at your country estate, Lady Pembroke."

Mary fights back tears, disheartened by her impending separation from a young woman she has come to adore. "And I wish you well on tour, Miss Daggett. While you travel, beware of wolves of all kinds."

"Wolves, m'lady?"

She levels a warning glare at Shakespeare before reengaging Jane. "Cecil knows."

Jane's eyes go wide, and she nods understanding. Shakespeare clears his throat, and Jane turns away. As the pair steps onto the road for their journey back to Southwark, Mary watches them go. She is torn in two. On the one hand, the prospect of continuing to write plays warms her soul. However, aligning herself with a players' company might increase the risk that someone will guess what she, Emilia, and Jane are hiding. And all this without knowing what Robert Cecil might or might not know. She must warn Emilia as she has warned Jane, and soon. She must not falter now. As Jane disappears from view, Mary makes a firm decision. She would rather die as a writer than live as a cipher.

16

Two months later, Henley-on-Thames

The minutes before unearthing a plot are to John Harwood like making love to a woman. He is giddy, flush with anticipation, and trembling like a battle steed on a tether.

Nearly three months of insinuating himself into the community of Henley-on-Thames have borne fruit at last. Today he will reap the harvest. Harwood creeps toward the Regan family barn as the lengthening shadows reach across the afternoon toward nightfall. A new wave of clouds rolls in to obscure even those with another round of misting rain. The spray methodically fades the telltale traces of footprints in the grass, all leading toward the ancient barn. Constructed of stone with a thatched roof, the structure normally provides shelter for sheep, geese, and a pair of cows during the harsh winter months. Today, the dead middle of summer, finds the animals in the farmyard or field. However, the barn is occupied. The footprints tell the story, and Harwood knows the ending.

A lad of perhaps eight stands watch by the barn door and paces. He peers repeatedly toward the road, clearly too young to understand that danger rarely arrives from the direction you expect. Harwood slips up to the side of the barn and waits for the boy to pace away. He is on the child in a heartbeat, his hand clasped over the boy's mouth. The barrel of his pistol nestles against the tender white expanse of neck just below the jawline. The boy freezes with grim understanding. Harwood leans into his ear until he can smell the boy's fear.

"When I release you, run away as fast as you can without a word. One sound and you will be the first to die. Do you understand?"

The boy nods frantically, so Harwood shoves him toward the road. The boy stumbles and nearly falls before gathering his legs beneath him. He sprints away with limbs akimbo, never looking back. Harwood grunts approval and turns his attention to the door. It is old, rotting along the bottom, where the moist earth extends its constant touch.

A voice leaks through the rot, steady and droning—a voice he now knows. He readies his pistol, draws a breath, and flings the door open. A dozen heads yank upward to stare at him with alarm. The Regan family. A neighboring family. A servant. All on their knees, with hands clasped at their waists. Beyond them stands a small altar presided over by a white-robed figure holding a chalice in one hand and a gold crucifix in the other. The briefest of moments passes—maybe three heartbeats at most—without so much as an indrawn breath.

Then the servant leaps to his feet and bolts toward the opposite door. Harwood puts a bead on him and pulls his trigger. The ball catches the man in his shoulder and spins him to the straw floor, but the servant bounces back to his feet and barrels through the doorway. Not one of Harwood's better shots.

The others react to the shot by clambering to their feet and pushing toward the far door. Before Harwood can pull his second pistol from his belt, Burnham is on top of him. The rogue priest rides Harwood back through the first doorway and into the mud. Harwood rolls Burnham aside and shoves himself to his knees. The priest becomes still when Harwood lifts the second pistol to point at the space between his eyes.

"You shouldn't have done that, Burnham."

He pulls the trigger. The clink of the hammer is loud in the absence of an explosion. A misfire. Wet powder, no doubt. Harwood drops the weapon and lays his hands on the old man when stars burst across his vision. He wobbles to one side and clutches his temple. Burnham scrambles to his feet with the heavy crucifix dangling from his fingers, no doubt spattered with Harwood's blood. The priest ducks back into the barn in a flurry of white robes. Harwood rises, falls to his backside, and rises again. He blinks heavily to stop his vision from swimming. Inside the barn, the priest has retrieved his chalice and holy book and is ducking through the far door of the now-empty barn.

Harwood rocks forward to give chase. Upon emerging through the second doorway, he scans the yard urgently before finding the priest running toward the river, his robe billowing at his back. He is fast for an old man. Harwood presses a hand to his bloodied and throbbing temple and continues his pursuit. After losing sight of Burnham, he spies him again as the man mounts a horse that he'd clearly hidden in the undergrowth lining the water.

"The devil take it!"

The curse rips from Harwood's lips when he realizes that he will not catch the priest on foot. He lobs mucous into the grass and returns toward the woods past the farm where he has tethered his mount. His mind roils with the logistics of the hunt. Where will Burnham go? He cannot stay in Henley-on-Thames now that Harwood has unmasked him. The priest was riding west away from the river. West. What lies west? Harwood stops in his tracks with rising horror as the answer comes to him.

The queen.

Her summer progress into the west took her and Robert Cecil away from nearby Reading just a week ago, on a line toward ... Ramsbury! The home of Mary Herbert, the plot's ringleader. He stumbles forward with barely restrained panic. Is Burnham bound for there? With the intention of murdering the queen now that the plot has been exposed? While the queen is surrounded by Pembroke soldiers and at their mercy? If ever a Catholic plot could unfold, it would be there. What a disaster! He must reach Cecil before the priest does, even if he must ruin his horse in the attempt. Her Majesty's life is balanced on a knife edge, and only he can stop the inevitable. He must make the forty-mile ride into the night in hopes that Burnham will rest at some point. He cannot fail in his mission. He must not fail. His dead father would never forgive him for it.

Overhanging clouds blanket Mary with a vague sense of dread as she stands on the gravel drive of Ramsbury Manor. She cannot precisely identify the source of her unease, which bothers her also. Tangible threats she can face. Shadows, though—they leave her in a constant state of alert that erodes the edges of her sanity.

"Bear up, Mary." Lord Pembroke stands firm beside her, emanating reprimand. "You must not falter under Her Majesty's gaze."

Mary inhales a breath, partly to swallow a retort, and tilts her chin higher. She will not be the one to falter this day. Within minutes, the long parade of the queen's court emerges from behind a dark stand of forest. Mounted liveried soldiers lead the way, followed by the queen's advisors and her behemoth and ornate coach. Behind them trail a dozen more coaches, three hundred carts laden with baggage and supplies, and five hundred servants and armed guards. The train seems more a hostile invasion than a social visitation.

Mary steels herself and draws slow breaths to order her scattered resolve. During her fifteen years of marriage to Lord Pembroke, this is the first time Elizabeth has called on them to host the court, and with only eight days' notice. Though her husband had grumbled over the inevitable cost of the three-day visit, he had accepted the point of honor and had challenged Mary to make Ramsbury the queen's most memorable stop along her journey. He need not have thrown down a gauntlet, though. This is Mary's house and she the ruler of her domain. Here she exerts control. Here everyone bends to her plans. However, the dread nags her, warning her against . . . what? Her only notion is the question she has asked herself since the queen sent word of her coming. *Why now, after all these years?*

As the procession draws near, Mary recognizes the three men riding horseback directly before the queen's coach. The Lord Chamberlain carries his white staff of state while Lord Essex appears to be regaling him with some tale. Sir Robert Cecil, the third rider, glares ahead as if the men do not exist. Is he looking at her? As the parade makes the turn to run along the front of the house, Elizabeth is a blur of color inside her coach. Mary's attention drifts to the next coach in the procession.

"God help me!"

She swallows the outburst and returns the stare of the woman in the second coach. Emilia! The young woman, so full of grace and confidence, pins Mary with a look of restrained distress. To Mary's knowledge, Emilia has never traveled with the court on a summer progress, remaining instead at one of the palaces. Yet here she is and in a place of supreme visibility. The nagging question surges back to the forefront of Mary's thoughts.

Why now?

Has the queen discovered what Mary and Emilia are doing? Has their shadow sisterhood come to light? Is the visit an elaborate mechanism to bring them into account? She has no time to wallow in hypotheticals, for the queen is descending from her coach with the help of two resplendent footmen. Mary dips a deep curtsy, and Pembroke bows low.

"Your Majesty." Her husband's voice booms with pride. "Welcome to Ramsbury Manor and House Pembroke. Our every possession is yours for the taking, our every diversion yours for the enjoyment."

Elizabeth saunters forward with the lithe steps of a dancer and dips her head. "You have my gratitude, Lord Pembroke. I will hold you to your word."

Mary peeks at her husband to find a line of worry forming above his nose. She almost chuckles. The queen has cowed the great and mighty Lord Pembroke, even if just a little. He recovers by extending his elbow.

"It would please me to escort Her Majesty inside."

"I am certain it would." The queen flashes him a tight grin and faces Mary. "However, it pleases me to walk with Lady Pembroke."

Mary blinks before extending her elbow. Elizabeth slips her gloved hand through the opening and pulls Mary close. She flicks a finger at Mary's husband. "Carry on, Pembroke."

Lord Pembroke's eyebrows lift, and a shadow crosses his face. He bows curtly and spins on his heel to lead the way into the manor. As Elizabeth prods Mary into motion, she leans near enough that the warmth of her breath tickles Mary's ear.

"Do you remember," she whispers, "what I told you on your return to Court last winter?"

The question jolts Mary. She had not expected anything so familiar from the one who sits the throne. "I do, Your Majesty."

"And what did I tell you then?"

"You said, *'We must exert our will within the shadows of men or possess no will at all—and we must exceed them at their own game.'*"

Elizabeth breathes a laugh. "Very good, Mary Herbert. Your memory does you credit." She motions toward Pembroke as he strides ahead of them. "See how I shaved your husband's arrogance by refusing his arm? The pride on his countenance gave me some offense, so I remind him of his place. I remind him who wields the scepter here."

Mary tries to keep her mouth from falling open. She has never experienced such familiarity from the queen and suspects that the reason for it might serve a darker purpose. As they enter the house, Elizabeth sweeps her scrutiny over the grand entry.

"A lovely space."

While the bulk of the court remains outside to erect tents, the luminaries gather in Ramsbury's large hall and fall into knots of conversation. Some of the talk is about the reimprisonment of Sir Walter Raleigh and his wife in the Tower for the sin of marrying without the queen's permission. Mostly, though, everyone discusses the captured Portuguese carrack that was brought into Plymouth three weeks prior. The vessel contains a mountain of pearls, gold, precious stones, amber, musk, and—best of all—pepper from the east. The ship is by far the richest prize ever taken by the English navy. Mary imagines that each of the nobles attending the queen dreams of a way to carve out a piece of the fortune for himself. She feels herself drifting away from the conversations, abdicating her role as hostess.

A shock brings her back into focus. Lord Hunsdon strolls into the hall with Emilia on his arm. Mary slaps her hand to her mouth to stifle a gasp. Keeping a mistress is accepted if not expected of highborn men, so long as they remain discreet in the where and when of their liaisons. Bringing a mistress on the queen's tour is brazen. Though she tries to maintain a bearing of nonchalance, Emilia appears to be failing. The tightness of her lips and the haunting shadow in her eyes tell the story. She would rather be elsewhere than in the presence of noblemen and noblewomen who watch her with predatory stares. Anger bubbles through Mary's detachment. She must protect Emilia in some way. She steps into the middle of the room and claps three times.

"If it pleases you, my lords and ladies, Lord Pembroke and I wish to present a gift to Her Majesty."

The ploy works. The nobles abandon their scrutiny of Emilia to murmur with intrigue. The hostess gift is always a subject of great speculation when the queen arrives at a new house. A good gift can curry favor with the queen, while a mediocre gift can virtually banish the gift giver from Court. Elizabeth lifts her chin with interest.

"What have you for me?"

Caught by surprise, Lord Pembroke snaps at a footman to retrieve the gift. The man runs away with stiff-legged strides and returns breathless with a paper package. Pembroke takes the package and extends it to Elizabeth with a bow.

"In appreciation of your visit, Your Majesty, we wish you to accept from us this humble offering."

The queen accepts the package and pulls the paper apart. Mary's heart stops while Elizabeth studies the posset bowl that the paper has concealed. It is covered in fine gold leaf, and the end of the handle features a small globe containing an agate, which itself contains a red rose. She releases a sigh when the queen smiles.

"How lovely. Exquisite workmanship."

"Thank you, my Queen." Lord Pembroke bows again, and his wide shoulders loosen. "If I might invite you to rest, Lady Pembroke has prepared a poetic dialogue for your entertainment."

Elizabeth hands the bowl to an attendant and regards Mary with those quick, dark eyes. "You are writing again, then?"

"Yes, Your Majesty." Mary's heart quickens at the prospect of virtually lying directly to the queen. "Mostly translations, but I also dabble in poetry and dialogue for the entertainment of guests."

"Wonderful." Elizabeth nods and accepts the plush chair offered by the Pembroke steward. The other nobles collapse around her, jockeying for the nearest seats. Emilia remains standing behind them, fading into the shadow of a corner. Mary understands. The large room is suddenly tight and close. However, as the hostess of the court, she does not have the luxury of fading from view, much to her chagrin. Instead, she sweeps to the adjoining room, where the impromptu players await—two servants of the household. Both appear ready to melt into the floor like spent candles.

"The queen is ready." She gives them what she hopes is a convincing smile. "You have my utter confidence. I commend you for your contribution to House Pembroke this day."

Both men swallow hard and bow before shuffling into the hall. Mary elects to stand aside at the archway, afraid to sit for fear of collapsing. One of the players produces a courtly bow.

"May it please Her Majesty, a dialogue between two shepherds, Thenot and Piers, in praise of Astrea, made by our excellent lady, the Lady Mary, Countess of Pembroke."

As the men recite the lines Mary had penned not a week earlier for this occasion, she finds herself glancing repeatedly at Emilia to find the young woman staring at her. Her brows draw together with concern, which surprises Mary. Why the angst? And why has Hunsdon brought his mistress when such a thing is so rarely done on summer progress? Mary shifts her focus to study the queen in profile. She appears intent on the dialogue of the players, with one hand resting against her topmost toggle. As Mary starts to look away, she finds Robert Cecil watching her intently. He narrows his eyes at her in a manner she considers too forward, too intense for propriety. He smiles and swivels his regard to Emilia, then back to Mary. Her knees begin to tremble. What is happening here? What does Cecil know?

In self-defense, Mary forces her attention to the players, only to remember another worry. Lord Pembroke's Men are slated to present a play to the queen after the evening meal—*Henry the Sixth*. They were due yesterday but have not yet arrived. Where are they? How will she entertain the court in their absence? And what of Jane? Is she still with the players' troupe? The flood of anxiety is nearly too much for Mary to bear. She leans against the archway to let it hold her up, for surely no one else will.

Emilia watches the players perform Mary's dialogue from a thousand leagues away. The nobles gathered before her seem just an extension of the play—a fiction, a phantasm. This state of unreality is not new, but has persisted since Lord Hunsdon demanded her presence on the queen's summer progress three weeks past. Lady Hunsdon, he'd assured her, was both unable and unwilling to join him. No one would breathe a contrary word, he'd told her. He was the queen's cousin, and Her Majesty did not concern herself with the unsanctioned dalliances of others. Only ensuring that marriages were between people of equal station mattered to the queen. Who filled a person's bed from night to night was an afterthought.

This much Emilia might have taken in stride, but then Hunsdon had mentioned Ramsbury, Mary Herbert's estate. Warning cries had erupted in her mind, and the fog of disassociation had descended to whip her with a gale of questions.

Why now after so many years of leaving me behind?

Does he know about my clandestine playwriting and wishes to keep me close?

Or...

Or does he perhaps truly love me?

She has not yet spoken to him of the child she carries but clings to the trembling hope that he will find joy when she breaks the news.

Tonight, though, Mary's expression cuts through the fog. She has spent enough hours with the countess to know when the woman is under a cloud of worry. Is she simply struggling beneath the burden of hosting the queen? Every time Emilia catches Mary's furtive glance, she feels a darker reason.

When Cecil studies Emilia with a shadowy smile, her suspicion hardens. He knows something. But what? She slides her palm to the corset that constrains her growing belly. Hunsdon has not yet called her to his chambers during the journey, but today her baggage has been taken to his private chamber. She will share his bed tonight. The change to her body will be obvious even to him. Her moment of reckoning has come.

Emilia tries to ignore Lady Pembroke across the hall but fails. Their anxious gazes meet again and again. Though Mary valiantly hides her fragile state, she appears near breaking. As for Emilia, she fears the whole world might break at any moment, shattering her into a thousand joyless pieces.

Because she trudges behind the tall wardrobe cart, Jane does not notice Ramsbury Manor until Burbage calls for a halt to the caravan just short of nightfall. Her curiosity forces Jane around the vehicle, and she gasps at the splendor of Mary's country estate. One of her country estates, she reminds herself. There is also Wilton House as well as the residences of Tickenhill and Ludlow. If the splendor of the other houses matches this one, then Lord Pembroke is surely wealthier than the queen. The three-story stone house stretches sidelong in the embrace of a garden, and light emanates from dozens of windows. Jane finds the overall effect warm and inviting, an extension of the Mary she has come to know and adore.

"Why do you smile so, Jane?" She finds Will Shakespeare at her side. "Are you not exhausted? Have you not dreaded this arrival for days?"

Her smile fades with Will's reminder. "That much is true."

Only four days prior, while on tour, Pembroke's Men had received a letter from Mary requesting their presence at Ramsbury Manor to entertain the court—and the queen. A belligerent creditor and his band of brutes had delayed their departure by a day. Heavy rains had forced the troupe to slog along mud-sloshed, rutted roads from sunrise to sunset for three straight days, bringing them to Ramsbury at the last gasp of daylight on the evening they are to perform.

While her troupe mates had grumbled over the slow progress, Jane had welcomed it. Melancholy dread has dogged her steps for sixty miles, nipping at her shins and dragging her spirits low. She fails to understand the reason for her state of mind. Over the course of two months, she has exchanged several letters with the countess, ferried back and forth by the still magnificent Captain Dansby. She takes too long to decipher Mary's letters and scrawl responses, but she dares not ask for help. The letters are too secretive, too indicting. Instead, she continues to pester Will for lessons in reading and writing, and he obliges with an inordinate level of patience.

So, why has she dreaded her arrival at Ramsbury? Jane doesn't know for certain, but suspects that it has something to do with her recurring dream where Mary snatches away Jane's paper and quill and banishes her into the darkness. A tap on her shoulder draws her chin up, which has drifted nearly to her chest. She finds Will pointing toward the manor.

"I find that man familiar. Don't you?"

She follows his extended finger and spies Captain Dansby approaching on foot. Her heart leaps as it always does when she first catches sight of the man after an absence. He is glorious, striding toward them with a burnished helmet under one arm and his other hand atop his sword hilt.

"I have seen him before," she says.

"Only that?" Will grins at her. "Is he not your friend who met you secretively at the theater twice or thrice? And delivers missives from our benefactor from time to time?"

Jane shudders. Will is too observant by half. "Yes, he is."

"And he serves Lord and Lady Pembroke? How interesting."

Dansby's arrival saves Jane from trying to explain what should never be told to anyone. The captain regards Will with narrowed eyes before dipping his head to Jane. "May we speak without lurkers?"

Jane follows him as they step away from the caravan. The failing light casts his broad angular features in shadow, drawing warmth into Jane's neck. He scrutinizes her for the space of a few heartbeats and grows a slight smile. "I am pleased to see you in good health, Miss Daggett. The plague runs hot to the east."

She instinctively dips a curtsy to the soldier. "I thank you for your concern."

"You may not thank me for long."

She draws her brow into a tight knot. "Oh? Why not?"

"Miss Bassano is here as well, apparently under some duress. I did not want you to betray surprise when you saw her."

Jane's heart skips a beat as the dread returns. Mary *and* Emilia are here? Alongside the queen and her spies? She wrings her hands and sways on her feet. Dansby grips her wrist to steady her.

"Remain calm, Miss Daggett, and do your work as if you don't know them. All will be well. You'll see."

The warmth of his large hand stays Jane's trembling. When *he* says it, she believes it can be done. She exhales a deep sigh. "Is that the way of the soldier?"

"We are all soldiers, you not least among us." He smiles softly and releases her wrist. "Are you prepared to march onward?"

"I am, Captain." She returns his smile but must fight to hold it. "Thank you."

"My pleasure."

He steps away and motions to the players. "Come this way. I will show you where you might pitch your tents and prepare for tonight's entertainment."

"How much time have we?" This from Burbage.

"Two hours, no more."

Grumbles erupt from the players, but they follow Dansby like dutiful children. As Jane falls back into the caravan, the dread resurges. She casts a glance over a shoulder, certain that a demon is at her heels. She finds only Will Kemp, who belts a laugh at her.

"What ails you, seamstress? Have you never stood before Her Majesty while splattered with three days of mud?"

Jane faces ahead, doubly concerned. Pembroke's Men are to stage *Henry the Sixth* for the queen in the intimate confines of a great house. Mary and Emilia will be nearby. Along with the entire court of England. So much could go terribly wrong. She only hopes she can see it coming when it does, but fully expects her inevitable downfall to take her by surprise.

※

For all its grandeur, the great hall of Ramsbury Manor doesn't quite live up to its name. As Will peeks from behind the curtain while awaiting his next entrance, he studies the intimate space. Bathed in the soft light of five score candles, the court nobles who crowd around the queen press to the edge of the hastily assembled stage. Lord Essex has set a bottle of wine and two wineglasses on it, but the players have managed to avoid kicking them into the lord's lap during the first two acts.

The Lord Chamberlain is already drunk, mewing the villains and cheering the protagonists as they come and go. His mistress—the Italian musician, Miss Bassano—seems mortified as she tries to fade away from him. However, her stunning beauty conspires against her. No eye can move past her without stopping to blink. Lady Pembroke perches beside the queen, shifting in her chair as if sitting on a pinecone. The queen, on the other hand, wears a casual smile and has already loosened the top toggle of her dress.

Just when Will decides to step back from the curtain, he notices it. Miss Bassano cranes her neck around Lord Hunsdon to peer at Lady Pembroke. As if sensing the gesture, the countess looks back. They hold each other's gaze for far too long. The frowns on their faces deepen, and their foreheads furrow. Then, as one, they break the standoff and swivel their attention to the far end of the stage. Will steps backward to discover the object of their study. It is Jane. The seamstress peeks around the edge of the curtain that separates the stage from the tyring area. When she pulls back, she rubs her temples with her eyes closed, the image of a woman about to empty the contents of her stomach. Then she peeks around the curtain again, her hands clearly trembling. Will looks back through the curtain and for the next minute watches with bewildered fascination the game of cat-and-mouse eye contact among the Bassano woman, the countess, and Jane.

The truth wallops him like a left-hand roundhouse. Jane is more than just a seamstress to these women. She *truly knows* Lady Pembroke and Emilia Bassano. And they know her. They know her well. Jane is more to Mary than the maker of a dress. The only possible explanation for such an oddity follows hot on the heels of his first realization.

Are these his secret playwrights? Lady Pembroke and Miss Bassano?

His gut insight makes perfect sense. He has long ago determined that there are two hands at work on the foul papers. The fact that they are women perfectly explains the secrecy. Were they to be found writing plays for the vulgar London stage, their reputations would become mud. And the queen? She likely would not take the news well, knowing that members of her court were walking ground only she is allowed to tread. He knows nothing of the musician, but Mary Herbert is the sister of a poet and a patroness of other poets. The skill of her writing is well known, and now she funds Lord Pembroke's men from her own purse. Of course! As for Jane? She is clearly their conduit to the players.

He releases the curtain and turns away to ponder his epiphany. Vivid memories of Jane come to mind. How she bristles when the players fumble lines that she has clearly committed to memory. How she frets when they fail to understand the story and stray from the meaning. How she pesters Will as bookholder to rectify both situations. How does she—a barely literate young woman—know the stories and the lines so well for every play she has brought him?

Could she . . . ? No. Perhaps. Is she more than just a courier? Are these stories hers as well? Her intelligence and depth of imagination certainly render such an improbability possible. If so, then are these plays the work of *three* women? Operating beneath the very noses of competing male playwrights and overshadowing them with ease? A chuckle escapes his throat. Oh God! How glorious that would be.

"Will!"

The harsh whisper draws his attention to Richard Burbage.

"Yes?"

"Make your entrance!"

Will flinches and jumps through the curtain, hesitating before he remembers his next line. As he plays the scene with two fellows, he cannot help but glance at the countess and the musician. If this is their play, should they not be rejoicing? Why do they appear so uneasy? He stammers another line as a terrible new thought occurs to him. Have Dutton or Greene uncovered the truth and shared it with an ally at Court? He had hoped that his writing of sonnets for Lady Southampton would quiet any suspicions of his authorship of the plays, but perhaps he has been wrong. The presence of the queen and her spymaster, Robert Cecil, could explain the women's concern. It also might explain Lady Pembroke's cryptic remark to Jane two months earlier in the courtyard of Baynard's Castle. *Cecil knows.* If Cecil knows the truth, then the queen soon will. And Her Majesty does not abide social rebels, especially those who act without her knowledge or consent. She keeps empty cells in the Tower of London for just such people. If she punishes women of high station in such a manner, what will become of him? A commoner who struts the stage? Newgate Prison to rot into a corpse? A gibbet? His head on a pike at London Bridge? He barely manages to finish his lines and exit the stage. His stomach feels weak. John Hemings settles a hand on his shoulder.

"Are you well, friend? You seem a bit green."

"I suppose I am." He wriggles away from Hemings. "Too much meat after we arrived. Nothing more."

"Can you finish?"

"I can. Worry not for me."

Hemings shrugs and begins changing his costume for his next entrance. As Will does the same, the queasiness fades, and a slight grin slowly returns to his face.

Three women! Writing plays in the shadows of the court and taking the London stage by storm!

His chest fills with pride to be associated with such bold and audacious determination. If his guess is correct, then he must do everything in his power to protect his benefactors. And to protect himself. He is, after all, the smallest dog in this fight.

Mary vows to ignore every person in the great hall except the players on the stage. She fails mightily. The queen to her right exudes palpable authority while Cecil burns slowly behind Mary in the recesses of the torchlight.

Despite knowing that the small man watches her, Mary finds her attention drifting to Emilia on her left. Every rustle of the curtain at the edge of the stage yanks Mary's focus aside to find Jane peeking at her. And at Emilia. And at the queen. And at Cecil. Her expression inhabits a place between awe and terror, trending toward the latter when it drifts past Mary to where Cecil sits. Emilia notices as well, for she cuts her eyes toward Mary again and again. Perhaps Jane and Emilia are thinking what Mary has tried to ignore—that Robert Cecil has come to expose them as the source of Will Shakespeare's plays and to accuse them before the queen.

Mary shudders and forces herself to watch the players. She begins whispering lines beneath her breath, to maintain focus on the play instead of the menacing specter of impending disaster that consumes the chamber. This new strategy carries her through to the end of the performance and the bows of the players.

"Magnificent," says Elizabeth as she taps the fingers of one hand against the palm of the other. "No less than we have come to expect from Mr. Shakespeare."

Mary gathers calm to steady her voice. "Yes, Your Majesty. I quite agree."

When Elizabeth stands from her seat, the rest of the nobles rise with her implicit permission and immediately congeal into huddles of intrigue, as is their custom. Mary curtsies to the queen.

"With your leave, I shall inquire of my staff regarding evening refreshments."

Elizabeth flicks two fingers of approval even as she engages Lord Essex in conversation about the play. Mary scurries to the kitchen in a servile manner that would surely earn a rebuke from Pembroke if he saw her doing it. After stirring the staff into action, she returns to the great hall at a statelier pace. As she rounds a corner, she skids to a stop. Her hand flies to her mouth and she gasps. Robert Cecil leans against the passageway wall with arms folded and lips slightly upturned. She drops her hand to her waist.

"Sir Robert. I did not see you there."

"You would not be the first." He leans away from the wall, with a sharp gaze that hints of impalement. "Many disregard me until it is too late."

"Then they do so at their peril."

"Ah, so you understand."

Mary nods, though still uncertain if his comment is casual observation or deadly threat. When he doesn't move to allow her to pass, she suspects the latter. She needs a change of strategy before she flounders.

"Did you enjoy the play, Sir Robert?"

He cocks his head and maintains the slight smile. "I did. I have watched it twice already at the Rose, though I have yet to see Shakespeare's other plays about the Civil Wars. I particularly enjoy the rich dialogue and the thorough understanding of the conflict between Lancaster and York. Do you find the historical events accurately represented?"

Mary suspects that Cecil lays a trap. She should adopt the expected role of female nonchalance and blindly agree with the man. However, he is deeply intelligent. Any attempt at deflection might ramp up his suspicions further.

"No, it was not perfectly accurate. The playwright clearly manipulated a few historic facts in the service of drama."

Cecil's eyebrows arch. "You know the subject well, then?"

"I read Edward Hall's *The Union of the Two Noble and Illustre Families of Lancaster and York*, as have most educated gentlefolk of England."

His soft smile widens into a grin. "Gentlefolk, you say. Nobles aside, I suppose that might include the lesser gentry such as the court steward, Popkin. And even the court musicians and their kin. Perhaps, say, Emilia Bassano. Do you know her?"

Mary's heart thuds briefly to a standstill. She starts to lift a hand toward the wall to steady herself, but stops. She harbors little doubt now that Cecil knows something specific . . . but what? Though her breathing has become shallow, she gathers a steady reply. "She is impossible to miss. Don't you agree?"

He chuckles low in his throat. "The queen's dear cousin Lord Hunsdon surely thinks so." He steps nearer to Mary and leans perilously close. "Do you know the true travesty of Henry the Sixth's reign?"

Mary shakes her head, unable to offer a single word. Her deep unease erupts into barely constrained fear as Cecil leans closer still.

"That kin from the same royal house killed one another, goaded by those in their company. Those in their trust. All of them lesser lights of society. It is an old tale, Lady Pembroke. A tale that repeats every generation or two with the predictability of the next chime of the clock tower. Why, one of the queen's other cousins, Mary Queen of Scots, sought to mount a murderous rebellion against Her Majesty. She failed, at the cost of her life. Is the tale not sad?"

Mary fades away from Cecil to reclaim her space. Is he comparing her secret playwriting to attempted assassination of the queen? If so, his reaction is extreme. She cannot make sense of it. She inhales deeply and lifts her chin to remind Cecil of their comparative stations. "It is a sad tale, though I cannot imagine what depravity might infect a mind that a person would seek to endanger the queen."

Cecil's grin fades. He rocks his head left and right, threshing Mary's soul with his scrutiny. "Believe me, Lady Pembroke, such depravity exists in the minds of Catholic firebrands throughout this land. One can never predict where the next popish plot might originate. From Spain. From royal cousins. From servants with Catholic sympathies. Stewards. Footmen. Maids." He pauses. "Even seamstresses."

Mary's eyes threaten to water. *He knows.* She is as certain as death about this. But why the threats? Why the comparison of playwriting to Catholic plots? She shakes her head defiantly. "As a loyal subject of Her Majesty, I pray that all plotters are uncovered and brought to justice."

Cecil steps back, half turns, and eyes her across one shoulder. "Oh, they will be, my lady. They will be. Our queen has ruled wisely, but she lacks a successor and is beyond the age of birthing one. As such, it remains in the best interest of all to extend her longevity until she might transition the rule to her cousin's son, James the Sixth of Scotland."

"I concur. A smooth transition remains our best hope." Mary means what she says, though she is still bewildered by why Cecil would take such a tack to expose her clandestine theatrical efforts.

"Good," he says. "Not all agree, though—even some in the highest of houses. Those of House Pembroke, however, are seen by all as good and godly Protestants and loyal to the Crown. Imagine the terrible shame if the queen were to learn otherwise."

His threat can be no plainer. He equates Mary's actions to treason. But why? She nearly asks him directly how he believes the writing of plays can possibly threaten the queen the way the Spanish Armada did, but she swallows the question. Once asked, it cannot be unasked. As seconds pass without her response, Cecil's smile grows. He dips his head.

"I see you truly do understand, Lady Pembroke." He steps aside to open the passageway. "Do not let me interfere with your hospitality."

Her chest tightens. She gathers her resolve and strides past him into the great hall. Though she presents an air of calm competence, she is anything but. Cecil has ordered her to stop what she is doing or face the wrath of the Crown. His demand places her on the edge of a blade tottering between heaven and hell. To continue doing what she loves might destroy her. To stop, though, would certainly crush her to dust.

Although the bedchamber given to Lord Hunsdon is richly appointed for comfort and style, Emilia sees only an inquisition court. She avoids the bed to pace, to fret, to sigh. Loud laughter and music that has trickled up the stairs for at least two hours has begun to fade, a harbinger that Hunsdon will soon join her. She flexes her fingers and attempts to slow her hurried breaths by envisioning a less anxious event.

This evening's play.

Henry the Sixth.

Even several months and a half-dozen viewings later, the sight and sound of players on stage, speaking her lines, swells her pride and ignites her joy. A year ago, such a notion would have been unimaginable. She shakes her head with disbelief over the manifestation of such an improbable dream. *Her* poetry. *Her* prose. Played for thousands to thundering applause and cascading delight. If the public learned that the play was the product of her hand, of Mary's hand, of Jane's imagination, they would cough into their fists and scoff over the very idea that three women could overtake the hearts and minds of London with the power of story.

Emilia's breath catches. The general public doesn't know, but certain individuals do. Her short-lived joy shatters as the reality of the evening invades her thoughts. Robert Cecil and the queen had shared the same room with the secret playwrights for the staging of a play that could wreck Mary, crush Emilia, and obliterate Jane if higher powers learned the truth. She stops pacing and leans her forehead against the cool stone of the manor house wall as a tempest rages in her soul. She is in that state when the door creaks open. Emilia looks back to find Hunsdon filling the doorframe, with a candle in one hand. He sways slightly, either from age or too much wine but likely both.

"Why do you inhabit the darkness?"

Emilia frowns at the question before realizing that the single candle in the corner has guttered out without her noticing. "The night does not require illumination."

He hums interest. "Still, I would see you better."

Hunsdon closes the door, ambles to the extinguished candle, and lights it with his candle. He repeats the process with a second candle at the bedside. He pats the bedclothes and throws her the very smile that had first attracted her to him those many years ago. "I would see all of you tonight, my Italian rose."

A shudder passes through Emilia. She can no longer hide the gentle swell of her belly beneath the compressing corset. She closes her eyes and clenches her fists while considering Hunsdon's smile and dancing eyes, his gentle demeanor in the bedroom, his unabated delight in her. She comes to a decision. Yes. He will welcome the news. He will share her joy. She opens her eyes and rests both hands across her belly.

"I am with child, my lord."

The confession rushes forth faster than she intends, driven by a gust of anxiety. The Lord Chamberlain stops swaying, and his brows draw together. "What did you say?"

"I am with child."

He blinks and his eyebrows lift. "Are you certain of this?"

"Yes, my lord. Already, the child quickens."

Hunsdon's expression draws into a blank. He steps to the end of the bed to face her across a few feet of open floor. His attention sweeps to her hands, her belly, her face. "Are you certain the child is mine?"

Emilia staggers from the question as if he has struck her cheek. Her hands begin to tremble as anger rises from the pit of her stomach. "You question my fidelity? My loyalty to you?"

He flips a hand and shrugs. "And why not? Many at Court lust after you. I imagine you have ample opportunity to stray."

Her anger spills over, throwing heat into her cheeks. Her lips draw tight, and she raises a finger to him. "Others at Court have treated me like a harlot for years, but never you. Instead, I was as a wife to you. A trusted confidante. A kindred spirit both in the bedchamber and in the halls. You made me believe I was important to you. Until now."

Hunsdon cocks his head and frowns. "You *have* been important to me, Emilia."

"Have been?" She steps nearer to him. "What about now? Will you care for me now? For your child?"

He waves a hand to her belly, stopping short of touching it. "Can you not rid yourself of the condition? 'Tis commonly done. Otherwise, the court would be awash in bastard children."

Emilia's anger gives way to shock and shame. He is disavowing the child. She should have expected as much—should have prepared herself for this reaction from him. But in the basking glow of her playwriting success, she had forgotten her rules of war. She had forgotten herself. The court is a chessboard, and she is but a lowly pawn to be shuffled and sacrificed by more powerful hands. For a glorious time she had forgotten. Hunsdon's expectant expression reminds Emilia how far she has slipped from the vigilance that has protected her and guided her for most of a decade. Now is her chance to reclaim the watchtower. A simple remedy, a simple procedure, and she can remain in his good graces and in his bed.

"I will not. I want this child, even if you do not."

Hunsdon's eyebrows arch, and his mouth opens to an oval. However, he is no more surprised than Emilia is. For an instant, she had intended to acquiesce. To return to the battlefield in full armor. However, her heart wants otherwise.

The Lord Chamberlain half turns to peer sidelong at Emilia. He lifts an index finger and shakes it three times. "I have kept you well these past many years, in clothing, jewelry, and allowance. I have paid you well enough to live comfortably at Court. However, I cannot afford to have a bastard child wailing at Her Majesty's feet. You promised me that you would take care of such a circumstance, but now you renege."

Emilia's shock spirals. She has never made such a promise. She has always assumed that his age left him unable to produce another child. How wrong she has been. In the silence following his pronouncement, she corrals her dismay and stiffens her spine.

"I *am* taking care of the circumstance. I will birth this child. I will raise this child."

Hunsdon grunts and nods. Though his eyes grow large with sadness, he strides to the chamber door and opens it. "Then you will sleep with the musicians tonight, as your station demands. Upon our return to London, you will leave the court, never to return."

"Surely, you do not mean this."

Hunsdon sets his jaw and turns away. "Surely, I do. I cannot have another bastard whelp. Not now. Not with the threats against me from inside the court. You must go now."

Emilia stifles a sob and stumbles through the door. As she turns back toward him with an imploring gaze, he sighs and closes the door in her face. Devastation washes through her soul. She is shipwrecked, cast on a dark shore without a beacon or a friend.

No.

Not without a friend.

Alfonso was right about Hunsdon. He had been right all along, but she had been too full of importance and vanity to understand his warning. Where is he now? All her dreams are dashed. After years of climbing toward respectability, she has been thrown from the battlements into the mud below. She presses the heels of her hands to her watering eyes and finally releases the pent-up sob. When the heaving passes, she clenches her fists and goes in search of the musicians. In search of Alfonso. He will know what to do. He always has when in the service of her best interests.

Not even darkness stands in the way of Harwood's desperate ride. He pushes his horse beneath a gibbous moon along the night-soaked road, knowing that an obscured pit or rock could cripple his mount and throw him headlong to his death. He does not relent, though. The stakes are too high and the potential outcome too dire for him to let prudence overrule his mission.

He cannot miss Ramsbury Manor when it comes into view. Every window glows with candlelight, and a dozen campfires dot the expansive grounds. Harwood urges the horse off the road and toward the great house, passing an array of tents along the way. He slides from the saddle and pauses only long enough to tether the horse to a post near the main entrance. Is he too late? Has the plot unfolded already? After mounting the steps, he pounds the door with a gloved fist. He does not shout, though, for fear of betraying his arrival to potential adversaries. When the heavy door creaks open, it reveals a pair of guards armed with short pikes and wearing blue livery and dour expressions. Their general lack of alarm or hostility tells Harwood that no violence has occurred—yet. He expels a pent breath. The older of the two, a man of gray grizzle, sweeps a discriminating gaze over Harwood and his mud-spattered clothing.

"What business could you have at this hour?"

Harwood tries not to bristle at the condescension. "I have urgent news for the queen's secretary, Sir Robert Cecil. I am in his employ, and my information cannot wait."

The man lifts one eyebrow, clearly skeptical of the claim, and tosses his head at his partner. "Fetch the captain. We wait here."

The guard spreads his stance and leans the tip of the pike toward Harwood while the other man hurries off. Harwood glares at him, but the guard fails to flinch. Within a moment, the captain arrives—a man Harwood recognizes. Dansby, the constant escort of the countess during her secretive meetings at the Temple Church those many months ago, and the courier of her letters to the Bassano woman and the seamstress. Harwood weighs his strategy carefully. Dansby is no doubt privy to the plot and likely a fellow plotter, and he is armed. Nothing is to stop the man and his two subordinates from seizing Harwood, hauling him into the fields, and slitting his throat. Harwood steps back from the door and bows.

"Captain. I am John Harwood, in the service of Sir Robert Cecil, and bring him urgent news of the Portuguese carrack at Plymouth. He will want to know immediately."

Though Dansby's iron expression does not waver, the lie appears to work. The captain turns away and beckons. "Come, then."

Harwood steps through the door, and the pair of guards falls in behind him. Only then does Dansby pause to face him again. He glowers at Harwood so intently that his eyes might skewer the man.

"If Sir Robert disowns you, then we will run you out with extreme vigor. Do you understand?"

Harwood does understand. Only a plotter would make such a threat. "I understand."

Dansby resumes his march, guiding Harwood past a scattering of drunken noblemen and up the wide central stairs to a hall of doors—bedchambers, no doubt. He stops beside one and raps it three times, softly.

"Yes?"

The voice behind the door belongs to Cecil, which brings Harwood some relief. He had half suspected that Dansby would drag him into an unused room, for interrogation or simply to murder him.

"A man to see you," says Dansby.

"At this hour?"

"A Mr. Harwood."

The soft thud of footfalls precedes the opening of the chamber door, to reveal Cecil. He is in a state of half dress, clearly preparing to bed down for the night. And he appears stone sober, another reason to admire the man. While others allow wine to overtake their good sense, Cecil remains always the model of self-control. He assesses Harwood's disheveled condition.

"Why now, John?"

Harwood cuts his eyes at Dansby before subtly lifting one eyebrow. The lines on Cecil's forehead fade with comprehension, and he beckons with his fingers.

"Come inside, then. Captain Dansby, you may resume your duties."

"Yes, sir." Dansby bows curtly and drags his men back toward the stairs, but not before throwing Harwood a deeply suspicious parting glance.

Harwood steps through the gap that Cecil opens, and the little man closes the door behind him. Cecil folds his arms. "Well?"

"I fear the plot may unfold tonight in this very place."

Any semblance of annoyance fades from Cecil's features, replaced by a steely frown. "Tonight? Tell me everything."

Harwood recounts the failed arrest at Henley-on-Thames and makes known his suspicion that Burnham is on his way to Ramsbury—and may already have arrived. Cecil unfolds his arms and paces back and forth with his lilting gait, one hand massaging his chin. After three turns he stops to face Harwood.

"I fear the plot might be wider than I first suspected."

"Sir?"

"Tonight's play," Cecil says. "*Henry the Sixth*. Do you recall that the letter you intercepted used a cipher that invoked names associated with the Civil Wars? And that King Henry was a central figure in that conflict?"

Harwood does not have a firm grasp on historical details, but every child in England knows the dread tales of those dark days. He nods to Cecil. "I do recall. What meaning do you find in the connection?"

"There can be only one meaning." Cecil peers at Harwood beneath a hooded brow. "The playwright, Shakespeare. He is more connected to this plot than I'd assumed. Perhaps he is even the architect of the cipher on behalf of Lady Pembroke. He is clever with words, after all. Even more, perhaps the very lines of his play speak instruction to unseen rebels who champion the Catholic cause."

Harwood shakes his head, but not with disbelief. "I do not know of such tortuous politics, Sir Robert. I simply hunt for those who hold them."

Cecil chuckles lightly. "That you do, John, that you do. And tonight, you've done well as always. Now, go fetch the seamstress without causing a fuss."

Pride and excitement course through Harwood, and he clenches his fists to contain his eagerness. "Where might I find her?"

"With the players' troupe in their tents on the south lawn. Can you snatch her away without inviting trouble from her troupe mates?"

"I can, sir. I boast of few things, but my stealth is second to none."

"Very well. I will wait here for your return."

Harwood slips through the door and into the hall, bound for the south lawn. He caresses the sword at his hip and the dagger on his belt, finding comfort in their presence. He does not prefer violence but is always prepared for its inevitable arrival.

※

Though it is high summer, the chill of nightfall and the presence of virtual deities drive Jane to the communal fire among the troupe's tents. Her pallet inside the covered cart affords her privacy but offers little warmth. She squats beside the cooking pot, to warm her hands over the dying coals, and recalls the astonishing evening.

When she had dared to peek around the curtains at the gathered nobles, her first glimpse of the queen had struck her with terror. For a lifetime, Elizabeth has represented to Jane the epitome of terrible authority, unbridled power, and unassailable heights. The sight of the woman not thirty feet away had threatened to unravel Jane's substance into a pile of disorganized threads. However, she had been drawn again and again to sneak a look at the queen, and at Mary and Emilia. Only the sharp glare of a little man behind the countess had convinced Jane to remain behind the safety of the curtain. His penetrating regard had unnerved her.

Now, though, she is safe. The nobles are ensconced inside Ramsbury's walls while she huddles in the midst of her sleeping comrades. She will be glad to leave the wolves of Court behind when the troupe moves along two days hence. How Mary and Emilia survive the consuming fire of the court day by day remains a mystery to her. Jane shakes her head and retrieves a poker to stir the coals. She is reaching toward the embers when an arm encircles her waist and a rough hand closes over her mouth.

"You are to come with me." The penetrating whisper in her ear speaks of malice, of rape or murder. "Shout and I will push a blade through your neck."

As the man drags Jane to her feet, a dozen traumatic memories stampede through her brain. She remembers the crowds who chased her through the streets, shouting "Witch!" and "Whore!" She thinks of the two times they caught her and of the one occasion when they beat her bloody, stole her virtue, and left her for dead in a ditch.

Visceral panic rises from the pit of her bowels to animate her limbs. She pulls at the malicious embrace and swings the poker at her unseen attacker. He grunts and releases his hold, allowing her to spin away. A closed fist to her cheek drops her to the dirt and fills her eyes with stars. The attacker yanks the poker from her hand and slings her over his broad shoulders. She rubs her cheek and blinks away confusion as the man hauls her toward the great house. When he reaches the back wall, he dumps her onto the damp grass. As his figure looms over her in the darkness, she clenches her knees together and grabs her skirt. The man leans low and puts a hand on her throat.

"You papist witch." His accusation spews bile. "I know that Burnham is a Catholic priest. I witnessed him performing mass, and now he is in the wind. Do not deny your association."

Jane's eyelids flutter rapidly as the confusion returns. Mr. Burnham a priest? Performing mass for Catholics? Her mind reels briefly before finding its balance. Of course, Mr. Burnham is a priest. He is one of the few who has shown her true kindness in a world of ridicule. He is compassionate. He is loving. He is good.

"Well?"

Jane stares at the shadow of the man leaning over her. "What do you want from me?"

Her question emerges as a choked whisper. The man loosens his grip on her throat. "A confession. I saw you place coins in the priest's hand only a few months ago. You support the papist cause."

"But I don't!"

"Do not deny it. My eyes do not lie. Tell me everything you know about the plot, and I will ensure that you aren't put to the sword this very night."

Coins? Plot? Jane had only repaid Burnham what she owed him. And what had that to do with her secret playwriting?

Her soul chills with the freeze of impending disaster. The world is collapsing on her head in ways both familiar and novel, and she cannot pick apart the threads. Her confusion mounts when the shadow abruptly jerks aside, and the pressure against her throat disappears. Jane pushes up to find another man grappling with her accuser.

"Jane!"

She startles and rolls to her knees at the sound of her name. Captain Dansby! One shadow rises atop the other, pinning it. The ascendant shadow pumps an arm at her.

"Run, Jane! Hide yourself! Do not stop!"

Dansby's command cuts through the gloom of Jane's confusion. She trusts the guardsman implicitly, as she has trusted Mr. Burnham, Mary, and Emilia—and no others. Against all odds and despite her unworthiness, Dansby works for her benefit with no expectation of repayment or ulterior motive. Jane scrambles to her feet and flees through the tents.

"Miss Daggett!"

Will Shakespeare calls her name as she brushes past him toward the dark open field, but she does not make the mistake of Lot's wife by looking back. She hikes her skirt and high-steps through knee-tall plants that bruise her shins with a thousand gentle slaps. A solid form reveals itself as a low stone wall in her way. She climbs over. Dansby told her not to stop, so she runs farther to escape the menacing stranger.

As her legs pump and her lungs heave, Jane begins to understand what has happened. She is tied to a Catholic priest and has been seen giving him money—a crime punishable in the extreme for one of her low station. If the stranger catches her, she is dead. Upon reaching the edge of the second field, Jane plunges into a night-soaked stand of trees. When her knees begin to buckle, she crawls deep into a thicket and huddles in a ball, gasping for breath.

In the embrace of her newfound stillness, Jane considers her plight. She is marked for death for a situation far beyond her control, and no one will believe that she is innocent. She has nothing now but the clothes she wears—no food, no money, not even a sewing kit by which she might earn her bread. Dansby has sent her away, and Burnham is on the run. They cannot help her now. She refuses to turn to Mary and Emilia for fear they be dragged into her dire misfortune. Where can she go, then? Where can she hide that she might find the means to survive? A place where no adversary will consider searching for her? The answer comes to her mind's eye, clear as spring water.

London.

The city is hot with the plague and rapidly emptying of those who can afford to flee. Nobody will expect Jane to return to the most dangerous place in all of England—in all the world.

Yes! London!

She has stashed two dozen coins beneath the floor of the Rose alongside the chests containing props and costumes. She will retrieve the coins and use them to pay for lodging, food, needles, and thread. Then she will find work. Surely, some remain who are in need of a seamstress, even if only to sew tight the shrouds of the dead. Her brief elation fades in the night, giving way to tears and muffled sobs. The dream is ended. Her shining hour of peace and belonging has shattered into a thousand jagged shards that will carve new scars into her wounded soul.

Her life on the run has begun anew, as if she could ever truly escape it.

⁕

Though most fear the night for its mysteries and unseen terrors, Emilia embraces the darkness. Ever since her beauty began to blossom, she has found solace during the times when the host of jealous watchers cannot lay eyes on her. This night is no different. She circles before the tents of the musicians, using a pair of nearly dead fires as markers for her turns. Sleep is leagues away, a destination made distant by the twin specters of shock and shame that dog her heels. The sound of soft footfalls draws her attention and an intake of breath. A familiar face greets her, however, his shadowed features lined with concern.

Alfonso.

She lunges into his open arms and buries her head against his chest. He strokes her curly hair and rocks her gently side to side but says nothing. His silence is a gift. How can she explain that she has been cast out from Court, discarded like a pair of worn shoes by a man who expects no complications?

"Miss Bassano."

The whisper of her name yanks her away from Alfonso's embrace to find Dansby two steps away. "Captain?"

"Sir Robert demands your presence in the manor immediately." His voice carries a weight that stands in contrast to his customary military delivery.

"Now?"

"Now."

"Is this about Lord Hunsdon?"

Though the coals throw little light, Emilia sees a shadow pass over Dansby's features—pain, perhaps even fear. A tremor climbs her spine.

"No," he says. "This is about Jane. Come now."

Bewildered, Emilia leans forward to walk, but Alfonso grasps her elbow. "I will go with you."

The captain holds up a palm. "You cannot, friend. I will watch over them. You have my word."

"Them?" Alfonso says.

"Miss Bassano and the countess. We must delay no longer."

Dansby strides away and Emilia follows, leaving Alfonso by the fireside. *This is about Jane? And Mary too?* A weight thuds in her chest, pressing against her heart and lungs. *This must be about the plays.* Her fear mounts as she walks behind the captain into the great house and up the central staircase to a long hall. He leads her to the door at the end of the hall and raps on it softly. The door cracks open to reveal Robert Cecil. The queen's man nods and opens the door wider, disclosing the presence of others—Mary, Mary's husband, and . . . Henry? Lord Hunsdon? Her former lover peers at her, clearly as befuddled as she is. She backs away but Dansby halts her.

"You must go inside."

She stares at the guardsman with wide eyes. "Will you come with me?"

"I cannot. I will remain just here, though. Take courage."

Emilia draws a deep breath, exhales, and walks into the lion's den. Cecil closes the door and lifts an eyebrow. "And so, the last player enters the stage."

Emilia tries to contain a shudder but is certain that her fear is as plain as the morning sun. This is definitely about the plays. She waits for Cecil to begin questioning her, but it is Lord Pembroke who seizes the floor.

"What is this nonsense, Cecil?" His stone features have become ice-dusted granite. "Why do you drag us to my wife's chambers in the middle of the night?"

Sir Robert does not wither beneath Pembroke's glare, but instead bows curtly with a flourish of the hand. "I beg your forgiveness, Lord Pembroke, but this gathering pertains to dire matters of state."

"Matters of state? Involving my wife and this, this . . ." He motions toward Emilia but doesn't say the word that is clearly on his tongue.

"Matters of treason, my lords."

Pembroke opens his mouth but closes it. He eyes Mary and Emilia before flicking his fingers at Cecil. "Say it directly."

Cecil grows a sly smile. "The Lady Pembroke, Miss Bassano, and a seamstress called Jane Daggett have been meeting in secret and exchanging coded missives for the past nine months in the service of a Catholic plot. Can I be more direct than that?"

Pembroke sways and lifts a hand as if to steady himself. Failing to find anything, he closes his hand into a fist. Hunsdon, though, grips Cecil's shoulder. "Explain, sir! If you lie, Pembroke will cut you down regardless of who your father is, and I will obtain the queen's blessing for his action."

"Of course." Cecil steps away from Hunsdon's hand and glances at Mary. "My spies bring word of a rogue priest performing mass not far from here, and the seamstress connects him to the countess and Miss Bassano. I have reason to believe he hatches a plot to assassinate Her Majesty and that these women might be involved, along with the Shakespeare fellow."

Emilia's knees nearly buckle, but Mary steps forward to steady her, watching her through wide eyes brimming with shock. They hold each other up as Cecil recounts the details of a plot involving Jane's former employer—Burnham—who is a secret papist priest. Jane was seen giving him money when he visited her in London. Letters between Mary and Emilia were intercepted and deemed to be coded messages involving the queen's assassination at the hands of other nobles. The priest escaped arrest and was last seen riding in the direction of Ramsbury. Each new accusation threatens to drive Emilia to the floor. She wants to scream at the falsehoods, but vertigo stills her tongue. It is the last detail, though, that nearly stops her heart.

"And finally," says Cecil languidly to the horrified lords, "the seamstress has fled this place only minutes ago, with what I can only assume was inadvertent assistance from the Pembroke captain of the guard, though that requires further inquiry. I have sent men to hunt her down."

Silence descends in the chamber as Pembroke and Hunsdon pin alternating glares on Mary and Emilia. Mary lifts her chin to Cecil.

"Have you reported this utter nonsense to the queen?"

He quirks an eyebrow and hides a smile. "I have stayed my hand to uncover further details before making accusations to Her Majesty. This would be a fine moment to refute what I have been told."

Pembroke's startlement breaks like an ice dam, and he wheels on Mary and Emilia. "Is this remotely true, Wife? Have you conducted these clandestine meetings and exchanged secret missives?"

Mary flinches at his vitriol. "We have met and exchanged letters, but . . ."

"To what end? Treason? Betrayal?"

Mary stiffens in Emilia's grasp, and her features lock into a mask more authoritative than what even her husband can muster. The cords of her jaw flex before she speaks. "You of all people, Lord Husband, should know better than to doubt my absolute loyalty to Her Majesty, the Church, and the Crown. I am no plotter, neither is Emilia Bassano nor Jane Daggett. You deeply misunderstand the nature of our meetings. Sir Robert's assessment of our missives would be comical if not for the fact that he cries treason."

Pembroke cuts his eyes at Cecil, who appears mildly troubled by Mary's response.

"Explain to me, then," Pembroke says from low in his throat, "the nature of your meetings."

Emilia's head swims. She wants to slap her hand over Mary's mouth to contain the secret of the playwriting, but to do so might cost them their lives. Mary returns her husband's glare but tosses her head toward Cecil. "We should discuss this privately. The four of us."

Cecil shakes his head. "Whatever you must discuss surely requires my presence, as your fate will be determined by my understanding and patience. Do you not agree?"

Pembroke peers deeply into this wife's eyes before nodding slightly. "Leave us, Sir Robert. We will manage this affair."

"I am the queen's secretary, not a footman to be dismissed."

"This is my house." Pembroke's brow knots. "And my wife. You will do me the courtesy of allowing me to speak to her about your claims. When all is said, I will serve the interest of the Crown. Of that you can be assured."

Cecil appears prepared to argue further, but instead dips his head. "Sort it out, my lords, or I will."

He leaves, shutting the door behind him. Hunsdon wastes no time before grabbing Emilia's arm. She tries to twist away, but he yanks her to him with a strength that belies his years, sending a jolt through her shoulder. "What is this, Emilia? What have you done to me? Speak, girl!"

Emilia opens her mouth, but her words fail, emerging as an incoherent stammer. Mary touches Hunsdon's chest and dips her chin. "Allow me, Lord Hunsdon."

Hunsdon releases Emilia, and she rubs her arm where his hand had gripped. Pembroke sets his jaw and spreads his palms. "Well?"

Mary cuts her eyes at Emilia with apology and clenches her hands together at her waist. "We have been writing plays."

Pembroke frowns and cocks his head. "Plays? House plays?"

"No, Lord Husband. Plays staged in the London theater, including the one we watched this evening."

"Surely not."

"Surely so."

Mary returns to that first meeting in the warming house at Whitehall Palace and describes the chain of events that has led them to the present time. She makes it clear that Will Shakespeare knows nothing of their identities and that Alfonso and Captain Dansby remain ignorant of their activities. Emilia knows otherwise but respects Mary for sparing as many as she can from whatever retribution will fall as a result of the admission. Still bereft of words, Emilia nods and hums agreement whenever Hunsdon snaps, "Is this true?"

When Mary finishes the telling, Hunsdon's cheeks are red with rage, and they wobble as he shakes his head. "A ridiculous tale. How can three women produce such sophisticated works, and only one of them a noblewoman? Surely, you lie, but for what reason?"

Emilia's ire breaks through her silence. "She does not lie! We have done as my lady claims! All of it. Every word and every line."

Hunsdon gathers a response, but Pembroke holds a hand of restraint. He frowns at Mary. "How can we be certain of this tale? What is your evidence?"

Mary grits her teeth, grabs her skirts, and sweeps to her writing desk. She reaches beneath to what can only be a false bottom and retrieves a sheaf of paper. "This is my evidence."

She returns and shoves the papers into her husband's hand. He squints at the title. "*Titus Andronicus*?"

"One of our newest plays, still in progress."

Pembroke scans three pages in silence before reengaging Mary. "So, this is true."

"As we have claimed."

Hunsdon puts a hand to his forehead. "This is a disaster. If the queen were to learn of this, we all would face social disgrace and invite Her Majesty's wrath. However, if we allow Cecil's claims to stand, we face the Tower or worse.

Pembroke runs a hand through his graying hair. "Treason is not an option. There must be another way."

Hunsdon freezes and raises a finger, his features lit with epiphany. "There *is* another way."

Emilia's heart plummets. She has witnessed Hunsdon at work too many times not to recognize that he is preparing to hurt someone. Pembroke lifts his brow. "What are you considering, Hunsdon?"

The Lord Chamberlain sidles up next to Pembroke and faces Mary and Emilia. "You must concoct a tale of meeting for prayer with the seamstress as a mere attendant. You must explain away the missives as a simple game between two bored women. You must claim ignorance of the seamstress's Catholic connections and fully support Cecil's efforts to arrest her. When she is taken into custody, you must refute everything she says as nonsense. Once she is in hand, I can arrange to have her silenced forever. And the playwright, Shakespeare. He too might meet with an unexpected and tragic accident. Only this way might our reputations be spared."

Before Emilia can square what Hunsdon has said, Pembroke claps his hands. "Yes. This is what you will do. The girl is common. Your story will be believed. I will instruct Cecil to refrain from informing the queen until the girl is found."

Mary clenches her fists. "Can we not simply tell Her Majesty the truth?"

"No! Never that." Pembroke lifts a finger to Mary when she starts to rebut. "I forbid you from speaking a word of your playwriting to the queen. From this day forward, you will cease all such activity and sever your association with Miss Bassano. You will do as I say, Wife, or face an annulment."

"As will you." Hunsdon lifts his chin to Emilia. "Not one word to the queen. You must depart from here at first light and never acknowledge me again. If you breathe a single word of your playwriting twaddle to the queen, whether spoken or written, I will see that every Bassano is severed from the court. There are many who would fill the role of court musician. Do you hear what I say?"

Emilia's lungs clench. He threatens the livelihood of three generations of Bassano musicians to keep her quiet. She can do nothing but nod understanding. He acknowledges it with a sad smirk.

"It seems your trouble for me this day is compounded, Emilia, and after all I've done for you."

In the aftermath of Hunsdon's statement, Emilia sees him for what he truly is. A weak man. A man with a spine of straw, blown by circumstance and bowing to power so that he might indulge his desires without fear of discomfort. Hunsdon gives a single, sharp nod and leaves the chamber. Pembroke glowers at Mary from beneath his brow.

"Do you understand *my* directive?"

She stands stiffly, her features locked in storm. "I understand precisely."

"Very well. Prepare your story and ensure that you agree on the specifics. I will manage the rest. Do nothing to further endanger us, or I will be forced to put you away. I do not wish that."

Pembroke strides out of the chamber, slamming the heavy door behind him. Emilia imagines that the sound is akin to the slamming of a coffin lid on a corpse.

The darkness that has overwhelmed Mary in the past threatens to descend again, to engulf and immobilize her. What her husband has asked her to do is an abomination—to construct a lie to destroy an innocent. How could he make such a demand of her and simply stroll from the room? Does she really know her husband at all? As Mary treads the lip of the abyss, Emilia touches her cheek. She flinches.

"They demand that we sell our souls for their reputations," Emilia says. "How can we possibly do what they ask?"

The commiseration of the question allows Mary to pull back from the brink. She breathes deeply to gather calm, to marshal conviction. "We cannot."

Emilia's eyes widen as if she had not expected Mary to agree. "Yet if we do not betray Jane, then all three of us face judgment from the queen for an imaginary crime. How can we possibly escape the trap the men have set for us?"

Mary considers the two options—betraying Jane or allowing Cecil's accusations to stand. One sentences Jane to death while the other risks all their necks. The third option—telling the queen the truth—has been removed from the table by her husband and Lord Hunsdon. To do so would end her marriage and destroy Emilia's extended family. No matter the course, someone else pays a price so that the lords might maintain their reputations. She rubs her forehead.

"I have no answer now. We need more time to devise another way, if such a way even exists."

"Yes, more time." Emilia opens her palms. "But how? Cecil hunts for Jane even now."

A spark of inspiration allows Mary to disentangle herself from the darkness. She steps to the door and opens it. "Captain Dansby."

"My lady?" He is waiting outside the door just two steps away.

"I am sending you to find Jane before Cecil's men do."

A grim smile crosses his face. "I was prepared to ask you to let me do so. I told her to run without stopping. She will do as I say in the manner that she does everything—with enthusiasm. Cecil's men beat the bushes nearby, but they will not find her. I believe she will be far gone from here by first light."

Emilia joins them in the hallway. "Where do you suppose she goes, then?"

Dansby cocks his head. "If I know Jane, a girl long without a family, she will return to the place where she has been the most welcome. The place that feels most like the home she never had. The place Cecil would least likely search for her."

Emilia's eyes widen. "London!"

"Exactly my thinking."

Mary agrees with the logic. By her own admission, Jane had found true happiness for the first time in her life these past months in London, and most prudent folks dared not approach the city as plague deaths mounted. "Go to London, then, Captain Dansby. Obtain a sufficient stipend from the steward to allow a long absence."

Dansby frowns but nods. "You do not intend me to bring Jane here should I find her?"

"No. Keep her hidden until I send word."

"Very good, my lady." He bows and touches his forehead. "I will gather my kit and horse and leave within the hour."

Mary smiles softly as he turns away. "You are a good man."

Dansby glances back across one shoulder. "I only hope Jane Daggett believes the same."

Mary takes Emilia's hand, draws her into the chamber, and closes the door. "There is little we can do now but wait."

"I fear the same," Emilia says. "I will return to the tents and prepare to leave."

Mary recalls what Hunsdon had said about her departure. His reaction was too extreme, too prepared. The devastation on Emilia's face tells her that something else has happened. "Why did Hunsdon send you away so quickly? The action is rash even for him."

Emilia wipes the tears that abruptly overflow her eyelids. "He has thrown me out because I am pregnant with his child and refuse to dispose of it."

Pregnant? Mary had thought Hunsdon too old. She gathers Emilia into her arms and pulls the young woman's head to her breast. "I am pleased for you, then. You have always been too good for the Lord Chamberlain, and now you will become a mother."

Emilia coughs a laugh and then sniffles. "Thank you."

Mary releases her and waves toward the bed. "Here. Share the bed with me tonight. It is large enough for a small army, and the night is chill."

"Oh, I couldn't possibly."

"I insist."

"But the lords have demanded our disassociation."

"They may hang, if only for one night."

Emilia dips her chin as color invades her cheeks. "Very well. You do me a great kindness, my lady."

As she and Emilia settle into bed, Mary tries to remain optimistic for Emilia's sake. But she knows the truth. Her companion has committed the mortal sin of allowing herself to become pregnant by a man who has bedded her for years, and poor Jane wanders alone in the night for the transgression of knowing the wrong man. She sighs. It seems to her that every act of a woman other than abject groveling is in some way a sin in the eyes of those who rest their boots on the necks of women.

A surge of resolve rises within Mary. She will not grovel—not this time. And she will not allow her sisters to pay a price for the myopic vision and misdeeds of men. She will find a way to save them. She must. The alternative is an end of living, whether she continues to breathe or not.

17

The London to which Jane returns is a cadaverous shell of the one she had left. The road toward London Bridge from the south tells a story of headlong flight. Broken carts, discarded household goods, and what can only be the remains of the dead litter the ditches, left behind by those fleeing the plague. Everyone she encounters is hurrying *away* from the city. They cross to the far side of the road and eye Jane with disbelief as she trudges toward the bridgehead at Southwark. Surely, they wonder if she has lost her senses by marching into a pit of death and despair. They must also puzzle over her appearance. Six days on the road, mostly at night to avoid any who might be tracking her, have left her one with the mud—filthy, ragged, and famished.

As the bridge comes into view, she veers away from the river toward the Rose Theater. The place so vivid in her memories seems fast asleep, perhaps even dead. The infamous writ of closure is pasted to the main doors with large, shouting text. Someone has nailed boards across the doors as well, as if the writ isn't clear enough. Rubbish has gathered at the walls, a mute testament to the building's three months of disuse. Jane pulls half-heartedly at the boards, in the hope that they are for show. When they fail to budge, she circles the theater to the rear door—the one where she had last met Dansby. It is similarly boarded, but someone has already pried one loose and kicked the door open. She wishes for a candle but carries nothing but a bag of overripe pears and plums she has collected along the way.

Jane steels herself and slips through the doorway. The open roof allows the early afternoon sun to imbue the interior with a dreamy murk of half-light. Silence runs deep, a requiem for the theater's recent raucous past. After slipping onto the stage, Jane fumbles around until she finds the trap door that allows for dramatic entrances and exits. It also conceals the area where boxes of props and costumes are stored. She grunts as she unlatches the door, and it falls open with a cry of stiff hinges and a ringing thud that she swears can be heard across the river. After a moment of frozen silence, she drops through the hole.

The space beneath is not quite pitch black as muted light trickles through the seams between the planks. She bends at the waist and shuffles forward like a woman of seventy, to avoid banging her head on the low ceiling. With hands extended, she moves by memory, rather than by sight, to the rear wall of the stage. As expected, the typical stack of boxes is missing. She had helped the troupe remove them for their road tour. However, her hands find the one box that they had left—stuffed with old garments no longer fit for a performance. Jane wrenches off the top and rummages for the item she seeks—a blue cloak with a distinctive but ratty fur ruff. She yanks it free, replaces the lid, and returns to the trap door. Because of her hunger, she can barely pull herself back onto the stage. Lifting the door to latch it proves impossible in her weakened state, so she lets it hang limp while hoping no one will stumble into the hole later.

As she catches her breath, Jane runs her fingers along the edge of the cloak to find the line of coins sewn into the hem. Not a fortune, but enough to sustain her for at least two months. She pries several coins free of the hem, wraps the cloak around her shoulders, and bids farewell to the Rose—perhaps for the last time. That thought fills her with melancholy, both deep and unexpected. She brushes aside the promise of tears and puts the theater to her back as she trudges toward the bridgehead.

Jane's shock at the state of London deepens when she enters London Bridge through the Great South Gate. Normally teeming with vendors, buyers, and travelers, the bridge is empty save for a tomcat that lifts a lip at her as she passes. Even the severed heads of traitors spiked to the gate appear surprised at the fallen state of the city. She crosses the long expanse in silence, certain that people will boil out of the shops and houses at any moment. However, the haberdashers, textile sellers, and grocers are nowhere to be seen, their shops shuttered and forlorn. Jane begins to wonder if *anyone* remains in London, when movement catches her eye. An elderly woman steps from the shadows, startling Jane. However, the woman maintains her distance. She is thin and gaunt, and her white hair barely clings to her head.

"Seeking groceries, my dear?"

Jane blinks before noticing the few bins of vegetables and cabbage at the woman's feet. A grocer. Perhaps the only one remaining on the bridge.

"I am. May I see?"

The old woman steps back. "Look your fill."

Jane's stomach growls as she picks through the beet roots, peas, radishes, carrots, and cabbage until she has filled her bag to nearly overflowing. She haggles only half-heartedly with the woman before leaving coins beside the bin and stepping away. "Thank you."

The woman eyes Jane speculatively. "Going *into* the city, are you?"

"Yes. I must find a place to stay."

The grocer frowns. "I'd reconsider, dear. The plague still burns inside the walls."

"I have no choice."

The woman nods, though her eyes droop with sadness. "Go to the house with a green door at Milk Street and Cheapside. Belongs to a wealthy family that abandoned it a month past. Left behind two maids to fend for themselves. They will let you stay given that you bring food. You willing to share?"

"I am."

"Good, then. Tell them Gertie Packwood sent you."

Jane thanks the woman and continues toward the north gate. A pair of lanky soldiers guard the gate with long pikes in hand and the lower portions of their faces swathed with scarves. They glare at her with suspicion but don't move to impede her.

"Cover your face," says one as she passes, "or the miasma will surely give you the death."

Jane pulls the cloak over her head and pins it together at her chin with one hand. She certainly doesn't want to catch the plague from bad air now that she has reached the one place in England where she might disappear for a time. The approach proves immediately useful when she encounters the stench of rotting bodies that overcomes even the persistent odor of sewage and rot. She draws her cloak tighter when passing the shrouded forms of the dead, who silently await the arrival of the ragged men who remove bodies to pits outside the walls. Many houses bear the painted cross, indicating that they have been sealed for forty days to contain the plague within. Watchmen linger beside of few of those, paid to ensure that no person inside the house leaves. A shudder knifes through Jane. She puts her head down and strides to the corner of Milk Street and Cheapside.

As Gertie had claimed, one house possesses a tall double door painted vivid green. Jane climbs the pair of steps and slaps the door three times with the heel of her hand. After a stretching silence, she thumps the door again. It opens a crack to reveal a single wide brown eye.

"What do you want?"

The voice belongs to a woman, and she sounds young. Jane backs down a step. "I seek shelter."

"We've no room."

As the door is closing, Jane slaps a palm against it. "I have food. Gertie Packwood sent me."

The door opens again, but wider, to reveal the young woman. Her cheeks are drawn, and her reddish hair lies limp against her skull. A pockmarked girl of perhaps fifteen peeks over her shoulder to stare at Jane as if one of them is a ghost. The first young woman studies the heavy bag in Jane's hand. "Will you share?"

"I have enough for all. I only wish to stay."

"Show me your neck."

Jane hesitates but removes the cloak to show her unblemished neck. The girl nods. "Now beneath your arms."

Jane understands the request perfectly. She has witnessed the arrival of plague before and knows that the sickness manifests as angry boils on the neck and in the pits beneath the arms. She sets the bag down, wriggles one arm free of her ragged, mud-spattered dress, pulls the collar low, and lifts her arm. The woman sniffs and whispers something to the girl. They step aside, and the door opens wider. Both throw an arm across their mouths and noses.

"You may stay. But you must go to the attic for ten days and leave the groceries with us."

Jane picks up the bag protectively. "But this is for me as well."

"We will leave food and water outside your door until we know you don't carry the plague."

A wave of injustice washes through Jane, but she lets it pass. Would she not demand the same of a stranger? And what choice does she have? Besides, who will search for her in the attic of a house on Milk Street? She retrieves her cloak, enters the house, and reluctantly drops the bag. The young woman points toward the stairs. "Top floor. Three flights. You will find a straw mattress with blankets and a chamber pot. We've no candles to spare."

Jane collects a handful of vegetables and grips her blue cloak to her chest. "Thank you for your hospitality."

The woman nods and manages a half smile. "I am Maggie. This is Libby. What are you called?"

Jane opens her mouth but hesitates. "Bess. Bess Wright."

As Jane trudges up the stairs, she chastises herself. She had not wanted to lie, but if men come looking for her, she does not want her new housemates to know the truth or be pronounced guilty by association. She absently scratches the back of her hand as she mounts the third flight of stairs. Cursed fleas. Jane is breathing hard when she reaches the attic. The steep roof allows her to stand fully upright if she doesn't stray too far from the middle. She settles onto the promised mattress and stares out the dingy, round window at the houses across the street. The melancholy she has kept at bay for days finally engulfs Jane, wrapping her in its cloying embrace. She is alone again. Invisible. A cipher. But except for a single glorious season, hasn't she always been?

～

Maggie does as she has promised, leaving a ration of food and water outside the attic door every morning while Jane haunts the small, attic room with recurring thoughts of isolation and despair. To lift her spirits and pass the time, she spins stories in her head—stories that the shadow sisterhood might have written had not reality stormed the walls to destroy it. Stories of shipwrecks and doomed lovers and haunted princes. Stories about misconceptions and miscommunication and false identities. Stories about the mighty and the weak and all those in the great middle. They sustain her for three days. On the fourth day, the food and water fail to arrive. She calls softly down the stairs, and from the recesses of the house, Maggie answers back.

"Not just now. Later. Later."

Three days of food have restored Jane, and she is accustomed to extended periods without food anyway. She decides not to bother Maggie and Libby for fear of driving them away. When the fifth morning comes and goes with no provisions, though, she calls again. The lack of response convinces Jane that her housemates have taken the food and abandoned her. She chides herself for having been so trusting, and her stomach rumbles in agreement. She runs her fingers through her long locks to remove the tangles, and carefully creeps down the stairs. As she treads down the final flight, Jane hears a soft moan. She stops and clenches her fists before continuing to the large drawing room. The sight that greets her opens a deeper pit in her empty belly. Maggie and Libby lie on the floor beside the cold fireplace, deathly pale. Light leaking through the windows reveals a sheen of moisture coating their faces. Jane inhales a stuttered breath.

Fever.

She finds rags in the kitchen, wraps one around her mouth and nose and others around her hands like oversized mittens. With the timid footfalls of a woodland fawn, Jane approaches the two women. Every step more clearly reveals the dire truth. They are terribly sick. She stoops over Maggie and gently prods her. Maggie's eyes flutter open to stare blankly for a moment.

"Bess?"

"Yes, from the attic. Might I feel beneath your arms?"

Maggie's eyes glaze with despair, and she turns her head away. Jane reaches beneath the young woman's arm to find . . .

She recoils, yanks the hand away, and stands. Maggie turns her woeful gaze toward Jane again, her eyes wet with tears. "I am sorry."

Jane rubs her face with disbelief before remembering where her hands have been. "What of Libby?"

"The same. Two days now. Is she dead?"

"No." Libby's left hand has been clenching and unclenching repeatedly. "She still lives. I will fetch you water to cool your fever."

Jane searches the kitchen but finds both buckets empty. These women need water before they burn with the heat. She hoists the two buckets and moves toward the door.

"Do not leave us to die."

Maggie's plea is barely more than a croak. Compassion washes over Jane, and tears wet her eyes. "I will not leave you. I only go to fetch water for your fever. I shall return, as the Almighty is my witness."

Jane slips out the door and hurries to the water fountain she had spotted before arriving at the house on Milk Street. While she is filling the buckets, a shadow falls over her. She jerks her head up to find a soldier armed with a pike, standing off her shoulder. He holds a handkerchief over his nose, and a pomander overflowing with herbs hangs from a chain at his belt.

"Show me your neck, lass."

Jane erupts into a tremble. In her single-minded attention to Maggie, she has not felt her own neck and armpits. Dread descends as she pulls down her collar to reveal the expanse of tender skin. The soldier leans forward with narrowed eyes before returning upright.

"On your way, then. Report to the authorities if plague visits your house."

"Yes, sir."

"Take care, miss."

Jane waddles back to the house with a heavy bucket in each hand while trying not to appear in a rush. Once inside, she drops the buckets to the floor, sending water sloshing over the sides to puddle on the parched planks. Once again, she has lied, but she hopes God will forgive her for a benevolent discretion. Watching over these women will be her penance for all the wrong she has done in her life, and perhaps all the wrong still to come. She gathers rags, soaks them in the cool water, and drapes them over the foreheads of her delirious housemates. Then, she waits.

By nightfall, she can no longer rouse Maggie from her stupor, and the girl's fever feels like a dying fire. Deep in the night, Libby's hand falls still, and her shallow breathing fades to nothing. Just after sunrise, Maggie joins Libby in that undiscovered country that lies beyond death's door. Jane considers fleeing the house but cannot bring herself to abandon the bodies of the two young women she has only just met. Her watch becomes a wake, the only one the women will ever receive. She falls asleep on the hard floor next to the dead women while wondering what it must be like on the other side.

The sun is already high when Jane awakens. Sand fills her eyes, and her head is like a hollowed gourd. She gathers her cloak and pulls it to her chin to ward off the chill of the dank house when the truth assails her. A finger to her neck reveals the gentle swelling, a mark of death's intimate touch and a promise of the agony to come.

With her strength fading, Jane collects the two half-full buckets and what vegetables she can carry and lugs them to the cook's quarters behind the kitchen. She falls onto the soft bed with exhaustion, her cloak grasped loosely in one hand. She pulls it over her head to plunge her gritted eyes into a darkness that matches the despair in her soul.

This is the end, and she will face it alone. That part makes her saddest of all.

18

Dread creeps up on Mary every afternoon to wrap its claws around her throat and draw her into the depths. Only bursts of writing keep the infernal demon at bay. Two weeks have passed since Jane fled Ramsbury and the queen departed with her court. The lack of word from Cecil on the young woman's whereabouts serves as a hopeful sign. The seamstress remains free, then, for now. But where is she? Mary is further concerned about the absence of Emilia. After that terrible night of accusation, Mary had been so absorbed by entertaining Elizabeth and two score nobles that she had missed Emilia's mysterious departure. She understands the disappearance, though. The twin specters of Lord Hunsdon's disdain and Robert Cecil's agents had driven Emilia to slip away without notice. As with Jane, her whereabouts remain unknown to Mary.

She might have searched for them herself if not for Lord Pembroke's order that she remain confined to the house until otherwise instructed. She still bristles over the condescension of his command, as if she were no better than their small children, lacking judgment and reason. She dips her quill in the inkwell and resumes writing with a fury that leaves smudges and spatters on the page while unleashing desperate and biting dialogue.

Light has nearly faded from her room, with the setting sun, when a scratch sounds at her chamber door. She massages her hand and blinks in surprise that the day has all but gone. The scratch becomes a gentle knock.

"Who calls?"

"Apologies, my lady." The muffled words belong to Lady Dalia, one of her neglected ladies in waiting. "Captain Dansby asks to see you."

Mary lurches from her chair and crosses the floor in three strides. She flings the door open, revealing the startled teen. "Captain Dansby? He has returned?"

"Yes, my lady."

"Where is he?"

"Foyer, my lady."

Mary forgets to thank the girl and brushes past her toward the stairs. She further forgets herself as she rushes down the steps like she hasn't since before her marriage. Neither Pembroke nor her dead parents would approve of the lack of decorum. Philip, on the other hand, might have found it amusing and would have told her as much. As promised, she finds Captain Dansby waiting near the main entrance, with his helmet beneath one arm. He is muddy and looks exhausted, but he offers a bow.

"Lady Pembroke."

She motions for him to follow her into the library that abuts the foyer. He guesses her desire for discretion and closes the library door behind him. Mary draws close to him so she might whisper.

"Have you any word of Jane?"

A quirk of his lips tells her the answer to the question before his reply does. "She has gone to London as we suspected she would. A shopkeeper in Southwark saw her leaving the Rose not one week ago, walking toward London Bridge. I missed crossing her path by only a day."

"So, she has entered the city walls?"

"Without a doubt. A guardsman at the gate recalled her because of a blue cloak she wore. I spent a day asking others if they saw her, but no luck. Afterward, I returned quickly here to beg your permission to search door to door, and for enough money to entice people to talk. Those who remain are paralyzed with fear over the plague. Maybe a few coins will stir their recollections and loosen their tongues. Perhaps they will be inclined to watch for her and report to me if they see her."

Though news of Jane's sighting is welcome, it churns the dread she carries in a sticky mass beneath her breast. London. The plague. Poor Jane. "Of course, you have my permission. However, you risk your life by staying in the city for long. I cannot ask that of you."

Dansby smiles and shakes his head. "You do not compel me, my lady. I choose this. I will find Jane if I must pound on every door in London, plague be damned."

His uncharacteristic enthusiasm lifts Mary's spirits. Maybe—just maybe—he can find Jane. "I believe you, Captain. Obtain whatever you need from the steward. Stay the night to refresh yourself, and then return to the city on the morrow. And as always, take care of yourself, and watch over Jane when you find her."

"Very well, Lady Pembroke." He bows again. "Please pray for Jane."

"I never cease doing so."

Dansby strides away, already intent on his new mission. He leaves behind a modicum of hope that Jane might be found and protected as she deserves. The hope struggles against the doom that lingers in Mary's thoughts, though. Pembroke ordered her to turn Jane over to be tried and executed. If she fails to do as commanded, Cecil won't wait long before laying his ridiculous accusations before the queen. And three weeks removed from the ultimatum, no third way has presented itself in the morass of Mary's tortured thoughts.

She returns to her chair and retrieves the ink-stained quill. She rolls it between her palms while studying her final lines of *Titus Andronicus*—a condemnation of a dead woman who had committed evil against others and received harsh justice for it.

No mournful bell shall ring her burial; but throw her forth to beasts and birds of prey.

Mary sighs, sets the quill down gently, and holds her head in her hands. Will this be Jane's epitaph? Will it be hers and Emilia's as well? Despised for what they have done? Or condemned for what they have not done? Neither epitaph is fair, but Mary can think of no way to avoid falling prey to at least one.

The rose garden at Lady Cumberland's house at Cookham remains as soothing for Emilia as it was a decade earlier, when she lived here as ward of the countess. Margaret Clifford is the best of women—keen, deeply educated, and warm. And now, because Lord Cumberland has joined the queen's progress through the countryside, he is not in residence to pester Emilia for services in bed when he is certain his wife is not aware—which she always is. Emilia huffs a breath. Another cocksure nobleman is the last thing she wants, given how easily Lord Hunsdon has cast her aside.

She drops a hand to her belly, feeling the novel tautness of her growing womb. What will become of her? Of the child? Lady Cumberland has extended her hospitality with no caveats, but Emilia knows she cannot stay indefinitely. Lord Cumberland will return eventually. She remains lost in thought until her hostess slips up the path to the bench where Emilia rests.

"Too much sun might harm the child."

The words take the form of criticism, but Margaret's tone is one of gentle concern. Emilia flicks her wrist. "My Venetian roots protect us both. I won't stay long, though."

Lady Cumberland joins Emilia on the bench. "Have you made a decision about your next course of action?"

"Perhaps."

"You may remain here as long as you like." She shoots Emilia a smile that fades as a shadow crosses her face. "As long as *he* stays away, I imagine."

Gratitude surges within Emilia's breast, but she tempers it with reality. "I thank you for your continuing kindness to one so common. However, I do not wish to press your hospitality. I will find a suitable alternative. My uncles and cousins would wish me to return to London when the plague has passed, where they might aid me. I need only ask."

Margaret cocks her head and grows a wry smile. "Perhaps the alternative finds you."

"What do you mean?"

She tips her head toward the house. "A young man has arrived to call on you. A cousin by marriage, he claims."

Emilia heart jolts. She leaps from the bench, barely remembers to curtsy to Lady Cumberland, and hurries into the house. Alfonso is waiting just inside the door that leads to the garden. She throws herself into an embrace, invited there by his extended arms. "Alfonso!"

He grips her in silence for a moment, rocking her gently as he would a newborn. "You left without so much as a farewell. I had the devil of a time finding you."

Emilia sniffles, surprised by her eruption of tears. "I am sorry. I was ashamed."

Alfonso gently pushes her away to arm's length. "Do not feel shame, Emmy. Hunsdon has treated you ill, the scoundrel. The shame belongs to him alone."

"Thank you." She ducks her eyes until he places a finger beneath her chin. The warmth in his expression threatens to unravel her.

"What will you do next?" he says.

"I have just been discussing that with Lady Cumberland." She turns her head aside and sighs. "I will wait for the plague to cool in London and then return to my family. Your stepmother would take me in, or perhaps our cousin Isabella. They know much about birthing babies and raising them up."

Alfonso goes silent until Emilia looks at him again. His gaze is intense, like a smoldering candle. "Your son should not be born a bastard."

"Lord Hunsdon thinks otherwise. I have no choice."

"But you *do*."

Emilia draws her brow low and frowns. "What could you mean?"

Alfonso takes her hands in his. "I still wish to marry you, Emmy."

She recoils with mild shock and fights to gather words. "You would marry me still? Despite everything? Despite my exile from Court and the discarded child I carry?"

"Why would you even question me?" He pulls her closer until his breath plays over her cheek. "We understand each other, like two halves of the same mind. And though I am but a minstrel for Her Majesty, you know well of my ambition to obtain a knighthood. I have attached myself to Lord Essex, and when he mounts his next expedition, I will join him and earn my title. Then you will become a lady of the court as you deserve."

Emilia sways against Alfonso. She is unmoored, but by more than her ongoing confusion. She puts her lips to his ear. "Do you love me, Alfonso?"

"Since you were a child and I had yet to reach my adolescence. You awed me from the beginning. Nothing stands before your magnificence, so what chance did I have?" He sighs into her hair. "I should ask the same of you. Do you love me?"

Emilia spins his question in her racing thoughts. He has always been her confidante. Her coconspirator. Her rock against the gales of life. She is startled to realize that she does love him, and differently from the way she has loved Hunsdon. The Lord Chamberlain gave her status and a heady life of courtly leisure. Alfonso represents something deeper, more eternal. "I do love you, Alfonso. And you will claim my child despite who the father is?"

"The child is yours, and nothing else matters beyond that fact." He lifts his head to peer into her eyes from inches away. "Are you accepting my proposal, then?"

She giggles. "Did you propose?"

Alfonso drops to one knee, keeping hold of one of her hands while placing his other hand over his heart. "Miss Bassano, my Italian queen, will you lower yourself to become my wife as long as we may live?"

She covers her mouth to stifle another giggle. "I will, Alfonso Lanier."

He bounds to his feet and embraces her anew. "Wonderful. We will remain here until the plague breaks in London—time enough for the crying of the banns at the family church in Aldgate. Then we will return there to marry. You have always said you would marry at St. Boltolph's or nowhere."

"You remembered," she whispers. "We will do just as you say."

And she means it despite the niggling of regret. Can the happiness she shares with Alfonso as a friend survive a marriage? Will he keep his word and love her child? Will he eventually make her a lady so that she might gain the respect she has so long craved? Emilia squeezes Alfonso with determination. She *must* make this work. Anything for her unborn baby. And such is the plight of a woman—to obtain what she can rather than all she deserves.

✦

Jane crawls into a stony crevice to huddle as the horror crashes across the rocks outside. She has been running headlong from her pursuers nearly nonstop for hours, days, months. They are formless and ever-shifting shadows that reek of cold and damp rot, and entangle her feet and hair with grasping tendrils. They are angry villagers with frayed ropes and bloody eyes who snatch at her clothing with clawlike fingers. They are a harsh voice in her ear belonging to the man with the knife who whispers "Catholic witch" and "papist whore" over and over until it flows through her blood like a hateful song. Sometimes, Mary and Emilia manage to wrench her free from those who would destroy her, but they are soon snatched away by the howling wind. She searches for them until the pursuers are again at her heels, and she runs anew.

When exhaustion overcomes her, she calls for Captain Dansby. Once or twice, he has called back over the gale, distant and fraught. Even now, he calls over the beating of drums. Where is he?

Jane squints one eye open as she struggles to escape the crevice now, climbing toward a blinding light. A crucifix of the murdered Lord swims into her vision. She twitches her other eye open and shrinks from the light. The crucifix is not in her face, but farther away. On a wall next to a door. Past the foot of the narrow bed in which she lies. Memory—true recollection—rushes in like the Thames at flood. Her flight from Ramsbury. The house on Milk Street. Her dead housemates. The swelling in her neck that spread to her jaw and groin. The excruciating boils that erupted in the tender hollows beneath her arms. The hot knife of a headache that stole her capacity for thought. The sapping fever that dragged her ever deeper into darkness. The rest is fog and running and hiding and running again. When will the plague finish her? How long has it waited already?

She inhales a painful breath and coughs until she retches into her hand. The mucous she deposits there shows hints of pink and red. Her mouth is sand, her throat a briar patch. She dips the fouled hand into the bucket beside her bed and it comes away dripping. She sucks on her moist fingers, reveling in the blessed chill against her ruined tongue. A relief, if only minor. But, what does her relief matter? Death will take her soon, in minutes or hours. She closes her eyes, and the drumming begins again.

"Jane Daggett!"

Her name comes from a distance, from Captain Dansby. This time, though, she fights to escape the encroaching sleep, to again find the crucifix on the wall.

"Jane!"

She tries to answer but erupts into another coughing fit. A crash reverberates from somewhere in the house, and a figure fills the doorframe. She cowers, pulling the sour blanket to her chin.

"Jane?"

Captain Dansby blinks at her with an ashen face. A scarf covers his mouth and nose, but she would recognize the strong brow, piercing eyes, and pitted cheek anywhere. Is this a dream? Death masquerading as a savior instead of a reaper? She extends a palm to him.

"Stay away. I am dying of plague."

Jane realizes her mistake. Her admission is an invitation for Death to act swiftly if this indeed a trick of her eyes. However, the man remains in the doorway, swaying on his feet. Devastation sweeps through his eyes and knots his features.

"The plague?"

"Yes." Her voice is a frog's croak. "How did you find me?"

"A grocer remembered you."

"Gertie?"

"Yes. Her." Dansby glances at the room behind him before staring at her until she expects him to turn away, to leave. He lifts his chin instead. "How long ago did the illness strike you?"

"I don't know. Days ago. The day after my housemates died."

His brow knots further. "Your housemates? Those women beside the fireplace?"

She tries to nod, but her neck is painfully stiff. "Yes."

Dansby takes a single step into her room. "Those poor women have been dead for at least a week. More likely two, I think."

Jane frowns with concentration. A week? "How do you know?"

He slides forward to stand at the foot her bed and pulls down his scarf to reveal his lips. They soften as she watches. "I have seen too many corpses to be mistaken about this. How is your neck?"

"Sore." Jane steels herself and touches the side of her neck. She flinches, but not from pain. The swelling, which had felt like an egg before, has diminished to the size of a pea. She widens her eyes and stares at Dansby. He approaches to stand beside the bed, inches away.

"Are you willing to show me the underside of your arms?"

Without a word, she pulls low her neckline. The garment clings to her side and elicits a stab of pain as she peels it back to wriggle her arm free. She carefully extends the arm and watches his eyes, afraid to even glimpse the cursed boils, let alone touch them. He inhales sharply and whispers a curse. No. Not a curse. *Mon Dieu*, a French phrase that means "my God." She recoils again when he grips the hand of the extended arm, but he does not let go. She continues to stare into his eyes with desperate question, suspended between life and death, light and shadow, hope and despair.

"The boils have burst, Jane." He kneels beside her bed. "They have burst."

"What does this mean?"

He shakes his head softly. "I know only this. One in twenty survives this plague. Those who remain alive after a week, those whose boils burst—they recover. What day did you fall ill?"

Befuddled hope surges in Jane, pushing aside the engulfing despair. Did not the plague kill everyone it touched? No. She has met a few who somehow twisted free of its deadly grip. She calculates the days—on the road, in the attic, caring for the doomed young maids. "Twelve days after I left my lady's house. Thirteen perhaps."

"The eighth of September, then." Moisture lights Dansby's eyes, and he sighs softly. "Today is the nineteenth, Jane. You fell ill eleven days ago."

A sob erupts from Jane's raw throat, an animal wail. A stuttered breath climbs her throat. "I am afraid."

Dansby settles on the bed and gathers up Jane to his chest to hold her tight. She circles her arms around his waist, ignoring the throbbing pain of the broken boils. He buries his face in her matted hair and exhales what sounds like a quiet sob. "Fear not, sweet Jane. You have beaten back Death. You have survived. You are the one in twenty. The one. And I will not abandon you now—not ever. Do you hear what I say?"

She nods, unable to muster a reply. For a lifetime, Jane has been alone and mostly accepting of her solitary nature. Until now. She has never been happier to end her isolation, to hold a hand, to embrace a friend.

❧

Mary reads the letter from Emilia a fourth time before dropping it into her lap. She looks out the window of her library into the haze that has descended over the course of the dying afternoon. The leaden clouds of the previous two days are finally making good on their promise of cold autumn rain. Droplets drift down the windowpane, joining with others to fling their combined weight toward the sill. The overall effect is an imperfect spider-web of falling water that shifts continuously, driven to a new course by each new drop of rain. She heaves a sigh.

"Only the dead may resist change," she murmurs to herself.

Mary rubs the paper between her thumb and forefinger. Emilia's letter is rife with new drops. She has found refuge at Cookham with Lady Cumberland, which Mary should have guessed if not for the strain of her husband's ultimatum. Emilia's strategy is sound. Margaret Clifford is the best of women, far superior to her faithless husband, who travels the countryside with the queen's court.

The young musician will be safe at Cookham for a time—especially now that Alfonso Lanier has joined her there and asked for her hand in marriage. This surprising news brings a smile to Mary's lips when all else rallies against her. He seems a good man—good enough to earn Captain Dansby's approval. Dansby does not give his approval lightly, and she suspects that even Lord Pembroke has yet to earn it. Emilia writes of her and Alfonso's intention to return to London when the plague abates, which it always does, and to marry at the family church. Mary whispers the question again.

Should I attend?

The answer does not change. She cannot. Her husband and the Lord Chamberlain have strictly forbidden any association between Mary and Emilia. In fact, the letter in her hands represents an enormous risk. No less risky, she thinks, than Dansby's mission to find and safeguard Jane—if he can. Voices in the foyer draw her scattered attention. Her steward, a decent but overly blunt man, is berating someone. That someone bites back. Footsteps announce the approach of the argument to the library before the steward steps inside and bows.

"My lady. A courier has arrived with a letter for you and refuses to allow me to deliver it. He insists on placing it in your hands." The steward's eyeroll indicates his disdain for the courier's brash reach above his station. Mary, though, has other suspicions.

"Does he come from Court?"

"No, my lady. From London."

Mary's back stiffens. London! "Send him in straightaway."

Tamping down his clear surprise, the steward bows and motions to his left. A man appears, travel stained and drenched from the rain. He holds a letter in one ungloved hand, pinching it by the corner to keep it dry. The man removes his hat and bows deeply.

"Lady Pembroke, I served under a mutual acquaintance during the Spanish invasion. He has entrusted me with this sealed missive and ordered me to hand it to you directly."

Mary's stomach roils with dread, angst, anticipation. "Bring it to me, then."

The courier marches in and stretches his arm so she may take it. He backs away three steps, with soggy hat in hands and eyes downcast to wait. The steward remains in the doorframe, sniffing with contempt. Mary breaks the seal with a trembling hand and consumes the brief letter—only half a page. Her heart hammers as she reads Captain Dansby's concise report. He has found Jane, and she is safe! Then a cryptic line about his pleasure over her survival. Survival of what? He asks Mary to send further instructions with the same courier, a trusted friend from the war against Spain.

"A moment," she tells the courier. She stands up and moves to Pembroke's desk, rifles through it for paper and quill, and leans over the desktop. The words flow without pause.

Captain,

My joy over your extraordinary news illuminates a dismal run of days. Pembroke keeps the wolves at bay for the present and endeavors to extend our season of reprieve until a certain person might be found. Remain where you are with any cargo in your possession and stand over said cargo with a watchman's eye until I issue further word.

Mary pauses to stare out the window before dipping the quill in the inkwell.

When the plague abates, send word here so I might alert our mutual friend. She wishes a return to the city for the purpose of marrying the young man of your acquaintance who so faithfully attends her when she prays. As always, your service to this house brings me great satisfaction and renders me in your debt.

Mary signs the letter, "Your Lady." She has kept it sufficiently vague in the event that Cecil intercepts it. Only the courier will know its source, and if Dansby trusts him, she must as well. She folds the letter, heats her husband's stamp, and seals it with a blot of wax.

"You may return this to our mutual acquaintance with my gratitude. My steward"—she lifts her voice—"will pay you for both trips. He will also show you to the kitchen, where you might receive a hot meal and a night beside a fire before you leave at first light."

The courier bows again. "My lady, I am grateful for your kind hospitality."

The steward lifts an eyebrow and sets his jaw. "This way, then."

When alone again, Mary burns the letter from Dansby while wondering at her luck. In a world of blue-blooded cutthroats, she has managed to collect an ensemble of truly decent people—Emilia, Jane, Dansby, and even Will Shakespeare—that her equals would consider common and expendable. Mary whispers a vow never to take such blessed associates for granted. In fact, it is her duty to continue protecting them from her equals who would seek to bury them. She will recommit herself to that mission, heart and soul. However, she cannot help but worry over a nagging question: She will strive to protect others, but who will protect her?

19

October 1592, two months later

The man pinning Will to the wall of his apartment at least does him the courtesy of not crushing his windpipe. Lady Southampton's behemoth footman, Perkins, is superior to Robert Greene's hired muscle in that regard. The orange-liveried man lifts an eyebrow but otherwise maintains a deadpan expression.

"Her ladyship expected a new pair of sonnets in September. As is it now half past October, the number has risen to three." He cuts his eyes toward Will's writing desk. "Such a pile of paper, and yet you claim no new sonnets have been written."

Will is certain now: he has made a deal with the devil, or at least with one of his minor attendants who happens to style herself a noblewoman. He tries to stretch his toes to the floor, but they do not reach. In the interest of preventing his imminent demise, he grows the warmest smile he can under the circumstances and draws on his reserve of amiable charm. "See here, friend. My troupe returned to London only three days ago, now that the plague has cooled here, and writing poetry on the road is a tall task. I surely would have explained this to her ladyship had I known of her similar return to the city."

Perkin's sprawling features do not change, but he releases the pressure against Will's chest, allowing his feet to settle against the floor. The big man looms toward Will. "Lady Southampton has *not* returned—hence my presence and not hers. Going back to my mistress with no sonnets in hand would plumb the depths of my disappointment. Friend."

Will fights to retain a shallow grin, but his forehead dots with perspiration despite the chill October air clawing through his open door to defeat the fire in the hearth. "You have an eloquence about you, sir. Have you considered trying your hand at poetry?"

"The only poetry of interest to me consists of fourteen lines in iambic pentameter and signed by you for the pleasure of Lady Southampton's beloved son. Now, which one is your writing hand?"

"My right . . ."

The footman engulfs Will's left hand in a meaty paw and squeezes until the joints begin to pop. The pain lasts three seconds before Will decides that a loose association with the truth is better than mangled fingers.

"I have them! I have the sonnets."

Perkins releases his hand. "Why did you simply not say so? Kindly bring them to me."

Will cradles his left hand in his right and spins another fable. "They are not quite finished. A few lines each and they will be worthy of her ladyship's generosity. I need only the evening to complete the work; then you shall have no need to disappoint your mistress."

The man nods, but Will is certain he has seen through the lie. "Quite reasonable. I will return at first light to collect the papers and pay your fee. Do not force me to search for you."

"Of course. First light, as you say."

"Good evening, Mr. Shakespeare."

"And to you, Mr. Perkins."

Will sags like a deflated bladder when the door closes. "Terribly rude."

He faces his unkempt writing desk and sighs. He must write three sonnets by morning or endure the snapping of some bone or another. This is his fault, though. He has allowed his preoccupation with Jane's disappearance to push his agreement with Lady Southampton to the hinterlands of his thoughts. Since fleeing Ramsbury at the end of August, Jane has gone unseen for more than two months. Will has wondered alternatingly if she is dead, held prisoner, hiding in the woods, or on a ship to France. Worse, he doesn't know precisely why she fled in the first place, nor why a man as powerful as Robert Cecil would send his agents to hunt her down. Regardless, the whole affair has kept Will looking over his shoulder for danger in the event that her flight somehow implicates him.

"First light," he says. "Curse the morning sun."

Will settles at his desk, pulls a blank sheet of paper, and stares at it for an eternity before penning the first lines of a new sonnet. He has written eight lines when a knock sounds on the door. His breath hitches. The footman again? There is another knock, accompanied by his name. "Will Shakespeare! Open the damnable door. The wind bites tonight."

Will unfreezes and rises to open the door. John Singer sails inside and squats beside the fire with his palms outstretched. The player is still with the Queen's Men, last Will heard, which has been . . . well, a few months. The old man grins at Will with yellowed but gapless teeth.

"I was told you had returned to London, and here you are. Braving the remnants of the plague and the rotting dead, I see."

"Uh, yes. And you?"

Singer struggles to his feet, his knees popping like logs on a fire. "Me? I never left. My elderly mother is too ill and immovable, and my general lack of good sense convinced me of a son's duty."

Will blinks with surprise. Singer is three score if he is a day. His mother must be the most ancient crone in England if she is yet alive. "In that case, John, I am pleased to see you still breathing."

"My favorite pastime. Breathing. However, I did not come to impress you with my respiration." He digs inside his vest and produces a sheaf of paper. "I came to show you this."

Will reads the cover of the pamphlet that Singer holds toward him. He shakes his head. "I refuse to give my consideration to anything written by Robert Greene."

Singer nods, thumbs through the pages, and holds one to Will. "You should read this part, just there by my finger, as it pertains to you."

Curiosity seizes Will. He accepts the pamphlet and reads the paragraph in question. There, Greene launches an attack on a playwright who, though unnamed, is clearly him. He alludes to a line from *Henry the Sixth* and calls him "Shake-scene." Greene also turns Will's use of the term *crow* against him, retribution for his humiliation by Will in the tavern those many months ago. However, it is what the attack implies that shakes him. Greene insinuates that Will pays other writers to put his name to their work. That he is an imposter. That he doesn't belong in the hallowed ranks of playwrights. Will's cheeks heat, not because Greene is wrong, but because he wends perilously close to the truth. He shoves the pamphlet at Singer and forces a laugh.

"This troubles me not. Let Robert Greene attack me if he dares."

Singer stuffs the pamphlet back into his vest. "Alas, that will not happen now."

"No?" Will draws his brow low. "Why not?"

"Greene is quite dead."

When he sees that Singer is not joking, Will frowns deeply. Greene was an enemy, yes, but still so young. However, the man kept dangerous company and was involved in shadowy endeavors. "Was it foul play?"

"No." Singer chuckles and winks. "Foul liver is more like it. The man never passed up a drink, until the practice pickled him."

"What of John Dutton, then? Has he taken up Greene's mission now that his attack dog is dead?"

"I don't know, but I have heard that John has thrown in his lot with Lord Essex, who schemes for control of the court spies. This puts him at odds with Robert Cecil, and as everyone knows, Cecil is an absolute badger of a man. He will not be cornered by anyone, even an earl." Singer leans nearer and lowers his voice. "Regardless, Will, if you are hiding anything, then I suggest you bury it well and deep."

A shudder races through Will, and he is certain that Singer notices. "Thank you, John. You are a true friend. I have a half bottle of stale wine just over here. Might I offer you some?"

"No, no." Singer waves a hand and steps to the door. "Mother calls and she does not abide tardiness. Take care of yourself, Shakespeare."

"And you, Singer."

Left alone again, Will paces the floor of his small apartment. With Robert Greene dead, perhaps the worst has passed. However, given that Dutton has allied himself with a powerful nobleman, he suspects that the worst may be yet to come. He rubs his temples rhythmically to massage away the angst. He could write a hefty volume on all the things he doesn't know, and that fact threatens to kill him. The chaotic desk draws his eye.

"Yes," he whispers. He needs to write. The act of transferring words from his thoughts onto paper is like a form of folk magic, driving all other concerns from his mind as if banning them to the ether. Besides, he must produce three sonnets by morning, or a certain footman will acquaint him with the subtle methods of a medieval torturer.

⁕

The child kicks furiously in her womb as Emilia stands at the altar of St. Boltolph's Church in the shadow of the Tower of London. She stares ahead at the glorious stained-glass window that shatters the October afternoon sunlight into a thousand shards—a match for her scattered wits.

When news had reached them from Mary of the plague's waning in London, Emilia and Alfonso had traveled swiftly to Aldgate from Cookham, arriving only three days prior. The journey and its aftermath are a whirlwind in her head, a run of reunions and conversations and preparations. The members of her extensive family standing at her back have said nothing about her clear pregnancy. Perhaps they believe the child belongs to Alfonso. To his credit, he has not dispelled any such rumors, behaving instead as the proud father. However, she suspects that her many aunts, uncles, and cousins know the truth—that she is pregnant with the Lord Chamberlain's child and has been exiled from Court as a result.

To worsen matters, Emilia worries for Jane. She has heard no word of the seamstress's whereabouts since she disappeared from Ramsbury. Mary's recent letter was intentionally vague and mentioned nothing of Jane. Emilia remains in utter darkness regarding the dire situation. Pure darkness.

"Emmy."

Emilia finds Alfonso watching her. Only then does she become aware that the Anglican priest has addressed her. "Pardon?"

The man leans close with a barely suppressed smile. "Is the bride ready to begin, or do you wish to reconsider?"

Reconsider? Too late for that. "You may proceed."

The priest straightens and begins reading from the *Book of Common Prayer*. "Dearly beloved, we have come together in the presence of God to witness and bless the joining together of this man and this woman in Holy Matrimony."

As the man orates through a ceremony that she has heard a dozen times, Emilia considers how handsome Alfonso is at her side. He is dressed in his finest doublet, breeches, and hose, those complemented by a tan cloak and tall boots. Despite Alfonso's splendor, Emilia has chosen her second-best gown and kirtle— yellow with gold threading and draped by a red velvet cloak. Her best attire was a gift from Lord Hunsdon and would have overshadowed Alfonso's best efforts. She breaks her study only when the minister addresses her directly.

"Emilia Bassano, will you have this man to be your husband; to live together in the covenant of marriage? Will you love him, comfort him, honor and keep him, in sickness and in health; and, forsaking all others, be faithful to him as long as you both shall live?"

An unwelcome image of Lord Hunsdon flashes into Emilia's mind. She ducks her eyes to study the minister's feet. "I will."

Alfonso smiles as he moves the ring he gave Emilia from her right hand to her left. It is beautiful, gold with onyx and four small rubies. She has not the foggiest notion of how he has afforded it.

With droning authority, the priest completes the ceremony, prays over the couple, and releases them like a pair of greyhounds set to run. Emilia wades through the flood of well-wishing Bassanos and slips from the church on Alfonso's arm.

Her husband's arm.

She had never given much thought to marriage before Alfonso's proposal, content to enjoy her life as a court mistress, borderland lady, and secret playwright. The child had changed everything in an instant. Oh, and the false accusation that she wishes to assassinate Queen Elizabeth. That did not help.

"Are you happy, Emmy?"

Alfonso's breath tickles her ear but rings of anxiety. With some surprise, she realizes that she is—for now. "I *am* happy."

Still, she grieves over what she has lost. Her station. Her income. Her honor. Marriage to a court musician is a steep downward step from warming the bed of the Lord Chamberlain. Her dream of becoming a lady in the eyes of the nobles has become tenuous at best. However, she maintains some trust in Alfonso and his determination to obtain knighthood. Perhaps in time, she will regain a measure of her lost status. Until then, despite the death of the shadow sisterhood, she remains a writer. If all else fails, she will turn her hand to poetry, make a name for herself, and hopefully reclaim her fading glory. That is, if Robert Cecil does not decide to throw her at the feet of Her Majesty with false charges of treason. What if he doesn't find Jane? What if he does? It is a demon's dilemma, and Emilia can't decide which outcome is worse.

Jane pulls her wimple forward when the young grocer peers at her too intently. His frown deepens as he retrieves two loaves of bread and places them on the table between him and Jane.

"Nothing more today, miss?"

"'Tis all this time, sir."

She pays the man from her coin purse, collects the bread, and strides away. She reminds herself to slow down to avoid suspicion, but lightning crackles in her shoes as she makes good her escape. According to Dansby, during his previous visit a week earlier, Robert Cecil has turned his attention to London in his search for Jane. She counts it a small victory that her face and name have yet to appear on a poster. On the other hand, perhaps she is too common to warrant the expense of ink and parchment. Jane's journey carries her toward the city's north wall over a circuitous route intended to confuse anyone who might notice her passing.

Within minutes, she arrives near the cramped hovel that she has called home since Dansby carried her away from the plague house. He had selected the place for its nondescript isolation. Tucked at the end of an alley and backing the city wall, the two-story, two-room sliver of a house borders an unused warehouse on one side and the humble residence of an elderly couple on the other. Once she enters her hovel, she will be alone again in the gloom of a windowless room as the days and nights drag slowly. She sighs and leans against the wall of the empty warehouse, inside a shaft of sunlight that battles the chill autumn air.

Be grateful, Jane.

Her self-counsel rouses her from creeping dismay. After all, with days and weeks alone, she has been able to practice reading and writing until her eyes grow dry and her hand aches. She spreads the fingers of her right hand, exposing ink stains and callouses, and recalls how she had envied Mary and Emilia for their marks of writing. Though she has started far behind in the journey, at least she is climbing the ladder now. A wave of warmth spreads through her breast, a rising tide of accomplishment, satisfaction, and worth that surprises her anew when it happens. She travels new and glorious ground every time she picks up a quill.

She should not tarry too long outside, though. The population of London is swelling day by day, and her ancient neighbor is watching her with narrowed eyes through a filthy window. Jane studies the alley before unlocking the hovel door and ducking inside. She bolts the door and drops a bar in place—the latter installed by Dansby for her protection. When she turns toward the room, she lets loose a sharp cry—a man is standing there.

"Be still, Jane. 'Tis only me."

Jane drops the loaves, steps into Dansby's arms, and buries her head in his chest. "You always come by night, when prying eyes cannot see."

"I was quite careful." He pushes her to arm's length to study her face. "The solitude is wearing on you."

"How can you tell?"

"The tilt of your eyes. The lay of your lips. Little things."

Jane finds another miracle to be grateful for—that a good man would notice her concern and speak of it. She notes that his beard is newly trimmed, a departure from its less groomed state for the past two months. She reaches for it but stays her hand halfway. "Are you leaving?"

"No," he says. "The skeleton staff at Baynard's Castle does not concern themselves with the condition of my beard. However, the steward has just arrived to whip the place into shape should his lordship and ladyship decide to return."

Jane's heart begins to race. "Lady Pembroke is coming to London?"

"Not yet. However, the steward did bring me a letter from her." He cuts his eyes aside and sighs. "And I must take this opportunity to confess that I have not been completely honest with you, Jane."

A herd of dismal speculation stampedes through Jane's soul. Has he lied about his regard for her? His pledge to protect her? Her face must betray the dismay, because Dansby places a knuckle beneath her chin to raise it.

"Perhaps it is not what you think, but also no better." He pulls his hand away. "After you fled Ramsbury, Robert Cecil gave Lady Pembroke and Miss Bassano a desperate ultimatum. Their association with you, and by proxy, your former employer, has put them in jeopardy of being branded papists. At a minimum, they are seen to have aided one who helps those who plot against Her Majesty."

Jane's heart turns to lead in her chest, and her knees threaten to buckle. "They are in danger because of me?"

Dansby nods grimly and exhales a deep sigh. "It gets worse."

"Worse?"

"Cecil will spare their honor if they turn you over to him, deny any knowledge of your actions, and denounce you as a Catholic plotter."

Tears begin leaking from Jane's eyes as wave upon wave of distress batters the shores of her resolve. "But I am no plotter."

"I know this," he whispers, "as do the countess and Miss Bassano. However, this is the offer extended to them. A horrific trade. A devil's deal."

Jane stumbles to the lone chair and plops onto it. She stares at the floorboards with mounting despair and fading hope. She is the cause of her friends' peril, and they would be foolish not to accept Cecil's offer. When boots appear beneath her gaze, she looks up to find that Dansby has followed her. He squats and grasps both her hands.

"If it brings any comfort to you, the countess has not agreed to the ultimatum. In fact, she instructed me directly to keep you hidden for as long as I can. In the meantime, Lord Pembroke buys time for his wife, even though he demands that she do as Cecil says. Which brings me, unfortunately, to Lady Pembroke's latest letter."

"What does she say?" Jane can barely meet Dansby's eyes. She settles for watching his lips.

"Cecil demands that you be given to him by the first day of the new year or he will accuse the countess and Miss Bassano before Her Majesty of plotting against the Crown."

Jane's devastation begins to grow roots, entangling her in a quagmire of regret and distress. However, if she has learned one thing from her shadow sisters, it is the value of a woman's will. The world has taught her to be powerless, but she has begun to unlearn the pernicious lie. She remains powerless only if she agrees to do so. And she does not agree. Jane forces herself to meet his eyes. "You should take me to Cecil, then. I will go this very instant to preserve Lady Pembroke and Miss Bassano. They will not suffer on my account."

A wistful smile grows across Dansby's face, deepening the pit in his cheek. "You are wonderfully good and truly courageous, Jane Daggett. However, her ladyship has instructed me to keep you hidden until she says otherwise. She needs time to solve the dilemma."

Jane's newfound resolve is further stirred by a flicker of hope. "What can she do?"

"I do not know. Though you might find some peace in the knowledge that she tries her best."

"What should *I* do, then?"

"Just wait. Lady Pembroke will send me instructions before the new year. Until then, we hope—and you remain a ghost."

Jane nods agreement with the plan, but she has already decided what to do. Should Mary fail to find a better solution, Jane will turn herself over to Cecil, confess to plotting against the queen, and deny that her associates had any knowledge of it. Although the decision will result in her execution, the choice is not difficult. After all, Mary and Emilia are willing to risk themselves for her. How can she not do the same, and more, in return?

20

December 10, two months later

Harwood slaps his gloved hands together and spits a curse over the bitter cold that has gripped London for days. His toes have surrendered all feeling, and his ears sting with searing complaint.

Night has swallowed Baynard's Castle into shadow across the road, though the structure's looming outline carves a jagged swatch across the starry sky. Only the watchman's meager fire illuminates the stones of the gate arch. The man's misery appears nearly equal to Harwood's as he huddles near the fire. The desire to find a flame of his own nearly overcomes Harwood, leaving him in desperate envy of the man across the road. However, he dares not leave his post.

As his search for the fugitive seamstress stretches into a fourth month, his employer grows impatient. Harwood has never failed a mission before, but success in this one grows tenuous. Nearly two months have passed since he followed the Bassano woman back to London on a hunch. However, she has failed to lead him to the seamstress. Her swollen belly and new husband conspire to keep her at home, much to Harwood's disappointment. Tonight, though, he follows a different intuition—that perhaps someone in Lady Pembroke's employ knows where the girl is. A daylight vigil had produced no fruit, so he decided to wait by night instead.

Harwood wraps his arms across his chest and resumes pacing, to stir his blood. With Lord and Lady Pembroke absent, Baynard's Castle is a shell of itself, housing only a skeleton crew. A watchman. A handful of caretakers. A cook. Harwood maintains his pacing in the shadows, measuring time with the march of stars across the night sky. He will wait all night if he must, but fears his vigil is for nothing. So mired is he in frosted misery that he doesn't notice movement at the gate until a horse clops onto the cobblestone road. The tall man astride the horse is half consumed by shadow by the time Harwood gets a good look. He recognizes the stature, though.

Dansby. The captain of the Pembroke guard.

A tremor courses through Harwood and draws him rigid with epiphany. Why would Dansby be at Baynard's without his lord master unless he is furthering whatever plot embroils the countess and the seamstress? Knowing that his horse could expose his presence, Harwood leaves it tethered down the road and follows on foot. Dansby pushes his mount at a trot, forcing Harwood to run. He ducks through the shadows perhaps a hundred steps behind—near enough to keep the guardsman in sight without the sound of his steps alerting his quarry. By the time Dansby approaches the north wall of the city, Harwood fears his heavy breathing will betray him. He has not run this far since he was a much younger man, and his lungs and knees cry in protest.

Mercifully, Dansby draws his mount to a halt at the end of a narrow lane and slides from his saddle. Harwood remains at the head of the alley, hands on knees and spitting mucus onto the frozen mud of the street. He watches as Dansby approaches the door of a narrow house.

"A copper for the poor, sir?"

The high-pitched voice yanks Harwood's attention to a ragged boy of perhaps seven, who has emerged from the shadows. He jerks the boy to him and presses him against a wall, his hand covering the boy's mouth. Dansby peers over a shoulder and remains unmoving for a long time. Then he taps the door. A sliver of light cuts over him, and a woman appears in the gap. Harwood bites back a cry.

The seamstress!

When Dansby enters the house, Harwood spins the boy to face him. He grips a pair of bony shoulders, bringing the boy to a proper tremble.

"Do you live nearby?"

The boy's eyes are wide in the darkness as he nods. "A shelter against the city wall."

"Have you no parents?"

"They lie in a plague pit, sir."

Harwood points to the house at the end of the lane. "Do you know who lives there?"

"A kind lady. She shares bread with me sometimes."

"And the man?"

The boy's tremble increases, no doubt a product of the cold and the fear of Harwood's single-minded intensity. Harwood relaxes his grip and pats the boy's shoulders. "There, there, lad. What can you tell me about the man?"

"I've seen him a few times. He comes at night. He is a friend of the lady, I think."

Harwood chews his lip and glares at the door at the end of the alley. Dansby owns a formidable reputation and swings a heavy sword. Any attempt to take the seamstress alone might cost Harwood his head. Meanwhile, Harwood's employer is with the queen at Hampton Court, not far outside of London. Now that the girl has been found, perhaps Cecil will lend him enough men to cut through Dansby, if necessary, to fetch the seamstress. Yes. He will ride there tonight to meet with Cecil after daybreak, and return before nightfall on the morrow. He snatches the drifting boy's arm, drawing him close again, and produces a coin.

"You asked for a copper?"

"Yes, sir."

He presses the coin into the boy's rag-wrapped palm. "This is silver. Watch the woman who lives in the house. If she moves to another place, return here until I find you. There is more silver in my pocket for you, should you do as I ask."

The boy clutches the coin and nods happily. "Thank you, sir. I will watch the lady."

"She is no lady."

Harwood leaves the boy and returns through the quiet, frozen streets toward his horse. All the while, he imagines Cecil's pleasure when he reports success at last. That vision warms him more than any meager fire possibly could.

○———○

Emilia tries not to waddle like a barnyard fowl as the queen's guard ushers her through the Great West Gatehouse and into Hampton Court proper. Her hips disagree and sway of their own accord, leaving Emilia to manage the swell of her belly unaided.

"Worry not," says Alfonso at her side.

"Cease telling me not to worry." Her retort is perhaps too tart. "You simply worry me further."

As the four guards escort her and Alfonso inside, though, her angst continues to spiral upward, as it has since she received the summons the previous day to appear at the palace. Her theories about the reason for the summons are legion, and even now tramp up and down the pathways of her thoughts, with no regard for subtlety. Alfonso knows this.

"Tell me again," he whispers, "why you believe we have come."

She rolls her eyes but appreciates the opportunity to speak her fears aloud. She rests a hand on the top curve of her belly. "Perhaps Lord Hunsdon has decided to claim this child."

"Does this please you?"

"I don't know." She is confident in her lack of opinion. "Does it please you?"

He shakes his head as the guards lead them to the left into a hallway abutting the Master Carpenter's Court. "Not at all. He does not deserve this child. The boy—or girl—is ours to raise."

The frown on Alfonso's face does nothing to settle Emilia's opinion. If the Lord Chamberlain claims her child as his, the child's prospects would improve dramatically. Surely, any mother would wish that for her unborn. However, the roots of Emilia's struggle run far deeper than she can admit to her new husband. Acceptance of the baby by the queen's cousin might offer Emilia an inroad for returning to Court. She wants this, even while despising herself for what she might lose to gain it.

"And what about your other notion of why you've been called here?" Alfonso's eyebrow quirks upward. She has no time to answer, because the guards halt before an oaken double door at the end of the hallway. Beyond lies her answer, one way or another. When the guards push the door open, Emilia's heart thuds in her chest at the revelation that her alternative guess was correct. The man waiting inside the small dining chamber is not Lord Hunsdon, but Robert Cecil.

"I am to be arrested." Her statement is more an expulsion of breath than a whisper. Alfonso grips her hand and supports her weight against his elbow.

"Look there."

Emilia tears her gaze from Cecil's blank expression to find Mary Herbert sitting alone at the table. The countess meets her perplexed stare with a grim countenance and a subtle headshake. They are both to be arrested, just as Cecil had threatened.

"Miss Bassano." Cecil's flat greeting draws her attention back to him. "Or shall I say, Mrs. Lanier."

"Sir Robert."

"Please, avail yourself of a chair."

"I require no chair."

Even as Alfonso squeezes her hand, Cecil pulls a chair away from the table opposite Mary. "I'm afraid I must insist. Her Majesty would not abide the abuse of a woman with child, and I shall not be the one to test her limits. Even concerning those who plot her downfall."

Emilia shuffles to the chair and settles on its edge. A guard prevents Alfonso from joining her, leaving him standing beside the door. Cecil waves a hand at the two guardsmen who had entered the room.

"Leave us. Take him with you."

Their eyebrows arch, and one man leans forward. "Sir Robert?"

"I will be quite safe, I assure you."

The men bow, collect an alarmed Alfonso by his elbows, and leave the chamber. The heavy doors thump shut in their wakes. Emilia is still blinking with bewilderment when Mary breaks the silence.

"We are no plotters."

Her ironclad statement echoes in the chamber while Cecil twists his lower lip left and right. He places his hands on the back of the empty chair at the head of the table. "So you have claimed repeatedly, though I remain dubious. Nevertheless, I do not wish for one of your station to be hanged without the opportunity for repentance."

At the word "hanged," Emilia's breath hitches. Mary, however, straightens her spine and clasps her hands together in a white-knuckled knot on the tabletop. "We require no repentance, for we have plotted nothing."

Something of Mary's demeanor appears to break Cecil's certainty. He pulls the chair from the table, sits, and leans on his forearms toward Mary. "Tell me, then. What have you been doing with Miss Bassano and the fugitive Miss Daggett?"

Emilia's heart jumps when Mary opens her mouth. However, the countess swallows whatever she might have said and shakes her head.

"I thought as much," says Cecil. He taps the tabletop with his forefinger. "Then I must assume the worst—that you mean Her Majesty ill."

"We do not." Mary's response frosts with the ice that encroaches on Emilia's heart. She wants to shout agreement, but her tongue is frozen. Cecil rises from his chair to face them again.

"Then I require proof."

"What proof?"

"A test, really." He tucks his hands behind his back and begins pacing with the wobbling gait that has become such a fixture at Court. "I have found the seamstress, and my man of eyes watches her even now."

Emilia slaps a hand to her mouth to stifle a gasp. "Jane?"

"Yes. Miss Daggett."

"What have you done to her?" Mary's question rings with accusation. Cecil pauses long enough to hold up a palm of restraint.

"Nothing for now. My man wished to kill your guard captain and take her by force. However, such an act would lead to consequences beyond any of our control. In the interest of pragmatism, then, I have devised a test."

Emilia knows she should remain silent, but her tongue fails to comply. "What test? What would you have us do?"

He waves a hand between them. "Simple, really. You must fetch the girl yourself and turn her over to me willingly. If not, I will take her by force and tell Her Majesty that you work against the Crown in association with a Catholic priest who has managed to escape to France."

Mary's eyes flash with anger. "You wouldn't."

"Oh, I would. The queen already knows of your clandestine meetings at Temple Church. I have kept further details from her for some time now and will wait no longer. However, your voluntary surrender of the seamstress to me and your oath that you knew nothing of her Catholic association would demonstrate your loyalty to the queen sufficiently for me to forget the particulars of the entire sordid affair."

A wave of nausea washes over Emilia. His ultimatum, only inferred until now, has become stone. Jane's life for hers. Jane's life for Mary's. Two may live or all may die. She stares at Mary, whose eyes have gone hollow. The countess drops her face into her hands, an act of capitulation. She rubs her temples with slow circles of her fingertips and inhales and exhales labored breaths. Cecil appears content to let Mary stew, and folds his arms to watch the countess unravel. Emilia doesn't know what to do, but can't tear her eyes from the slowly collapsing Mary.

That's when she sees it happen. Mary's circular caresses freeze, and her breath falls silent. She calmly lowers her hands and lifts her chin. Her countenance, so twisted with concern for the duration of the meeting, has gone placid. Emilia imagines the beatific face of the Virgin Mary portrayed in paintings and in sculpture as she watches *her* Mary. The countess nods to Cecil.

"We will do as you say. We will return to Court with Jane Daggett and hand her over to you."

"No." The harsh whisper escapes Emilia's throat despite her desire to melt into the floor like a spent candle. "We cannot do this to Jane."

Mary shakes her head. The sparkle of her eyes, the subtle quirk of her lips, the twitch of an eyebrow—these tell Emilia what words cannot. Mary has a plan.

"We must do this," Mary says, "for all our sakes. It is the only way." She faces Cecil. "However, I ask one caveat."

Cecil chuckles. "Three steps from the end of a rope or the blade of an axe, and you demand a caveat?"

"I do."

He flicks a hand at her. "What, then? Let's have it."

"Give us a fortnight, until the day after Christmas. Then we will turn the girl over to you."

"The day after Christmas? The Feast of St. Stephen?" He strokes his short beard. "You would martyr the seamstress at the feast of a martyr?"

"We would consider it a Christmas gift to Her Majesty as evidence of our loyalty."

Cecil chuckles again, louder this time. "Very well. You have a fortnight to do as you have promised, or I will have your heads. Understand?"

"Completely," says Mary.

"I believe we are finished here, then." Cecil taps the door. "Guardsmen!"

Emilia's thoughts are a whirlwind as the guards reenter and whisk Mary, Emilia, and a deeply concerned Alfonso away from the dining chamber. Only Mary's expression keeps her from collapsing into Alfonso's arms. The countess does not betray any sign of grief, anger, or dismay. Her expression is sharp, as if she is plotting a scene for a play. Emilia waits until they exit the grounds before she dares ask the question that she has kept leashed like a surging hound before the hunt.

"What are you thinking?"

Mary's lips tick upward into what might become a smile. "I just thought of a third way."

"A third way?"

"A means to save us all. But I will need you to deliver a missive to Mr. Shakespeare on the morrow."

Emilia slips free from Alfonso's arm and clutches Mary without any regard for the propriety of station. She shakes Mary softly. "Tell me. Tell me now, Mary Herbert."

The countess's smile emerges fully. "When I returned to Court a year ago, Her Majesty gave me prudent advice about maneuvering as a woman within the den of powerful men. *'Men endure only through the persistence of the female sex,'* she told me, *'We must exert our will within the shadows of men or possess no will at all. And we must exceed them at their own game.'"*

The queen's words jolt Emilia. She has long striven to enforce her rules of war, often to the point of personal pain. Elizabeth, however, suggests another path—subverting the very rules constructed by adversarial men to instead defeat them. "How do you see the game, then?"

"At this point," says Mary, "Lord Pembroke and Lord Hunsdon have dictated the rules of the game. We are to hand over Jane to the Crown and breathe nothing of the truth to the queen, under the threat of ruination. This, then, is how we will turn their rules against them." She leans into Emilia's ear and shares the specifics of her plan to save them all from the executioner. Emilia lifts her eyebrows as the plan unfolds, and gasps twice.

"Can this possibly meet with success?"

Mary grunts in a very unladylike manner. "I cannot say for certain, but it remains our only path to save Jane. Do you accept your part, then?"

"Of course." Emilia nods for emphasis. "I must convince Lord Hunsdon to invite Lord Pembroke's Men to stage *The Shrew* at Court for the queen on the day after Christmas, even though the play is the property of the Queen's Men, and the plague is still abating."

Mary tilts her head. "Are you certain you can accomplish this?"

"Convince God to strike down the plague? No. I fear he has stopped listening to my prayers. However, I will convince Lord Hunsdon to do as I ask."

"How?"

A laugh escapes Emilia's throat, taking with it a large measure of the dread that has invaded her bones. "Because the Lord Chamberlain talks in his sleep, and I kept notes of everything he said."

Mary joins Emilia in laughter and links an arm through her elbow. "I would never wish to become your adversary, Emilia Bassano."

"Nor I yours, Mary Herbert."

Though she means it, Emilia does not speak aloud of the dread that remains. She, the countess, and Jane remain at the mercy of Robert Cecil, the plague, and the queen. If the plan fails, at least one of them will die. And if it succeeds? Perhaps the same.

⁂

"Had I no eyes but ears, my ears would love. That inward beauty and invisible."

Will watches the frost of his breath scatter as he considers the words he has just spoken to the air. He nods and scratches them on a scrap of paper with a stubby pencil. "Oh yes. That's very good, Mr. Shakespeare," he murmurs, talking with himself.

"Is it? How kind of you to say so.

"Natch. Think nothing of it, friend."

Writing and mumbling done, he returns his attention to the street that he wanders when composing his sonnets, or in this case, lines for his epic poem about Venus and Adonis. His latest line has Venus employing her senses of sight and hearing to profess how she pines for Adonis. But are there not five senses? Can he make use of the others, perhaps? Will shoves the pencil behind his ear, to think, but blinks when he finds a young milkmaid staring at him with dismay. She is clearly wondering if he has lost his mind and might be dangerous. Will flings a smile at her. "'Tis just poetry, miss."

"Poetry?"

He sweeps one arm toward her and clutches his chest with the other hand. *"Or were I deaf, thy outward parts would move each part in me that were but sensible. Though neither eyes nor ears, to hear nor see, yet should be in love by touching thee."*

When the woman hurries away, Will snatches the pencil again and writes furiously. "That is very good as well, sir," he says, continuing his conversation with himself.

"Why thank you, sir," he responds.

"You are quite welcome, sir."

As he resumes his wandering, further lines come to him, until the paper is a mass of lead scratches. He is in this state of distractedness when a coach clatters to a halt before him. He jumps aside and cowers, with visions of Lady Southampton's behemoth footman racing through his head. He owes her two more sonnets. However, the coach door opens to reveal a different woman altogether.

Emilia Bassano.

She holds out her gloved hand. "Mr. Shakespeare?"

"In the flesh."

"I wonder if I might have a word with you in private." She nods to the bench opposite her. Curiosity overcomes Will, and he climbs inside the coach. The late stage of her pregnancy surprises him somewhat. Most high-born women would have been put to bed a month earlier. He sees that she has noticed his scrutiny and drapes a hand across her belly, as if in self-defense.

"We have not met, but I am called Emilia Lanier, née Bassano."

Given his suspicions of the woman's activities, Will opts for more boldness than he would normally risk with one above his station. "I know you by reputation only."

The subtle narrowing of her remarkable eyes communicates her chagrin over his response. "By reputation, you say? By my antics at Court, whether true or not?"

He lifts a palm to her. "No, not at all. I know you by your heavenly lute. And by your wonderful plays. You and Lady Pembroke must be as pleased by them as Jane is."

Will holds his breath as alarm captures her features. Her eyes dart to look at the door as if she means to escape the cab. Instead, she leans forward to clutch his wrist. "Did Jane tell you this? The truth of us?"

Triumph surges within him. Her reaction confirms the truth—that the three women have composed the plays and let him take the credit. He swallows a chuckle, given the lowering of the musician's brow. "She did not."

"Do you laugh at me, then? Smile at my expense?"

He peels her hand from his wrist. "No, Mrs. Lanier. Jane Daggett is as honest and discreet as anyone I've ever met. She told me nothing. However, I have suspected for a while the identity of my secret benefactors. I smile because of the amusing notion that three women have overshadowed an entire industry of pompous men who believe women incapable of such a thing. Do you not find it amusing as well?"

Emilia relaxes her scowl and settles back against the bench. "I do, Mr. Shakespeare. But as you might also suspect, our clandestine playwriting has landed us in a fair heap of trouble, but of a far more serious variety than the disdain of pompous men. And I hate to say that you face some danger by association. For that, I am sorry."

Her blunt assessment troubles Will, but what she claims is not new to him. He has sensed his vulnerable position ever since his visit to Ramsbury. "Do not apologize. I accepted the task of staging your plays in my name in return for serving as bookholder. Is that why you have come? To warn me of impending doom?"

"No." Emilie places a hand on a loose pile of parchment beside her that Will just now notices. "Lady Pembroke asks a favor of you."

"Name it. I will do it."

"But I have not yet explained—"

"It matters not. You have risked everything for your art. I would be less than a worm if I did not rise to the same challenge."

Her eyes twinkle as she smiles warmly at Will. "Jane was right to trust you, sir."

He bows in his seat. "I thank you for the compliment. Now, what can I do for our lady countess?"

She pulls the papers into her disappearing lap. "The countess will arrange for Lord Pembroke's Men to stage *The Shrew* at Court on the day after Christmas, during the Feast of St. Stephen."

This is news to Will. After the Queen's Men made it clear they would not risk performing yet, the Lord Chamberlain did not ask another troupe to perform at Nativity. And the specified time is only twelve days away. However, they have faced tighter schedules and larger stakes before. "I will prepare the troupe and appear at Court on the appointed day. However, *The Shrew* is the property of the Queen's Men. Lord Pembroke's Men have no rights to stage it."

The musician shakes her head. "The play as it was intended is *our* property. What the Queen's Men staged was a pale imitation of what *The Shrew* should be."

"Such as the ridiculous sterilization of Katherina?"

A smile stretches across Emilia's face, lighting the interior of the coach. "Precisely! Then you understand what she was meant to be."

"Oh yes. A lady of iron who works Petruchio like a reluctant mule, not a whining footstool of a woman."

"Your insight lifts my heart, Mr. Shakespeare. But I am afraid there is one more detail." She extends the papers to Will. "Her ladyship asks you to amend the final scene to what she has written here."

Will knots his brow and accepts the pages. He reads through the familiar lines, finding them unchanged—until they are not. The modification amounts to the addition of a few lines, nothing more. He looks up at her. "Did the countess explain the changes?"

"She has her reasons, and they affect all our futures."

Will folds the pages and stuffs them into his vest. "We will prepare our Kate to present the modified lines. I know just the lad to play her. Anything more?"

"That is all, and perhaps enough. Good luck, Mr. Shakespeare, and thank you."

Will steps down from the coach and bows low. "No, my lady. Thank you. And take heart. What you have accomplished can never be stolen from you so long as you live."

Her eyes well with tears while he closes the door, and she nods through the window as the coach lurches away. He watches it go and pats his chest where he has secreted the papers. Somehow, those altered lines will determine his fate and perhaps the fate of many others. He doesn't understand what they mean, but understanding is not his mission. He must trust those who have entrusted him with no less than the outpouring of their hearts. He must not fail them in their hour of need. More pressingly, he must find Richard Burbage, and quickly.

21

December 26, 1592

Disaster anticipated is more insidious than disaster realized. The former paralyzes the soul with promises of unimagined suffering. The latter breaks the shackles, releasing the prisoner to stand against the fall of darkness with an upraised fist.

Jane's fists, though, lie limp in her lap as Lady Pembroke's coach bounces her along toward her doom. Only a day earlier, she had been huddling alone beside the fire in her small hovel, recalling Christmas days past, nearly all of them spent in solitude. She had never much regretted the lack of company before, but then she had never known such friendship before.

Captain Dansby had arrived at the fall of Christmas night with the terrible news. Jane was to be handed over to the Crown for her association with Mr. Burnham, and her act of surrender would save Mary and Emilia from certain condemnation. The fact that she had already decided on that course of action brought Jane little comfort. Dansby had tended to her crushed spirit by draping her with blankets, brewing a pot of tea, and hovering nearby throughout the long, dark night.

Now he rides his horse alongside the Pembroke coach with a face of stone, a man robbed of life by a death yet to come. She is watching him through the window when he spurs his horse ahead and shouts for the driver to halt. While the coach is still rolling, he flings open the door.

"I will not have this, Jane."

Her eyes must rival the size of dinner plates as she stares at him. "Have . . . have what?"

He points down the road ahead toward Hampton Court. "Any of it." He leans into the door and grasps Jane's hand, startling her. "I can take you away with me now. We can run together. We can go to France or Italy or Spain. I have friends in all those places, who will help us."

His use of the word "us" nearly rips a hole in Jane's chest. For a fleeting moment, she imagines the joy of escaping her impending doom to run away alongside the most wonderful man she has ever met. Just the two of them on a grand adventure, linked as one by hearts and minds. As Dansby waits with expectation, Jane's brief surge of joy fades into the muck. She squeezes his hand and regards the floorboards.

"I cannot, Captain Dansby. I will not leave my friends to suffer the worst of penalties on my behalf. Nor will I sentence you for aiding in my escape." Fat tears roll down her cheeks. "I thank you, though, for your kindness to a simple, common girl."

Silence stretches, broken only by the raucous call of a distant raven. He grips her hand tighter. "You are not simple, Jane Daggett. You were never common. Not to me."

His motion draws her attention, and she finds that he has clambered up the coach step. He stretches forward until his lips hover over hers, his warm breath light against her cheek. After a heartbeat, he closes the gap between their lips, holds the tender touch for a too brief instant, and withdraws.

"If only..." He does not finish his thought and instead closes the coach door. Seconds later, he is mounted, and the coach is moving again toward Court. Jane returns her regard to the floorboards and drowns in devastation. She has been on the run for a lifetime, leaping from shifting sand to wobbling boulder in a frantic dance of preservation, alone and without a future. Just when a miracle seemed within reach, ridiculous circumstance has snatched it away. And she can run no more.

As the coach rolls onto the grounds of Hampton Court, Jane inhabits the misery of the most heartbreaking words in the English language:

If only.

⁂

With a chasm of uncertainty before her and imperial dragons at her back, Mary intercepts Captain Dansby and Jane as they reach Anne Boleyn's Gateway below the stairs leading to the great hall. Mary cannot help but note the irony of the location, named for another woman sacrificed by the Crown for political expedience. At least she has managed to escape her husband's suffocating vigil long enough to meet Jane before she enters the fray. He does not trust Mary to follow through with his instructions, simply not to tell the queen the truth. And his trust is not misplaced, for Mary is on a counter mission. She tries to affect a smile that might put Jane at ease. However, Jane exhales a plume of frosty air and pulls her cloak tighter as she regards Mary with large, frightened eyes.

Does she fear me now? the countess wonders.

Mary would not blame the seamstress if she did. Jane knows nothing of Mary's desperate and risky plan, given her long isolation. To her, Mary must be just another of the dragons with lofty titles who gather in the great hall for the Feast of St. Stephen.

Unable to tolerate the prospect of Jane's disdain, Mary steps forward to meet the approaching couple. When Dansby bows, Jane appears to remember her place, and drops a deep curtsy.

"My lady."

The stilted formality of her greeting confirms Mary's worst fears. Jane has resigned herself to having been betrayed by those she trusted, and she intends to bear the consequences with as much grace as her terror will allow. She flinches when Mary darts out a hand to gently touch her cheek.

"You have my deepest apology for what is happening, Jane. Circumstances have run beyond my ability to corral them, to my everlasting shame."

Jane watches Mary's hand as she draws it back, and then the seamstress looks up with misty, blinking eyes. Oh, those eyes! Behind them spin worlds and wonders beyond the imaginings of most mortals. Mary thanks her lucky stars that she has been allowed a glimpse behind the majestic curtain, even if only for a while.

"You need not apologize, my lady." Jane's voice tremors, perhaps from the chill air but more likely a response to her fear. "I was nothing when first you met me. You gave me the opportunity to do what I never thought possible. You offered me your friendship, undeserving as I was to accept it. All that I have become I owe to you and Emilie. It is my great privilege to preserve your honor, no matter the cost."

A mountain of heartbreak falls on Mary, and she sways on her feet. The urge to embrace the young woman seizes her, but she does not forget where she is—in the shadows of the Court, the center of English intrigue. No doubt, there are many watching her now at the direction of Robert Cecil or the Lord Chamberlain—or the queen herself. Any untoward familiarity with Jane at this juncture might turn the tide against Mary and extinguish what little hope remains for them both. Instead, she dips her chin subtly, a show of deference only Jane and Dansby might notice.

"You might want to know, then, that Mrs. Lanier will be joining us anon."

"Emilia comes too?"

"Yes."

Jane's eyes well with tears, and she leans into Dansby's chest. "That is most kind of her."

The heartbreak within Mary redoubles, bolstered by a wave of shame. She would rather Jane shake her fist and cry foul than express any sort of gratitude for the situation in which Mary has placed her. A situation that will likely condemn Jane—and perhaps doom Mary and Emilia as well. The darkness in her soul that has remained at bay for more than a year threatens a dreadful return. She must resist it. She must fight back. With every ounce of will she can muster, Mary stiffens her spine and calls upon her best oratory skills.

"Have faith, Jane Daggett, and pray like you have never prayed before."

Jane squeezes away tears and stares at Mary with wonder. "For . . . for what should I ask?"

"That revelation might occur before this night is finished."

Jane's chin falls and her shoulders slump. "Yes, my lady."

Unable to look upon Jane any longer, Mary engages Dansby. "Do not leave her side even for a moment, Captain. Cecil and his men are not to lay finger on Jane until after the play. Sir Robert has sworn an oath to me on the matter."

Dansby taps his heels together and dips his head low. "Yes, my lady."

"A play?"

Jane's expectant whisper draws Mary's attention back to the young woman. Of course, she has no idea about the play. "Yes, a play. Lord Pembroke's Men will stage *The Shrew* in the great hall after supper." She leans toward Jane where she might whisper. "Your story, Jane. Your Katherina, this time as we intended her."

Improbably, a smile breaks through Jane's astonishment, and she curtsies. "Then I thank you for this one last kindness."

Mary spins hard and marches away from Jane before the young women can witness her tears. As she mounts the stairs into the great hall, with Dansby and Jane at her heels, Mary wipes her eyes with anger. A kindness? Hardly. A salvation? Only if fortune smiles on them. As Mary tops the stairs, she collects her resolve and sails into the great hall.

The die is cast, and she can do nothing to influence its roll. There is only one who might save Jane now—or condemn them all equally.

The child Emilia carries is none too pleased by the deeply rutted road. Every bounce of the coach results in a flurry of movement in her womb, an outpouring of disagreement from the unborn child. The tiny, pressing limbs shorten Emilia's breath and inflame her lower rib on the left side. She takes it as a good sign that perhaps the child will be as spirited as she is. A proper Bassano in fortitude and vigor. When she stretches her torso and sighs with discomfort, Alfonso takes the opportunity to lean toward her from the opposite bench and renew his complaint.

"You should be resting at home, Emmy. Not enduring a frigid ride to Hampton Court for the sole purpose of witnessing a travesty."

Emilia does not disagree but won't tell him as much. Dismal dread has hung on her like a funeral shroud since Cecil's ultimatum only days earlier, and now she just wishes for this day to end. For the matter to be decided one way or another. However, she has tried to keep her fears hidden from Alfonso. As far as he knows, Jane will be handed over to Robert Cecil tonight so that Emilia and Mary might escape dire consequences with their honor intact. He does not know that if Jane fails to appear, Emilia will be arrested on the spot. He does not know that if Jane does arrive, Emilia's and Mary's subsequent actions might propel them into the fire anyway. He does not know any of this. He need not know until the plan falls apart and she is being clapped in irons. Until then, she will keep him content through enforced ignorance, as she has for nearly a fortnight. Emilia gathers her courage and lifts her chin.

"Resting at home? Really, Alfonso. Women have been chasing after wandering men for thousands of years, birthing babies and raising children along the way, dragging home and hearth in their wake and making sure the entire venture doesn't fall to pieces. And yet we are still here—our entire capricious race. Two hours in a chill and jolting coach is nothing against what my forebearers faced."

"I did not mean to insinuate—"

"Hush, Husband. I am not finished speaking." He falls silent, and she twists her fingers into the fabric of her tightening cloak. "All that aside, if Jane is to be sacrificed tonight on the altar of my honor, I must be present to see what I have done. To bear witness to my craven act for which I can never forgive myself. This I will do, child or no."

Alfonso settles back against the bench. "I see. As you wish, then."

His abrupt capitulation surprises Emilia. "You would drop your argument so easily? You would not fight harder to keep me safe from the terror I must witness tonight?"

"I would," he says, "if I thought it possible to counter your intentions. But do not forget that I know you too well. Your determination exceeds my own, and you never surrender high ground once you have taken it. That is what I like best about you, if you must know."

"Not my beauty?"

"That as well, yes. However, there are many beautiful women at Court, and none are worthy to carry your train."

His blunt compliment heats her cheeks, which delights and annoys her. "So long as you do not forget that fact, we shall remain thick as thieves."

"I look forward to it." His slight grin fades, and his brow draws lower. "We are nearly arrived at Hampton Court. Are you certain you wish to witness the betrayal of a girl for whom you hold such fondness? Are you convinced you can live with that burden?"

No! I do not! I cannot!

What Emilia wants to say she must not say. Not directly, anyway. "I have no other choice, Alfonso. Besides, if another course plays out and I am instead in the fire, then Cecil will know exactly where to find me."

The crease above the bridge of Alfonso's nose deepens, and he tilts his head to one side. "What do you mean by 'another course'? What are you not telling me?"

Emilia bites her lip while cursing letting slip even that much. She has been right to keep him in the dark—for his sake. She reasserts her resolve and lifts her hand toward him.

"No questions, Alfonso. Just hold my hand and inhabit the silence for a time."

His contorting expression makes it clear that he is now bursting with concerned questions. He emits a grunt of frustration but accepts her hand. "Of course."

Despite the looming disaster that awaits them at the palace, Emilia cannot help but smile over Alfonso's willingness to grant her request without question or relentless argument. She peers at him until he returns her smile.

"And that," she says, "is what I like best about you."

They gaze at each other from across the cab, conversing with their eyes and subtle expressions, alone together at perhaps the end of all things. Her opportunity to cherish the moment is fleeting before the coach bounces to a stop and a footman opens the door. She steps into the frigid night air at the Great West Gatehouse, drawing her cloak as tight as she can, but the rebellious shape of her abdomen stymies the effort. A hand on her shoulder restrains her. When she turns to do battle, she freezes. Lord Hunsdon stands inches away.

"I would speak with you."

Alfonso begins to step between them. "We were just . . ."

"'Tis alright, Alfonso." Emilia stays him with her hand. The injustice of what will happen to Jane flares within her, igniting the rage that she has so carefully buried. She clenches her jaw and nods at Alfonso. "Wait by the gatehouse. This will take but a moment."

He stares a dagger into the smug expression of the Lord Chamberlain but does as Emilia asks. Emilia bottles her wrath and faces Hunsdon with an expression of stone. "What can I do for you, my lord?"

"So, I am 'my lord' now. No longer 'Henry'?"

"By your choice, not mine."

He grunts and then reaches to hover a hand over her belly. If he touches her, Emilia decides, she will break his fingers. However, he pulls the hand back. "How is the child?"

"If it is a boy, then I will name him Henry for his father."

When a contented smile grows across Hunsdon's face, Emilia's anger begins to crowd the banks of her soul. Only when Hunsdon offers a handkerchief does she feel the tears leaking down her cheeks. She accepts the offering and dabs the moisture. Hunsdon tucks his chin and peers at her from beneath his beetled brow.

"You have always understood the ramifications of my position, Emilia. I am a close cousin to the queen. Loyal and above reproach. A credit to her family name. You know well that I cannot risk my standing by having bastard children bumping around the court."

Her rage bubbles and churns. However, he is not done. He lifts his chin to her.

"I wish you and the child well."

The lid flies off the boiling kettle, and Emilia punches the center of Hunsdon's chest. "You wish us well? You wish us well? Is that all? Is that all you have for your unborn child?"

"Emilia, I only meant—"

"You do not speak, my lord, until I am finished." She stabs his chest with her finger, driving him back a step. "I will be more than well. I have what I need, no thanks to you. It is the way of my family to survive the torments of society. It is the way of my sex to survive the torments of men. I will certainly survive you."

When she stops to breathe, Hunsdon circles her finger in his fist. "I know you will, Emilia. I knew you were strong enough to manage without me. I only ask that you understand my position and absolve me of the pain I've caused you."

She glares at him until his eyelids flutter, and he cuts his eyes away. She withdraws her finger from his hand. "I will not grant you absolution. The Lord God will be your judge, Hunsdon, not me."

He shakes his head. "You cannot mean that."

His lack of contrition cuts through Emilia's desire to fight and instead reveals the truth in all its awful glory. She can never forgive him because he can never deserve it. She can only try to forgive herself for dwelling so long in his sway without understanding that she was never more than temporary in his world. The revelation allows Emilia to do something she has never done before. She turns her back on him without a nod, a curtsy, or a farewell, and leaves him standing forlorn beside the coach, like the callow creature he is. Alfonso rushes to catch up with her.

"What did he want?" His voice trembles with anger and perhaps terror. "You? His child?"

Emilia stops to grip his short beard in her hand. "Listen well, Alfonso Lanier. I am yours. The child is ours. The magnificent Lord Chamberlain is worthy of neither, nor did he want us."

"What did he want, then?"

Emilia releases his beard. "My goodwill."

"Did you grant it?"

She leans her head into his chest, and he pulls her close beneath a comforting arm. "I did not. My goodwill belongs to our little family, to my friends. I have none to spare for a foolish old lord, despite his lofty title."

Alfonso breathes softly into the curls of her hair and kisses the top of her head. "You mean this?"

She wriggles closer to him. "More than I've meant anything in my life."

Emilia withholds the rest, for there is time enough to explain it later. In violating her rules of war, she has gained many insights:

That ground must be ceded when it is not worth the cost of keeping it. That taking no prisoners only results in a mutual bloodbath. That trusting no one is a recipe for a lonely and joyless life. After tonight, her days at Court, that insidious and bloody battlefield, will lie behind her. If she survives the evening, the horizon holds only the miracles of her new family, her cherished friends, her blessed writing. These define her stature as a woman, not the regard of lecherous lords and jealous ladies. The noblemen may have their cursed Court. She will choose joy for as long as she lives. And somewhere, perhaps, God hears her after all.

<hr />

Jane cannot help but gawk as the cream of English society gathers in the great hall for the feast. She lingers against a side wall of the long room, trying to blend in with the army of footmen and maids who will serve their betters this evening. Besides Dansby at her side, only one arrival pays her any notice: Robert Cecil. He pauses before Jane as he ambles along and casts an appraising eye.

"Miss Jane Daggett?"

Her knees become water, and she clings to Dansby for support. "Yes, my lord."

He lifts one dark eyebrow and smirks. "As at Ramsbury, you appear far more harmless than you are."

Jane does not respond. What can she possibly say at this point to save herself? She clutches Dansby tighter and waits for Cecil to pull her away or to give the order for her arrest. However, Cecil simply nods at Dansby and continues to his seat near the head of the table. In his absence, her heart races like an untethered colt. Dansby strokes her white-knuckled hand until the tremoring passes. Otherwise, Jane remains unnoticed—the most shadowy of the shadow sisterhood. Even Mary avoids glancing in her direction, though perhaps because of the hovering presence of Lord Pembroke. Dansby whispers to Jane from time to time, but her power of speech has evaporated. Not even the sumptuous food that is hauled to the table manages to entice her envy. Her stomach is filled with lead.

"See there."

Jane follows Dansby's motion to find that Emilia has arrived on Alfonso Lanier's arm. In times past, Jane's friend might have found a place at the long table with the other notables. However, Dansby has told Jane about Emilia's pregnancy, her banishment from the inner circles of Court as a result, and her marriage to Alfonso. Instead, Emilia joins the musicians, at least four of whom are uncles or cousins. Emilia catches Jane staring but quickly averts her eyes.

Jane does not blame her or Mary for what is happening. They do what they must to save themselves, to avoid being branded as papist plotters. Jane turns her attention to the stage and tyring house at one end of the hall. It stands ready for use, though the members of Pembroke's Men are nowhere to be seen. No doubt, they remain inconspicuous but nearby until the queen calls for them after supper.

Where is the queen, anyway? Shouldn't she be here by now?

Within moments, her silent question is answered. A herald appears at the far end of the hall and squares to face the guests. "My lords and ladies! Her Majesty, Queen Elizabeth!"

The guests rise from their chairs to face the door, and the queen sweeps into the chamber. Jane shrinks away to hide behind Dansby with fascinated terror. The queen! Again! In all her awful glory. Jane remembers her from Ramsbury, but there Her Majesty had been seated and Jane had been concealed behind a curtain. Now, Jane stands exposed, and the queen is on the march. She is like a mythical creature, a capricious god, dripping power and resolve while casting her baleful eye on all those she passes. Even the nobles seem cowed. Jane cannot tear her terrified gaze from the monarch as she strides the length of the table to its head. When she halts there, the guests shout as if prompted, "God save the queen!"

Without so much as a nod, she sits in the chair offered by the Lord Chamberlain. Only then do the nobles return to their seats and raise again the din of conversation. Dansby continues to hold Jane steady, saying nothing. It is just as well. Her senses become fogged as she repeatedly steals glances at the queen, knowing that to make eye contact is to invite Her Majesty's immediate wrath for such impudence. Jane cannot help herself, though. Elizabeth exudes authority in a manner she has never witnessed from a man, let alone a woman. And she will use that authority to condemn Jane to death before the night is finished.

The fog thickens, and Jane loses track of time. Her feet begin to ache, but she dares not move from the wall or sit. Perhaps if she remains motionless, Cecil and the queen will forget about her. Perhaps she can become one with the shadows, after all, and slip away when everyone else leaves.

"Your friend is here."

Dansby's first words in a while pull her focus to his face. Though he wears a grim frown, he nods toward the stage. Jane finds Will Shakespeare watching her from behind a slivered gap in the curtain. He wears an inscrutable expression, but even from here she can tell he is chewing his lip. He lets the curtain drift closed, leaving Jane again to her fog.

℘

No sooner has Will turned away from the curtain than he meets a wall of resistance clad in orange livery. He lifts his eyes to find a deadpan Perkins peering down at him, Will reactively pats his empty pockets for sonnets he has not yet written.

"My lady wishes a word," says the footman. "This way."

Will swallows the lump in his throat and follows after Perkins, out of options and with nowhere to run. His heart races as he approaches an alcove where Lady Southampton awaits. He bows to her, hoping that his panic isn't too obvious. "My lady countess."

"Mr. Shakespeare." Her eyes narrow and she pokes a fan in his direction. "I have heard a terrible rumor questioning your credentials as a playwright."

Will's knees become liquid. "A rumor begun by John Dutton?"

"Indeed. What say you?"

Will inhales a deep breath as spots dot his vision. "I am a writer, just as I claim."

Lady Southampton's compact frown melts into a softer expression that stops a twitch short of a smile. "Of course you are, given the delight of what you've written for my son. Thus, it might please you to know that John Dutton will trouble you no further with slanderous accusations."

Will lifts his eyebrows until his forehead grows tight. "Begging my lady's pardon, but how can you be certain of his abandoning the matter?"

The pending twitch produces her smile at last. "I sent Perkins to discuss the accusation with the man." She cuts her eyes up at the behemoth footman. "What, again, were your parting words to Mr. Dutton?"

Perkins quirks one eyebrow but remains otherwise deadpan. "I said that should he compel another of my visits on behalf of her ladyship, I would be obliged to fracture his other arm."

Will blinks three times. "His other . . ." He shakes his head and fails to hide a smile. He dips his chin to Lady Southampton. "Thank you, my lady. I owe you a debt."

She shakes her head without losing the slight smile. "No, Mr. Shakespeare. It seems I owe you."

"You owe me? How could you possibly?"

She pokes her fan in his direction a second time. "It seems that your sonnets have produced the desired effect on my dear boy. As a result, he and I have come to an understanding. The next five years, he may do as he pleases. Afterward, he will marry a young woman of my choosing and will waste no time in fulfilling his duty to extend the family line."

The countess's explanation surprises Will. His words have had such an effect on a powerful young lord? Truly? He must look like a haddock with his jaw agape, for Lady Southampton chuckles.

"As such," she says, "you have met your commitment to me and are thus freed from our agreement. Write your plays and poems as you see fit, Mr. Shakespeare. Meanwhile, I will see to any of your detractors."

Despite his still quivering knees, Will drops a courtly bow that threatens to scrape his forehead against the floor. "Your benefaction honors me, my lady countess."

He returns upright to find that she is again all business, as evidenced by her imperious frown. "I must make an entrance now. Be a good lad, Perkins, and show me to the table."

"My lady."

Will blinks away astonishment. Free from Dutton's scrutiny and his deal with the devil? He can hardly believe the luck.

However, visions of a pallid Jane return to him. Something momentous will happen this night—of that, he is sure. If Jane's expression is the harbinger, then disaster might await them all.

<hr />

Supper finished and announcements made, Pembroke's Men storm the stage and begin belting their lines. The table has been shoved aside, and the guests watch from their well-padded chairs. The queen sits nearest the stage, with Robert Cecil on her left and the Lord Chamberlain on her right. From where she stands, Jane can clearly see the glorious and terrifying woman in profile. The other nobles cluster behind the queen in a pecking order befitting their titles, wealth, and authority.

Not Mary, though. She should be near the queen but has elected to sit alone to one side, well behind Elizabeth. Her husband is pressed to her side, though his scowl indicates that he appears displeased about their peripheral position.

Emilia remains with the musicians, who have taken up a position to the right of the stage. She virtually ignores the play, instead glancing between the queen, Cecil, and Mary.

Unable to contain her recurrent tremble, Jane decides on a distraction. She pins her attention on the players and silently mouths their lines, scene after scene, act after act. Her periodic glances at the queen find the woman attentive and sometimes smiling as she fingers the toggle nearest her neck. Gradually, Jane forgets to watch the queen and falls fully into the embrace of the story. *Her* story. *Her* Petruchio and *her* Katherina. *Her* unfolding plot. Even after all that has befallen her, Jane remains proud of what she has put into the world, and wonders if this is the feeling of a mother for her children. And tonight, Lord Strange's Men present Katharina as Jane had intended—a raging fire of a woman rather than an insipid complainer. The world falls away as she whispers line after line.

When Katherina—or the boy playing the role—rises for her final speech, Jane's whispers grow louder. The boy rages his lines, flinging them like daggers at Petruchio and his friends. Katherina's poetic protest rings in Jane's soul as it never has before. The pain of injustice catches in her breast and knots her heart, drawing out her frothing and fuming anger.

And then her lips freeze.

The lines Katherina is speaking are unknown to her. Jane pricks her ears to catch the fleeting words.

"*Men endure only through the persistence of the female sex, and that is our secret.*" The player pumps a fist to make the point. "*We must exert our will within the shadows of men or possess no will at all—and we must exceed them at their own game.*"

The next line is a return to form—a line Jane knows. However, the boy does not finish his delivery.

"Cease talking."

Jane darts her gaze from the stage to find that the queen has risen from her chair and is pointing at the player. The boy shrinks away, his features frozen with mortification. Elizabeth glares at him in a stretching silence before she lowers her hand.

"Speak those last two lines again."

Will, who plays Petruchio's friend, Hortensio, steps to the boy's side and thumps him into action. With a wavering falsetto, the young man repeats the strange lines for the queen. The monarch lifts her hardening chin. She slowly turns toward Mary, clearly having been aware of where the countess was sitting. Elizabeth's eyes are wide, like an eagle's glare before its prey. Mary stands from her chair, clearly befuddling her husband. She dips her head to the queen and then pins her gaze on Emilia in the corner. The queen follows Mary's eyeline and studies the musician. Emilia rises, one hand draped across her belly. She tucks her chin and then fires a stare at . . .

Jane.

As Elizabeth slowly pivots to face her, Jane prepares for a breath of consuming fire that will reduce her to cinders where she stands. When the queen's terrible scrutiny falls on her, she cannot look away. She has been captured, body and soul, with no hope of escape. Some part of Jane knows that she does great disrespect to the queen by daring to look upon the all-powerful woman's eyes. But she is frozen. She is helpless. She is ruined.

"The seamstress, I presume?"

Jane cannot believe that the queen has spoken to her. Her tongue fails to dislodge, but she nods three times. Then, improbably, the queen allows the hard line of her lips to soften into the merest hint of a smile. She lifts her chin higher and blinks softly at Jane. "How wondrously delightful." The queen sits again and rolls a hand toward the mortified boy. "If only *I* had thought of such delicious words, perhaps I might be a playwright. You may proceed."

The boy stumbles into action, and the final lines of the play resume. The guests frown sidelong at one another, clearly baffled by the strange interlude. For once, Jane is their equal. Her head spins as she tries and fails to determine what just took place.

༄

"What just happened, Mary?"

Lord Pembroke whispers the steely question into the dying applause as the players take their bows. Mary responds with a frown. "Of what do you speak?"

He lifts a hand toward Elizabeth, who sits in cloistered conversation with Robert Cecil. "She looked keenly at you and the Bassano woman. Then she addressed the seamstress directly. Why did she do that?"

Mary pushes to her feet. "I do not deign to know the mind of Her Majesty. Now, if you will excuse me."

"Where are you going?"

Mary pins her husband with a hot glare. "Henry Herbert. You have never mistrusted me until these past few months. Is this to be our lot now? Your wife an object of your disdain?"

Pembroke uncoils from his chair and places one hand softly on her shoulder. "Never disdain, Mary. However, you have kept much from me. Your secrecy causes me . . ."

He cannot finish, but the twist of his cheek reveals the pain he bottles inside. Mary places her hand on his. "I shall not make that mistake again, Lord Husband. You have my word."

His countenance relaxes. "Then you have my trust, Mary. And my apology."

"Apology?"

"For underestimating you yet again. A mistake *I* shall not repeat."

She dips her head. "Thank you. Now, I must attend to one final matter. I will explain later."

He lifts one eyebrow but nods. "Do as you must."

Mary sails away to find Jane. The seamstress remains glued to the wall, clinging to Dansby's arm as a drowning woman to a stick of wood. Her cheeks are flushed, and her large eyes betray confusion. Mary motions subtly to Captain Dansby before sliding through the milling nobility and the archway exit beyond. Emilia meets her along the way, as planned. Her expression remains blank as she studies Mary, perhaps searching for a sign that they will survive the next few minutes. Mary has no answer, though. They proceed down a dog-legged hallway to the same small dining chamber where Cecil had confronted them a fortnight earlier. The doors are open, and a servant has lit a half-dozen candles to illuminate the place. Dansby arrives seconds later with Jane on his elbow. The seamstress studies the room with wary eyes.

"What do I do, now?" she asks.

Mary wants to comfort Jane but cannot, given the uncertain circumstances. "We wait for Sir Robert."

Jane sags on Dansby's elbow and stares at the floor. The captain stands unmoving, his gaze a thousand-yard stare. Emilia settles onto a chair and stretches her back, clearly weary from the long pregnancy. She groans quietly, perhaps from discomfort, perhaps from duress.

Mary rests one hand on the dining table and prepares herself for the worst. They wait in silence for several minutes before the clop of asymmetric steps echoes on the wooden planks in the hallway. Robert Cecil appears at the door—with a hollow-eyed Will Shakespeare trudging in his wake. However, no guards, no pikes, no swords. His expression grim, Cecil coolly appraises Mary and Emilia. When he turns his attention to Jane, she ducks her eyes with barely restrained terror. Cecil shakes his head, grabs the edge of his vest with one hand, and faces Mary.

"Mary Herbert, Countess of Pembroke."

She stretches her neck as if for the executioner's convenience. "Sir Robert."

"Let it be known that the queen has changed her opinion of Miss Jane Daggett, a seamstress formerly in the employ of the Queen's Men. She is hereby pardoned of any offense against the

Crown, whether real or perceived. Furthermore, your ladyship and Mrs. Emilia Bassano Lanier are now free of any suspicion regarding your loyalties to Her Majesty. The Crown holds you now in its former esteem."

Mary's hand on the tabletop prevents her from stumbling to her knees. She notices that Jane is overcome as well, remaining upright only with Dansby's help. Emilia has buried her face in one hand and strokes her belly with the other, and Will has sagged against the doorframe.

"You are surprised." Cecil's droll remark matches his half smile.

"Why?" Mary says. "Why has Her Majesty decided this?"

"She did not say precisely, but when the queen speaks on such matters, it is law. However, she knows well the insidious games forced upon the female sex. It has made her what she is—more than any man but less than any woman. You, of course, understand this well."

"More thoroughly than I wish."

"I thought as much." Cecil grunts and taps a finger to his chin. "And on another matter, I am particularly fond of Katherina's final speech but was puzzled tonight by the addition of new lines. Lines I have heard only once before but from a quite different source. I would ask Mr. Shakespeare here about the reason for this, but now realize I should ask all of you instead, while reminding you of the need for utter secrecy on the matter. If you obey only one rule, it must be that one. I have called off my dog, but he remains hungry."

Mary nods. "Sir Robert. It will be as you say."

"Very well, Countess. Godspeed to you all." He returns through the doorway but taps Will on the shoulder as he passes. "A word, Mr. Shakespeare."

Will follows the secretary into the long hallway, blinking shock as he goes. In Cecil's absence, Mary finds Jane staring back and forth between her and an open-mouthed Emilia. Jane lifts a trembling finger and struggles to find words.

"You . . . you saved me somehow. With the words of the play."

"Yes," Mary says. "It seems that we did."

"But . . . but why?"

Mary finds herself in motion toward Jane, and Dansby silently hands her over. She gathers the surprised seamstress in her arms.

"For you, Jane. For us. For our secret alliance."

⁂

Emilia throws her arms around Mary and Jane, nearly falling into them. Her eyes are bleary with tears, and her heart is fuller than she can ever remember. Her rules of war have burned to blackened cinders, leaving her to wander in a strange new world. A world of friendship and solidarity. A world of peace.

"Yes, Jane," she says. "For us. And for all the bright and curious minds that have been relegated to ignorance and silence by custom and by law. We write for them. We speak for them. We do not abandon them."

Jane sobs on Mary's shoulder, her words of gratitude mostly incoherent. Emilia softly strokes Jane's hair until Mary carefully breaks the huddled embrace. She tangles her fingers together at the waist.

"So, to the remaining point: we must decide if this shadow sisterhood is finished. If this grand experiment has staged its final act and has bowed to the world for the last time. What say you?"

Though the same question nags Emilia, the abruptness with which Mary raises it catches her off guard. She hesitates to gather

her thoughts. "The queen knows what we have done, and yet we remain free of condemnation. If I understood correctly Cecil's implication, we have Her Majesty's blessing. Perhaps even her protection."

Mary hums assent. "I interpret him the same, mostly. So long as we remain in the shadows, we may continue our efforts. However, if our work becomes exposed to public scrutiny, the queen might forget her blessing and punish us to preserve her reputation."

"You believe continuing the work to be a risk?"

"I do. Our great initial risk is reduced, certainly, but it could flare into a conflagration should the wrong nobleman learn of our work and decide to make an example of us. Threats to the queen extend beyond Catholic plots. She knows this well and will do as she must to maintain her grip on the throne. Our reputations are an easy sacrifice."

Emilia nods solemnly and looks at Jane, who has mostly contained her sniffling. "You have remained silent thus far. What is your wish, sweet Jane? Is the risk worth the potential price?"

Jane studies her fingers, particularly the ink stains on her right hand, while Dansby rests a hand on her shoulder, barely touching. When she raises her eyes, they are shining. "I am what I have become because of us. I do not wish the dream to end until it must, and I am willing to pay whatever price might be exacted from me. You have more to lose, though. I will respect your decisions on the matter. Either way, I will always love you both and will remain forever in your debt."

Jane's declaration draws an audible stuttered breath from Mary. She regally regathers her composure, as is the obligation of her station. "I am willing to continue."

Emilia nods firmly and suppresses a shout to the heavens. "As am I."

Jane lets loose a giggle before slapping a hand to her mouth. "Can I say this pleases me?"

Mary chuckles, her kindly amusement with Jane never more evident. "You most certainly can." Her smile just as quickly gives way to a firm set of her jaw as she regards Emilia. "In that case, how proceed your foul papers?"

Emilia shakes her head softly with admiration. Mary Herbert is nothing if not driven toward a goal. "I have nearly completed the story about the two gentlemen of Verona, although we must think of a clever name. What of yours?"

Mary hums approval. "My draft of *Titus Andronicus* is ready for you—and Jane—to read."

Jane's mouth draws into a frown. "I am a slow reader, my lady."

"But you *are* a reader. These are your stories, your imaginings. We must have your approval as always, or otherwise shelve the play."

Jane's frown is subsumed by the blush of her cheeks and a beaming smile. "You are too kind."

"No." Emilia hopes her reply does not sound too curt. "We are mercenary, Jane. Without you, these plays are simply a jumble of words. Do you have other story notions?"

Jane tilts her head back and forth. "A few, yes. While hiding these past months, I had little to do but imagine stories." She spreads her fingers to show the ink stains. "I began writing them down, though I left the papers at home. I am sorry."

"Not to worry," Mary says. "Tell us what you remember."

The seamstress turned playwright stares upward, her eyes unfocused. "Let me see. There is one about twins separated as children who are mistaken for each other when they arrive in the same town on the same day. And one about four men who devote themselves to celibacy just before a princess and her three comely attendants arrive. Oh, and a story of two young people from warring houses who fall in love, to the horror of their families."

Emilia claps her hands with delight. "Wonderful. My fingers itch to write such fanciful tales. And we simply must write of Richard the Third to round out our telling of the Civil Wars. What a fine villain he could make."

"Then it is settled," Mary says. "Let us meet again at the Chapel of St. Anne three days hence. Two o'clock in the afternoon. Are we agreed?"

"Yes, of course," says Emilia.

Jane merely nods, though her body trembles with agreement. Mary tosses the seamstress a soft smile. "Remain near to Captain Dansby now. He will see you safely home." She motions toward the doorway. "Shall we, Emilia?"

Jane dips a curtsy and sniffles. "My ladies."

Emilia spontaneously kisses Jane's cheek, surprising herself, and follows Mary as they return toward the great hall. Though heavy with child, her feet are light on the floor, and she basks in the wonder of having threaded an impossibly small needle. Of having won a war.

Mired in disbelief, Jane watches Mary and Emilia leave the small dining room. Her head pounds from hours of terror and gallons of tears, but her seizing lungs finally begin to fill again. She looks to Captain Dansby for confirmation that what just happened isn't a waking dream. The stone planes of his grim expression have shattered, flaring his nostrils and smoothing his forehead. He places his hands on her arms just below the round of her shoulders.

"I thought I'd lost you, Jane."

His voice breaks against her name, like a ship shattered on a reef, leaving her bewildered. She tips her head to one side and peers so deeply into his eyes that she might lose herself there. "Lost me? When was I . . . when did you ever . . . ?"

"Oh, sweet seamstress. You captured my interest that night we first met. I don't know how or why, but it has caused me no end of surprise and consternation. Then, over time, you took from me what I have never given to anyone, not once in my entire unremarkable life. You stole my heart." He swallows. "I have yet to retrieve it, nor do I wish to. I suppose it is yours now to do with what you will."

Jane's lungs close again briefly before she releases a bursting sob. "You mean this?"

"As God is my witness."

She corrals her wildly surging disbelief and stumbles over an appropriate response before simply nodding. "I will be sure to take good care of it."

He grasps her right hand, lifts it to his lips, and kisses each finger individually. He watches her with the eyes of a hound before its master, smiling and content.

"Your fingers are stained with ink, Jane. Are you also now a writer?"

She chokes a sharp laugh. "A pitiful one, but I suppose so."

"There is nothing pitiful about you. You do nothing by half, leaving me in awe of your resolve."

He laughs gently, and they stare at each other. Her warm smile surely matches his, and she must fight not to break eye contact. How can he find her worthy of his affections after all she has been through? How can he overlook her strange mind and odd ways, as if she is perfect?

His continued smile, warm as a summer picnic, begins to convince her that the silence between them holds answers to questions she has never dared to ask but is anxious to explore.

Dansby gently pulls Jane into an embrace, folding her frame into the fortress of a soldier's muscled arms. She loops her arms around his waist, a landscape she knows well from her many rides on the back of his horse. This is far different, though. Now *he* holds *her*.

Dansby places a curled forefinger beneath her chin, to lift it from his chest. She blinks with wonder as his lips fall on hers, and for the first time in her short life, tastes of the forbidden fruit that is true love. His lips are softer than she has imagined, a contradiction to his hardened exterior. He smells of musk and leather, and she is lost in it. After a far too brief time, he lifts his chin with a rumbling sigh and leans it atop her head. She presses her cheek against the expanse of his chest, unable to draw him near enough. She clings to him, one with the beating of his heart, rejoicing in the security of his embrace. He is like a mighty rock in the sea, a place of refuge from the tempest that engulfs the world. Jane imagines the scene—a storm-tossed ship that surrenders to the waves. A woman clinging to a rock in the howling storm. No—a man tossed onto a beach. A duke, and those who serve him. And there is a sorcerer who caused the storm and shipwrecked the men to right a wrong. In Dansby's sacred embrace, Jane's imagination soars as it never has before.

Will trails Cecil to a quiet alcove before the man stops to face him. Will scans the nook to his right and the stairwell just behind Cecil, suspecting that the secretary has men-at-arms at his disposal within calling distance. More than that, he has the ear of the queen and can condemn a man like Will with a word. Commoners hold no power and no recourse when the Crown decides to burn them.

Cecil's thin beard shifts to one side as he grows a restrained but lopsided smile. "Mr. Shakespeare. You seem deeply uneasy. Have you been plotting foul deeds, then?"

Will nearly chokes. "No, my lord. I am loyal to Her Majesty."

Cecil waves a hand and chuckles. "I only jest. How could I accuse one who produces such marvelous plays? You did write them, yes?"

"I . . . yes. I wrote them."

"No." Cecil taps his chin. "That will not do. I will ask you again, and you must claim the work with enough conviction to persuade me. Did you write the plays that bear your name, *The Shrew* and *Henry the Sixth* among them?"

Will's eyes begin to open to what might be happening. He stands as tall as he can. "Yes, Sir Robert. I am the author of the plays that bear my name."

"Much better. Henceforth, that will be your story, for now and for all time. The plays are yours, no matter what others might claim, by the order of Her Majesty, Elizabeth, Queen of the Realm. Do you understand?"

"I understand clearly."

"Of course you do, as you are shrewd and intelligent. This arrangement should serve you well. However, should you change your story by accident or intention, you and I will have a new conversation with a far less pleasant ending. Is my meaning clear?"

"Yes, Sir Robert."

"Excellent. Then we are of an accord on the matter."

"We are." He waits for Cecil to turn away, but the man does not. Will picks at his vest. "How else may I serve you?"

"Fortunate that you should ask." Cecil steps closer. "As your company travels about the kingdom, I expect that should you overhear any words of treason or disparagement of Her Majesty, you might feel obligated to send me a missive on the matter."

Will does not expect the request, but he is not surprised. "Of course."

"Very good." Cecil slips aside to allow Will to pass. As Will steps by, Cecil taps his arm. "By the way, the young Lord Southampton shared a number of your sonnets with me. They are yours, yes?"

Will spreads his shoulders and lifts his chin. "They are mine. Deeply mine."

"I thought as much. They are distinct from the plays but also quite good. Your talents as a poet are without question."

The compliment surprises Will. Normally, he relishes praise. But this? From the man he feared would kill him? "I am pleased you think so."

Cecil chuckles quietly. "Mind yourself, Mr. Shakespeare. You are an object of scrutiny now."

Will nods firmly and bows again. "I will. Thank you, Sir Robert."

He backs away from the man before returning to the great hall, his jaw practically agape. He now has the blessing of Sir Robert and the protection of a dowager countess? How has his fortune turned so dramatically rosy? He chokes a laugh and returns to the stage to join his fellow players as they pack the trunks. His heart is racing again, but not from dread. Joy is rising in his breast, a bright and glorious sunrise after a fitful, dreamless night. He loves writing poetry, and regard for his poems by noblemen only adds kindling to the fire already blazing in his soul. He jumps into the fray, packing gear with abandon. The sooner he finishes, the sooner he can return to his London apartment and his small writing desk beside the dirty window. After all, no less than Venus and Adonis await.

Mary and Emilia part ways before entering the great hall. In the interest of maintaining their secret association, it is no longer prudent for them to be seen together. Lord Pembroke meets Mary with a wrinkled forehead and a lifted eyebrow. She loops a hand through his elbow and gives it a reassuring squeeze.

"All is well, Lord Husband. Our house is safe."

He releases a sigh that she feels but does not hear. "*Your* safety is my primary concern."

The earnestness of his confession stirs a flame within Mary's breast that threatens to burst into light. She grips his arm tighter and smiles up at him. "Then in service of our safety, let us take a turn about the hall that we might make conversation with a number of our peers."

His eyebrow arches again. "You wish to visit? Not flee to your chambers? Of your own volition?"

The knot that has clenched like a fist in Mary's gut for a year is conspicuously absent, releasing her spirit from a chain she cannot name. She feels truly liberated, perhaps for the first time since Philip died. "Yes, my dear. That is my wish."

He shakes his head and grows a half smile. "You surprise me, Mary."

"I surprise myself," she whispers.

As Pembroke leads her through the great hall, Mary can't help but ponder how far she has traveled since her return to Court a year earlier. It had always struck her as a tragedy that the serpent offered Eve the key to all knowledge, but the price was death. Now, she recognizes the offer for what it truly was—an opportunity for freedom. A brief lifetime of knowing instead of an unending age of incomprehension.

Not a curse.

A gift.

As such, a woman must never cease to struggle free from her constraints, for even an eternity of blissful ignorance cannot compare to a single stroke of the tortured pen.

Acknowledgements

This novel is the end result of a few sparkling ideas, an immense amount of research, and the critical support I received along the way. First, I'd like to thank my son, Nathan Nix, who pitched the idea to me in 2018.

After sitting on his notion for a while, I came across Elizabeth Winkler's article in the June 2019 edition of *The Atlantic*: "Was Shakespeare a Woman?" Her article convinced me that a believable and historically coherent story was possible, so she has my thanks.

After a long slog of research and then the writing of the first several chapters, I pitched the story to my agent, Jill Marsal, in late 2022. She became an early champion and assembled a stellar submission list that resulted in the sale of the completed manuscript in June of 2024. I am forever grateful for her excellent feedback and efforts on my behalf.

My gratitude extends to my editor, Tara Gavin, who believed in the draft manuscript and provided critical feedback that tightened up the story. I'd also like to thank a couple of those dear to me who helped along the way—Dusty Davidson, and my wife, Karen Nix. Dusty is an old friend and theater guy who gave an early draft his seal of approval. Karen was, as always, my sounding board for ideas, one of the first readers of the work, and my inspiration for female characters who possess backbones of steel.